All REGENCY Collection

A TIMELESS Romance ANTHOLOGY

All REGENCY Collection

Anna Elliott
Sarah M. Eden
Carla Kelly
Josi S. Kilpack
Annette Lyon
Heather B. Moore

Mirror Press

Copyright © 2016 by Mirror Press, LLC
Print edition
All rights reserved

No part of this book may be reproduced in any form whatsoever without prior written permission of the publisher, except in the case of brief passages embodied in critical reviews and articles. This is a work of fiction. The characters, names, incidents, places, and dialogue are products of the authors' imagination and are not to be construed as real.

Interior Design by Rachael Anderson
Edited by Annette Lyon, Cassidy Wadsworth and Whitney McGruder

Cover design by Mirror Press, LLC

Published by Mirror Press, LLC
http://timelessromanceanthologies.blogspot.com

ISBN-10: 1-941145-72-8
ISBN-13: 978-1-941145-72-2

TABLE OF CONTENTS

The Wedding Gift: A Pride and Prejudice *Story*   1
by Anna Elliott

Dream of a Glorious Season   53
by Sarah M. Eden

The Mender   115
by Carla Kelly

Begin Again   179
by Josi S. Kilpack

The Affair at Wildemoore   237
by Annette Lyon

The Duke's Brother   295
by Heather B. Moore

MORE TIMELESS ROMANCE ANTHOLOGIES

Winter Collection
Spring Vacation Collection
Summer Wedding Collection
Autumn Collection
European Collection
Love Letter Collection
Old West Collection
Summer in New York Collection
Silver Bells Collection
California Dreamin' Collection
Annette Lyon Collection
All Hallows' Eve Collection
Sarah M. Eden British Isles Collection
Mail Order Bride Collection
Road Trip Collection
Blind Date Collection

The Wedding Gift

by Anna Elliott

OTHER WORKS BY ANNA ELLIOTT

Georgiana Darcy's Diary
Pemberley to Waterloo
Kitty Bennet's Diary
Susanna and the Spy
London Calling
Twilight of Avalon
Sunrise of Avalon

A note to the reader: Because this story takes the form of a diary written in Regency-Era England, British spelling and punctuation conventions have been used in a departure from the usual TRA style. —A.E.

Monday
2 November 1812

I have never kept a diary before. I suppose, strictly speaking, that I am not keeping one now, either. Not properly, at any rate. A proper diary ought to be leather-bound and suitably official and solemn-looking. At least I am certain that that is what my sister Mary would say.

I am just jotting these words down on a sheet of paper from my aunt Gardiner's writing desk. Somehow I want to keep a record of these days, even if it is only dashed off in bits and pieces on haphazard scraps.

Darcy came to see me today. We see each other every day, or nearly, so that was not so very remarkable. But—

But I have just realised that in addition to failing at giving these words a proper leather-bound setting, I have also failed to properly introduce myself.

Does one introduce one's self to a diary?

If it is to be forced to be the silent recipient of all one's private thoughts and confidences—yet never allowed to offer any return thoughts or confidences of its own—I suppose it seems rather rude not to.

Very well. I will be courteous to my diary. It is not *its* fault, after all, that thus far my diary consists of just a single sheet of slightly dusty writing paper.

To begin, my name is Elizabeth Bennet. I am nearly twenty-one years of age. I have dark hair and dark eyes, and—

And really, I am hurrying through all these boring particulars so that I may have the pleasure of writing: I am engaged to be married to Mr. Fitzwilliam Darcy in just two short weeks' time.

It is rather lucky that my diary does not have a mouth with which to protest, considering how quickly I have abandoned courtesy in favour of boasting. *Is* it boasting to tell of one's own happiness?

I'm sure my cousin Mr. Collins would say that it is.

I also seem to have developed a strong streak of my mother—speaking of my engagement as though it is the culmination of all my accomplishments. As though having informed the world—or this page—that I am engaged to marry, there can be nothing more of value to say.

But that is not true. There is more to me, of course, than my engagement to Darcy. I love music, and can lose myself for hours within the pages of a good book. I love to be out of doors, and, much to my mother's chagrin, I have to be bullied, tortured, or bribed into suitably feminine pursuits like quillwork or embroidery.

It is just that right now it still seems such an unlikely miracle that Darcy should happen to love all of those various bits and pieces of me.

That is really why I took up this paper and pen to begin with.

The Wedding Gift

They say that time moves swiftly when one is happy, and it is quite true. I seem to spend my days both wishing that the days between now and Saturday next will fly by—and at the same time wishing that I could somehow slow time down, sink fully into every minute the way one sinks into a warm bath.

Perhaps that is how every bride feels two weeks before her wedding day—but of course, never having been married, I cannot be sure.

In any event, to continue my lamentably circuitous introductions, I am currently staying in London, with my aunt and uncle Gardiner, for the purpose of selecting wedding clothes.

To be honest, I would have been perfectly content to marry Darcy in my last year's workaday gown. Or in my nightshift. But it seemed cruel to deprive my mother of the delight of seeing me outfitted in a perfectly outrageous number of new things. Jane, my oldest sister, was to accompany me to London, as well. Our wedding is to be a double one; Jane and Mr. Charles Bingley are to be married on the same day Darcy and I are wedded.

But at the last moment, Charles heard word of an estate in the north that has come up for sale. The place is not so very far from Pemberley, where Darcy and I will live, and it sounds ideal in practically every regard. Charles elected to travel there at once to see the place for himself and decide whether he wishes to make an offer for it.

Jane, of course, being the happy possessor of the sweetest temper in all of England, told Charles that she would be entirely content with his decision, whether he chose to buy the property or no.

But Charles would not hear of that. He really is Jane's perfect match. Not only that, but he loves her so truly that it practically radiates from him whenever they are in the same room. He insisted that Jane ought to see the place too, before he committed to buying it. After all, it would be her home, as well.

So they have gone off on a hurried journey to the north—properly chaperoned by Charles's sister Mrs. Hurst. I told Jane that Mrs. Hurst's presence was the only part of the arrangement that made me pity her a bit. But Jane is too sweet tempered to mind even Charles's slightly dreadful sister.

I hope, hope, *hope* that the estate in the north is as charming as the estate agent claimed it to be.

It almost seems like too much happiness, to think of myself living at Pemberley with Darcy, and Jane and Charles settled not far away.

I had to break off writing earlier. My little cousins—Aunt and Uncle Gardiner's children—came bursting into the room. There are four of them: Anna and Charlotte, who are seven and nine, and Thomas and Jack, ages three and five. They are all so utterly adorable that I was forced to drop all other considerations and play at spillikins and hunt-the-slipper with them.

Then it was time to dress for dinner.

Only now that I am back in my room getting ready to go to bed have I realised that I never did write down what I set out to say earlier, which was an account of Darcy's visit this morning.

I was in the morning room, writing a letter to my mother—who had just written to inform me that I am a

The Wedding Gift

terrible daughter for not giving her better accounts of the balls that I am attending, the gowns that I am wearing, and the expensive presents with which Darcy is (presumably) showering me; because what is the good of her daughter's being engaged to marry a fabulously wealthy man, if she cannot crow about all of said items of interest to our neighbours?

(That, of course, is my own interpretation. My mother's actual words were slightly more subtle. *Very* slightly.)

Rose, Aunt Gardiner's maid, came in to tell me that Darcy had arrived to call on me, and a moment later, he entered.

He looked almost impossibly handsome, wearing buckskin breeches and a blue superfine coat that set off his broad shoulders and dark hair.

I suppose the truth is so patently obvious that I may as well admit it straight out: I am hopelessly, helplessly, utterly in love.

But more important than good looks, he was smiling. Not the polite, stiff quirk of the lips that passes for his social smile—the one he gives people whose boring company he is forced to endure. A *real* smile—the one that reaches his eyes, and that I have seen only since we have been engaged.

"I met Mrs. Gardiner on the front step," he said. "She was just going out to pay some morning visits. But she kindly allowed that I might come in and visit without a chaperone, seeing as how, for one thing, we are engaged to be married in two weeks' time, and for another, she said she has the highest estimation of my gentlemanly character."

"Ah." I pushed the letter to my mother aside and got up to greet him. "I, however, am not gentlemanly in the slightest. How does she know that I will not take ruthless advantage of your honour?"

Darcy laughed. Until we were engaged, I had never heard him laugh before, either. Actually, there was a time in our acquaintance when I would have believed him utterly incapable of laughter. "I shall resign myself to being thoroughly compromised."

The way he looked at me then—his dark eyes somehow at once wondering and tender and filled with need—stopped my breath and made my heart feel as though it were expanding inside my chest.

The morning room, the noise of carriages in the street outside, the entire world around us, all seemed to fade as his lips settled over mine. Finally he kissed me one last time, then lifted his head and said, "I have something for you."

"Really?" I had to stop to draw in a breath. "I must warn you, after that, no gift can possibly compare."

My breath caught again, though, when he brought out a small velvet-covered box and opened it to let me see inside.

It was the most beautiful article of jewellery I had ever seen: a necklace, worked in a delicate design of twining leaves and vines and flowers. Diamonds formed the vines and leaves, while the flowers were accented with tiny rubies.

"It belonged to my mother," Darcy said. "My father gave it to her when they were married."

I touched one of vines, just with one fingertip. It was so lovely, I was almost afraid to do more. "My mother will finally have no reason to complain that I am failing in my filial duties."

"I beg pardon?" Darcy looked more than slightly confused.

I shook my head and blinked a sudden press of tears from my eyes. "It is beautiful. Absolutely, utterly lovely. Thank you." I looked up at him. "I wish that I could have known your mother. Or—" I stopped as a sudden thought struck me. "Perhaps she would not have been happy to know about your marrying me?"

Darcy's mother was, after all, the Right Honourable Lady Catherine de Bourgh's sister. And to say that Lady Catherine is less than pleased that her nephew and I are betrothed is a little like saying that Marshal-General Wellesley is less than a good friend to the Emperor Napoleon.

In Lady Catherine's eyes, I rank somewhere around the level of an unpleasant insect stuck to the sole of her shoe. *Insolent, headstrong girl* were the most complimentary of the epithets she hurled at me on our last meeting—and if she could prevent Darcy's and my marrying by sacrificing an arm and a leg, I have a strong suspicion that she would lose no time in calling for a surgeon.

Darcy only smiled again, though, and pulled me close. "My mother used to tell me that one of her fears for me was that I should marry a meek wife—some timid, spiritless girl who would do nothing but pander to my own good opinion of myself. She would have been delighted to find that with you, she need not have feared anything of the kind."

I made a slight face. "Because I am the opposite of meek and timid and spent the majority of our courtship subjecting you to teasing and general abuse? I am not sure that that is entirely a compliment." I leaned my head against his shoulder. "Though I am desperate enough to marry you that I will accept it as such. So you see, perhaps after all I *am* meek and cowed and . . . what was the other word?"

Darcy laughed. "*Spiritless*. And I am happy beyond words to say that the day the word applies to you is the day I shall expect a freezing snowstorm in July." His arms tightened around me. "As for my mother, she would have liked you very much the moment she met you. She would have loved you, if she could have had the chance to know you well."

It is almost frightening to be so perfectly happy.

Tuesday
3 November 1812

I am *almost* perfectly happy. The only slight blemish on my spirits is that I should like to find a gift for Darcy. Nothing I can give him would match his mother's diamond necklace, of course—at least not in expense. But I should like to find some present for him. Something that would mark how much I love him. Something that would surprise and delight him.

The difficulty lies in thinking of such a gift. Lady Catherine would probably say that I ought to give him an engraved snuffbox or some such. Or a diamond-studded watch fob.

But Darcy does not take snuff, and I suspect that he would make affronted noises—or laugh—at the idea of adorning his pocket watch with diamonds. Besides, if he wished for either of those, he could well afford to buy them for himself ten times over.

And doubly besides (Can one double a *besides*? I

suppose it is lucky that these are only my own private musings), even if I thought Darcy would like either of those articles, *I* could not afford them.

So, I require a gift that is unique, clever, delightful, and thoughtful. Something Darcy cannot or would not purchase for himself—yet at the same time something inexpensive.

I suppose it is small wonder that my mind was absolutely blank of useful ideas.

I spoke of the dilemma to Georgiana, when she was here this morning to see the latest set of gowns come from the *modiste*.

Georgiana is Darcy's younger sister—and if I am of necessity deprived of Jane's company for these weeks in London, I am consoled by having the chance of spending time with Georgiana. She is such a dear. When we first met, I thought that she was lovely, but terribly shy. She *is* shy—occasionally even still with me. But now that I know her better, I have discovered that beneath her reserve, she is both intelligent and good-humoured, with a surprisingly sharp wit.

She understood at once my difficulty in thinking of a suitable gift, and nodded when I explained what was required.

"I do see what you mean," she said.

Georgiana has her brother's very dark hair and tall figure, and is very pretty in a stately, classical way. Though she looked considerably more informal perched on the edge of my bed and fingering the fringe on the new paisley shawl that arrived this morning.

"There is so little, really, that one can get for a man like my brother. Although—" She stopped and looked at me intently. "You do realise—at least, I hope you do—that my brother truly does not *need* a gift from you. Simply in agreeing to marry him, you have given him all that he could wish for. I have never seen him so happy as he has been these last weeks."

"That is truly good to hear. But—"

"Oh, I do understand." Georgiana nodded. "It is so often far better fun to give gifts than to receive them." She laughed suddenly, a dimple appearing at the side of her mouth. "I remember one Christmas, I got Edward—"

Edward is Colonel Edward Fitzwilliam, Georgiana's second guardian. I like him very much—and I should have liked to know the full story of Georgiana's Christmas gift to him. But she stopped abruptly, a touch of colour warming her pale cheeks, then went on a little hurriedly, "But I am sorry. I am rambling on, when what you require is for us to think of a gift for my brother."

"I thought perhaps . . . that is, you have known him longer than I have," I said. "I wondered whether you might have any ideas."

Georgiana frowned, plainly deep in thought. "I do not think . . ." She shook her head, but then stopped abruptly. "I wonder. There was Nero."

I felt my eyebrows lifting. "Apart from being an unpopular Roman emperor, who was Nero?"

"He was my brother's hunting dog. Our father purchased him when Fitzwilliam was eight or nine, I think—before I was born, I know, and that was when my brother was ten. Nero and my brother were inseparable all the way up until Fitzwilliam went away to school. And even then, whenever Fitzwilliam came back to Pemberley for a visit, Nero would be a permanent fixture at my brother's side. Nero lived to be a good age for a dog of his breed—ten or eleven, I think. But he died years ago, and my brother has never got another dog, though he has spoken of doing so at times. He has a kennel and dogs at Pemberley, of course, for when he and Charles and their other friends go hunting. But not one dog that is *particularly* his more than any of the others, if you know what I mean."

"You think I ought to get him a dog for a wedding gift?" I asked.

I liked the idea at once—very much indeed. A dog is a far warmer and more personal gift than a snuff box or a watch fob. And seems as though it ought to be less expensive, besides. Though actually, I am not sure of how much a well-bred hunting dog may cost.

"What sort of a dog was Nero?" I asked Georgiana.

"Oh. A greyhound. His coat was white and tan."

"A greyhound" I nodded decidedly. "Very well. I believe that I *may* have to credit you with being a genius. Although you would secure your status of being my own personal *deus ex machina* completely if you could tell me where in London I may go about procuring such an animal."

Georgiana, however, proved to have no more idea than I did of where we might find a breeder of greyhound puppies.

"I suppose I could ask my uncle," I said, frowning. "Or—wait a moment. Edward is still in town, is he not?"

Properly speaking, I ought to call him Colonel Fitzwilliam, still, since Darcy and I are not yet married. But neither of us is particularly good at standing on ceremony.

Georgiana nodded. "Yes. He is staying with us, at Darcy House. He has leave from his regiment until the wedding."

"Do you think that you could ask him whether he knows of any reputable greyhound breeders?" I could not be sure that Edward would be able to locate one for us, but he seemed our most likely resource.

"Of course," Georgiana said slowly. "I mean, I will

directly return to Darcy House." She seemed to hesitate a long moment. When she spoke again, the words came all in a rush. "You do not . . . I do not mean to be impertinent, but . . . that is to say, if you will forgive my asking such a personal question—"

She stopped again, her cheeks flaming.

I raised my eyebrows. "Goodness. After that sort of beginning, you absolutely *must* ask your question, impertinent or no. I am quite agog with curiosity to hear whatever it may be." I stopped, smiling, and added in a different tone, "Truly, you may ask me anything. I will not be offended, I promise. We are to be sisters in a fortnight's time, after all. There is no such thing as an overly personal question between sisters. Just ask my sisters Lydia or Kitty—or even Jane."

Georgiana's cheeks were still flushed, but she dropped her eyes to the fringe on the shawl again, and said, in a low, hurried voice, "I was wondering whether you ever wish . . . whether you ever regret that you are marrying my brother instead of Edward."

I felt my jaw drop open slightly as I stared at her. Whatever I had been expecting, it was not that. "Good heavens, no. Whatever put such an idea into your head?"

Edward and I were good friends when we met at his aunt's estate a few months ago. He is charming, intelligent, well mannered, and altogether a delightful young man.

"I do not—," I began. I could feel the blood rushing up to colour my own face. "I suppose that I sometimes find it difficult to express my sincerest feelings. It is one of the defects in my character, I'm afraid. I like to hide behind humour and banter and wit. But if you doubt that my affections for your brother are sincere—"

"Oh, I do not!" Georgiana broke in quickly, looking

distressed. "Not really. I mean . . . it is just that Edward admired you a great deal. I know he still does. But being a younger son, he cannot marry without his father's approval, and—"

"And I am too poor to be a suitable bride for the younger son of an earl?" I finished for her. I shook my head. "Georgiana, you know Edward. If he had *truly* fallen in love with me, do you think that the lack of his father's approval would have stopped him? I like him—I esteem him very much, and I hope he feels the same liking and esteem for me. But that is all."

A wash of relief seemed to cross Georgiana's face, and I had a sudden suspicion that it was not worry over *my* feelings that had led her to begin this conversation.

I did not like to embarrass her by asking, though, or to strain our newly begun friendship by pushing her to confide more than she might wish.

Besides, she is very young. Only sixteen. And it was not so long ago that she was nearly seduced into an elopement by George Wickham, who is unworthy of her in every way.

She has plenty of time to make a suitable match with the *right* sort of gentleman, one who truly deserves her. Whether that may be Edward, I suppose, only time will show.

"I ought to be getting back" —Georgiana rose to her feet—"if I am to beg Edward for any intelligence he may give about possible suppliers of greyhounds."

"Thank you," I told her. "Truly."

I got up too and hugged her quickly. "I may joke and laugh and talk a great deal of nonsense at times. But I *do* love your brother—more than I ever thought it possible to love anyone. If you can help me towards finding him a wedding gift, I will be forever in your debt."

Wednesday
4 November 1812

Samson?
    King?
    Midas?

I am trying to think of a suitable name for the puppy currently lying at my feet and gnawing one of my slippers with a look of the fiercest concentration. But so far, every name I try out seems more preposterous than the last. More preposterous even than his appearance—and that is saying a great deal.

I could *not* have done anything else. I have told myself as much, at a rough estimate, approximately four hundred and thirty-two times since I purchased the small creature and brought him home to my aunt and uncle's. I could not.

However, I am as much at a loss to imagine what Darcy will say when he sees the puppy as I am to think of a good name. I vacillate between picturing Darcy dissolving into fits of mirth, and feeling sure that he will decide he must have been mad to ask me to marry him at all.

Edward *did*, in fact, know of a breeder of greyhounds. The man has an establishment in the Seven Dials district—a not terribly salubrious neighbourhood near to Covent Garden. I am not normally nervous going about in London, even in the poorer streets—of which there are many, not too distant from my aunt and uncle's home in Cheapside.

However, I was glad today that Edward had offered to escort Georgiana and me to the dog breeder's—and not only because I am unsure whether we could have found the place without his assistance. We took the carriage as far as we could. But the streets soon became too narrow, and Georgiana had to ask her coachman to wait for us while we proceeded on foot.

We made our way through a series of narrow, crooked streets—some barely more than alleyways—with tumble-down-looking tenement houses, and lines of washing strung overhead, nearly blotting out the view of the sky. Drunken men in labourer's garb came lurching at us out of the doors of seedy-looking gin shops and taverns. Despite winter's chill coming on, the children playing in the streets had no coats and very often not even shoes.

All the time we were walking, I had the oddest feeling of being followed. But when I looked round, there was no one behind us whom I recognised, so I supposed the feeling must have been only nerves.

We finally reached the breeder's house. It stood next to a cow house—a rather miserable place where the poor cows who provide milk for London markets are housed. It is no wonder to me my aunt insists on buying her milk from country farmers, now that I have seen the way their city counterparts live.

The Wedding Gift

However, the dog breeder's home was quite clean and well kept—and on knocking, we were welcomed inside by a rotund, cheerful little man who introduced himself as Mr. Meakes.

Edward explained what was required and asked whether Mr. Meakes might have any puppies that would suit our purpose.

Indeed, Mr. Meakes had. One of his best dogs had whelped some six weeks ago, and her puppies would be ready for sale quite soon.

He brought us through the house and out into the rear yard to see the litter. There were six of them, all wriggling and tumbling about their mother in a pen as clean and well kept as the house.

Georgiana and I admired them for a time, while Edward and Mr. Meakes spoke of breeding and bloodlines. And then I heard a high-pitched *yipping* coming from a shed at the back of the yard, and wandered over to investigate.

I found a puppy. Quite the most ridiculous-looking one I had ever seen in my life. It looked rather as though someone had taken bits from various wildly disparate breeds and glued them together into a single animal.

The head—or rather, the face—had the sleek, thin, and elongated muzzle of a greyhound or whippet. But the ears were enormous, drooping like a basset hound's. Its coat was curly—like a poodle's—but with the brown and white spots of a spaniel. Its basset hound ancestry was visible once more, though, in a long body—rather sausage-like, truth be told—and preposterously short legs. When it tried to walk—or rather, when it waddled—it kept tripping over its absurdly long ears and winding up sprawled on the ground.

Mr. Meakes came up behind me, eyeing the puppy with

a mixture of resignation and dislike. "You don't want to be botherin' yourself with that 'un, miss."

"What is it?" I asked.

Mr. Meakes sighed. "That there? That's a bit of a mistake, like."

He gave me the story—an expurgated version, to be suitable for a lady's ears. Apparently, some three months ago, one of his breeding females broke free of her pen and escaped for a wild, solitary adventure on the London streets.

Just how wild, Mr. Meakes only discovered some weeks after she had returned. Apparently in addition to being an adventurer, his dog proved to be a shameless light-skirt, having returned carrying a litter of puppies "of uncertain paternity."

Mr. Meakes spoke the last words with a pronounced shudder.

Luckily—luckily according to Mr. Meakes, that is—the rest of the litter of ill-bred puppies did not survive. There were four, but the little fellow before me was the only one to live. Mr. Meakes had allowed the mother dog to nurse it for a time, for the mother's sake. According to his theories of dog raising, that is somehow vital for the breeding dog's health. But now the rogue puppy was ready to be weaned, and his mother was to be bred again—with a suitably chosen mate this time.

The puppy was rolling on the ground, pouncing on little scraps of straw and making tiny, high-pitched growling sounds—apparently trying to frighten the straw into submission. I would have defied even Lady Catherine de Bourgh not to smile.

"What are you going to do with him?" I asked.

Mr. Meakes shrugged, unconcerned. "Drown him, most

like. Haven't got around to it yet, but I don't see as how there's anything else to be done with the little wretch."

"Drown him!" I looked from the pouncing, tumbling puppy to Mr. Meakes, appalled. "Oh no. But you cannot."

Mr. Meakes shrugged again, looking entirely unmoved. "Who's going to want him?"

The words were out before I could stop to think. But even if I had paused for consideration, I would have said the same thing. "I do! I want him."

And that is how, instead of the handsome greyhound puppy I had intended to buy Darcy for a wedding gift, I found myself carrying my preposterous little bundle of curly brown and white fur back to our waiting carriage.

Georgiana smiled every time she looked at him, and Edward's mouth was twitching suspiciously.

"I could not have done anything else!" I said, before either of them could say anything. That was the first time I made the above-mentioned assertion.

"No, certainly you could not." Georgiana's voice still held an undercurrent of laughter, but she caressed the puppy's soft little head. "You could not possibly have allowed this sweet love to be drowned."

"Certainly," Edward agreed. His lips were still twitching. "Not to mention that had you not rescued this fine fellow, I would have been deprived of the pleasure of one day witnessing Darcy striding onto the hunting field with his loyal ... what breed would you say the animal is?"

Georgiana said, very straight-faced, "A greyhound-spaniel-basset-hound-poodle, perhaps? Would that make him a ... *groodle*? A *boodle*?"

Edward made some choking sounds. "I vow there is some pug in his ancestry somewhere as well. Perhaps you might tell Darcy that he is a *grug*."

I cuddled the puppy more closely against my shoulder. "Pay no mind to these philistines," I told him. "It will not be long before greyhound-spaniel-pug-poodle mixes are the height of fashion. The Duchess of Devonshire herself will feel sadly behind the times and lacking in sophistication without her faithful groodle trotting at her side."

Now that I have the puppy home at my aunt and uncle's, however, I begin to have misgivings. Darcy will not be angry with me; I am not worried about that. Nor, I am certain, will Darcy declare, as hateful Mr. Meakes did, that my small rescuee ought to be drowned. I would not be marrying him if he were that sort of man.

It is just that I set out to find a gift that would demonstrate how utterly and completely I love him. And instead, I seem to have ended up procuring for him the world's most ridiculous-looking dog.

Thursday

5 November 1812

I am going to be very calm and not panic.

Witness how nicely and legibly I have written the date at the top of this page. I am not precisely sure whether it *is* the fifth of November, or still the fourth, since what with being bound and gagged and blindfolded and then driven to an unknown location, I seem to have lost track of the time.

But the point is that I could not be giving way to abject panic and still have laid this out like any ordinary diary entry. Clearly. Therefore, I must be remaining calm—and it is only my imagination that pictures a thread of terror pulling tight under my ribcage right now.

What happened is this:

Just as I was folding up the sheets of paper containing my last diary entry—preparatory to shutting up the writing desk for the night—the puppy (groodle?) made it known to me that he needed to go out. *Immediately.*

Since he had already misbehaved himself twice on poor Aunt Gardiner's nice floral carpet, I scooped him up and fairly ran with him down the stairs. I was in such a rush that without thinking, I simply thrust these sheets of paper into the pocket of my dressing gown.

I flung open the front door and charged out, puppy in hand. It was, of course, improper in the highest degree for me to be outside in nothing but my nightdress and dressing gown. But it was an emergency. Aunt Gardiner is the best-humoured and kindest woman imaginable, but even she has a limit on how many puppy-related stains she can be expected to tolerate on her best rug.

However, the dog—who apparently also has a sense of humour, and not entirely a benevolent one, at that—refused to . . .

I have been sitting here for what must be a solid minute thinking of more delicate ways of phrasing this. Which, considering the circumstances I am currently facing, is patently absurd. I suppose the effort is not entirely wasted, though; it has at least distracted me from listening for the sound of approaching footsteps.

At any rate, I will go on by simply stating that the puppy refused to do as he ought. Had he been capable of folding his tiny paws across his chest and looking at me with lowered brows and stubbornly outthrust lip, he would have done it, I feel sure.

I waited. What else could I do?

I was certain that the moment I took him back upstairs, my aunt's carpet would once more be in mortal peril.

The street was silent and utterly deserted. My aunt and uncle's street is a quiet one. At eleven o'clock at night, their neighbours were all fast asleep in their beds rather than driving to or from dinner parties or theatre performances, as

The Wedding Gift

would be the case in Hanover Square or one of the more fashionable London neighbourhoods.

There was only one carriage in sight—a hansom cab—parked near the end of the street, as though waiting for someone. When the driver picked up the reins and urged the horses into motion, I was surprised, but not alarmed. It never occurred to me that there would be any danger.

The carriage came towards me, and I saw that the driver was muffled up to the eyes with woolly scarves, a greatcoat round his shoulders, and a broad-brimmed hat pulled down low over his forehead. But that did not seem unusual, either. The night was cold. I was already regretting that I had not thought to catch up a shawl before coming out.

Then—

I have replayed what happened next in my mind a hundred times or more. My insides still clench and my heart hammers with remembrance every time.

As the carriage rolled past me, the door opened, and a man leapt out. Likewise cloaked and muffled, he was little more than a shadowed shape in the dark. But big—I could see that much. A veritable giant of a man, and tremendously strong.

He seized hold of me, threw a thick layer of scratchy woollen blanket over my head, then picked me up like a bundle of washing.

At first I was too utterly stunned to react. It felt so unreal, as though I must be having a nightmare. Then I heard the sound of the puppy's frantic yipping, followed by a high-pitched yelp of pain. I suppose my abductor must have kicked him.

That snapped me free of my temporary paralysis. Rage swept through me, and I fought him—as well as I *could* fight, bundled as I was like a baby in swaddling. My attacker had a wad of the blanket clamped over my mouth so I could not bite or even scream, and he had my arms pinned at my sides. But I kicked and thrashed and tried with all my strength to wrench myself away.

I might as well have tried to kick a stone statue. His grip on me did not relax or even falter. Hauling me with him back to the carriage, he flung me roughly inside.

My head struck the hard edge of one of the seats, and my shoulder struck the floor. It aches yet, even now. I lay there, momentarily stunned, trying to breathe through the smothering layers of blanket. Trying above all to *think*.

My thoughts felt like rabbits, scampering frantically back to their burrow at the sight of a fox.

I felt the carriage sway as my attacker climbed into the compartment with me, and then a lurch as the wheels started to move, carrying me with every turn farther from Gracechurch Street and my uncle and aunt.

The realisation made me start upright, struggling to throw off the blanket. I had some idea of screaming out of one of the windows. The street had been deserted, but surely someone would hear if I made enough noise.

Before I could wrestle my way upright, though, a heavy weight settled on my back, pinning me to the ground.

"Now, now." The voice was deep. Heavy and ponderously slow, with a soft burr of a country accent. "You don't want to be doing that now, miss. Just keep quiet, and you won't be harmed."

I could have pointed out that my aching head and shoulder spoke to the contrary. I could also have pointed out that it was rather absurd to call me *miss*, considering the nature of our acquaintance thus far.

But the breath had been knocked out of me—and I was also not sure that I could keep my voice from shaking if I did speak. Large, calloused hands seized hold of my wrists, and I felt a rope being tied round them, binding them together so that I was truly helpless to move.

I do not know how long the journey lasted—somewhere between an hour and an eternity, at a guess. My attacker did not speak any more, and—to my slightly cowardly relief—he made no move to touch me again. I lay with my head and shoulder throbbing, jolting uncomfortably with every bounce and jounce of the carriage, and taking stock of my position—which was, as far as I could make out, depressing enough.

My aunt and uncle and all the servants had been asleep when I ran downstairs to take the puppy out-of-doors. Unless one of them heard me—which I do not think they can have done, since none of them came down during the time I was outside—no one will have any idea that I am gone. I cannot expect that anyone will miss me until morning, when they realise that I am not in my room and that my bed has not been slept in.

What will they do then? I keep trying to imagine it. They will notify Darcy. Of course he will mount a search. But by that time, I will have been gone for hours and hours. And there were no witnesses to my abduction that I know of. London is a vast, sprawling city, and neither Darcy nor my uncle and aunt will have the least idea of where to begin looking.

I do not know where I am myself, come to that. I have not the least notion.

To continue, though, since I have nothing else to do but try not to give way to abject panic.

After what seemed an age, the carriage drew to a halt. I heard a thump as the driver jumped down from his box, followed by a low murmur of voices—too soft and indistinct for me to make out the words.

Then the second man—my giant of an abductor—moved to lift me up and haul me out of the carriage. I debated whether to try and fight him again, but there seemed little point. Besides, I thought that I might be better off feigning unconsciousness so that I would have the advantage of surprise if an opportunity to fight back successfully and escape *did* come along.

Accordingly, I hung limp and lifeless while I was carried across what might have been cobblestones, to judge by the sound my attacker's boots made. Then we seemed to go inside a house or building and up some stairs. At last I was lowered to the floor. I felt a knife blade slide along my arms, and I froze, heart pounding sickeningly. But the man was only severing the rope that held my wrists.

I was bruised and sore from the carriage ride, and stiff from being bound in one position for so long. By the time I could manage to make my arms move and—at long last—throw off the smothering blanket, a door had closed and my attacker was gone.

That must have been about . . .

Again, it is nearly impossible for me to guess the time. An hour ago? Two?

I have examined every inch of the small chamber in which I am imprisoned—not that there is much to see. It is a tiny, dingy room with mildew-stained walls and a bare wooden floor. The air smells sour: a mixture of dust and dampness, and the smell of old cooking.

The only furniture is a rough mattress of sorts lying directly on the floor, so lumpy that it feels as though it must be stuffed with corn cobs. There is a window—or at least, the remains of one—but it has been bricked shut, leaving no way out. Despite the general decrepitude of the place, the door is of solid oak, heavy and strong, and barred from the outside. I have tried putting my shoulder to it, but it does not budge even a fraction.

The fireplace has the charred remains of a fire in the grate, the ashes long since gone cold. It looks as though someone has been burning letters or other documents, as I found the charred remains of thick, cream-coloured paper that looked as though it had once been used for writing. There were no legible scraps, however. Only a few meaningless fragments of letters, and one elaborately curling *B*.

I would not be averse to trying to climb out through the chimney. Actually, I would try it willingly, right now; that was my sole reason for inspecting the grate. But the opening is far too narrow for me to fit through.

I do have light, at least. A single candle burns in a dirty, chipped saucer on the floor. I ought to blow it out and conserve it, perhaps. The candle will not last forever, and there is only the one. But if I do blow it out, I have no striker with which to light it again, and so far I have not been able to give up the small, friendly-looking point of light, which is all that is enabling me to write these words.

Well, that and the stub of pencil I found in one dusty corner. I suppose that is a second dubious blessing to be counted right now—that I have both paper and the ability to write, though it is growing increasingly hard to hold my hand steady enough to form the letters.

The truth is that I am afraid. Horribly afraid.

I am worried about my poor little nameless puppy. I suppose that is ridiculous, considering my own predicament, but I cannot help it. My attacker kicked him, I suspect—but I have no way of knowing how badly the puppy might have been hurt.

He is outside on the street alone—and the nights have

been cold enough lately for frost to form on the windowpanes. If he cannot find shelter, I am afraid that he could easily freeze to death before anyone finds him.

And—I suppose there is no use trying to distract myself or deny it—I am afraid for myself. However hard I try to push it back, the fear keeps creeping in.

Fear and questions, besides.

Why have I been abducted? My mother, when she speaks of the dangers of London, is full of stories of girls sold into debauchery. But I cannot escape the conclusion that the carriage and my abductors were waiting for me—me in particular. The only explanation that seems to fit the facts is that they were watching my aunt and uncle's house for a chance to snatch me—just such a chance as I presented them with tonight.

And however hard I rack my brains, I cannot imagine *why*—

My hands are still shaking. It is entirely likely that my handwriting will henceforth be even more illegible than before. But at least I am once more alone.

I had to break off writing, for I heard the sound that I had been both expecting and dreading: footsteps mounting the stairway outside my door.

I had just time enough to thrust my paper and pencil under the edge of the mattress before I heard the sound of a key rattling in the lock. Then the door began to move.

My heart was beating in short, hard bursts. I was expecting a man—my giant of an abductor, maybe, or the carriage driver. But instead, a woman entered.

The Wedding Gift

I did not know whether to be relieved or further alarmed.

She was of medium height, middle-aged, and extremely thin—really, almost gaunt. She had a pale, narrow face, the skin stretched tight over sharp bones. Her eyes were a steely shade of blue and set just a little too close together, and her lips had a discontented look, pinched and sour. Her hair was greying, and looked thin as well.

Altogether, she looked like someone once respectable who had since fallen on harder times. Her brown silk dress was of a good cut, and had once been of fine quality, but it now appeared wrinkled and worn, nearly threadbare. Her ruffled cap had a limp and slightly dingy air.

She carried a lamp—it was this that allowed me to see the particulars of her appearance. Holding the lamp aloft, she stepped into the room, and then stopped.

For a moment, we simply stared at each other without speaking. Anything I could think of to say—*What do you want with me? Where am I?*—sounded in my own ears like something out of a gothic novel. Besides, I was not perfectly convinced that I could keep my voice from shaking.

I may have admitted in writing to being afraid, but I was determined not to reveal my fear to my captors.

I might have tried pushing past her out the door. She was taller than I am, but did not look strong. But I caught sight of the hulking form of my original captor standing just behind her in the doorway.

In the lamplight, he was revealed to be a young man—perhaps my age, or a year or two more—with fair hair plastered down over his forehead and a broad, slightly vacant-looking countenance.

Escape was still impossible. So I simply sat motionless,

my hands locked together to keep them from shaking, and stared.

I was faintly comforted by the odd impression that the woman was nervous too. Her eyes kept darting about the room, and her movements were simultaneously jerky and controlled, as though she were trapped in a children's game and expected at any moment that someone would jump out at her and shout *boo!*

She swallowed several times and then at last said, "You need not worry. If you do exactly as we ask, you will not be harmed."

I cleared my throat. "That is more or less what your muscular companion there told me. Just before he tied my hands, bundled me in a blanket, and locked me in this room." I was surprised to find my voice quite steady. "So you will, I hope, forgive me if I treat your assurance with some skepticism."

The woman swallowed again, the muscles of her throat contracting above the dingy lace ruff of her dress. "You will not be harmed," she repeated. There was something firm and precise about her way of speaking. Nervous as she was, I had the impression that she was accustomed to giving instructions. "All you need do is write a letter."

"A *letter*?" It seemed the most improbable reason for a kidnapping I could possibly have invented.

"Yes, a letter," the woman snapped. A sudden, cold look of dislike glittered behind her nearly colourless eyes. "You will write a letter to Mr. Fitzwilliam Darcy, stating that you are putting an end to your engagement and explaining that you do not wish to marry him after all."

The Wedding Gift

Despite all appearances to the contrary, I did not actually break off writing a short while ago for dramatic effect. I ran out of room on the few blank sheets of paper I had stuffed into the pocket of my dressing gown.

I am writing this now on the extra sheets which Mrs. Younge brought me. I suppose that if she is determined to see me blight my life, she is at least not stingy about the supplies with which she is forcing me to do it.

But I am getting ahead of myself. I have not even set down how I came to be aware of her name.

There is nothing else for me to do but write—well, that and think, but thinking is a thoroughly unpleasant occupation at present. So I will keep on with my narrative.

I believe my jaw dropped open, and I must have stared at the strange woman for nearly half a minute before managing to articulate any words in response to her demand.

"You wish me to end my engagement?" I stared at her. "But why on earth . . . I mean, why should you possibly care whether I marry Darcy or not?"

The woman's eyes narrowed as she looked at me. "You do not even know who I am, do you?"

"Should I? I beg your pardon if my ignorance gives offence, but I cannot recall that we have ever met."

My sarcasm more or less bounced off her like dry peas off a wall. I am not even sure she knew I had spoken. Her eyes, still bright with angry dislike, were fixed on my face. Her thin lips twisted in a sneer. "I know your sort. You believe yourself superior to the rest of us simply because you have schemed and connived and managed to attract the notice of a rich man."

I said nothing. Really, I could think of nothing to say. I was hardly about to agree with her. But if I tried to deny it, she would say that I was clearly protesting too much, and her opinion of me would only be confirmed.

So I waited, and after a moment, she went on.

"I served your precious Mr. Darcy. I took charge of his dullard of a sister and guarded her with the most tender care. And what thanks did I get for it?"

Her voice grew shrill with indignation. Behind her, the blond giant shifted his weight as though uncomfortable.

"Your Mr. Darcy threw me out into the street—without a penny, without a single care for my well-being!"

The words blazed through my mind, forging a sudden connection and making sense of the whole insane plot.

A few years ago, Darcy employed a woman called Mrs. Younge as Georgiana's governess-companion. He terminated her employment when she tried to manipulate Georgiana into an elopement with George Wickham.

At that moment, I realised this woman must be the same Mrs. Younge.

I sat up straighter. My situation had not materially improved, but all the same, I was far less frightened than I had been.

"I believe that your definition of the phrase 'guarded her with the most tender care' is somewhat at variance with the generally accepted meaning. Most people would not see attempting to engineer an elopement between a thorough scoundrel and a fifteen-year-old girl the act of one who had the welfare of her charge at heart."

Mrs. Younge's lips thinned with anger. "We are not here to discuss that. You will write the letter as I dictate it to you." I could hear the authority of a former governess in her tone.

I raised my eyebrows. "Or?"

"Or we will not release you until you do." Mrs. Younge's

pale eyes regarded me coldly. "I will venture to say that after a day or two in this room with nothing to eat or drink, you will be in a far more compliant frame of mind."

I stared at her, my thoughts churning rapidly. Every instinct stubbornly rebelled against capitulating without as much fight as I was capable of putting up. Yet, what else could I do but give way?

I could refuse and let them try to starve me into submission. But that would take time. I did not want to spend another moment in this ugly little room than I could possibly help. Besides which, my odds of escape seemed greater if I did not wait until I was weak from hunger and thirst.

As I met Mrs. Younge's wintery gaze, the faintest glimmer of a plan began to form in my mind.

I dropped my head, trying to let my whole posture droop in a way that I hoped suggested defeat. "Very well," I said. "If you bring me paper and pen, I shall do as you ask."

Mrs. Younge did so. She stood over me, too, and dictated the words I was to write. The letter was very brief and stiff. Though I suppose, really, there is no particularly good way of breaking off an engagement two weeks before one's wedding.

The whole time that I was faithfully transcribing Mrs. Younge's words, I kept thinking of Darcy. What will he think when he reads the letter? Will he believe it?

I hope he will not. Yet the letter is unquestionably in my hand, stating categorically that I have no wish to marry him after all. And the whole of this affair is so wildly fantastical, that I cannot hope for him to suspect the truth.

I hate the thought of the pain he will feel on reading the missive. I hate whatever insane impulse led Mrs. Younge to concoct this preposterous scheme.

Is it simply a desire for revenge that has led her to this point? Anger at Darcy for having dismissed her from her position as Georgiana's companion? Certainly that must be part of it.

But sitting here alone, I have begun to have a glimmer of an idea that the desire for revenge does not constitute the whole of her motivation.

I am also coldly, sickeningly aware that even if Darcy does not believe the contents of the letter, my position is still ugly enough.

After I had finished transcribing the letter, I looked up at Mrs. Younge. I tried to appear meek and pleading. It did not take much effort to allow my voice to shake. "I have done as you asked. Now may I please go?"

An ugly, satisfied little smile curved Mrs. Younge's lips as she read over the letter and blew on the ink to dry it. "Oh no. We must allow time for word of your scandalous disappearance to spread. Your aunt and uncle will surely insist on mounting a search for you, even if your fine Mr. Darcy is too offended by what you have written to care whether you are missing or not."

Darcy *will* care—I know he will.

I was not really surprised by Mrs. Younge's refusal to release me. But I was angry enough that I forgot to make my voice timid and shaking as I asked, "For word to spread? What is the point of that?"

The twisted little smirk deepened at the corners of Mrs. Younge's mouth. "Why, because that way it will be the scandal of the Season when you are discovered in St. James's Street, wearing nothing but a nightdress and dressing gown." She looked at my attire. "To be sure, it was good of you to give the boys the opportunity of snatching you up at night. I daresay we could have managed equally well had we been forced to abduct you during the day. But this will create far more of a sensation."

It certainly will. St. James's Street is where the most exclusive gentlemen's clubs in London are located. It is also a street on which no woman—no respectable woman—is ever seen. It may be stupid; it may be unfair. But a woman who so much as walks down St. James's Street has her reputation forever compromised in the eyes of the world.

If Mrs. Younge and her companions drive me there and abandon me as I am now—dishevelled, hair unbound, and wearing nothing but my nightclothes ...

Mrs. Younge is correct that it will be the scandal of the Season. I may even flatter myself that it will be the scandal of the *decade*.

Regardless of what I may say to defend myself, it will appear in the eyes of the world as though I have broken my engagement to Darcy to run off with another man. Possibly a married man? Gossip will probably hint as much.

Gossip will likewise speculate that said married gentleman must have broken off our association and cast me out into the street.

When my sister Lydia eloped, our sister Mary took the opportunity to point out that a woman's reputation is no less brittle than it is beautiful, and that one false step involves her in endless ruin.

At the time, the sentiment made my fingers twitch with the urge to smash something. Or possibly to throw something at Mary.

I feel that way still—especially considering that a gentleman found wandering London in his nightshirt would be laughed at and deemed either drunk or eccentric, but nothing more.

The fact remains, though, that if Mrs. Younge has her

way, a patch of mud will look positively clean and sparkling when compared to my reputation.

Darcy's reputation will be ruined, too—even if I get out of here and have the chance of explaining to him what has occurred.

If he believes me.

My imagination keeps painting horrible pictures of him being so much offended by the letter Mrs. Younge forced me to write that he will not even listen if and when I try to explain.

But no. I spent the better part of a year doing Darcy every sort of injustice in my estimations of him. I will *not* doubt him or the strength of his feelings for me now.

Besides, if I am successful, I hope that I may yet escape both this nasty little room and the scandal Mrs. Younge hopes to create.

I am going to stop writing now, lie down on the abominably lumpy mattress, and try to sleep a little, as best as I can.

And I am going to hope, with every part of my energy and will, that I have a chance in the morning to execute my plan.

Friday
6 November 1812

I have decided that being forced to wait without occupation or distraction is the vilest state of being imaginable.

I have paced the narrow confines of this room half a hundred times. It is five steps each way, if I pace back and forth. Twelve if I pace in a circle.

The opportunity I spent last night praying for did, in fact, arrive. Though I am not sure right now whether that makes the waiting more endurable or less.

I felt sure last night that Mrs. Younge would wish to deliver my letter to Darcy's residence herself. She dare not let him see her, of course. But she will also wish to be certain that the document arrives. Apparently I was right. At least, she did not appear this morning, when I heard the sound of a key once more scraping in the lock.

It is difficult to judge time in a windowless room. But it *felt*, somehow, as though it was morning.

It was my giant of an abductor who entered—the big, burly, blond-haired young man. He was carrying a tray of some stale bread and a cup of weak-looking tea.

He stumped slowly into the room, deposited the tray on the floor without speaking a word, and then turned to go. But I stopped him.

"Wait!"

He made a slow turn to face me. I had the impression that *slow* is more or less a watchword with him, and had a moment to wonder how Mrs. Younge had found him. Is he simply a common ruffian, hired for the purpose of this scheme, or do they have some previous acquaintance?

At any rate, his expression as he looked at me was somewhere between bemusement and surprise. He looked as though he had not taken into consideration that I might speak to him, and now had to (slowly) readjust his plans.

"Yes, miss?"

He still spoke politely, at least.

I swallowed. Now that the moment had come, my heart was hammering so hard in my chest that it seemed impossible he should not hear it.

I said, choosing my words with care, "Are you being paid for keeping me here?"

The giant frowned, looking at me warily. Plainly he had not been instructed as to whether or not to answer questions from me.

Finally, he made an indeterminate movement with his head, which I took to be a nod.

I swallowed again. My throat felt painfully dry, and not only with thirst.

"Mr. Darcy has given me a necklace. A very expensive necklace. It is at my aunt and uncle's house now. If you would be willing to deliver another letter for me, I could send for it. I could reassure my aunt and uncle that I am well and unharmed, but wish to have the necklace with me. They will give it to you for delivery, and then you can bring it to me here. It should fetch a handsome price if we find a way to sell it."

The proposal had so many holes that I could have driven a horse and cart through them all. Mrs. Younge would have seen through such a scheme in a moment. But her blond-haired accomplice was another matter entirely. That is why the whole of my plan hinged on being able to speak with him alone.

As it was, even the giant's eyes narrowed as he regarded me. "What would you be wantin' to do that for?"

I shrugged, trying to look both casual and sincere at the same time. "If I am no longer to marry Mr. Darcy, I will need money. He will, no doubt, ultimately demand the necklace back, since our engagement is at an end. But he cannot have it back if we manage to sell it first."

I looked up at him. "I will make you a bargain. If you will go and fetch the necklace for me and bring it here, I will let you have half of the proceeds from its sale." I smiled at him. "I will leave it to you whether or not you want to tell Mrs. Younge anything about our arrangement."

The blond giant's eyebrows drew together as he frowned, clearly trying to work out the implications of my scheme. My heart seemed to stumble to a stop as I held my breath, waiting for his response.

As it turned out, he did not so much as try to drive a harder bargain or demand a larger share from the necklace's sale.

Or, thank heavens, ask why he shouldn't just take the necklace straight away to be sold, instead of bringing it first to me.

He gave a ponderous nod, and said, "That's a bargain, then."

I seized my pen and paper and wrote the note I had been planning all night long between attempts at sleep.

It read thus:

> *Dearest Uncle and Aunt,*
>
> *Find, I pray you, the necklace that I have locked in my jewellery case On my dressing table. Let me assure you that I am well, but simply have need of it. Leave the necklace in the charge of the gentleman with whom I am entrusting this note. Once my business is taken care of, I Will return.*
>
> *Yours,*
> *Elizabeth Bennet*

The blond giant left me.

Now I have nothing to do but hope with all of my heart that he will deliver the message—and that whoever reads it will understand.

Later...

It is over. *Over.*

I feel as though I must be dreaming—as though I will at any moment wake up and find myself back in that grim, nasty little room again. I suppose that is why I am writing this now instead of sleeping in my own bed: I am trying to shake off the last, clinging bits of anxiety and convince myself that I no longer have anything to fear.

After I finished writing before, I waited—and paced some more—for what seemed like hours. It seemed as though my blond friend should have had time to collect fifty necklaces, and at every moment, I was afraid that either he had decided to simply steal the necklace and keep all of the profits from its sale after all, or that whoever read my note had not understood the message hidden therein.

When at long last I heard footsteps mounting the stairs outside my door at a run, my heart tried to leap up into my throat. There was a rattle of keys, the door was flung open—and Darcy exploded into the room.

I have been glad to see him before, but *never* so glad as I was in that moment. An overwhelming relief hit me like a physical force, weakening all my muscles, so that I had to steady myself against the wall. I still might have fallen, had Darcy not come in and caught me up in his arms.

He held me very tightly, and for a moment I could not speak at all. I think he was saying something—asking whether I was hurt—but I could not even make out the words. I could only close my eyes, resting my forehead against the hollow of his shoulder.

"How did you find me?" I managed to say at last. I had not cried at all during my night spent alone in that horrid room, yet now, at the sight of him, I felt myself perilously close to tears.

Darcy's hands shook slightly as he reached to smooth my hair. "I followed your messenger. Or rather, I followed the instructions in your letter. Your *second* letter." He drew back enough to look down at me. "What has happened? First I received a letter from you this morning that fairly made my hair stand on end. Then when I went directly to your uncle and aunt's house, hoping to beg you to reconsider, I found a messenger with a second letter from you. One that seemed to contain a message. So I did as your letter asked—I followed the ruffian who came to deliver it. Then, when he reached this house, I approached him and . . . *persuaded* him to tell me where you were."

I gave a shaky laugh. "Persuaded?"

The grimness of Darcy's tone suggested that there had been decidedly little in the way of calm reasoning involved.

"I might have informed him that I would shoot him in both legs if he did not first of all tell me where you were, and second, return my mother's necklace to me."

For the first time, I noticed that Darcy carried a pearl-handled revolver; it protruded from the pocket of his greatcoat.

"You have the necklace?" I let out a breath of relief. "Oh, thank heaven. I was worried about taking the risk of using it this way—"

Darcy dismissed the question of his mother's diamonds as though they were cheap imitation paste. "I would have counted fifty necklaces well lost if they led me to you. But yes, I got it back. I have it here."

He touched the pocket of his waistcoat. "Our large friend's valour being apparently inferior to his physique," Darcy went on, "he gave way and handed over both the jewels and the key to this room. When last I saw him, he was beating a hasty retreat down the road." Darcy shook his head. "But what has happened? Are you all right? The first letter, saying that you did not wish to marry me after all—"

Before he could finish, the tears that had been threatening abruptly broke. All the horrors and fears and tensions of the last night suddenly seemed to strike me all at once, and I started to cry.

"I'm sorry—I'm so sorry for everything! You and my aunt and uncle have been caused the most terrible worry, *and* you were very nearly exposed to the most vicious sort of gossip, besides. If anyone should ever hear of this . . . and in addition to everything else, I've lost your groodle!"

Darcy only held me closer during most of this more or less incoherent flood. But that last made him blink. "My . . . what?"

"A dog." I hiccupped and made an effort to wipe my eyes. "Well, not precisely a dog. Truth be told, he looks more like a sausage with curly fur, but—"

Darcy looked at me more closely. "Are you quite certain that you are not hurt? If you were struck over the head—"

I hiccupped another laugh and made an effort to regain control. "I am not hallucinating or suffering a concussion, I assure you. Ask Georgiana and Edward. It is just that . . . I purchased a dog. Well, a puppy. A greyhound-spaniel-pug-poodle. But I lost him!"

Apparently I had not managed to regain control after all; on the last words, my voice broke all over again.

Darcy looked at me in alarm. "If you will promise that we are indeed still engaged to be married, I will buy you all the greyhound-spaniel-pug . . . what was the last one?"

I sniffed. "Poodle."

"Yes, poodle. All the spaniel-greyhound-pug-*poodles* you could possibly wish for."

Despite myself, I started to laugh. "That must be the strangest incentive for marriage in the entire history of the institution." I wiped my eyes again. "Yes, as far as I am concerned, at least, we are still engaged. And I will explain everything—only, please, can we first get away from this dreadful place?"

The house proved to be deserted. Mrs. Younge had apparently still not returned, so we were able to leave without impediment.

I had not seen the outside of the house or the street at all before. It proved to be a shabby little dwelling on a narrow street near to the river. Darcy and I had to walk several blocks before he could find a cab—for of course, following my blond-haired abductor, Darcy had come on foot.

Once we were settled inside the cab, I leaned my head against the leather seat and finally allowed myself to relax.

"It was lucky that you understood the meaning of my message," I said.

Outside the cab's window, the sun was shining; it was a

chill, crisp late-autumn morning, and every turn of the carriage wheels took us farther away from my whole ordeal. "I was not sure anyone would realise that the capital letters spelled out the word *Follow*."

"Luck?" Darcy gave me a look of mock affrontment. "It was only my superior intellect that allowed me to filter out the extraneous capital *I*'s to get from F-I-I-O-L-I-L-I-O-I-W, or what have you, to F-O-L-L-O-W."

He was sitting beside me instead of on the seat opposite, as though he wanted to remain as close to me as he possibly could. He put one arm around me, his face turning sober once more. "I thank heaven that I *did* understand. That you were able to convey such a message. When I think what might have happened—"

"They intended me no harm. Well, not really. Only to prevent our marriage."

Darcy's face grew grimmer still as I finally explained the whole of what had occurred. He would, I think, have turned straight around and waited for Mrs. Younge to return to the shabby little house if I had not persuaded him otherwise.

"Let her go," I said. "If we attempt to bring criminal charges against her, it will make the most dreadful scandal."

Darcy snorted. "If you think I care more about scandal than I do about your welfare—"

"But *I* care. I do not want your good name dragged through the mud. Besides, if we accuse Mrs. Younge of the crime, Georgiana will inevitably hear of it—and I should hate that. She already feels guilty enough for nearly being persuaded into eloping with George Wickham. If she learns of Mrs. Younge's attempt at revenge, she will feel as though it is in some way her fault—you know she will, even though it is plainly nothing of the kind."

I believe it was my mention of Georgiana more than

anything else that persuaded Darcy to let the matter go. He frowned, the corners of his mouth still compressed, but finally nodded. "Prosecuting Mrs. Younge would involve a public explanation of her grievances against me, which would, in turn, expose Georgiana to ill-natured gossip." He rubbed his forehead. "I wish that I could see her happily settled with a man worthy of her esteem."

I thought of Georgiana's face, the way her expression and her voice changed at the mention of Edward's name. "I am sure you will—in time. She is still very young."

Darcy nodded. Then he frowned again, returning to the subject of Mrs. Younge. "I still cannot believe that Mrs. Younge can have conceived such a scheme for revenge on me. If she really believed that such a clumsy attempt to dishonour your reputation would alter my feelings for you in the slightest—"

I smiled up at him. "Apparently she does not understand how entirely irresistible I am."

Darcy laughed. And then—despite our being inside a cab, in full view of a busy London street outside the window—he lowered his head and kissed me, long and lingeringly.

"Irresistible indeed," he said. His voice was husky when we finally drew apart.

I leaned against him, letting myself soak in the feeling of his arms about me. I debated for a moment whether or not to speak of my own private suspicions. But they would only cause Darcy pain, and I have not the smallest shred of proof, besides. Only a letter *B* inscribed on a sheet of burned paper.

It is perhaps only my suspicious nature that leads me to wonder whether that *B* was once part of the signature of Lady Catherine de Bourgh. Whether this whole scheme for preventing our marriage originated in *her* mind, not Mrs. Younge's.

The Wedding Gift

She could have paid Mrs. Younge for enacting my abduction. I am certain that Lady Catherine would consider it money well spent if it succeeded in putting a halt to our wedding.

But I said nothing of that out loud. I have no proof, as I say. And if Lady Catherine wishes to persist in her efforts of driving a wedge between Darcy and me, she will find me a far more formidable opponent than she thinks.

It is very late. My candle has nearly burned itself out, and I ought to stop writing and go to bed.

But I nearly forgot. There is a further happy ending to my tale.

As our cab rolled to a stop outside my aunt and uncle's house, I saw a young man in stablehand's garb walking down the street with a small, furry bundle under one arm.

"Good morning, miss. Sir." He tipped his hat to Darcy and me as we climbed down from the carriage, and I recognised him as John, the stable boy who works for my aunt and uncle's next-door neighbour. "I'm trying to find out whether this little beggar belongs to anyone on the street. I found him this morning inside the horse's stall—curled up in the straw, comfortable as you please. Shouldn't think he's worth much—looks like some street mutt to me. But you never know."

John looked down at the bundle under his arm, and I saw that it was my puppy. Looking more preposterous even than he had the night before, with dirt and muck and bits of straw stuck all over him. But I was too relieved to care.

"Yes, he's mine!" I took the little dog into my arms and kissed his head—which earned me a sleepy swipe of his small pink tongue. "That is—" I glanced a little tentatively at Darcy. "I suppose, properly speaking, that he is yours. If you do not think him too ridiculous to serve as a wedding gift."

Darcy looked at the small, dirty puppy cradled in my arms, and laughed. "I would not trade him for all the impeccably bred hounds in England." He rumpled the puppy's ears. "What do you think of Odysseus for a name?"

"Odysseus?" I started to laugh, too. "After the Greek hero? It is certainly a noble name. But why?"

Darcy smiled—then pulled me closer, looping his arms around my waist and resting his cheek against my hair. "Because today seems a good day for remembering adventurers who endure danger yet still find their way home."

ABOUT ANNA ELLIOTT

Anna Elliott writes historical fiction and fantasy. Her first series, the *Twilight of Avalon* trilogy, is a retelling of the Trystan and Isolde legend. She wrote her second series, *The Pride and Prejudice Chronicles*, chiefly to satisfy her own curiosity about what might have happened to Elizabeth Bennet, Mr. Darcy, and all the other wonderful cast of characters after the official end of Jane Austen's classic work.

She enjoys stories about strong women, and loves exploring the multitude of ways women can find their unique strengths. Anna lives in the Washington DC area with her husband and three children.

Visit her website at AnnaElliottBooks.com

Dream of a Glorious Season

by Sarah M. Eden

OTHER WORKS BY SARAH M. EDEN

Seeking Persephone
Courting Miss Lancaster
The Kiss of a Stranger
Friends and Foes
An Unlikely Match
Drops of Gold
Glimmer of Hope
As You Are
Longing for Home
Hope Springs
The Sheriffs of Savage Wells
For Elise

One

Miss Elizabeth Gillerford counted amongst her most notable realizations one she had at the very wise age of eight and three quarters. She came to the irrefutable understanding that her heart would forever belong to the twelve-year-old boy to whom her sister had already pledged a life of devotion: their neighbor, Julian Broadwood.

Falling desperately in love was painful enough for any eight-year-old girl, but having a heart so fickle as to devote itself to the object of the deepest longing of one's sister added another layer of acute discomfort. Thus Elizabeth spent the next ten years in various stages of misery and heartbreak.

Mary, her older sister, had made her first bows to Society two years earlier, and, seeing as Julian had made very few appearances, Mary remained unhappily unattached but determined to wring a proposal out of Julian. Unfortunately, their parents were sticklers for the strictest versions of social etiquette, so until Mary wed, Elizabeth simply had to wait for her own debut in Society. At nearly nineteen, she was quickly growing embarrassingly old to have not made her bows.

"Society doesn't entirely forbid a younger sister from being out before her older sister is married," Elizabeth argued to her parents a week before the Season was set to truly begin once more. "Especially if the older sister doesn't seem to be making progress and the younger sister is more than old enough to have a Season."

Her father was already shaking his head, the movement setting his jowls flopping about. "Some may be willing to flaunt expectations willy-nilly, but the Gillerfords are stalwart. We do not bend to—"

"—the fickle winds of ever-changing opinion," Elizabeth said under her breath in perfect unison with her father's declaration. She had long ago learned a deep appreciation for his opposition to fickle winds. In full voice once more, she argued, "I am nearly nineteen, Father, and will soon be so firmly lodged on the shelf that I may as well be a book in the darkest corners of a lending library."

Mother chose that exact moment to wander inside. "Oh, dear. You haven't been frequenting the lending library, have you? People will begin to form the wrong idea of you."

"They might think I read?" Elizabeth asked dryly.

"Precisely." Mother emphasized the declaration with a widening of her eyes and a desperate nod of her head. "A girl should read, of course; she simply shouldn't make a point of doing so. The ladies will think you a touch too blue for their company, and the gentlemen will think you a vast deal too educated for theirs."

This was an old argument that Elizabeth knew far too well. "Gregory does not think me too educated for *his* company."

Mother waved that off. "Brothers are supposed to overlook their sisters' faults."

"Faults." Lovely.

"What of Julian Broadwood?" Elizabeth asked. "He has never shown any disgust at my refusal to hide my literacy."

Mother had no immediate answer. Father filled in the gap.

"He is meant for Mary," he said. "No doubt he already views you quite as his own sister, and therefore has joined Gregory in turning a blind eye to your oddities."

"Has he at last declared his intention to court Mary, then?" She tried to ask the question casually. But how does one lackadaisically ask if one's heart is about to be crushed to a fine powder and sent adrift on, as her father would have called it, the fickle winds of change?

"Our family and the Broadwoods have always understood that young Julian and our dear Mary would make a match of it," Father said in a tone of scolding. "He needn't come to make a formal declaration."

"Well, if he means to marry her, I wish he would hurry and do so." Oddly enough, she very nearly meant it. "If she were engaged, I could make my bows and find myself a husband, since no one in the neighborhood bothered to conveniently produce a son for me to marry."

She refused to admit to anyone that, as far as she was concerned, Julian fit that description. She preferred to do her suffering in secret.

Mother dropped onto her chaise longue, pressing her fingers elegantly to her temples. "You do give me such headaches with all of your nonsense, Elizabeth."

"I know, Mother. I know." She left her parents in the sitting room and walked out of sight down the corridor before sighing aloud in frustration.

A girl should read, of course, she simply shouldn't make a point of doing so.

She had endured such ridiculousness for nearly nineteen years. She couldn't do so much longer. Heaven help her, if she was left on the shelf and had to live out her life in her parents' house, she would go mad.

Two

Julian stood beside his best friend, Damion, on the walk outside the Gillerfords' London home, attempting to convince himself to go inside. As an old friend of the family, he couldn't very well not make an appearance at their ball. More pressing even than that, his mother would summon him to Broadwood House before breakfast had even cooled the next morning to ring a peal over his head if he didn't spend at least a full hour at the Gillerfords' ball, dancing and socializing and generally pretending he was happy to be there.

"Don't turn lily-livered on me now, old boy," Damion, insisted. "You've ducked out of nearly every social obligation these past two years. I'll not keep making excuses for you."

Julian groaned and dragged himself forward.

"I doubt Miss Gillerford will be waiting on the other side of the door with a vicar and a license," Damion reassured him. "You'll be obligated to a single set with her. You've courage enough for that, surely."

"Dancing with her is like a prisoner tying the knot in his own noose."

Julian plastered a smile on his face as they stepped into the front foyer. There stood his row of anxious executioners: Mr. and Mrs. Gillerford grinned with glee at seeing him. Mary's eyes took on that eerie aura of possessiveness she'd first adopted when she was ten and he almost twelve. He liked it even less now than he had then.

He made his bows as quickly as possible without being rude. Mary opened her mouth to say something. Julian spoke first. "I do not see Miss Elizabeth."

Mrs. Gillerford hit him playfully with her fan. "You know full well that she is not out in Society yet."

He did, indeed, know, and it bothered him to no end. "But she is quite of an age to be so."

Mr. Gillerford's brow furrowed with indignation. "She'll have her come out when it is proper."

In all truth, the "proper" time had come and gone. Beth ought to have made her bows the year before. He could easily picture her upstairs, watching the carriages arrive and quite eloquently decrying the ridiculousness of her exclusion from it all.

He found her absence trying as well. She, along with her brother, who avoided London as one would a den of hungry wolves, were the only members of that family with whom he enjoyed spending time, Beth being preferable even to Gregory. She conversed with intelligence. Her sense of humor displayed her innate wit. She didn't flaunt her wealth or beauty the way her mother and sister insisted on doing. In short, she was pleasant company, a rare enough thing in Society. He'd always liked her.

"You will be pleased to know that our Mary has her supper dance open," Mrs. Gillerford said.

Julian was far too adept at side stepping such things to fall into that trap. "I shall be certain tomorrow to ask my mother what fortunate gentleman was granted the privilege of claiming her supper dance." He took a step closer to the ballroom. "Forgive me for holding up the reception line so long."

With that, he made good his escape.

"Excellently done," Damion said, slapping him on the back. "Does Wellington know your knack for stratagems?"

"I have had several years of practice." He glanced back at the reception line, barely holding back a shudder. "The Gillerfords have it firmly in their heads that I am destined to be their son-in-law. *I* am firmly convinced that they would take a supper dance, or an overly long glance, or my willingness to be in the same room as their older daughter as tantamount to a declaration. They'd have our announcement in the papers by morning."

They stepped into the ballroom with its din of voices. He and Damion cringed in unison. Together they'd survived more than their share of Society functions.

"Time for the 'two in a row'?" Damion asked the question to which they both knew the answer.

"I'll meet you at the punch bowl in an hour," Julian said. "Make certain to greet enough matrons to warrant whispers over tea tomorrow. If we're forced to be here, we may as well receive credit for it."

They set off in opposite directions, in search of two young ladies they could ask to dance. Experience had shown them that two sets within two hours, plus a few well placed "Good evenings" gave the impression they had spent far more time at a ball than they actually had.

Julian had made a point of choosing for his two-in-a-row partners young ladies who didn't seem likely to have any other partners. Those ladies relegated to the lonely corners were often neglected and ignored. They deserved to be treated with kindness. And he generally found they were finer company than the belles of the ball.

Out of the corner of his eye, he spotted a silhouette in an unused doorway. He couldn't say just how he knew, but he identified her in an instant. Did Beth always spy on her parents' balls, or was today a special occasion? He intended to ask her, though doing so meant abandoning his efforts at securing a partner for the first set of dances.

Damion'll have my neck. Still, he moved quickly in the direction of Beth's hiding place. He might manage to fit in two sets after speaking with her. But time or no time, he wanted to see his old friend.

Just as he reached the doorway, she disappeared into the darkness. With a quick look around to make certain no one in the ballroom saw him, he slipped out and stepped into the room beyond.

Only moonlight spilling through French doors illuminated the space at all—Mr. Gillerford's library, by the looks of it.

"I know you're in here, Beth," he whispered.

"If you give me away, so help me . . ."

He turned back in the direction of her voice and found her watching him from beside the door, arms folded defiantly across her chest. She'd always been firmly independent. That was one of the greatest things about her. Julian snatched up her hand and pulled her over to the French doors.

"Where are we going?" she asked.

"Outside," he explained. "If we're found in here, I'll have to run myself through with my own sword."

"Rather than be forced to marry me, is that it?"

Being caught alone meant not merely a forced marriage, but also leaving her reputation in ruins, painting himself as a cad, and destroying their friendship. So, yes. He'd rather they not be found out. He shrugged, keeping to the more casual tone they'd thus far employed. "More or less."

A few people wandered about on the terrace. Julian slipped Beth's arm through his. "Pretend this is commonplace," he whispered. "We'd best not attract too much notice."

"No amount of pretending will change the fact that I'm not dressed for a ball."

He hadn't noted her attire until that moment. Her dress was decidedly plain, but at least she wasn't in her nightrail or anything equally scandalous. They kept to the edges of the small, lantern-lit garden. Poor Beth looked deucedly uncomfortable. He wouldn't keep her but a moment.

"What is this nonsense I hear about you not having a Season again this year?"

"Didn't you know, Jules?" she answered dryly. "The Gillerfords are stalwart and cling stubbornly to even the most archaic of notions."

"That makes me wonder if you're actually a foundling."

Beth had more sense in her smallest toe than her entire family did combined. "What half-witted notion is your father clinging to this time?"

She picked a flower from an obliging bush. "He won't allow me a Season until Mary is married."

Julian eyed her sidelong. "Has he met your sister? You'll never get a Season."

"Believe me, I am fully aware of that." She spun the little yellow flower in her fingers. "I am hatching a plot to abduct an unsuspecting gentleman and force him to wed her."

He stopped right in the middle of the path. "Is that what this is? You're walking me to my matrimonial demise?"

"Don't be dramatic." She kept walking, leaving him behind.

He hurriedly caught up to her. "You didn't pick me for Mary?" He was busy enough disabusing *Mary* of that idea without Beth taking up the same notion.

"Good gracious, no," she answered. "If you ever set your cap at Mary, I'll—"

"—run me through with my own sword?" he finished for her.

She shrugged. "More or less."

Lands, Beth was always vastly fun to spend time with. She deserved her share of Society and diversions.

"Your banishment must be remedied," he said firmly.

"It's not banishment so much as forced hermitry." She sighed, though without any of the theatrics so many young ladies employed. "At times I feel trapped in this house."

"What would you do if you had London at your feet and the freedom of being out in Society?" He was honestly curious.

"Hatchard's. Hyde Park. Balls, dinner parties. At this point, I would settle for anything other than these corridors and this back garden." She held her hands up in helplessness. "I said 'hermitry,' and 'hermitry' it is."

"We must find a way of getting you out of this house." There had to be a solution.

Beth tossed him a lopsided smile. "Are you volunteering to sacrifice one of your friends for Mary's cause?" Her auburn eyebrow arched doubtfully.

"I have far too few friends to risk losing one in such a drastic fashion. They would all abandon me after that." He took her hand in his and met her gaze. "I *will* think of something, Beth. I swear to you, I will."

"I'll hold you to that," she warned.

He pressed a kiss to the back of her hand. "Now, sneak back in and up to your room. I'll return to the ball after I'm certain you haven't been spotted." No point working on her entry into Society if he'd ruined her reputation beforehand. "Dream of a glorious Season, my friend."

"Or Mary's untimely demise," she said.

He grinned. "Whichever brings you the greatest satisfaction."

He kept to the gardens for a long moment after she slipped away and around the back of the house. It was utterly unfair that she was denied Society and all its enjoyments simply because her older sister was too wretched to be courted.

"I will find a way to help her," he vowed. "I will."

Three

Since Elizabeth was destined to die a lonely old maid with a vast deal too many cats, the ten minutes she had spent with Julian at the ball were likely to be the highlight of her rather pathetic existence. He'd laughed with her, listened to her, swapped ridiculous observations on the absurdities of life. That had been their way for years. It was little wonder, really, that she was so fully in love with the thick-headed man. They were wonderful together, but he thought of her only as little Beth, with whom he'd grown up.

She sat on the window seat in her bedchamber, her stitching lying untouched on her lap. Sewing was possibly her least favorite occupation. She'd much rather read, but Father's Town library was severely lacking in anything with even the slightest appeal.

Mary stepped abruptly inside. "I need your green bonnet."

Elizabeth had long since stopped expecting her sister to *ask* for anything, let alone ask kindly. "You have boxes and boxes of lovely bonnets."

Mary rolled her eyes and sighed loudly. "But none of them are green. I cannot be seen in my cream carriage dress without a green bonnet. Now, where is it?" she demanded with a stomp of her foot.

I am going to die alone.

Fanny, the ladies' maid whom Mary and Elizabeth shared, rushed in. "Miss Gillerford! Miss Gillerford! Mr. Broadwood is here to fetch you already."

That brought a look of near panic to Mary's face. "The bonnet, Elizabeth. Give it to me."

"Mr. Broadwood is insisting that Miss Elizabeth come as well," Fanny said.

"Elizabeth? Come along on *my* carriage ride?" Mary's shout likely carried across the Channel. She flew from the room in an instant.

Elizabeth met Fanny's eyes. "Has he really invited me along with him?"

She nodded. "And he told Mrs. Gillerford that he'd not take Miss Gillerford unless you came as well. Your mother is in quite a state, I tell you."

Dear, sweet Julian. "It seems to me that, for the sake of my mother's health, I had best dress for a carriage ride."

Fanny was a step ahead; she had Elizabeth's carriage dress out of the wardrobe already and laid out on the bed. "If we are really quick, you can be downstairs before Miss Gillerford reaches the end of her tantrum."

"Excellent."

They had a speed borne of years spent helping Elizabeth dress during the rare few moments Mary wasn't demanding her maid's presence. Elizabeth hurried down the stairs just as Mary was storming up them.

"I don't know how you managed this," she hissed, "but do not embarrass me."

Elizabeth ignored the all-too-familiar warning and continued to the front entryway. Julian stood there, gloves still on, hat in his hands. He looked up as she approached, and his perturbed expression melted into a friendly smile.

"I see word has reached you," he said.

"To quote my beloved sister, 'I don't know how you managed this.'" She accepted her wrap from the maid at the front door.

"I simply chose to be stubborn about it," Julian said. "You being in a carriage with your sister and me—an old family friend—along with a maid, would be quite unexceptional. It isn't quite a Society function, but at least you will have left the house."

She tightened the ribbon under her chin. "When I inevitably join a convent, I will make certain to submit your name for sainthood."

His adorable smile surfaced on the instant. "You? In a convent?" He shook his head and chuckled. "The vow of silence alone would see you expelled."

Elizabeth shrugged. "Then I suppose you'll simply have to kidnap a husband for me."

"I thought we were forcing someone to wed *Mary*."

"Did I hear my name?" Mary was practically running down the stairs. She held her blue bonnet on her head with one hand and clutched her skirt with the other. "I am ready. We can be on our way now."

Mary stopped directly beside Julian, perhaps a touch too close for propriety. He held himself stiffly but quite civilly.

"How lovely it will be to make a turn about Hyde Park during the fashionable hour," Mary said. "Why, simply everyone will be there!" Her eyes darted to Elizabeth, and she added, under her breath, "And I do mean *everyone*, even those who aren't wanted."

Elizabeth ignored her sister. This was her one chance at escape, and she wasn't going to miss it. She waited patiently at the door, watching Julian expectantly. He flashed her the briefest of smiles, enough to set her heart fluttering about—a sensation she went to great lengths to keep hidden.

"Ladies," he invited, motioning to the door. "The park awaits."

A dark-blue landau with black trim sat in front of the house, its folding top down to reveal fine grey leather upholstery. A driver, in livery that perfectly coordinated with the vehicle, was already in position. Julian clearly didn't wish to prolong the outing any longer than absolutely necessary. She could appreciate that—Mary's company grew tedious after a matter of moments—but, for her sake, Elizabeth wished the ride could last all afternoon.

I will simply have to savor it.

Julian handed Mary up first. She sat on the forward-facing seat, directly in the middle. Elizabeth was handed up next. As she moved to sit rear facing, Julian spoke up.

"Do make room for your sister, Miss Gillerford," he said. "Surely you would not insist she ride rear-facing. Such a thing would be unforgivably rude."

To give someone a forward facing seat was an indication of their importance, or in the matter of gentlemen and ladies, it was an act of chivalry for him to give up that seat to her. Mary clearly would not countenance her younger sister being given as much consideration as herself, lest the two be viewed as equals. Elizabeth knew her sister too well to expect otherwise.

Mary sputtered a moment whilst Elizabeth stood on the top step, unsure where she ought to sit. "But my maid has a sad tendency to grow ill in a carriage if riding rear-facing." Formulating schemes and half-truths at a moment's notice was one of Mary's particular skills. "So Elizabeth simply cannot sit here."

Mary's brow assumed a triumphant arch.

But, then, so did Julian's. What had left him so decidedly pleased?

"I would hate for your maid to be ill," he said. "Miss Elizabeth, would you kindly assume the rear-facing seat?"

She did. She would have ridden up beside the driver if it meant a few moments out of the house.

Just as gallantly as he'd handed up Elizabeth and her sister, Julian offered Fanny his assistance and saw her situated beside Mary. "That leaves me the place beside Miss Elizabeth. I hope you do not mind."

"Not in the least." She managed the response in a tone of only casual interest despite the laughter begging to be released at the sight of Mary's thunderous expression. She would wager that her sister had only just realized how her fabricated story had cost her the opportunity to sit beside the object of her matrimonial ambitions.

But Mary never was long discouraged. "We may just as easily—I daresay *more* easily—make this outing without Elizabeth." Somehow the dismissive remark was made in a tone of utmost sweetness and innocence.

"Perhaps." Julian took the seat beside Elizabeth and motioned for the driver to set the horses in motion. "But her presence will prevent any unwanted whispers."

"Whispers?" Mary smiled and swatted in his direction with her hand. "Why, you silly man. What whispers could there possibly be? Our families are neighbors, and our connection is quite well established."

"Perhaps, but we are *not* actually related. I would hate for Society to take any notions into their heads that are neither accurate nor welcome."

Mary shrugged a dainty shoulder. "No one would ever suspect us of anything untoward."

"I am far more concerned that they would suspect us of courting."

Mary's coy smile dropped off quickly, and her demeanor grew more than a touch icy. But she did stop talking, which, Elizabeth would wager, was a welcome change for everyone present. She had never seen anyone handle Mary as neatly as Julian just had. She felt a real urge to applaud.

"Have you ever been in the park during the daily crush?" Julian asked Elizabeth.

"I haven't, but I have heard a great deal about it. Is the spectacle as ridiculous as I suspect?"

A laugh rumbled deep in his chest. She'd always liked his laugh, even when they were young and it had been more of a giggle. "There is a great deal of the ridiculous about the ritual. Once we reach the park, the carriage will all but come to a stop, perhaps inching forward now and then. Completing a full circuit will require vast swaths of time, far more than it ought."

"Perhaps the horses should be permitted a brief nap between the sixth and seventh hour," Elizabeth suggested. "Or a moment's respite for dinner."

Again his laugh filled the space between them. A lady could happily spend the rest of her days listening to the sound.

"Does everyone simply arrive at the park, come to a standstill, and then, once darkness falls, inch their way back home?" she asked.

"Nothing as painless as all that, I'm afraid." His brown eyes lit with mirth. "We will be required to bid good day to every person who passes by—at least to those we ought to consider not too far below our notice."

"And how does one know which are too lowly or ill-mannered to be acknowledged? Do they wear signs?"

"Signs?" Mary sputtered her way into the conversation at last. "How utterly ridiculous. Little wonder you have never had a Season. You wouldn't have the first idea how to go about it."

Julian gave Elizabeth a dry look. "Oh, there are signs, Beth. Irrefutable signs."

"You are going to make me laugh, and then I will be lectured about being properly demure, and that will ruin this entire outing."

"Who could possibly disapprove of seeing you laugh?" he asked.

Elizabeth rolled her eyes in perfect unison with Mary's huff of disapproval before she said, "If you are trying to make me jealous, Julian, you will have to flirt with someone other than Elizabeth. No one could possibly believe a gentleman of your standing would be interested in her."

Her sister's barbs had long ago stopped wounding. Julian, however, did not seem immune to the shock of her vitriol.

"And why wouldn't a gentleman be absolutely enthralled with Miss Elizabeth?" he demanded.

Mary smiled lightly, as though she truly thought Julian's question was an ironic one. "Even at the slow pace of the park, we'd not have time enough to list all the reasons, now would we?"

The barbs might not have wounded Elizabeth any longer, but she still didn't enjoy them. "I have complete confidence, dearest sister, in your ability to rattle off as much of the list as you possibly can during the course of this excursion."

That, apparently, served as an invitation enough for Mary. "You are here as a guest," she said firmly. "Inserting yourself into the conversation is rather ill-mannered."

"Reason number one," Elizabeth mouthed to Julian, holding up a single finger.

"And whispering is rude as well," Mary added.

Elizabeth added a second finger to the first. Julian seemed to only just hold back a grin. He looked away from them all, waving to someone familiar he saw not far off.

"Here comes Mr. Carson," Mary said. "He has four thousand a year and is related to some of the first families of England." She hissed under her breath to Elizabeth. "Do not—"

"—embarrass you," Elizabeth finished for her. "I know the rules, Mary."

"You know them, but you do not follow them."

Elizabeth caught Julian's eye once more. She held up three fingers, not bothering to hide her amusement.

"We are making remarkable progress, aren't we?" he whispered. Then, at full voice, he greeted a young gentleman who had just ridden up alongside the carriage. "Damion, I would like to introduce you to someone."

With a look that could only be described as approaching panic, Mr. Damion Carson said, "I have already made Miss Gillerford's acquaintance." He eyed Mary as if she were an owl and he a helpless rodent. It seemed that he really did know Mary.

"I wish to make you known to Miss *Elizabeth* Gillerford." Julian proceeded without hesitation. "She has not made her official bows yet, but I assure you, her acquaintance is well worth making."

Mr. Carson offered a proper inclination of his head. "Miss Elizabeth, it is an honor to meet you at last."

"At last?" That was an unexpected phrase to hear tagged onto the end of a sentence uttered by a gentleman she did not at all know.

"Julian has mentioned you many times before," he explained.

He had spoken of her to his friend? Her heart picked up at the thought. Perhaps her adoration of him was not so entirely one-sided.

"I understand you two grew up together," Mr. Carson added.

And with that her heart dropped once more. Had Julian said nothing more about her than merely the fact that they'd grown up together?

"We all grew up together," Mary interjected.

Mr. Carson kept his gaze on Elizabeth and Julian. "Yes, I understood that as well. And" —he actually seemed to be speaking to Elizabeth now—"I am told you are fond of books and have a similar taste in literature as Julian. I confess that histories and treatises are not entirely to my liking, though I have enjoyed a few."

So that was the topic of discussion with which she was concerned: her taste in books. How lowering.

"I do read other things, of course." She had always been plucky, something for which she was particularly thankful at the moment. "I simply have limited to access to anything else. Mr. Broadwood occasionally lends me volumes from his family's library, but he is often engaged elsewhere during the Season and no longer has time for his childhood friend, more's the pity."

Mr. Carson smiled broadly. He struck her as a genuinely happy person, and she was glad of it. Julian would do well having such a friend in his life. "I have seen our Mr. Broadwood at any number of Society events during the

Season, and I assure you his time would be far better spent perusing the shelves of a library than inexpertly navigating the social whirl."

"I look forward to one day watching his ineptitude in action," Elizabeth said.

"It is a sight to behold. And I hope that when you do have your Season, you will allow me to dance with you, as I find I would very much like to continue building our acquaintance."

Elizabeth blushed so immediately and so deeply that no one in all of Hyde Park could have failed to notice. "I would like that as well."

Mr. Carson looked past her at Julian. "Thank you for making this fortuitous introduction."

"My pleasure," Julian muttered, sounding as though it had been anything other than a pleasure.

What has come over him so suddenly?

"Miss Elizabeth." Mr. Carson bowed over her hand. "It has truly been a joy speaking with you." He looked over at Mary. "Miss Gillerford, it has been . . . as it always is."

Elizabeth watched Mr. Carson as he set his horse to a slow trot away from the carriage and disappeared into the press of people gathering in the park. She liked him. He had a sense of humor quite similar to Julian's and a kindness about him that she admired. For a moment she imagined Mr. Carson, married, and calling on her and Julian in their home, an abiding friendship growing between all of them.

She'd entertained daydreams of that sort for years, even during that long-ago time when she'd thought the only obstacle to her imagined happiness was Mary. She'd realized in more recent years that Julian had as little interest in courting Mary as he did in courting *her*. She hadn't lost her dearest love to her sister; she'd simply never had his *love* in the first place.

"I am firmly on the verge of throttling Mary Gillerford." Julian paced once more the length of his sister's sitting room.

"You have been on the verge of throttling her for ten years, Julian," Helene reminded him.

"Yes, but now she has gone beyond simply leeching the life out of me. She is attacking Beth, and doing so in public." He stopped at the mantle, tapping his finger on its edge. "Mary insulted her on the way to the park yesterday. She made sly comments about her to nearly every person we spoke with. And, as if she'd not done a thorough enough job of it, she spent a full quarter of an hour afterward criticizing Beth's conduct, her dress, her conversation, everything she could think of."

Helene set her sewing on her lap. "Mary's unkindness is the reason she has not had a single suitor despite being in her third Season. She, of course, insists that the real reason is being already promised to you."

Julian's jaw tensed on the instant. "I do not know what our parents were thinking, encouraging that idea all of these years. I have certainly never been in favor of it. Intelligent men dream of more noble deaths than being nagged into an early grave."

"That, we do." His brother-in-law, Robert Pinnelle, stepped inside at that exact moment. "And we choose our wives accordingly." He greeted Helene with an affectionate kiss on the cheek then sat beside her.

"I am so pleased you've come in," she said, "as I have

had an absolutely brilliant idea and need you to extol its virtues shamelessly."

"What is this brilliant idea?"

"As you well know, I have not hosted a dinner party in weeks."

"Do I know that?" He clearly didn't.

"Of course you do, love. After the last one, you told me, whilst you were kissing me, how much you'd enjoyed the evening."

That was a touch more information than Julian had bargained for.

"I remember the kissing part," Robert said.

Helene continued as though Robert were keeping up perfectly. "I must have guests over again. I am simply bereft of company."

"I know it is my duty to agree with you wholeheartedly," Robert said. "And yet I can't help feeling a little insulted."

"You know perfectly well what I meant. You do not always attend functions with me, and you are so often gone during the day doing your important things. This house—indeed, this city—is so lonely without you."

Julian jumped in once more. "That is quite a boon to your pride, old man. All of London is not companion enough for her without you."

"As I said, an intelligent gentleman chooses his wife wisely."

Helene tossed them both looks of sorely tried patience. "Neither of you is allowing me to share my brilliant idea, and I think it is very badly done of you."

"My apologies, dearest," Robert said. "Do tell us your idea."

Apparently mollified, Helene continued. "I mean to invite the Gillerfords for a small dinner gathering, and I mean to insist that Miss Elizabeth Gillerford be included in the invitation."

Brilliant indeed! Julian's heart lightened at the thought. Beth would have reason to leave her house once more, even if she was required to do so in the company of her irksome family.

"Gillerford?" Robert's brow drew in. "The family who are neighbors of your family in Surrey?"

"The very same," Helene confirmed.

"Hold a moment." Robert held up a hand. "Isn't their daughter the one with the crazed look in her eyes?"

"I do not believe I have ever heard Mary described so precisely." After taking a moment to ponder that fitting turn of phrase a little more deeply, Helene continued her explanation. "Mary, the older sister, is the frenzied one whom everybody avoids like an eel pie on a hot summer's day. Miss Elizabeth is the younger sister, and is a lovely person with very civilized eyes."

Robert's ponderous gaze landed on Julian. "Aren't you supposed to marry one of these sisters? I am certain your mother said something about that."

Julian shook his head in disbelief and took up pacing once again. He ought to simply flee Town before Mary's claws were lodged even further into him. But that would mean abandoning Beth to her family's unkindness.

"Mrs. Carson told me that her son met Miss Elizabeth just yesterday and mentioned her quite a few times last evening," Helene said. "I believe young Mr. Carson is near enough to family to be included in the dinner." A matchmaking gleam filled her gaze. "I believe they would get on quite famously."

"Beth is not yet out," Julian quickly pointed out.

Helene didn't seem the least bothered by that

information. "But she is of an age. After all, one need not have a Season to be courted."

"Courted?" He nearly choked on the word. "How have we jumped that far already?"

Robert eyed him with blatant curiosity. "What has you wound so tightly? Carson's your friend, as is Miss Elizabeth."

"I simply do not think that they would suit each other." He was pacing again. Something about the suggestion of Beth and Damion making a match of it did not sit well in his mind.

"Nonsense. They would be perfect together." Helene met her husband's eyes. "They really would be."

"It is settled then." Robert lifted his wife's hand to his lips. "Extend your invitation to the Gillerfords and Mr. Carson, and let my secretary know the date of your party so I can make absolutely certain I do not miss it."

Helene hopped to her feet, her eyes brimming with anticipation. "I shall make my list immediately."

"I am on that list as well, aren't I?" Julian called after her. He received no answer.

I had better be on that list.

Four

Elizabeth watched out the carriage windows as one grand house after another passed by. Helene's invitation had been nothing short of a godsend.

"But why should Elizabeth be asked?" Mary demanded to know for the hundredth time. "She is not yet out. First the park, and now this. It is utter nonsense."

Mother patted Mary's hand. "Mr. Pinnelle is a man of tremendous importance; your father told me as much, though he was unaccountably vague about the reasons for Mr. Pinnelle's consequence. We must make a good impression on him, as I do not believe he has taken much notice of our family."

"Besides all that," Mother continued, "Helene has known Elizabeth all her life and likely feels some obligation to include her, even if she would not normally do so."

Elizabeth didn't care if Helene *had* sent for her out of pity, and was simply grateful for yet another temporary escape from her imprisonment. Julian, no doubt, had found a way to make this evening happen.

"Do you suppose Pinnelle House has a library?" she asked no one in particular.

"I certainly hope you do not mean to embarrass the family while we are there," Mother said. "Reading when you are supposed to be socializing with the other guests."

"But then, she is not out," Mary said. "Perhaps it would be best if she didn't socialize."

The carriage pulled up at just that moment. They had arrived. Elizabeth bit back a grin of delight. A single evening's entertainment was not precisely a dream come true, but it was a taste of freedom. The anticipation of it was nearly her undoing. Somehow she maintained her composure right up until the moment Julian himself met them at the front door.

"Ladies," he greeted.

Mother and Mary executed perfect curtsies.

Elizabeth clapped her hands together and exclaimed, "Oh, Julian, this is the most wonderful thing."

He smiled at her antics, as always.

Mother, also as always, was horrified. "Elizabeth! I certainly hope you know better than to address a gentleman so intimately."

"I have called him by his Christian name all his life." Yes, she was in the wrong, but the promise of the evening had made her rather bold.

Julian stepped near her side. "Actually, I believe you generally called me Jules during our childhoods."

"Mother would simply love that, now wouldn't she?" Elizabeth said.

He lowered his voice, his gaze lingering a moment on her face. "*I* would love that, which ought to count for something."

Something in his expression, in his closeness, left her

quite upended. She covered her confusion with a quick change of topics. "Did you arrange for all of this?"

"It was Helene's idea." He motioned toward the doorway through which they were all to step. "But I will happily take credit. I did promise to help you escape your imprisonment, after all."

"You did, and I expect you to make my evening away as pleasant as possible."

Her teasing didn't have its usual effect. Rather than meet her jest for jest, he simply watched her more closely. He looked as though he was searching for the answer to some unspoken question.

Helene approached them, arms outstretched to take Elizabeth's hands. "My dear, old friend," she said. "I am so pleased you were able to come this evening. I feel as though we have not seen each other in ages."

"Thank you for the invitation."

Helene shook her head. "None of that. We are nearly family, after all." She hooked her arm around Elizabeth's and, without ceremony, walked with her further into the elegant drawing room. Almost as an afterthought, she glanced over her shoulder at Mother and Mary. "And you are, of course, most welcome as well."

"We always feel most welcome amongst your family." Mary latched onto the words like a terrier pulling a fox from its den. Her eyes quickly turned to Julian. "We are practically family, as your sister said. Or soon will be, at least."

Elizabeth fought to keep her expression neutral. If she laughed, her family would make her life a misery for the rest of the evening and beyond. That would be a shame and a waste of a once in a lifetime—she very much feared *lifetime* wasn't an exaggeration—opportunity.

Julian kept a noticeable distance without being outright

rude. "I see Mr. Gillerford was not able to join us this evening. Is he . . . at his club?"

"Father is indisposed this evening," Elizabeth said. "Gout being the persistent monster that it is."

"Elizabeth Mildred." Mother looked horrified. "A lady does not use the word 'gout' in public."

"At least I didn't say 'Jules,'" she muttered.

If the sudden combination of coughing and clearing his throat was any indication, Julian overheard.

Helene invited Elizabeth to the settee near the low-burning fire. Despite not being the coldest part of the year, the weather had been unfortunately damp and overly cool. Helene had ever been kind, but there seemed to be a pointedness to her attentions.

Julian saw Mother and Mary seated in the sofa facing the settee, and then, to Mary's obvious shock, he chose to sit beside Elizabeth.

"This is not the way to win Mary's affection," she warned.

"Is it not?" He didn't look worried. "What is the way, then?"

"The key, my friend, is opera."

Julian eyed her questioningly. "She will fall madly in love with me if I attend the opera with her?"

Elizabeth shook her head solemnly. "She will fall hopelessly and irrevocably in love with you if you *sing* opera to her. All the time. No words, only singing."

He leaned a touch nearer. "You have heard me sing, Beth."

She pretended to think deeply about that. "Actually, I believe I meant that if you sing to her every day you will *prevent* her from falling in love with you. Yes. That's what I meant."

"Excellent. I will never *speak* to her again." He sat up straight once more. "Helene's dinner will be ruined and that, my dear Beth, will make my evening an utter delight."

"I will do my utmost not to embarrass you or her."

"That sounds like Mary talking, and I will not stand for it." His was not an entirely joking tone. "You have never embarrassed me, not even when you were little and followed my friends and me all over the neighborhood while we were home on school holiday. Not then. Not now."

Not being embarrassed by her was a few too many steps away from loving her, but it was at least inching in the right direction.

A quick knock at the door announced the arrival of another guest. Elizabeth knew only that it would not be her brother, as Gregory was in the country, enjoying a quiet stay at the family's estate.

"Who else has Helene invited?" she asked Julian.

"Damion," he said.

"Your friend from the park? But why have you not gone to greet him as you did us?"

He folded his arms across his chest. "Damion is a grown man. He can find his own way inside."

Julian seemed to have been seized by a case of the doldrums. It had often been her task to tease him out of a difficult mood. So she took it upon herself to do so again.

"Are you calling me an incapable infant?"

He didn't take the bait. Instead, he watched his friend's entrance with precisely the look Elizabeth had always imagined Hamlet had given his uncle after piecing together the older man's role in the late king's death.

"What has Mr. Carson done to earn your wrath?" she asked.

Julian slumped a bit lower on the settee. "He accepted Helene's invitation to come tonight."

Damion, having stepped inside, seemed to sense Julian's glare of death, and, oddly enough, appeared surprised by it. Whatever complaint Julian had with his friend, the feeling was not mutual. As Damion made his bows to the ladies and Mr. Pinnelle, his gaze continually returned to Julian. After a moment, he came and stood near the settee.

"Miss Elizabeth, a pleasure to see you again."

"And you, Mr. Carson." Though Elizabeth didn't think of herself as slow-witted, she did have an unfortunate tendency to let her mouth run away at times when she ought to hold her tongue. "Perhaps, sir, you would be so good as to tell me why our friend here"—she indicated Julian with a brief wave of her hand—"is in such a sour mood this evening."

"Elizabeth," Mother hissed.

But Damion did not appear shocked by her lack of demureness. "I would wager his mood was perfectly pleasant whilst only the two of you were conversing." The devilish glint in his eye brought a smile to her face.

"Very perceptive, Mr. Carson. Though that means *you* are the culprit behind his disgruntlement."

"It would appear so." He made a bow to Julian. "Am I to expect pistols at dawn?"

Julian allowed the smallest softening of his expression. "I haven't decided yet."

Elizabeth was happy to see something of his usual cheeriness return, but she didn't like to see him act so unlike himself. She set a hand on his. "Are you feeling unwell, Jules?"

Mary quite suddenly appeared at her side. "Take a turn about the room with me, dearest sister." The request was made through clenched teeth; Elizabeth knew better than to deny her in such cases.

Mary pulled Elizabeth's arm through hers and dragged her away. They'd only moved a handful of steps from the group before Mary launched into a harshly whispered rebuke. "You are acting far too familiar with the gentlemen, Elizabeth. You are embarrassing us all."

Julian had said quite the opposite.

Mary squeezed her arm harder, and a little painfully. "If this is the way you behave in Society, it is little wonder you've not been given a Season."

"I rather think *you* are demonstrating the reason far more clearly than I am."

Mary's steps fumbled a moment. "I suspect I should be offended."

"Never mind." Elizabeth had no desire to spend her one and only dinner party arguing with her sister. "I will do my utmost to be well behaved."

"See that you do." Mary's possessive gaze settled on Julian. "I believe Julian means to press his suit tonight."

"Do you?"

"Why else would he be acting so skittish? The dear man is nervous."

Elizabeth was certain that Mary was not at all the reason for his behavior, though she couldn't quite decipher the real one. Perhaps Julian had realized Mary's expectations for the evening and was unhappy at the prospect of spending the night dodging her efforts to force a courtship. That very well might be precisely the cause of his sour mood. Fortunately, Elizabeth could help with that predicament. She'd acted as a buffer between her sister and Julian many times over the years; she could certainly do so again.

"I believe I will further my acquaintance with Mr.

Carson," Mary said firmly, pulling them both back in the direction of the other guests. "Being on friendly terms with the closest friend of one's intended is crucial, after all."

Poor Damion. "Will you not be stretched a bit thin, paying attention to two gentlemen? And you would do well to not neglect your hostess, either."

That brought Mary's glare back around. "Do not presume to tell me how to conduct myself in Society. I know more of it then you ever will."

"Something I have you to thank for," she muttered.

"I beg your pardon?" It was a rhetorical question if ever Elizabeth had heard one. "Do not act as though *I* am the reason for your lack of opportunities. You, Elizabeth, would never make a splash in Society. You are too plain, too unrefined. You are in the shadows not because of me but because that is where you best fit. Enjoy this evening away from your books; it is likely the last you will have. Few people will take pity on you the way Helene and Julian have."

Mary could cut deep when she chose to, tonight piercing even Elizabeth's fortified armor.

They were but a step from the other guests. Mary took a moment to add one more jab under her breath. "Do not monopolize Julian's time the way you always do. It was sweet when you were ten, but you are no longer a child, and he cannot be expected to continue enduring you."

Enduring.

Certainly Julian more than merely *endured* her. They were friends, good ones. Had he not vowed to help her have some enjoyment in London? Had he not taken her for a carriage ride despite the inconvenience of Mary's company?

Still, the word seeped into her, filling the most vulnerable cracks in her heart.

But, if Elizabeth could but endure Mary, she could

spend a nice evening away from home and in Julian's company. That would be worth all of the barbs and angry glares.

"Dearest Helene," Mary said, approaching their hostess with an overdone look of worry. "I am afraid my sister is not feeling well. She is too shy to say so herself; indeed, I fully expect her to deny the state of her health, but she is doing poorly."

Quick as that, Mary had brought Elizabeth's evening to an end. Mary had even circumvented any attempt Elizabeth might make to reveal the deception.

Mother jumped in, putting the final nail in the coffin. "She did feel under the weather earlier today," she insisted. "I knew she should have remained at home."

Helene didn't look entirely convinced. And yet, manners didn't allow her to contradict her guests, especially when one of the bold-faced liars was a mother speaking on behalf of a daughter who was not yet out.

Helene gave Elizabeth an unmistakably apologetic look. "I suppose there is little for it but to call up the carriage and see to it that you are returned home."

"I suppose not." Elizabeth was too disappointed, too frustrated, too angry to say more. She spun on her heel and marched from the room. She might be forced to leave, but she would do so alone and without the feigned attentions of uncaring family members.

She stood in the entryway for several long minutes, waiting for the carriage to be brought around. The driver had likely only just finished unhitching the team for the evening. Mary never did care who she inconvenienced.

One of the maids stepped into the entryway, buttoned in a light coat.

"Have you been commissioned to accompany me home?" Elizabeth asked.

"Yes, miss." The maid offered a curtsey.

"I hope doing so does not cause you too much inconvenience."

"No, miss." Any well-trained servant would say as much, whether or not it was true.

"And what if it causes *me* too much inconvenience?" Julian asked from a few feet away. The butler handed him his outer coat.

"Are you coming along, as well?" Her heart skipped about in hope.

"No gently bred young lady should be forced to traverse London entirely unprotected." He winked at her. "A great number of questionable areas of Town lie between here and your home, you realize."

There weren't any, actually.

"Why do I get the feeling you are using this as an excuse to flee a certain matrimonially minded lady?"

"Because you know me better than anyone."

And yet, you know so little of me.

Five

Throughout the ride, Elizabeth was pale and withdrawn. Even Jane, the maid Helene had sent along for propriety's sake, watched Elizabeth closely. Though Julian hadn't overheard the sisters' conversation, he knew enough of the older sister to be certain that her words hadn't been kind.

The carriage arrived and a footman handed them all out. Julian followed in Elizabeth's wake as she made her way up the front walk and stayed near her after she stepped inside. Jane, at the housekeeper's invitation, went down to the kitchens for a warm posset.

Upon reaching the front entryway, Elizabeth did not quite look him in the eye. "Thank you for seeing me home," she said quietly. "I hope the dinner is lovely." She turned and walked up the stairs.

Watching her slow ascent—shoulders slumped, head a bit bowed—Julian ached for her. She so seldom let Mary's unkindness affect her, but clearly it had injured her this time.

He took the stairs two at a time and caught up with her in the corridor.

"Beth. Wait, please."

She stopped but didn't look back.

He stepped around to face her. "I'm sorry that Mary—" His words ended abruptly. Tears hovered on her lashes even as one escaped in a trickle down her cheek. "You're crying."

"Only a little." She pushed out a deep breath.

He motioned for her to slip into the sitting room. He knew that Beth severely disliked showing emotions; she would be mortified if any of the staff came upon her while she was tearing up. She took the handkerchief he offered and wiped away the tears hovering at the corners of her eyes.

"Was Mary particularly vicious?" he asked.

She sighed. "She said I will never escape the shadows because I'm too inferior to belong anywhere else."

"Did she?" What an utter termagant Mary was.

"And that I'm plain and poor company. That no one other than my books would ever wish to spend an evening with me." She'd put on a brave face, but the slight quiver of her chin betrayed her upended emotions.

"Mary never was terribly bright." He set a reassuring hand on her arm, watching her for any signs of recovery. That her own sister could be so cruel was heartbreaking. "Her lies are so transparent, one can only assume she realizes that were your parents to come to their senses and allow you a Season, you would cast her into a shadow from which she would likely never emerge."

"You are saying that only to make me feel better."

"No, Beth. Truly." She needed to know the truth of her worth. "You are lovely, and your company and conversation would be coveted by everyone with whom you'd interact during the social whirl. You would be in demand in a way

Mary never has been, and that frightens her."

She shook her head. "You are obligated to say nice things like that; you're practically my brother."

Brother. That word carried a flavor he could not like. They'd always been something a bit deeper than mere friends, but *brother* didn't hit the mark at all.

He reached out and took her hand. That simple, familiar touch had always carried with it a feeling of comfort and peace, almost as if he'd returned home.

"Your sister will be wondering what is keeping you," she said. "And, as Mary pointed out, only my books are missing me. I should really get back to them." She pulled her hand from his. "Thank you for arranging this evening, even if it didn't work out quite as I'd hoped. The gesture meant a great deal."

A moment later, he was alone in the sitting room. He missed her the instant she was gone. It had ever been that way with Beth. Yet, there was something more to his longing for her this time. He ached for her to return, could hardly countenance climbing back inside the lonely carriage without her.

He returned to Helene's home every bit as lonely as he had been upon leaving Elizabeth. Dinner had been held for him, but he had no appetite for it. He merely picked at the food whilst thoughts spun and collided in his mind.

Upon the gentlemen rejoining the ladies after port, Damion launched directly into the topic foremost in Julian's mind.

"It is a shame Miss Elizabeth could not remain this evening," he said. "I was hoping to make her better acquaintance."

I wager you were. Julian sat a little apart from the others, eyeing his friend with growing suspicion. Was Damion the real reason Elizabeth was so distraught at missing the dinner?

"Yes, a shame." Mary's sincerity was nonexistent.

Helene patted Damion's arm as she passed. "We'll have Miss Elizabeth over again sometime and will be sure to invite you as well."

Julian did not like that idea at all. Helene sat beside him and turned her head toward him, a triumphant gleam in her eye. The rest of the room took up individual conversations.

"Is this not remarkable?" Helene said. "Damion is quite smitten with Elizabeth, I can tell."

"How could any gentleman not be?" His compliment was likely clouded by the monumental pout he couldn't seem to wipe from his face.

Helene apparently noticed. "Are you not happy for your friend? He and Beth got on famously."

Julian slumped lower in his chair. "I plan to toast their happiness at the first possible opportunity," he muttered.

"You are in a sour mood this evening." She eyed him scoldingly. "Are you jealous?"

He sputtered. "Jealous? Of Damion?"

Helene shrugged a shoulder. "He seems happy. Perhaps you would like to be happy as well."

"I am happy. Very happy. Deliriously happy."

Helene's eyebrows arched. "Your dry tone and dead eyes are truly convincing, Julian."

He pushed out a puff of air. "I don't even know why I am feeling so ill-tempered tonight. Although you did serve lamb this evening, and you know I prefer beef. Perhaps that is the reason for my bad mood."

"You like lamb well enough, Julian. My menu is not to blame." Her gaze narrowed on him. "Now that I reflect back on dinner, you weren't glaring at your plate, but at Damion.

Have the two of you come to blows over something?"

The answer that first jumped into his head was *"Not yet,"* but that made absolutely no sense, so when he spoke, he amended it to a simple, "No."

Helene made a sound of pondering even as her gaze took in the rest of the guests. "It is a shame Elizabeth couldn't stay. She is such a delight, far more so than her mother or sister."

"It was a lie, you realize. She wasn't actually ill."

"Of course it was a lie. Mary cannot bear the fact that her younger sister outshines her at every turn. But what could I do?" Helene always had possessed the kindest of hearts. "We may simply have to kidnap Elizabeth and sneak her into a ball or two."

Dancing with Beth at a ball. The idea was surprisingly pleasant, not that he'd ever thought that dancing with her would be *un*pleasant. He was remarkably confused.

"I have known Elizabeth and Damion for many years now," Helene said. "I cannot believe that I didn't realize sooner how utterly perfect they are for one another. Did you?" There was something a little too pointed in the question, as if Helene wasn't actually asking the question she'd voiced aloud.

"I never would have put the two of them together if you hadn't," he said. "Why did you, by the way?"

The question appeared to surprise her. "Is there some reason why I shouldn't have? Damion is young and unattached. He has a lovely little estate and a tidy income. And he is a fine gentleman. Elizabeth is also young and unattached. She comes from a good family with more than respectable connections. And she is a simply lovely person. How could I not encourage a match?"

"Because they—because I—" He couldn't seem to come

up with a good reason. At least not a logical one. "They wouldn't suit."

"I had my suspicions, but this confirms it." A sudden smile lit her face. "Oh, heavens, Julian. Good heavens."

"Good heavens *what*?"

She pressed a hand over her mouth, looking at him wide-eyed.

"I do not like that look." He'd seen it too often growing up, usually preceding either tears or a scheme that later got him into tremendous amounts of trouble.

"I had hoped, but now I know," she said from behind her hand. Helene often failed to get to her point.

"Know *what*?"

She patted his hand. Her brow furrowed in something very much like pity. "That you are in love with her."

Julian nearly choked, despite not having anything in his mouth or throat. "I am not in love with her," he insisted under his breath. "She's Beth. She's a friend."

Helene was already shaking her head. "She *is* Beth, though only you call her that, and she *is* your friend, but she is far more than that as well. There's such a fondness in your eyes when you look at her, a fondness that has grown considerably of late. And newly arrived in the picture is a surprisingly murderous glint when you look at Damion. The puzzle is not difficult to piece together, dearest brother."

Julian opened his mouth to object but was silenced by his own thoughts. His heart had broken for her. His temper had risen on the instant in response to her family's unkindness. Even before that evening's events, he'd thought about her when they were apart. His day improved on the instant when he was with her. He was happier in her company than in that of any other person he knew.

But that wasn't love.

"Tell me, Julian, what would you do if Damion were to come over here right now and declare himself madly in love with her? If he were to insist upon riding to her home and declaring his passion, kissing her senseless, and pleading with her to marry him with all possible haste?"

Julian didn't have to think about it. "I'd kill him."

"Why?" Helene asked on a laugh. "You like them both, and Elizabeth is, by your own declaration, only a friend."

"Beth is *my* . . . friend. She's my Beth. Damion doesn't know her the way I do. He doesn't understand her or cherish her like I do. He doesn't—" His words ended as the realization of what he was saying truly settled on him.

"He doesn't love her like you do?" Helene finished for him. "Ponder on that, Julian. Your mind and your heart have not been listening to each other. I, for one, think it is about time they start."

Six

"I haven't the slightest idea what you wish me to tell you." Elizabeth looked from each of her parents to the other several times. "I am sorry for Mary that Julian didn't press his suit last evening, but I am not privy to his thoughts or intentions."

"She said something to him on the drive home, I am certain of it." Mary sent her a look of such hatred that it nearly stole Elizabeth's breath. Mary had disliked her more and more over the past few years, but had been so openly hostile. "What did you say in the carriage that changed his mind?"

"We didn't say anything. You can ask the maid Helene sent along. It was a silent drive."

"Then what did you say *after* the drive?" Say what one might about the state of Mary's compassion, there was no denying the quickness of her mind.

Elizabeth chose to be honest, if incomplete, in her response. "He asked if I needed anything before he left, and said he was sorry I wasn't able to remain for dinner." She shrugged as though his words, his touch, from the night before hadn't been equally heavenly and torturous. "Then he left. It was nothing of significance." How she hoped that wasn't truly the case.

"Elizabeth," Father said, using the stern voice reserved exclusively for her, "Julian Broadwood has been dragging his feet where Mary is concerned. You ought to be doing everything in your power to help convince him that the time has come to fulfill the expectations he created."

"Expectations *he* created? What has *he* ever done to convince you that he had any intentions?" Her temper had been piqued, but and she couldn't seem to calm it. Julian did not deserve such besmirching. "Does he call regularly? Insist on claiming her for every supper dance? Has he declared himself in any capacity?"

"That is quite enough, young lady." Mother's lips all but disappeared. "Do not speak so boldly of matters about which you know so little."

"And how much do *you* truly know of it?" Her indignation sent her to her feet, too agitated and upset to sit any longer. "While the three of you have spent the past decade scheming and planning and assuming, *I* have spent those years coming to know the object of your designs. Julian Broadwood is decisive and determined, without being unfeeling. He would never allow a decision of this importance to be made without him, but neither would he lash out at anyone attempting to force it on him. He is a good man, and you" —she turned to Mary—"do not deserve him."

"How dare—" Mary stopped quite suddenly. Her narrowed eyes widened. "Oh." Her shock turned to disgust as she uttered the word again. "Oh. You are in love with him. You. Plain little Elizabeth, whom he has likely not given a second thought, are in love with him."

"That is not at all what this is about."

Mary's gaze grew calculating. "I notice you don't deny it." She turned to their parents. "Now we know the truth of it."

"Have you been sabotaging your sister's courtship?" Father demanded. "Is that the reason Julian hasn't offered yet?"

"Of course not," she said. No one was truly listening to her any longer.

"How long have you been nursing this ridiculous *tendre*?" Mary laughed through the words. "Look at the way she blushes, Mother. There is no question; she is in love with him."

Now they were both laughing, and Father was watching her quite as though she were a stranger to him.

"Does Julian have any idea of this, do you think?" Mary asked Mother, both ladies grinning as if they'd never heard anything so amusing in all their lives.

Mother gave it a moment's thought. "It may explain why he has been reluctant to undertake his suit; he fears hurting her feelings. Bookish girls always are the most easily overset, being too little acquainted with the world."

Mary nodded her agreement. "I think we had best send her to stay with Gregory in the country." Mary's triumphant look in Elizabeth's direction told her, in no uncertain terms, that her sister knew such a thing was hardly necessary, but she didn't mean to pass up the opportunity. "We do not wish to risk a repeat of this outburst when others are present."

As if on cue, the drawing room doors opened, and the butler stepped inside. "Mr. Julian Broadwood," he announced.

Elizabeth had never before wished to simply sink into the ground, but in that moment she would have happily procured a spade from the gardener and dug her way straight to the center of the earth. "Please, Mary," she quietly pleaded. "Do not spill your speculations into his ears."

But Mary stepped past Elizabeth and closer to the door. "Why, Julian, how wonderful to see you."

"And you, Miss Gillerford."

Elizabeth turned enough to watch Mary lead him farther into the room. *Please don't say anything, Mary. Please.*

"Do sit with us," Mary invited, indicating a seat very near the one she then lowered herself onto.

He didn't take the chair, however, first stopping to offer his bows to Mother and Father, and then he turned to face Elizabeth. "Miss Elizabeth." He offered her a bow as well.

She somehow managed the appropriate response despite her heart being firmly lodged in her throat. Mary looked far too pleased with herself for Elizabeth's peace of mind.

Julian was watching her a touch too closely. "You are pale," he said. "Is anything the matter?"

She looked quickly in Mary's direction, rather desperately hoping that her sister had softened. If anything, Mary seemed even more jubilant. The worst, Elizabeth was quite certain, was yet to come.

"Beth?" Julian whispered. "What is wrong?"

"Julian," Mary cooed. "We have been having the most diverting conversation. Your arrival could not have been better timed."

He didn't look back at Mary but kept his searching gaze on Elizabeth—on *her*. She had no doubt he could see the abject misery in her eyes. Mary wouldn't hesitate to humiliate her.

"Please don't do this, Mary." Begging wasn't likely to prevent humiliation, but Elizabeth had to try.

"Do what, sister? I simply wish to include our dear friend in our very enjoyable discussion." As innocent as a viper, she was.

Elizabeth stepped closer to her sister. "I will stay with Gregory for the remainder of the Season, if that is what you wish. I will stay there until your future is firmly decided, if need be. Only, please, do not do this."

Mary simply arched an eyebrow. Elizabeth looked to her parents but could see that she would get no help from that quarter. Too many years they'd spent making plans for Mary and Julian; Elizabeth's concerns had never been as important to any of them, and not always even to herself.

"Do you know what we discovered this afternoon?" Mary said, obviously addressing Julian.

"Please don't," Elizabeth whispered.

"My dear little sister is in love. How very quaint, don't you think?" There was a viciousness in Mary's declaration that robbed it of any degree of sweetness.

Elizabeth's heart shattered.

"Is she?" Julian didn't sound amused. He didn't even sound convinced.

"Oh, yes," Mother said. "She certainly is." Her voice added to the declaration would make it more convincing. "But I suppose every girl must have her hopeless fantasy. It is certainly nothing for the family to be ashamed of."

It was always about the family.

Don't read in public, Elizabeth, you'll embarrass us.

You can't have a Season until your sister is married; how would it look for us?

Keep to your quiet corner, Elizabeth, where no one will eye us sidelong upon hearing your impertinent questions.

"Would you care to hazard a guess who it is she fancies?" Mary offered to Julian.

Elizabeth couldn't bear it. She fled the room, not caring that doing so would only add fuel to her family's complaints about her lack of manners. She wasn't quite fast enough to miss Mary's next words.

"It's *you*, Julian. How adorably ridiculous is that? She is in love with *you*."

Whether he believed Mary's declaration, Elizabeth didn't know. It didn't matter. The next time he saw her, he would see the truth of it in her eyes. He would see how hopelessly she loved him.

And he would either find her ridiculous or pitiful.

She couldn't bear either one.

even

For a moment, Julian couldn't even think. He'd come to Elizabeth's home on the hope that she might take a turn about the garden with him, or sit a moment in the sitting room. Something. Anything. He'd wrestled with the realization that Helene's conversation had proffered him and had, in the quiet hours of morning, realized his sister was right.

He did love Elizabeth, with a steady and deep love built on years of friendship. He'd thought his distaste for Mary's was the result of her undesirable company and little more. How wrong he'd been. Elizabeth had claimed his heart, and he hadn't even realized it.

"Did you hear me, Julian?" Mary interrupted his thoughts. "Elizabeth, quiet, bookish Elizabeth, fancies herself quite in love with you. Is that not the most diverting thing?"

He met her victorious gaze. "Why are you like this, Mary? You inflict pain with glee. You didn't used to be this way."

Her smile disappeared on the instant. "I only meant to

share something amusing. Do you not find it funny?"

"Not in the least. For though I cannot approve of the way you went about it, hearing that there is even a chance that Miss Elizabeth might care for me is, perhaps, the most encouraging thing I have heard in this home these past three years."

Shock began to give way to panic in Mary's face.

He eyed Mrs. Gillerford but found himself with nothing to say to the lady. She'd allowed her younger daughter to be mistreated and hurt again and again, never protecting her, and never seeming to care. At times, she'd even participated in the cruelty.

"Mr. Gillerford, under the circumstances I feel I should tell you that I am in love with your daughter. Not this one." He motioned to Mary. "And should I be so fortunate as to earn her regard in return, I would very much like to have a conversation with you in the near future."

Mr. Gillerford's heavily creased brow pulled deeper. "We are speaking of *Elizabeth*?" He clearly didn't think that possible.

She deserved so much better than this family.

"If you will all excuse me," he said, addressing them as a whole, "somewhere nearby, the lady I adore is hurting, and that is a circumstance I cannot allow to continue." He sketched a quick bow and turned to go.

"Julian, wait." Mary caught up to him with alarming speed. "If I have offended you—"

"The one you ought to be apologizing to is your sister. And then, may I suggest you search inside yourself for the kindhearted girl you were when we were children. She got lost somewhere along the way, and you would do well to find her again."

For once, Mary was speechless.

"Good day, Miss Gillerford." He left her there with no more than that.

A short distance down the corridor, he came upon the housemaid who had accompanied them on the drive through Hyde Park. "I am looking for Miss Elizabeth."

"She's stepped outside, into the back gardens, sir."

"Thank you."

That is precisely where he found her, on a bench in a lonely corner of the manicured gardens, with her head in her hands and her shoulders shaking as she cried. She didn't look up as he approached, though she must have heard his footsteps.

He sat beside her, unsure what to say.

She spoke first, her voice tremulous. "Can we please pretend this day never happened?"

But the day had been a revelation for him. For his part, he could not wish it undone. He set his arm about her and gently nudged her toward him. After a moment's uncertainty, she accepted the unspoken offer and turned into his embrace, her face buried in his waistcoat.

Julian rested his head atop hers, marveling that he'd not sooner realized his feelings for Beth. He'd embraced her and held her hand and sat near her before, and always he'd experienced a rare and almost magical sense of belonging. But each time, he'd dismissed the feeling as nothing more than the result of their longstanding friendship. How blind he had been.

"I missed you last evening, Beth." He surprised himself with his own candor. Mary's words had given him hope and courage. "I am never as happy in anyone's company as I am in yours. I wish you could have stayed for dinner."

"Mary ruined that as well," she said from within his arms.

"What else has Mary ruined, dear? Her words were meant to wound, but they missed their mark." He stroked her back, wishing she wasn't so miserable. A gentleman didn't often pour his heart out. Doing so whilst his lady love was weeping added an element of worry to the undertaking. "Do you remember last evening when you asked Damion why I was in such a sour mood?"

She nodded against his chest, still not showing her face.

"Helene invited him with the hope that you and he would develop a fondness for each other." He still flinched at the idea, despite having reason to believe that Helene's efforts had been in vain. "*That* is why I was unhappy."

"I don't understand."

Nothing for it but to make a full confession. "Your sister made a declaration just now. And while I don't know the truth of it, I should like to make one of my own, if you will allow it."

She pulled a bit away, enough to look up into his eyes. So much pain, so much misery on her beloved face.

"Do you still have the handkerchief I gave you yesterday?" he asked.

She shook her head. "Not with me."

With a bit of maneuvering, he managed to fetch a square of linen from his coat pocket without fully releasing her. He gave it to her and allowed her to dab as necessary. Her gaze didn't leave his face.

"What is it you want to confess, Jules?" She looked equal parts hopeful and worried, no doubt matching his own expression.

He brushed away a lingering tear from her face with the pad of his thumb. "I love you, Beth," he said, diving right to the heart of the matter. "I cannot say with any certainty how long I've felt this way. It came on gradually, with the natural progression of our friendship."

Beth seemed to be holding her breath.

"Was Mary being truthful? Did she have the right of it?" Now it was his turn to hold his breath.

Her voice was quiet when she answered at last. "I have loved you since I was eight years old. But you have always been meant for Mary. Even when it became apparent that you didn't share her expectations, it hardly mattered. I didn't know who had your devotion, only that your heart would never be mine."

He cupped her face, his pulse leaping inside him. "Oh, Beth. It was *always* yours. I was simply too thickheaded to realize it sooner."

She closed her eyes, breathing what could only be described as a sigh of relief.

He kissed her, slowly, savoring a moment which had, unbeknownst to him, been a very long time in coming. His Beth, his dear, wonderful Beth. How had he not realized the true state of his heart?

They sat there for a long moment, she in his embrace, as he inwardly shook his head at his own stupidity. How fortunate he'd been that his idiocy hadn't cost him her love. What if she'd grown weary of waiting on him? What if someone else had captured her heart after he'd inadvertently broken it again and again for years?

"Mary will be unbearable now." Beth leaned more heavily against him. "Do you suppose she would ever find me if I simply refused to leave the garden?"

He hadn't thought much about the repercussions of his declaration on her home life. "I'd wager your entire family will be impossible."

She wrapped her arms around him. "Let's stay out here forever so I never have to face them."

"I have an even better idea. Let us go pay a call on

Helene. I'd wager she'd require little convincing to invite you to stay with her for a few weeks, perhaps even until the end of the Season."

"Do you think she would?"

He kissed the top of Beth's head. "I am certain of it. And I could come for Helene's at-homes, and awkwardly take tea, and attempt to catch your eye. Robert, I am certain, would enjoy playing the overprotective guardian, demanding to know my intentions and insisting I return you unharmed from every ride in the park."

He could feel her laugh, and it did his heart good. She'd been unhappy enough that day for a lifetime.

"It will not, perhaps, be a true debut as you deserve," he said, "but I hope it will make up for, in a small way, your lack of a Season."

"Promise to steal a kiss now and then, despite the watchful eye of my overprotective guardian, and I will consider myself well compensated." She pressed a kiss to his cheek then settled into his arms. "You are the only reason I came to London these past three years. I wanted to see you."

"I was so unforgivably blind, Beth." He held her ever closer. "But I will atone for it. I promise you, I will."

Eight

All of London had likely heard Mary's tantrum after Julian had announced that Elizabeth would be spending the remainder of the Season with his sister. While Elizabeth had taken no satisfaction in the display, she'd seen it as an insight to her sister's character. Mary had always been given everything she'd ever wanted without question, and usually without delay. Julian had been firmly on her list of intended acquisitions, but he had chosen Elizabeth.

The passage of a month had neither lessened her memory of Mary's anger nor left her in any less a degree of awe at Julian's affection for her. That he loved her, she was absolutely certain. His devotion could not have been more evident. He held her hand at every opportunity and never bid her farewell without a kiss, however protracted, given Helene's vigilant presence.

Elizabeth's parents had still not given their approval for her to have a true Season, so her days were spent as something of a companion to Helene, accompanying her on shopping expeditions, sitting quietly nearby during her at-homes. She didn't accompany the Pinnelles to the theatre or musicales or balls. But Julian came for dinner every evening before the social whirl began to spend a precious hour or two with her before propriety required that he leave. She loved those brief moments with him but longed to have the right to be with him always.

Four weeks to the day of Elizabeth's departure from her parents' home, Helene held a dinner party. The guest list matched precisely that of the previous dinner Elizabeth had been forced to quit early. As the appointed time came and went, however, she could not help a feeling of disappointment. Julian had not yet arrived.

Mary did not wear the smug look Elizabeth might have expected. Indeed, she noted something quieter and more ponderous in her sister's expression than Elizabeth had ever seen. She didn't know at all what to make of it.

Just as she began to wonder if Julian meant to come at all, she heard the arrival of a carriage. As it always did, her heart lightened simply knowing that he was nearby. A moment later, the butler stepped into the drawing room.

"Mr. Broadwood and Mr. Gregory Gillerford."

Her brother had come? From Surrey?

Only Helene, Mr. Pinnelle, and Julian did not appear surprised. Elizabeth's gaze darted from Julian to Gregory and back again. Her brother made a quick succession of *good evening* to their parents and Mary before turning an enormous grin to Elizabeth.

"Haven't you an embrace for your favorite brother?" he teased.

She adored him; she always had. Eagerly taking his invitation, she embraced him for a long, drawn-out moment.

"I do wish you had come to London with us. I've missed you ever so much."

"And I wish you'd stayed in Surrey. The old pile of rocks isn't the same without you." He released her, still smiling all the while. "Julian here insisted I make the journey to Town. It seems he has some scheme up his sleeve."

She turned her attention to her dearest love once more. "A scheme? Dare I ask what it is?"

"I had meant to wait until after dinner, but seeing as everyone is here, and staring at me, I suppose I would do well to I jump straight to the heart of the matter."

What was he hinting at?

He took her hand, holding it both gently and earnestly, and led her to where her father stood watching in confusion.

"Mr. Gillerford," Julian began. "It will come as no surprise to you, seeing as I told you as much only a few short weeks ago that I love your daughter. I have loved her for a very long time, and my feelings have only grown. She is the dearest person to me in all the world."

She'd once worried that he merely endured her. But he'd declared her the dearest person in the world to him, and he'd said it without hesitation or qualification. The dearest. *His* dearest.

"As she was not permitted a proper Season, I have not been able to court her in the manner she deserves. The chaperonage of my sister and brother-in-law has allowed me to call on her, and have done what I could to press my suit. I have cherished every moment of her company this past month. But I find I can no longer be content with mere snatches of her time."

Elizabeth had to remind herself to breathe. She knew what he was saying, the declaration he was building toward. She had imagined this moment so many times and wondered if, perhaps, she was dreaming yet.

"Our families are well enough known to one another that I need not make you acquainted with my social standing or financial situation," Julian continued, still addressing Father. "Further, you have known that I was courting your daughter these past weeks yet made no objection, so I do not believe you are opposed to the idea."

Father shook his head firmly. "I long ago decided you'd be a good match for my daughter, though I'd assumed you would court a different one. Everyone assumed that."

For a moment she allowed her father's words and her family's lack of enthusiasm to dampen her happiness. But for *only* a moment. They might not be happy for her, but how could she be anything but overjoyed?

"I, for one, think this match is brilliant," Gregory tossed in. Little wonder he was her favorite, if her only, brother.

Julian turned and faced Elizabeth, taking her hands in his and holding her gaze. "Dearest, dearest Beth. I have cherished these past weeks with you, but I can no longer bear being limited to mere snatches of your time. I do not wish to take dinner with you and then say goodbye. I do not want to spend week after week counting the hours until I may see you again. I want to be able to simply turn around, and there you are. I want to be able to call you *my* Beth, and to be *your* Jules."

How was it possible that a person could smile and tear up at the same time? She didn't know whether to throw her arms around his neck or keep still and quiet so he would continue declaring his love for her. She'd waited ten years to hear these words.

"Please, Beth, do me the honor of becoming my wife so we need never be apart again, my dearest, most darling friend. I cannot promise to never be as thickheaded as I have hitherto been, but I solemnly vow to love you with every breath and every thought and every beat of my heart for the rest of my life. Will you marry me, Elizabeth Mildred Gillerford?"

She couldn't speak. She didn't have the breath left in her to do so.

Gregory moved ever so slightly closer and loudly whispered, "The word you are searching for, Elizabeth, is 'yes.'"

She laughed through her amazement and bubbling emotions. "Yes. Of course I will, Jules. *My* Jules. My darling friend. Of course I will."

Despite the audience and her mother's gasp of surprise, Julian kissed her quite thoroughly, holding her to him as if he meant never to let her go. He held her even after ending their kiss, smiling at her, his eyes filled with unmistakable love.

"I've been waiting for this since I was eight years old," she said. "I've known since then that this was what I wanted."

"I hope, my love, that you will tell me everything else you've ever wanted." He pressed a kiss to her forehead then rested his head against hers. "I mean to make all of your dreams come true. Every last one."

In that moment, she believed that even the most impossible of dreams could, indeed, come true.

ABOUT SARAH M. EDEN

Sarah M. Eden is the author of multiple historical romances, including *Longing for Home*, winner of *Foreword* magazine's IndieFab Gold Award and the AML's 2013 Novel of the Year, as well as Whitney Award finalists *Seeking Persephone* and *Courting Miss Lancaster*.

Combining her obsession with history and affinity for tender love stories, Sarah loves crafting witty characters and heartfelt romances. She has twice served as the Master of Ceremonies for the LDStorymakers Writers Conference and acted as the Writer in Residence at the Northwest Writers Retreat. Sarah is represented by Pam van Hylckama Vlieg at Foreword Literary Agency.

Find Sarah online at SarahMEden.com

Follow Sarah on Twitter: @SarahMEden

The Mender

by Carla Kelly

OTHER WORKS BY CARLA KELLY

Reforming Lord Ragsdale
Miss Drew Plays Her Hand
With This Ring
Summer Campaign
Softly Falling
Her Hesitant Heart
Miss Wittier Makes a List
Borrowed Light
My Loving Vigil Keeping
Safe Passage

1805, New Bedford

"Thankful, thee is a pest."

"I merely want to accompany thee on thy voyage to Italy, cousin."

"The world is at war. This is folly."

"Cousin, what year is it?"

"Thankful, thee *knows* it is 1805."

"What did I do in 1805?"

"Thee stayed at home here in New Bedford and helped my aunt. If I remember right, Abner Whittier sat with thee—sits with thee—in the parlor Sunday night. H'mm, and David Starbuck and Joseph Winslow, on occasion."

"What will I do in 1806?"

"Probably marry one of these."

"In 1807?"

"Thee will probably undergo a birthing and tend a home."

"In 1808, 1809, 1810?"

"More of the same, God willing." Pause. "I begin to understand."

"Just one trip, Cousin Loum Snow. I will ask no more of thee."

"Everyone on the *Ann Alexander* must serve a useful purpose. What is thine?"

"I mend things."

One

If Thankful had thought Mama would not agree to an adventure taking her youngest child to Italy, she was happily proved wrong. Mama had done no such thing. With her usual vigor, Mama had recommended warm drawers and a thicker cloak, which appeared on Thankful's bed as she packed her trunk.

"Mama, it is beautiful," Thankful said, hugging the cloak to her and then rubbing the soft wool against her cheek. "I will be warm, thanks to thee."

Patience Winnings was a practical woman. "Thee is too fanciful for thy own good. When has thee ever been cold in this household? We are in Massachusetts, not the North Pole. Besides that, dark green looks well against auburn."

Thankful had to ask. "Why is thee not objecting to such a voyage? Even Loum keeps reminding me the world is at war, and water is choppy in November."

Patience sat on Thankful's bed, which sat under the eaves. "Thy cousin is young, but he is a good captain, and the *Ann Alexander* is new built. As for war"—She patted the space beside her, and Thankful sat down—"I would remind thee of Job, who tells us that 'man is born unto trouble, as the sparks fly upward.'"

"That makes me think that thee would be inclined to keep me in safety here," Thankful said, for she was no fool.

"I could," Mama agreed. "Your father and I could end it right here for you, but no."

"Why?" Thankful leaned her head against her mother's shoulder, and sure enough, her mother's arm went around her waist.

Patience Winnings chuckled and inclined her head against her daughter's auburn hair, so like her own. "Could it be that thy mother wishes she had taken such an adventure herself?"

"*Thee*, Mama?" Thankful had not thought her practical, careful mother would ever have craved the unknown.

"Yes!" She touched her daughter's hand, then picked it up and kissed it." I am grateful beyond measure for my life here in calm New Bedford . . ."

"Say it, Mama—boring New Bedford," Thankful teased.

"*Calm*," her mother repeated. "With a good, steady husband. But between thee and me, I might have enjoyed an adventure when I was eighteen."

"Mama, may I remind thee that thee was married by eighteen?" Thankful said.

"Precisely! And that is why I have no objection to this voyage."

"I believe I understand."

"I knew thee would. God keep thee."

Two

The *Ann Alexander* cleared the port of New York on October 5, 1805, laden with kegs of flour, hogsheads of tobacco leaf, and great barrels of flour and other sundries. She was bound for Livorno, Italy (called Leghorn by the English, because they were persistently stubborn people, as Captain Loum Snow pointed out to Thankful).

At the last minute, Loum had succumbed to an offer he could not refuse, and took on a substantial lading of lumber, which had been lashed to the deck—lumber he had paid for himself.

"I intend to make a profit from my lumber," he told his cousin, who stood beside him on the quarterdeck.

Thankful looked at her cousin, captain of the *Ann Alexander* at the tender age of twenty-six, knowing she could match his shrewdness. "Does thee intend to impress Nancy Swift with this profit when thee returns?"

Loum laughed and made no reply, his attention taken up with the business of getting his vessel underway. Entirely satisfied, Thankful looked around at the disorderly order of a merchant ship. She gazed with pride at the rope that made up the ship's rigging, manufactured in her father's New Bedford ropewalk. But when the undulations of the water beneath the ship became more pronounced, her smile slipped a bit. She was ready to cut loose her own moorings, and Loum had already furnished her miniscule quarters with a bucket. If she was to be seasick, that was the will of the Almighty.

She wasn't delighted that sea sickness gave her ample time to contemplate saying goodbye to her parlor visitors. True, Abner Whittier had pouted, then showed her his dairy herd, and acres of recently harvested corn and barley. "When thee returns from this adventure" —funny how he could make such an exciting word seem foolish—"I will have a house ready."

He didn't say for what, and Thankful didn't ask, particularly since only the day before, David Starbuck had showed her his own plans for a whaleship he was to build with his father and brothers. "We have more and more orders every year," he told her. "Starbuck and Sons will be known around the maritime world."

She had nodded over the plans, wondering what Joseph Winslow would come up with to give her reason to stay home. When all he did was shake his head and bid her good day, she marveled at how easily some men folded. Better to know such character defect now, perhaps, but her pride stumbled a bit, which was probably good for her character.

Leaving New Bedford had caused her more than one pang. As the *Ann* cleared New Bedford on her way to New York, Thankful's father had blown his nose several fierce times and had made mention of pollen flying in the streets. Thankful kindly did not inform him that August had seen

The Mender

the last of the pollen, because she was suffering the same affliction. Mama, on the other hand, had remained dry-eyed.

The *Ann* had hugged the sound on the voyage to New York, which had also meant no need to kneel over the bucket in her cabin. Loum had assured her that the Atlantic rollers would be a different story.

Thankful did not care. Beyond kissing her parents and promising all manner of good behavior—and swallowing the lump in her throat as her beloved New Bedford slid from view—Thankful was ripe for the future.

New York had not disappointed, even though Loum firmly turned down any excursions off ship, saying he was too busy to chaperone her, and that there was plenty to see from the *Ann's* deck. Thankful made no objection. What she saw reminded her that the world was a harsh place: wives and children weeping as ships docked with missing crew members; one-legged beggars, probably former seamen, begging on the docks; women lurking in shadows.

But the excitement! Great cargoes of all description were swung from the dock into the *Ann's* hold, and the surrounding ships as well, all as eager as greyhounds to slip their moorings and take good American commerce to the world. Just leaning over the rail acquainted her with the sound of accents she did not hear back home. A Jew with curly sidelocks and wearing a long, black coat haggled with a bluff fellow with a Scottish accent so strong that she wondered how the men could communicate. Sailors swaggered about with the peculiar drunken walk of men newly ashore. Wives and sweethearts waved handkerchiefs as other vessels shipped anchor and moved from the port. It was almost too much, but Thankful Winnings faithfully recorded everything in her mind and heart. When she was old, married and settled, she would remember.

Finally, it was the *Ann Alexander's* turn to bid farewell to American waters and hail other lands. Thankful's view from the quarterdeck left her nearly trembling with excitement at the booming of the sails and the shouts of the captain and his number one as the merchant ship made her graceful way into the Atlantic.

Loum had been right about the swells. For two days, Thankful took to her bunk and welcomed death as the *Ann* moved up and down the troughs of the sea, bound for Italy. She puked everything she had ever eaten, petitioned the Almighty for a quick and merciful end, and then, on the third day, recovered and staggered into the wardroom, where Loum and his two mates applauded.

She kept down pea soup to smiles all around, then settled it with ship's biscuit and tea. "Now, sirs," she announced, folding her hands in her lap, a proper Friend again, now that the tumult had passed. "What can I do to help thee?"

"Cousin, did you bring your mending kit?" Bless her good cousin. He had work for her already.

She nodded, ready for anything.

The first mate took out his watch and pushed it across the table to her. "Stopped running only yesterday, Miss Winnings. What can you do?"

"Why, mend it. And please call me Thankful."

She fetched her leather-bound kit with tiny tools and let Cousin Loum escort her to the deck, where the light was good. She whispered, "Does thee not say 'thee' and 'thy' aboard the *Ann*?"

He shrugged. "Depending on the crew, sometimes, but both of my mates are not Friends, so I do not. Perhaps . . . you . . . should not either. Sometimes we Friends perplex the wider world."

The Mender

Thankful nodded, content not to perplex anyone. The sun was bright, and she blinked a few times, then sighed with the loveliness of open water everywhere, and all sails crowded on.

"My goodness, Loum, this is a wonderful sight."

And so it was. A sailor—Loum called him the ship's carpenter—brought up a clever chair, low-slung and with a canvas seat, which he anchored to the deck with a few well-placed nails to wooden blocks.

I want one of these in my own house someday, she thought, as she sank into it and took out her kit.

She set the watch on a small wooden board with raised edges and dismantled it, gradually accumulating a cluster of curious sailors, until Loum reminded them in what must have been his captain's voice of their own duties.

The timepiece only wanted cleaning, which was easily accomplished. At the noon watch, Loum shot the sun with his sextant and indicated a new course to the helmsman. Loum relinquished the quarterdeck to the first mate again, who held the timepiece to his ear and nodded. "You're a clever lass," he said. "Where did you learn this?"

Overcoming her shyness—when had she ever in her life spoken to someone who wasn't a Friend? —she told him of a winter two years ago when she'd contracted measles and languished in boredom until an uncle had brought over his own tools and repaired her father's watch as she looked on. Broken locks followed as her interest grew, increasing her skill. In a matter of three weeks, when the last of her splotches went away, Thankful was a locksmith.

"I have a sewing kit, too," she told the man with the healed and ticking watch. "You know, for more prosaic things."

On a small ship, word gets around. By the dog watch,

she was mending trousers and shirts. She blended a torn watch cap into its yarn again with a few judicious stitches. Before too many days, she had moved on to minor cuts and bruises, courtesy of her cousin's rudimentary medicine chest and book of instructions.

Her medical skills carried their own heavy burden. When she sutured a forearm laceration, she had so many tears in her eyes that the victim patted her cheek and said, "There, there," as she stitched.

Thankful Winnings passed the next eighteen days of the voyage, mending and fixing, until they sailed into a morning where her rudimentary skills paled into insignificance. Near the Cape of Trafalgar, almost where the Gates of Hercules opened into the Mediterranean Sea, they came upon the aftermath of a battle, and not just any battle.

Three

The day had begun as usual—one more day of sailing—although the water was choppier now, and there were more clouds than sun. A glance at the calendar in the wardroom showed it to be the 23rd day of October. Strangely, no one else was in the wardroom, even though she was certain that this was the usual breakfast hour. She started for the companionway, but Loum blocked her path.

"Cousin, stay below deck," he said.

His face was pale, and his eyes so serious. She went closer until she was just a step below him. "Loum?" she said. "Please tell me what is the matter."

He passed a shaking hand down his face and took a deep breath, this cousin who was the steadiest man she knew, discounting her own father.

"Such sights . . ." His voice trailed off.

"Are . . . are we in danger?" she asked.

"The danger has passed." He looked at her as though measuring her, something he had never done before. "Then again, maybe we can help." He turned slightly toward the hatch. "That is what the Lord expects of us, isn't it?"

She took another step. "Thee knows He does. What is life if not to serve? But Loum, what is it?"

She watched him visibly make up his mind. He took her hand in hers, kissed it, and pulled her up after him to the deck of the *Ann Alexander*.

Her eyes widened at the sight before her. She must have made an exclamation, because Loum's hand tightened. She swallowed and looked around.

To Thankful's shocked senses, the landscape appeared as if giant, cosmic hands had snatched up an ocean full of ships—some large, some small—raised them high, and then slammed them against the water, tumbling men and fragments of men, crumpling sails, and turning wooden walls into matchsticks. Ruin lay on the surface of the choppy water, the destruction so monumental that Thankful could only blink and wish it would all disappear.

"What can we possibly do?" she whispered to her cousin. "I . . . I wouldn't know where to begin."

"Nor I," he whispered back.

Maybe if she only looked at a smaller sphere, she could manage. She glanced at the sailors on deck, all of them staring at carnage that would not disappear. Typically when Captain Snow came on deck, his crew redoubled its efforts. Not so today. Loum Snow was one of them now, as horrified as they were. As she watched them, some of the men even moved closer to their young captain, like child to parent.

Thankful looked across the water. Several ships had burned to the waterline, a massive Spanish flag from one draped across the water like a shroud. Others were dismasted hulks, rolling like stodgy merchantmen, no longer elegant and deadly ships of the line. Little cutters and pinnaces darted from one British ship to another, reminding her of water bugs on a June pond back home. One cutter pulled toward the three-deck ship of the line directly in front of them.

She had no doubt this was a British victory. Far more ships bearing the Union Jack patrolled the water. None of the still-floating wrecks bore flags, because their Spanish and French crews had been forced to strike their colors. Even a landlubber could tell that.

Some of the Royal Navy ships had taken a dreadful pounding, especially that ship of the line directly in front of the *Ann*. Smaller ships clustered around the massive vessel, and signaling flags raised and lowered repeatedly.

Loum must have caught her gaze. "It's the *H.M.S. Victory*," he said in a more normal tone, as the shock had worn off and he'd become a captain again. "Lord Nelson's ship."

On the tattered deck of the *Victory*, a man she assumed was a midshipman put a speaking trumpet to his mouth and gestured toward the *Ann Alexander*.

"Ahoy! Ahoy!" came the tinny call. "Name, port of origin, cargo, and whither bound?"

"Can they—"

"—stop us? Of course they can," Loum said. "You are looking at the Royal Navy." He hurried to the quarterdeck railing and reached for his own speaking trumpet. "The *Ann Alexander*, Loum Snow commanding, eighteen days out of New York Harbor, New Bedford berthed," he shouted. "Flour, apples, sundries and lumber, bound for Leghorn."

Thankful ran to his side, childlike in her urge to stay close to her cousin.

Loum smiled at her. "Don't be a goose, Thankful," he told her. "Thee wanted an adventure."

"Not this one," she replied, which made him shake his head.

"Thee cannot pick adventures like clams in a basket."

The midshipman was hailing Loum again, an officer standing beside him now. "Captain Snow, come aboard the *Victory*. Handsomely, now."

"We've been summoned," Loum told Thankful as he put down the trumpet. "And look, they're sending a cutter. Want to come along?"

She eyed the approaching ship, rowed smartly by four sailors, and shook her head. "Not in a dress." She leaned toward her cousin. "Someone might see my drawers!"

"Didn't know thee was wearing any," he teased. "I'll rig a rope to swing thee down."

"I don't want to go," she assured him.

He turned serious then. "I'd rather keep thee close. Trust me, Thankful."

"Very well." *An adventure*, Thankful told herself. *Thee wanted it and thee has it.*

Loum was as good as his word. A quick rope around her waist and knees anchored her dress. One of the men ran another rope through the block and tackle, and she was ready. When the cutter bobbed far below the *Ann Alexander*, Loum stepped off the deck and descended hand-over-hand down the chains, timing himself to a rising wave. A whistle to his men, and Thankful was up and over the side, eyes closed, clutching the rope and praying her drawers didn't show.

If the sailors in the cutter were surprised to see a woman, they didn't show it. Thankful clutched Loum's hand as they crossed the space between vessels, a small one, but large enough for body parts and ship fragments to float by. Thankful bowed her head and prayed.

The men of the *Victory* were as efficient as the *Ann's* crew. In no time, she stood on the deck of the Royal Navy's most famous ship, so famous that even Quaker misses from New Bedford had heard of it. She looked around the *Victory*, wishing to see the same tidy disorder as on the *Ann*, but seeing only chaos. She took a deep breath, calmly taking in the deep stains on the deck, the splintered railings, the foremast that hung like a broken bird's wing.

"Poor, poor ship," she whispered. "She looks like a ruin, but still she floats."

"Thee would be amazed what stays afloat almost from sheer will, cousin," Loum said.

As they stood together on the deck, an officer with considerably more rank than a midshipman approached. He paused, eyeing the two of them, thinking heaven knew what.

"First Lieutenant Sir Donald Gatewood," he said with a slight nod. He raised his hat, then set it back on his head.

"Loum Snow, at thy service," her cousin said, making no move to doff his hat or bow.

Lieutenant Gatewood frowned. "Captain, the common courtesies?" he prompted.

"I am of the Society of Friends and take my hat off for no one," Loum said. "What can we do for thee, Donald Gatewood?"

"By God, you're impertinent!" the lieutenant exclaimed.

"I am a Friend," Thankful's cousin said patiently. "We do not doff hats *or* recognize titles. Please, call me Loum."

Gatewood opened and closed his mouth a few times, looking suddenly younger, and gave up. "I have been ordered to buy the lumber so visible on your deck, as well as several hogsheads of flour and one of apples," he said. "I need it now, Captain . . . uh, Loum."

"Now? I have promised cargo bound for Leghorn. I'll sell you what I can, but—"

"We will take what we need, if we must," Gatewood replied.

He opened his mouth to say more, but from below deck, up came a long-legged brown dog, followed by an even more distinguished gathering of gold trim and shoulder boards. Pleased at the distraction, Thankful knelt on the deck and held out her hand to the hound.

As the men came closer, the effect of battle became more obvious—torn sleeves and bandages. The officers surrounded the man with glittering gold trim lace, but the dog came closer to Thankful and sniffed her hand. "There now, thee is a friend," Thankful said.

"Madam, Bounce doesn't like just anyone."

Thankful looked up with a smile. "I am not just anyone, sir," she said. "I am Thankful Winning out of New Bedford, and this is my cousin Loum Snow, who captains the *Ann*." When Bounce started to lean against her, she laughed out loud. "I am not thy resting post, hound."

A snap of the officer's fingers, and Bounce returned to his side, even though the dog continued to observe Thankful, his tongue out, his eyes lively.

The glittering man came forward, effectively dismissing Gatewood, who appeared delighted to step back into less responsibility. "Captain Snow, I am Admiral Lord Collingwood, and this is my flagship now."

Loum nodded. "Horatio Nelson? What of him?"

The admiral took a deep breath and looked toward the mainmast, where a large keg had been secured. It was surrounded by a Marine guard, which made Thankful wonder what could possibly be inside it that was so important.

"Admiral Lord Nelson died the afternoon of the battle two days ago," he said after taking a deep breath. "We have placed him in this cast filled with brandy, and will transport him to England as a hero. Not for him a burial at sea, though I do not doubt he would prefer it."

Thankful swallowed her sudden tears—not from knowing Nelson, but from the reactions around her, of sorrow of the deepest kind. The other officers looked anywhere but at the cask. "Poor, poor man," she whispered.

"Captain Snow—"

"—Loum Snow."

"You Quakers are a nuisance! Very well, *Loum*, I sorely need your lumber. We will tow the *Victory* to the Rock and repair her there," the admiral said, in a voice unused to objection.

"The rock?" Thankful asked.

"Gibraltar, cousin," Loum said. "Come stand by me."

She did as he said, feeling more than seeing a wide gulf between the two of them and the Royal Navy. *They could take it all, couldn't they?* she thought.

Silence from Loum. She knew his nimble brain had to be weighing what price he could get from the admiral against what he'd said the Italians would likely pay. And there was Nancy Swift, waiting for Loum back in New Bedford, to consider.

"Sir, I do hope thee plans to pay him well for that lumber," Thankful said to the admiral, who waited for Loum's response.

"Thankful!" Loum hissed from the side of his mouth.

She plunged ahead, thinking of Nancy. "With the sale of the lumber, Loum will be able to build a house for Nancy Swift, and then he will propose marriage."

Oh, dear. Why did she have to say that?

To a man, the glittering assembly, began to smile. She even thought she heard a laugh turned into a sudden cough.

Maybe these naval officers had Nancy Swifts in their lives too.

She might as well blunder forward. "He needs a good price because Nancy Swift's father is more particular than . . ." She looked around, then clasped her hands together, eyes on the deck now. "I am an idiot."

The admiral gave her a famously large smile. "I doubt that supremely! What you are is concerned about your cousin and Miss Swift." He gave her a most proper bow, one foot extended, his bicorn hat doffed, which made many in his entourage smile. "We will pay Captain Snow exactly what he asks, so Miss Swift will have him." He named a figure. "Well, Loum? Do we disappoint Miss Swift?"

"N—no, no. Not at all, Cuthbert Collingwood," Loum stammered. "And as much flour and apples as you need."

"Done," the admiral said. He turned to a smaller man beside him. "Draw up a contract here and now, and you'll return to . . . to . . ."

"The *Ann Alexander*."

"The *Ann* with your money in hand."

"Aye, then," Loum said.

"I have one request, and in this I must be firm: You must follow our tow to Gibraltar and make the exchange there. We cannot complete all of the repairs to the *Victory* at sea."

"Aye again."

Admiral Collingwood nodded. "Deal with my paymaster now. I have other business." He turned to Thankful, and she gulped. "You, my dear, are persuasive. Have you other talents?"

"I mend things," she said promptly. "Clocks, watches. People, too, because I have a good medical book."

His face grew suddenly solemn, sorrow so evident that

Thankful felt tears in her eyes again. "Would to God you could mend us here in this fleet. Would to God."

"I can help," she told him.

"I believe you would try," he replied. "Good day to you both."

The admiral turned toward the battered quarterdeck of the *Victory*. A captain stepped toward him. His voice was soft, but, as he spoke to his admiral, he gestured several times toward Thankful, which made her slowly move behind her cousin.

"Thankful, thee is still a pest," Loum whispered to her.

"I know. I promise to be silent hereafter evermore."

"Ask her, Captain," she heard distinctly from the admiral. "I know your desperation. Good God, I know the fleet's desperation."

Please, please, don't let him look my way, Thankful thought as she edged farther behind Loum.

But there the man was in front of Loum, doffing his bicorn. She knew from his single epaulet that he was a mere captain. He was a youngish man who might have been handsome at one time, but who had been altered by war.

"Captain Snow . . . Loum . . . I have great need of your cousin," he said with no preamble.

Drat Loum, if he didn't step aside and leave her standing there.

"Thee will have to address any concerns to my cousin," Loum said, "although I do not precisely understand how she could help thee."

The man looked at her, as if measuring her competence. "I am Captain William Sanford and I command the *Tethys*, that 36 over there."

She followed his pointing finger to a battered frigate, its masts intact, but with a hole blown just above the waterline.

Men with planking and hammers were covering the hole from the inside and outside.

"I doubt there is anything I can do for thee, William Sanford." It sounded so cowardly, but what could the man possibly expect her to do?

"I contend there is," he said in a voice most firm. "Where *do* you Quakers get your effrontery?"

"It comes naturally to us," she replied, equally serious, which made the helmsman smile.

She looked around for Loum to shield her from what was already beginning to frighten her, but her traitor cousin was talking to the paymaster. Her mother had raised her better than to ignore someone talking directly to her, so she returned her attention to the frigate captain. Drat the man, but he would have a bloodstained bandage on his head, which someone had wrapped poorly. She could tidy that and maybe trim his hair a bit, too, so it wouldn't mat in the blood.

"In a battle such as this, frigates carry messages by repeating the signals from one warship to the other. When black smoke masks the water, we must move about in the fleet. Sadly, we came under fire and suffered a direct hit."

"I am so sorry," she said. "But what—"

"My surgeon lost his pharmacist mate and loblolly boy in the blast," he said, riding over her words, perhaps aware that he had to state his case quickly. "He sustained a most punishing sprained ankle." Captain Sanford came closer. For one terrifying moment, Thankful thought he might drop to one knee. "Please, Miss Snow..."

"Thankful Winnings," she said automatically.

"Thankful Winnings, I need you to help my surgeon. He cannot stand up, and there are men to tend. He has the matter well enough in hand because the surgical part of his duties are done, but the cleaning and the feeding are dragging him down."

"He needs to stay off a bad ankle," she said. "Find someone in thy crew to help." She almost winced with the heartlessness of her own words, but the poor captain obviously had an inflated idea of what she could accomplish. Best to disabuse him of it at once.

"There *is* no one else. There are no pharmacist mates or surgeons to spare in the fleet right now." He swept his hand from horizon to horizon, as though peeling back a curtain to reveal ships in all states of desperate need. "It would be only until we reach Gibraltar. We'll follow the *Victory* into port, and your cousin, as well. A matter of three days. Please, I beg you."

Thankful could tell he was not a man inclined to beg. She made the mistake of looking the captain in the eyes. She saw a man worn with worry for his ship, his crew, the fleet, and maybe even the fate of England. Perhaps she could help a little. Perhaps if she kept the ship's surgeon off his feet, he would mend faster.

A mender must help a mender, she thought, even though it was as illogical as anything she had ever told herself.

"Let me ask my cousin," she said, and crossed the deck to Loum. He nodded when she told him the captain's request. "Thee is supposed to tell me no," she whispered to Loum.

"Thee wanted an adventure," he reminded her. "Now thee has one. Go help the surgeon. Thee says the *Tethys* will follow us to port? I raise no objection. Go to it, cousin." He turned back to the paymaster.

Thankful returned to Captain Sanford's side. "I am not highly skilled," she temporized, still hoping to dissuade him.

"Do you faint or puke at blood?" he asked bluntly.

"No."

"I will pay you."

Pay me? she thought, astounded. *No one has ever paid me for anything.* Scandalized at the thought of payment for goodwill, her head went up. "I will do this for no wage, William."

In fewer than twenty minutes, Captain Sanford briefly returned her to the *Ann* for a change of clothing and her medical book. As he waited in the cutter that would take them to the *Tethys*, she snatched her watch repair tools, then stood in her cabin, wondering if the man would drag her from belowdecks if she did not return promptly. Deciding that he would, she continued the adventure she was already regretting. The *HMS Tethys* it would be.

Four

Captain Sanford was silent on their brief journey from the *Ann* back to the *Tethys*. He stared at the fleet, then shook his head, as if trying to tumble out bad memories. He spoke only once, after he himself had made the rope secure around her knees and waist.

"I have a daughter," he said, right before he gave the rope a tug. "She is seven now, and I have not seen her since she was three. Do ye think she has changed much?"

She nodded, feeling instantly small-minded to quibble about having to tend a few men. As the men of the Royal Navy hoisted her onto the deck, with her eyes shut in terror, she reminded herself that not all duty was pleasant.

The bosun piped his captain aboard, careful to remember the tributes even when all around them was in shambles. Captain Sanford took her by the hand, startling her further.

He faced his men and spoke in his captain's voice. "This is Thankful Winnings from New Bedford by way of the *Ann Alexander* on our starboard beam. If any of you so much as look at her cross-eyed, I will hang you personally." He released her hand. "Come now. There is work to do."

She followed the captain down the companionway, minding her steps because the *Tethys* listed to one side. The ship's depths smelled no better than the *Ann*'s after eighteen days at sea, but there was another odor she couldn't identify, something cloying and foul.

"Careful," he said. "They'll go on deck tomorrow morning for burial. These will probably be the last."

The noonday sun would never penetrate the deck below the guns, but in the gloom, she made out three shrouded bodies.

"Ordinarily, the sick bay is closer to the forecastle," he explained as they threaded past the shapes. "We took a hit there, so moved everyone up a deck. In here."

The captain paused with his hand on the doorknob. "I should tell you this: I stand on terms of familiarity with Surgeon Farnsworth. On my father's estate in Devon, his father was an assistant to the steward. After a fashion, we grew up together."

Thankful nodded, wondering what "after a fashion" could possibly mean.

"You know each other well then?" she asked, merely to be polite. She was here for the purpose of helping the surgeon, and already she wished the onerous duty was concluded.

After a moment's hesitation, the captain replied. "We know each other rather too well. Ah, but never mind. There is work to do, and I greatly appreciate your assistance, Miss Winnings."

Thankful followed Captain Sanford to what she suspected might be the officers' wardroom. Five men lay on cots, two sleeping and the remainder eyeing her with the inward gaze of the wounded. Wearing a bloody apron, a sixth man sat beside one of the sleeping invalids, his foot propped on an overturned bucket. He seemed to be dozing, too, but when the captain cleared his throat his head snapped up.

He appeared younger than the captain, his brown hair cut so short that in the low light, she wondered at first if he was bald. His lips were thin, his face gaunt, softened only by an improbable beauty mark beside his right eye. He possessed not a single handsome feature except that beauty mark, but his overall look intrigued Thankful. She knew, in some unknown fashion, that this was an intensely capable man. Maybe it was the set of his shoulders. She couldn't explain it, but she found Surgeon Farnsworth sturdy and entirely to her liking. How odd; he hadn't spoken a word, and his eyes were barely open.

Thankful came toward him with no urging from the captain—she who had hung back all across the deck and down the companionway. She went directly to the surgeon, knelt by his leg, and touched the swollen ankle, even as he looked at her in startled surprise.

"Thee needs to wrap it tighter," she told him, then realized she was telling a surgeon what to do. "I do beg thy pardon."

"As it happens, you are correct, so do not apologize. I have been too busy to tend myself, which is always an awkward business. Captain, kindly explain this Quaker lady who is fondling my ankle."

Thankful laughed, which probably was what the surgeon had intended, to alleviate both his surprise and her embarrassment. She chose to see it as an open invitation from an equal.

With a smile of his own, Captain Sanford divulged her

name, which brought a slight smile to the surgeon's lips and explained her presence. Surgeon Farnsworth absorbed the narrative without a murmur, as if the heavens always rained Quakers after major sea battles.

"Are you ready to go to work?" he asked.

"I am," she said as she got to her feet.

"Captain, please point her toward the galley. Miss Winnings, tell Cookie to give you a bucket of whatever he has." He tried to rise, but his effort only made sweat pop out on his forehead.

Thankful put a hand on his shoulder. "Please don't," was all she said.

"I would like to ease the men before you return, but I doubt I can. That will be your first duty when you bring back food. I could wish you were married, because this is dicey business. Are you married?"

"No. That is why I was allowed to have this adventure with my cousin."

"Adventure? More than you planned on, eh?"

"We'll see."

His face turned red, and she felt her own face grow warm. "Then I fear the Royal Navy will contribute to your more intimate education. I regret that everyone has to piss." In spite of his own pain, he chuckled.

"I have little brothers," she replied, determined to be useful, even if the homely business of easing the men suddenly mortified the surgeon, now that a woman had to assist.

"These are not little brothers."

"And thee is borrowing trouble from tomorrow," she said, and left the improvised sick bay with the captain.

"He's like that," Sanford said. Two spots of color burned in his cheeks, reminding Thankful that captains weren't likely involved in sick-bay duties.

She fetched a bucket of something that looked like mush from the galley, where a one-eyed, one-legged man held court, muttering to himself. He stopped his monologue long enough to stare at her and cross himself.

Thankful returned to the sick bay in time to watch the surgeon hobble to a cot, urinal in hand. He gave her a guilty look.

"Adam, thee is not to be trusted alone," she scolded. "I told thee I would do that."

Over his protests, she took him firmly by the arm and sat him on the unused cot, to the applause of two men who seemed to be enjoying themselves hugely. She fluffed a pillow behind his head. He leaned back, exhausted from the effort of even a few minutes on his feet, then gave her an appraising look.

"You called me Adam."

"It is thy name. We Friends do not recognize titles. I am Thankful."

"So am I," he said, with just the hint of a smile.

"Thee is too old for such a tease as that. Don't think I have not heard it before."

"Very well, Thankful, you win. Take the urinal to those two jokers over there. They can manage their own business. Then pour it in that canister, and one of us—probably you—will take it topside and dump it into the ocean."

She did as he said, averting her eyes even as her new patients did all they could under the shelter of their blankets to spare her further embarrassment. When everyone was finished, she marched the canister on deck and dumped it over the side, looking neither right nor left. She returned to the galley, requesting hot water this time, which she used to wipe every grimy face in the sick bay, including the surgeon's.

The mush had remained gratifyingly warm in the bucket. She spooned it into bowls stacked only two high on a shelf with a thick wooden lip. Everyone could manage his own meal except for the amputee.

"I'll learn," he said, as she fed him.

There was enough left for a bowl of her own, which she took to the surgeon's cot, pulling up a stool beside him. The mush was heavily sugared, which she found to her taste. When she finished, she told him—and all of them listening—the circumstances of the *Ann Alexander*, how she was bound for Leghorn and had sailed onto a watery battlefield. "So my cousin has sold his own lumber to the Royal Navy, and Nancy Swift will have her house," she concluded.

She thought the surgeon might provide some commentary, but he lay there placidly, with nicely veined hands—surgeon's hands—folded across his middle, his eyelids drooping, looking as content as a man could, which surprised her, considering their surroundings.

"I could probably listen to you all day," he said finally. "I have been at sea since 1793."

"Never on land?" she asked. "None of thee?" She looked around to see the others sleeping.

"Now and then. Long enough to stash my prize money with a banking house, get drunk, eat a meal that didn't threaten to crawl off my plate, sleep in a bed that remained stationary, then return to sea." His own frankness seemed not to bother him, or maybe he was just tired. "So you came to sea for an adventure before settling into humdrum marriage?"

Put that way, she wasn't so certain. "I . . . I suppose I did. I . . ."

She stopped and looked at the surgeon. His eyes were closed, and she thought at first that he slept, like the others.

But no, he was weeping—silent tears traveled down his cheeks and dripped from his chin. Horrified, she didn't know whether to walk away and spare him further embarrassment or stay where she was.

"Did I say something I shouldn't have?" she asked quietly. She took the cloth she had used to wash his face and dabbed his cheeks.

He shook his head and continued to cry silently. As she watched, she knew without anyone telling her that these noiseless tears were old friends. He had somehow perfected the dismal art of crying without anyone knowing, and here she was, staring at him, aghast.

She looked around and realized that he had waited until the men under his care were asleep. If he hadn't been injured himself, he probably would have held out until she'd left. At a total loss, she closed her eyes in quiet prayer, the kind of prayer Friends were famous for, and she meant every unspoken word.

Lord, give me thy light, she prayed. *I need it now.*

Hold him, the Inward Light told her, and she didn't hesitate. She edged herself onto his cot, then put her arms around him, this man she barely knew. His arms went around her, and he began to shake with his silent tears. She held him close, her arms under his back, and rested her head on his chest, because his grip was strong. She didn't say a word, because the Inward Light had not mentioned anything about talking. She held him and let everything leave her mind except comforting another of God's creatures, wounded perhaps more than the men he tried to heal.

In utter peace with the Light, she listened to the steady beat of Adam Farnsworth's heart and wondered about the toll that war took on everyone.

Some wounds are visible; others are not, the Light of Christ whispered.

As she held this man—an action alien to everything she had ever been taught by careful parents—she felt him gradually relax. The beat of his heart slowed, and his shoulders lost their rigor. Soon he was breathing deeply, asleep.

Thankful disentangled herself from his embrace, sat back, and then returned to the stool beside the cot. She felt drained and weary beyond words, as if his pain had transferred to her body through some curious alchemy.

She heard one of the men stir on his cot, and looked around. The sailor with one arm watched her, his eyes full of sympathy. She went to his cot and knelt beside it. "May I help you?" she whispered.

He shook his head, his eyes so tender as he watched the sleeping surgeon. "I wonder, miss, if he don't suffer for all of us in ways we can't imagine."

She nodded. "Do you remember what happened here?"

"Saw it all. I was laying there on the mess chests, waiting to part with me arm when—whoosh!—a ball hits the ship, and another." He closed his eyes against the memory. "The pharmacist mate had started up the companionway cuz two wounded men was stacked there. He hollered for help, and the surgeon, God save the man, ran to the stairs. The ball hit the mate and threw him back against the surgeon, who tumbled in his own heap. Break his ankle?"

"Sprained it. Was the pharmacist's mate..."

"Deader'n my aunt Sallie, his brains blowed everywhere." He winced and seemed to remember his audience. "Sorry, miss."

"Thankful," she said. "Just Thankful. What did he do?"

"Carried on as if nothing happened, walking on that swollen ankle. When he couldn't manage on his pins any more, he crawled on his knees and did surgery on the deck."

The sailor passed his hand in front of his eyes. "I'll see it the rest of me days—hands and knees, doing his job. This is the first time he has slept, I think." He held out his left hand awkwardly. "Nahum Partridge, foretopman."

Thankful shook his hand, shyer than when she had helped him with the urinal. "Sleep, Nahum," she said. "I'll see what I can do to tidy up."

Tidy up? She had a sudden, ludicrous vision of dusting the front room at home and cajoling her little brothers to take the rugs outside and beat them. *Tidy up.* She gathered bloody rags and gore-soaked sponges into a bucket, happy to set it aside. The surgeon's capital knives soaked in a pan that smelled strongly of vinegar. She looked around and found a keg of vinegar. With a clean cloth, she wiped down the fearsome knives, dried them, found their case, and replaced them, while everyone slumbered, even Nahum Partridge.

She saw other damage to the medicine chest. It lay on its face, as though thrown by a mighty hand, rendering the lock jammed. She looked around. All was orderly, and the men slept. She peered closer at the surgeon, dismayed to see his eyeballs moving rapidly under closed lids, a sure sign of nightmares.

Poor, poor man, she thought. *Thee needs to quit the war.*

"Tell him that, Thankful," she murmured quietly. "He'll greatly appreciate thy foolish advice."

Instead, she walked to his cot and put her hand gently over his eyes, keeping her hand steady until the motion stopped. In another minute, he was breathing deep again. She moved her hand and looked down at him, amazed that he could sleep now that someone else, even someone as little skilled as she was, could stand watch. Had anyone ever trusted her so much? Or perhaps the good man was so tired, he didn't care. Either way, the flattery warmed her.

It was a mystery, but Thankful had decided years ago that life itself was a mystery. She took out her watchmaker tools and sat next to the medicine chest. She studied it, then decided on a tool. A few minutes' fiddling rewarded her with a satisfactory snap. She tugged on the ruined lock, and it opened.

"You are a clever miss."

She looked around to see the surgeon watching her. "Just a little skill I picked up when I was home with the measles and bored," she told him. "Thee is supposed to be asleep. In fact, I insist upon it."

"Oh, thee does?"

She smiled, pleased that he could get Quaker speak correct. "Most people would tease me and say, 'Thou dost,' or some such thing," she told him. "That's so old and we don't talk that way."

"I know Quaker speak," he said, and nothing more on that subject.

His relaxed manner led her to suspect that he had no memory of terrible dreams or her hand over his eyes, and she was too shy to say anything, or maybe too kind. His eyes were on the medicine chest, which made her smile.

"I am a mender," she told him, not afraid that he would laugh or think it strange.

"Bored with the measles, and you learned to pick locks?"

"And mend watches," she added. "That sounds more dignified and less felonious."

"Silly lass," he teased. "I have heard that Sir Isaac Newton invented calculus on a dare."

"This is not calculus," Thankful said. "I am clever with my hands. Which reminds me." She looked around, happy that the others still slept, even though the hammering and sawing in the ship seemed so loud to her. "Let us see what we can do for thy ankle."

"You don't mind looking at a hairy leg?"

"It's not my first choice, but I am here to do thee some good."

He winced as he sat up, then struggled to lie down again. His hands went under his covers. "Tug off my trousers now. I want a bandage up high enough to do me good."

Cautious, Thankful lifted the end of the sheet and grabbed hold of his pant legs. She frowned at his sharp intake of breath, but she worked quickly. She pulled away his trousers, exposing his smallclothes. She thought a moment, then set his trousers far away from the cot, which earned her a fishy look.

"See here now, I need to put those on again when you're done."

"Maybe, maybe not," she said. She raised the end of the sheet and stared a long time at his ankle, swollen and purple and aggravated further by standing on it when he should not have.

"Thee is certain this not broken?" she asked, dubious.

"Who's the surgeon here?" he responded. "Nothing snapped, and it's not cocked in an odd direction. Here's what I want you to do."

He directed her to find a plaster in the medicine chest she had opened. "I made some plasters before the battle, and then that dratted ball sealed the chest shut. Dig around in the top shelf."

She found a plaster and several rolled bandages, each about three inches wide, and returned to the cot.

"Set those down here and find some pillows."

"And where might they be?"

"Check one of the other cabins."

She did as he said, doubtful. She found two pillows in the cabin next to the makeshift sick bay, and another in what was probably the captain's quarters. The hammering continued, and gradually the *Tethys* continued to right herself.

She returned to the sick bay and put all the pillows underneath the surgeon's bare leg. He had pulled up his smallclothes, and she couldn't help the observation that his leg might have been hairy, but it was nicely shaped. She retained that information in her mind.

"Sit down," he directed. "Grasp my leg about three inches above the ankle."

She did as he said, feeling the pulse in his ruined ankle, and the heat.

"This is the hard part."

"For me or thee?" she asked.

"Probably both of us," he replied. "I think thee has a tender heart, unlike the Royal Navy."

"Thee realizes that I will require an explanation for thy Quaker speak," she said, steeling herself against what was to come. "I am hopeful thee is not just teasing me."

"Thee is Thankful, remember, not Hopeful," he joked, even as sweat broke out on his forehead again, probably in anticipation. "Grasp my foot and flex it as best you can. I'll tell you when to stop. Press it against your stomach to free your hands. Sorry for the indiscretion, Thankful, but you wanted to be helpful."

She worked quickly, unable to help her tears when he gasped and clutched the sides of his cot. She pushed slowly against the mass of swollen, bruised tissue, wishing his pharmacist mate still lived and breathed; he could probably do this better.

"Don't cry, Thankful, there's a good girl," he managed to say. "Surgeons don't cry."

"Yes, they do," she said quietly. She pushed until he gasped for her to stop, then moved forward to rest his foot against her stomach and the space between her breasts. Now her hands were free.

His voice was faint, but he was in control. "Take that first plaster strip and wrap it diagonally against the distal tib fib. Yes, there. Now do it with the other plaster, same place. Make it strong. Oh, Lord," he said quietly, then fainted.

Thee can't do this to me, she thought, wanting to shake him awake. Instead, she stayed as she was with his bruised foot, still flexed, resting between her breasts. He had a handsome high arch and needed to clip his toenails.

The surgeon regained consciousness within a few minutes. He made no comment about his lapse, but instructed her on wrapping his foot just above his toes. "Make it tight. Go around the heel and up my calf, then down again," he ordered. "When you finish, rip the end and knot it, then do it again with another bandage roll."

She worked quickly, grateful that his poor foot remained flexed. When she finish, she moved out from under his foot and brought it to rest on the pillows again.

"I'd like some ice on that, but we're not in the Arctic," he murmured, his eyes closed again. "Dip a cloth in water, wring it out and wrap it around my ankle."

When she finished that order, he directed her to a deep drawer, where she found a wire cage. She was ready to wince with him when she gentled his foot into the cage, but he made no exclamation. Maybe she was a better mender than she knew, or maybe the surgeon was good at giving orders. She pulled the sheet down over the metal contraption.

"There thee is, and there thee will stay for a while," she announced. "Nothing is going on here that I cannot remedy."

Nothing, at least, until a sailor brought down a comrade with a bloody finger and terror on his face. Adam Farnsworth beckoned the man closer and took a good look.

"An avulsed finger," he pronounced. "Come closer, Thankful. This will tax you a bit, but you'll manage."

And so the day passed, with the avulsed finger being the worst of the lot. When she had finished that gruesome task under the surgeon's calm and clear directions, she walked up the companionway, made her dignified way to the side of the ship and threw up. The burned forearm and cheek laceration had amounted to less than nothing after that gory finger, which she knew she would see in her dreams.

She stayed at the rail a moment, looking across the water to the *Ann Alexander* nestled alongside the much larger *HMS Victory* like a chick with a mother hen. She knew it was within her power to summon the captain and demand to be rowed to the *Ann*, but she said nothing. A few more deep breaths of better air, and then she went below deck, full of purpose and duty and determination to keep the surgeon who had endured too much off his feet and out of his trousers so he could not make his injury worse.

She won the first skirmish. When he asked for his trousers, she shook her head and continued rolling a tangle of bandages into organized little soldiers. "Thee doesn't need to move anywhere."

He tried, and she gave him grudging credit. "Thankful, suppose someone brings down a man needing amputation. Here I lie, useless."

"Thee left out 'forgotten and alone,'" she said. "'Unfriended, outcast.'"

"You are well nigh heartless," he replied, but without any punch to his words, because his eyes were closing again.

She couldn't help smiling. "That is precisely what Abner

Whittier says when I won't let him kiss me beyond a peck on the cheek."

He gave a silent laugh that set his shoulders shaking, as he tried not to wake the others. "Good for you, Thankful," he whispered. "I've heard that Yankees are an unprincipled lot."

"We are," she agreed, which made him put his hand over his mouth because he had to laugh at that.

The sun continued its slow trajectory from high overhead to low in the sky. When she had tidied all she could, and the men slept in the drugged somnolence of the wounded, Thankful went on deck to watch how a mauled, though victorious, fleet regained its sea legs and prepared to sail again.

Although debris still coated the water, order was returning, and the sight relieved her heart. The *Ann* stood off from the *Victory*, the flour and apples obviously delivered and secured, probably in holds all across the fleet. She waved to the tall figure on the quarterdeck, and Loum waved back. She watched signal flags flap from the *Victory*, then run down, to be replaced by other flags with their messages. The constant stream of messages amazed her. As dark settled, the flags were replaced by signal lamps.

The hammering and sawing continued aboard the *Tethys*. Once the frigate heaved like a wounded thing, and Thankful clutched the rail, her heart pounding. It heaved again, then settled. She looked around, hoping not to see concern on faces besides her own. What she saw did not reassure her.

They know what they are doing, she thought, but the uneasiness did not go away.

She saw to dinner for the men, the food given to her in another bucket by the cook, who smiled at her this time and managed a sketchy sort of bow. She superintended the meal, kneeling by Nahum Partridge, who struggled into a sitting position and took care of himself. His triumphant grin when he finished didn't reveal too many teeth, but Thankful had lost her interest in perfection.

Brave men all, she thought, happy to mend and help.

The only person she had to assist was the powder monkey, who had trouble swallowing. She put her hand to his head, surprised at the heat.

Adam must have been watching the boy. He motioned her over and told her how to prepare fever powders. She followed his clear instructions and raised up the powder monkey—no older than her youngest brother—so he could drink the concoction. The simple act seemed to exhaust him. With relief, she watched him sink into drugged sleep.

Thankful was spooning out her own bowl of burgoo when the captain came into the sick bay. It touched her heart to see the men try to lie at attention, but he ignored their efforts. She wanted to call it to his notice, but that wasn't her place. He ducked his head because of the low ceiling and walked directly to her.

"Miss Winnings, will you dine with me in my cabin?"

Thankful hesitated, shy at the offer. "No, William, I will not."

He put his hands on his hips, exasperation all over his face. "God's wounds, I am not used to someone calling me by my first name!"

"Thy title means nothing to a Friend," she said quietly. "I'll remain here."

The captain seemed unwilling to give up, even though she wished he would leave. "The second lieutenant and one or two midshipmen will dine with us," he told her, his face flaming red.

She glanced at the surgeon for affirmation but saw no expression at all on Adam's face. She directed her attention the captain next, asking herself, *What is this bad blood?* Apparently, the only way to find out was to agree to dine with the man. Perhaps she could mend whatever rift there was. It might be a fitting last duty before she returned to the *Ann Alexander* at Gibraltar.

"I will dine with thee," she said.

Dinner wasn't much of an improvement on the lowly burgoo, which she suspected was all Cookie could come up with after a battle, except that it was served on good china. She shook her head over grog poured into cut glass, but lingered over dried-apple pudding. She felt awkward and out of place as the officers discussed ship's matters, and the midshipman stared at her.

She soon exhausted her limited supply of idle chatter with the midshipman, younger even than herself, as she half-listened to the captain and his lieutenant. She heard the words *danger* and *sinking* spoken in low tones, and hoped they were referring to another vessel. The sea at the Cape of Trafalgar fairly teemed with faltering ships on the injured list, as wounded as some of the men aboard them.

As the meal came to its dreary conclusion, another midshipman clattered down the companionway and burst into the room without a knock, which earned him a growl from the captain.

"Beg pardon sir, but you are requested on deck."

Captain Sanford threw down his serviette, gestured to the midshipman at the table, and the two of them stormed after the boy, the captain muttering over his shoulder for his lieutenant to see Miss Winnings back to the sick bay.

The second lieutenant looked at her and raised his eyebrows. Rather than do as his captain had commanded, he poured her another cup of tea and settled back. "Cheers, Thankful. I'm Samuel Arlis, and my friends call me Sam."

Thankful accepted the tea with a smile of her own. "Thee has some experience with Quakers?"

"Happens I do. Wasn't the Society of Friends started in northern England, where I was raised? Captain Sanford forgot he had a first name until you reminded him."

That is sad, she thought.

They both sipped tea in complete understanding. *I wonder*, thought Thankful. *It cannot hurt to inquire.*

"This is manifestly not my business, but what has William against Adam? The surgeon says they were boyhood friends, raised on the same estate."

She had read the second lieutenant right. He *was* chattier than his superior. "More like, what has Adam against William?" he said, his Yorkshire tones as plain as his face. He pointed with his cup toward an empty chair that no one had occupied. "There sat our late first lieutenant, as cruel a tyrant as you might entertain in a nightmare." He raised his cup in a mock toast.

She watched him, thinking of Adam's eyes moving under his closed lids, caught in bad dreams. She waited, suspecting that Sam Arlis was not a man to be silent.

"He came aboard the last time we hailed Portsmouth, two years now." Sam set down is cup. "Two years followed of coursing back and forth across the Atlantic, trying to pin down the Froggie fleet. Nerves were on edge, and none worse than Lieutenant Randall Babcock. He rode the foretopmen hard, which in itself is not unusual." He leaned forward to look her in the eye, something the captain hadn't done all evening. "But with this difference: there was never a pat on the back or an extra tot of grog for a job well done. These are skilled men, Thankful!"

"Wh—what did he do?"

"He'd line 'um on ta deck and harangue them. Ye'd

have thought they didn't know their own business, which wasn't the case. Nay, not at all."

"Why didn't the captain say something to his lieutenant?" Thankful asked.

"The first luff has the running of the ship, most generally," he explained, after another sip. "Captain Sanford relied on him to be firm and only come to him with problems or the enemy."

"Where does Adam enter the story?"

"Where ye'd expect, lass. Adam and his mate were the ones who patched up the cuts and bruises, and then the deep lashes that Randall had inflicted. Adam complained to his great good friend, and his great good friend did nothing." There was no mistaking the anger in the congenial officer's voice.

"I'm almost afraid to ask," Thankful said, holding out her cup for the last of the tea, which the lieutenant poured.

"Came the day—about a month ago—when we were sailing east under fair skies. Randall thought to exercise the foretopmen, and by now, every jack tar dreaded the man." He lowered his gaze as though suddenly finding the tablecloth fascinating. "I'm not proud of my own fear, but I'm second luff, with barely more clout than a minnow." He blew out his cheeks. "Babcock sent the tars aloft to furl and unfurl the sails. They did as he asked, then . . ." He paused and passed a hand across his eyes. "Then he told them that the last man down would get ten lashes on the grating."

"No, no," Thankful murmured.

"They tore down the ratlines, and sure enough, at about thirty feet, two of them tangled in a heap and dropped to the deck, one dead, the other barely breathing."

He stood up and walked back and forth, unable to hold still. "Davey Carlisle tumbled down into that same heap, breaking a leg and lacerating his face, poor man." He sat down with a thump. "All Babcock did was bawl, 'You get ten lashes!'"

Thankful dabbed at her eyes with her serviette.

"We've come this far, so here's the rest," Sam told her. He closed the door and returned to the table. "I wasn't on deck and didn't see it, but Lieutenant Babcock claimed that Davey tried to push him down. The midshipmen and others on deck said that Davey was just flailing about for a handhold to help him to his feet. Blood was streaming down his face, and he couldn't see who stood there." He took a deep breath. "Babcock grabbed him by the back of his shirt, yanked him to his feet, and told the Marines to slap him in irons. Striking an officer is a capital offense. Poor Davey would swing from the yardarm."

Thankful sucked in her breath, thinking of the firm but fair duty her cousin invoked aboard the *Ann*. "Surely the midshipmen and other sailors said something!"

Sam shook his head. "Too afraid they was. If they'd stood up for t' poor lad, wouldn't the lieutenant make their lives a misery next?

"The lads followed the Marines with Davey down the companionway, and Adam met them there. He countermanded the Marine's orders, which he had no warrant to do, except that of the surgeon. Even Lieutenant Damn-his-eyes Babcock bowed to that, though unwillingly. Once Davey was splinted and sewed, didn't Adam and Babcock go round and round in the captain's quarters? Y'could hear them all over the *Tethys*."

After a long silence, Thankful asked, "Where is Davey now?"

Sam lowered his eyes again. "The captain sided with his first luff. Once Davey was well enough to hang, that's what happened." He managed a sick smile. "The Marine drummed everyone on deck, and we watched a good sailor yanked up the yardarm."

Thankful sobbed out loud, convinced she'd had all the adventure she needed. This voyage couldn't end too soon. "Poor, poor man."

Sam nodded. He handed her his own serviette, and she took it gratefully. "Adam did get the last word, howsoever. When the Marines hauled Davey on deck to meet his Maker, his eyes were glazed and barely open. He probably didn't know what was going to happen to him, thanks to the surgeon's potion, whatever 'twas. Adam stood there and watched, his lips tight and his eyes so narrow." He shuddered. "Makes me blood run cold. And our Adam hasn't spoken to the captain since."

Thankful looked around, suddenly fearful. "Where is this first lieutenant?" she whispered.

"Davey got'um! Davey Jones, at any rate. He took a splinter through the neck three days ago. 'I'm bleeding! I'm dying,' he screamed.'" Sam shrugged. "It was heavy battle. I think the extras on his gun crew slung him down the companionway, because he was in the way." He rubbed his chin. "'Twas before the pharmacist mate died and our Adam was injured. I'll never forget t'sight of the surgeon at the foot of the stairs, knife in hand and bloody apron. He just stared down at the lieutenant and said, 'I'll tend you when I finish those before you, you fiend. Ship's orders: other wounded before you.'"

Sam fell silent, chin on his chest. "War is a hard business," he said finally, perhaps more to himself than to Thankful.

 Five

She nodded, at a loss for words. They returned to the sick bay in silence. Sam nodded to Adam and bid them good night. In the low light, Thankful saw a pallet on the deck.

"I can't offer you anything better," Adam told her, apology high in his voice. "I need you to stay here, in case something happens that I cannot manage." He rose up on one elbow. "Where did you put my trousers?"

"Where thee won't find them," Thankful said.

She made brief rounds of the five men, standing a long time by the powder monkey, whose breath came in fits and starts. She looked back at Adam.

"He'll die soon. I feared he might have internal injuries. Sadly, I was right. Just sit by him, Thankful."

She pulled up the stool and took the boy's hand. It was hot and dry, and his pulse fluttered. In another moment, she sat on his cot. The moment after that, she picked him up—he was just a boy—and held him in her arms, humming to him. Before she finished her tune, his eyes opened. He stared at her and a light came into his eyes. Then he breathed his last.

"I don't even know his name," she murmured, as she lowered the little body to the cot and covered his face.

"Billie. Just Billie. He came from a workhouse; we were his only home," Adam told her. "Thank you."

"For what?"

"For being the mother he never had, for twenty seconds."

Without a word, she tugged the pallet close to Adam's cot, lay down, and curled herself into a little ball. She felt his hand on her hair, and she put up her hand to cover his. It was her last memory before she slept.

She woke to feel that same hand shaking her. She sat up, alert, bumping heads with the surgeon, who had leaned down from his cot. He chuckled.

"Beg pardon, Thankful, but the lacerated leg in the far cot needs the pisser." He leaned closer. "Remind yourself that this is an adventure." He kissed her cheek then lay down again, still chuckling.

"Thee is feeling better, Adam," she whispered after she accomplished her task. She saw no point in feeling shy around the surgeon, not after his peck on the cheek. Funny, though, how her stomach had done a little flip. Abner Whittier had kissed her cheek several times in the past six months, but she had felt nothing.

She could barely see the surgeon in the light of the slatted lamp. He lay with his hands behind his head now, staring at the ceiling, his sprained leg still elevated by the pillows, the wire cage gone. She sat crosslegged, close to him, their heads on the same level.

"Sam Arlis told me about your falling out with the captain," she said, leaning closer, the better to disturb no one's slumber.

"A bad business all around. Take the pillows out from under my legs, please. I want to shift and talk to you. Just one pillow between my legs. Ah, yes." He moved until he could face her. "When Will Sanford went to sea, his father ordered me to accompany him."

"He could do that?"

"Aye. My father was his assistant steward on the family estate. The unspoken threat was that if I chose not to go with Will, Da would be dismissed. I went to sea as Will's servant. I discovered an aptitude for medicine, and Will's father gave me two years in London Hospital to learn the trade. After that, I was pharmacist mate on Will's ship when he was a second lieutenant. I earned my warrant two years later, and I was moved to Will's new ship when he made first lieutenant. David Thatcher, more properly *Sir* David Thatcher, had that sort of influence."

"Why did David meddle that way?"

"After what Sam probably told you, can you guess?"

She could, and it was a bleak prospect. "Will isn't good at his trade."

"He is not. What Sir David thought *I* could do about that, I never understood." He put his hand on her head and gave it a shake, much as Loum might do. "I am ambitious, Thankful Winnings. I now hold a warrant and am judged a skillful surgeon. Hopefully, William Sanford will be passed over for higher promotion and will eventually give up and retire on half pay."

He was silent, his hand on her shoulder now. She leaned her cheek involuntarily toward his hand.

"But there is a war on," she said. "And even Will's puny skills are needed," she added, filling in what she thought he might be thinking.

"Alas and true." His great sigh filled the close space

between them. "What a dilemma: Will should not command but will not leave, while I am desperate to set this life behind me." He couldn't suppress a half-sob, half-moan. "It's killing my soul, Thankful."

She moved closer and rested her hand on his chest. He moved her hand to his heart.

"I try to sleep at night, and my mind forces me to revisit case after case. Could I have saved this one, with more time? Had I more skill, would this one still breathe? And on and on."

"What would thee do instead, if thee could?" she asked.

"Deliver babies, physic for croup and piles, set bones, maybe amputate, if called for. I would be a country surgeon somewhere. Nothing grand, no heroics. No guns. No war."

He sounded so wistful, it broke her heart. She closed her eyes and felt a powerful yearning for New Bedford, a bustling maritime town that had, only a month ago, seemed so tame. The man lying next to her in such mental pain could easily manage a dockside practice because he had the skill and do the homely business of medicine, too. With her usual thoroughness, she thought through the matter.

"New Bedford, Massachusetts, would suit thee right down to the ground."

"How do I get there? I can't surrender my warrant in wartime." He laughed, but there was no humor in it this time. "And know this, Thankful—oh, the irony—a century ago, my own family was part of the Society of Friends."

"I wondered," she said. "You mentioned an understanding."

"More than that. One of my ancestors was George Fox, who began the movement."

"Sakes, that is impressive," she said.

"My great-grandfather buckled under the persecution

after the death of his wife at the hands of a howling mob, and he led his family out of meeting. They never returned."

"Such persecution happened in America, too, but independence ended it."

His hand caressed her head now, and Thankful found the gesture both soothing and oddly unsettling, and she didn't want him to stop. "Thankful, I came upon my grandmother one day, sitting in silence. I asked her what she was doing. 'Listening for the light,' she told me. 'Hush, boy, and listen too.'"

"Did thee?" Thankful asked, interested.

"No. With my schoolboy logic, I informed her that you don't *listen* for light, and I left her alone. I have thought of her words since, though, many times."

"I would call it *waiting* upon the Light," she said.

"Do you do that?"

"Every moment since I came aboard the *Tethys*," she replied. "I am here to mend the wounded."

"You're mending me," he whispered. "Come a little closer."

She did, and he kissed her—on the lips this time—just a little kiss, but followed by another with more intent, and then another, which meant her hands had to go to his face to steady herself and kiss him back. Abner Whittier would never have understood *this* kiss.

Astounded at herself, Thankful pulled away.

"Should I apologize?" Adam whispered, his forehead against hers.

"Nay, lad, kiss her again," came a highly entertained voice from Nahum Partridge's cot.

Thankful laughed, and the spell was broken.

Six

Under leaden skies and an oily ocean roll, the *Tethys* followed the *Victory* from the Cape of Trafalgar in the morning. Six cutters towed the *Victory* after them, and the *Ann Alexander* followed. By four bells in the forenoon watch, it was obvious to even a lubber like Thankful that the *Tethys* was sinking. Adam insisted upon the return of his trousers, and Thankful told him to look beneath the pillow under his head, which led him to mutter something best left unamplified.

The bodies in the companionway, accompanied now by the powder monkey, were consigned to the deep in record time as the frigate settled lower in the water. Adam unwillingly released the sailor with the deep powder burns to his gun crew again, then asked Thankful to find the second lieutenant and hurry.

Sam Arlis stood on the quarterdeck, bawling orders through a speaking trumpet when she approached. She climbed a few rungs and waited, knowing the rules of the sea from her brief tenure on the *Ann*.

"Samuel, can thee spare a moment for the surgeon?" she asked.

He glanced at the captain, who gazed moodily out to sea, away from the coast as they passed between the Pillars of Hercules into the more placid Mediterranean. Captain Sanford snapped something at him, and Sam leaped down the ladder and took her hand, running below deck with her.

"I have mere seconds," he told the surgeon, who was on his feet now, his face a mask of pain, but his eyes full of purpose, something Thankful knew that Captain Sanford would always lack.

"Get a jolly boat for the wounded and Thankful," Adam said as he pulled on his coat. He dug into his pocket and handed Thankful some coins. "You may need these if the boat pulls toward a Spanish port."

"Thee is coming, too," she said, taking his arm. "Thee is wounded."

"I wish I could," he told her. "From the bottom of my heart, I wish I could."

Stubborn man, she thought. *Wretched, stubborn man. Abner Whittier is far less trouble than thee.*

"I will not go without thee," she said.

"That is drivel and poppycock and all kinds of foolishness," he snapped. "Of course thee will."

She shook her head and sat down on the deck. "Thee cannot make me."

"Over your shoulder, Sam. Grab her."

The second lieutenant did as the surgeon said, snatching her from the deck and carrying her up the stairs as she cried and pounded on his legs. She stopped crying on deck because the Spanish guns of the old Moorish fort of El Tarifa began to find the *Tethys*'s range. The frigate answered back, and she put her hands over her ears, terrified.

Sam set her on the deck and shook his finger at her. "Don't you even *think* about going below deck."

Without a glance at his captain, the second lieutenant scribbled a note and thrust it at the midshipman who was signalman. The boy read the note, gulped, and looked at the lieutenant.

"Handsomely now," Sam ordered, and the midshipman snapped to his duty, raising one signal flag and then another, faster and faster.

The lieutenant collared a bosun's mate, who grabbed three sailors and pushed them toward the last jolly boat hanging in its davits. They began to lower the little craft slowly as Sam shepherded Thankful toward it.

The other wounded had reached the deck now, the worst among them sagging between the one-armed foretopman on one side and Adam on the other, his medical kit tucked under his free arm with Thankful's leather-cased tools.

"Thee can't be a mender without these," he said in her ear.

A volley from El Tarifa slammed into the *Tethys*, which shuddered like a living creature. Thankful fell to the deck, and Sam helped her to her feet. The wounded were in the boat now, and Adam pushed her after them, then shouted to the sailors to lower the boat.

"I can't leave thee," she sobbed. "Drat thee, I am in love!"

"So am I, Thankful, but thee wouldn't marry a coward, would thee?"

"I haven't mended thee enough!" she pleaded as the little craft inched down the side of the dying frigate.

Adam tossed her kit and what she knew were his capital knives bound in leather, to the one-armed sailor. "Take care of her," he shouted, because the guns were speaking.

What happened next Thankful could only credit to a merciful and all-knowing God who had the ear of His children. She stared, open-mouthed, as the second lieutenant, a huge grin on his face, pushed the surgeon into the water. Sam gave the outraged, swearing man as snappy a salute as the laws of Admiralty required. He blew a kiss to Thankful and returned to his doomed position on the quarterdeck with his captain as the surgeon floundered in the water until one of the sailors dragged him by his belt into the jolly boat.

As Adam lay gasping in the bottom of the boat, the sailors rowed away from the sinking frigate, protected by the bulk of the *Tethys*. One of them shouted to her, "Ship an oar, miss," and she took her place on the bench, happy to row and row. The seam in her dress ripped under her arms, and her hair streamed down her back as she bent to the oar and prayed.

"Praise God," she heard from Nahum Partridge. "Take a look, lassy."

She followed his pointing finger to see the *Ann Alexander*, that tubby, practical merchant vessel, crowd all sail and lumber toward the dinghy. Surrounded by other frigates flying the Union Jack, the *Victory*, under tow, stood far enough off the coast not to risk a Spanish bombardment.

The guns of El Tarifa took out their fury on the *Tethys*, pounding her until nothing remained but a hulk. A shot finally found the magazine, and the frigate exploded in a belch of flames, lumber, and flying men. Thankful turned away, shaken, and rowed with all her strength. She prayed for the soul of Lieutenant Samuel Arlis, and knew that if she and the stubborn surgeon no woman in her rightful mind would tolerate were to marry, she would insist upon that dear name for their first son.

They were a small craft on a large ocean, but the *Ann* homed in. Thankful was certain that Loum helmed the ship himself, because he had no stomach to face his cousin's parents with a sad tale. She knew the sudden curtain of rain that veiled all vision would not deter Loum Snow. They rowed through the odd shower as the guns grew fainter.

Thankful turned around to look at the surgeon, upright now and tending to the wounded man with the laceration, which had opened up during his own tumble into the jolly boat. Adam bound the wound tight, then wrapped the man in his own service jacket. The one-armed foretopman had his remaining arm around another of the wounded men, who sobbed into his already soaked shirt.

"His brother was on the *Tethys*," Partridge told her with a shake of his head. "Last living relative, so he is melancholy, is the lad."

When the squall lifted, the *Ann* appeared before them, huge and benevolent. Already ropes were dangling for the sailors in the dinghy to knot into bowlines and lift them to the deck one by one. And there was Loum, his face so anxious and looking years older, gazing down at her.

Thankful let out a breath she felt she had been holding for thirty minutes at least. Her shoulders slumped, and she felt the Inner Light carry her into another small world, probably for the last time. She knew she didn't belong just to Thankful Winnings anymore. Her life would be shared with Adam.

Thankful raised no objection to the rough and ready way the rope circled her armpits alone. This was no time to worry about her legs, not with the *Ann* inching closer to El Tarifa. She took first turn rising to the deck, not caring who saw what under her petticoat.

But trust Adam Farnsworth to whistle and hoot. That

man! What was she thinking? Did love mean every single brain in her head had sloshed out her ears?

Never mind. In minutes they were all on deck as the *Ann* wore out to sea again, blankets around their shoulders, and a stretcher provided for the sailor whose leg now gushed. Calling for bandages, Adam limped after the stretcher. She started toward him, but Loum pulled her back and brought her close to his chest.

"Cookie is on it. He'll have towels and wadding. Oh, Thankful, praise God from whom all blessings flow."

She closed her eyes, safe in the circle of her cousin's arms.

True to his word, Captain Snow followed *HMS Victory* to Gibraltar and offloaded his lumber, as well as more flour and apples. To his great relief, as he told Thankful and Adam later in his cabin, the Royal Navy had no particular interest in the leaf tobacco in his depleted hold.

"With the tobacco to Italy, plus my ample remuneration from the Royal Navy here . . ." He sketched a little bow in Adam's direction. "I will call this a most successful voyage, if a bit out of the ordinary."

Adam nodded in return. His sprained foot rested on another pile of pillows, and Thankful had decided that he would be even more comfortable with his head in her lap. "I haven't been to Leghorn in several years," he said. "The Italians will haggle, holler and do their best to make a shrewd bargain." He yawned and closed his eyes, the portrait of contentment.

"Loum is smarter than the Italians," Thankful said. "Cousin, I'm still fair dumbfounded at thy safe conduct letter from that admiral."

"I had to do something, since I have five contraband and highly illegal members of the Royal Navy on my ship," Loum replied. "Not to mention the three sailors who rowed thee here."

Thankful gathered Adam closer and he made no objection, beyond a comment about his view of her bosom that earned him a pinch. "Loum, thee is completely certain that no one saw the jolly boat leave the *Tethys*?"

"Completely. The bulk of the *Tethys* shielded it from view. Collingwood came to me in tears over the loss of my little cousin the mender, dead aboard the *Tethys*. I behaved touchingly sorrowful, of course, and he was only too happy to promise me in writing that no ship of the Royal Navy will tamper with the *Ann Alexander* on our return voyage." He turned to Adam. "And thee is completely certain that your wounded men and these seamen don't mind coming to the United States of America?"

"Completely. I am not the only man tired of war." The surgeon pulled Thankful's hand to his chest. "If they have a change of heart in Leghorn, we can leave them there."

"Then we'll sail with the morning wind. Cousin, what little bauble would you like from Leghorn? I promised thee a souvenir of the voyage."

Thankful caressed Adam's chest. "He will do."

"We can marry in New Bedford," Adam said, but she heard no conviction in his voice.

"Who would soothe thy bad dreams, if we waited?" she asked. "Loum, please. Right here and now."

When the *Ann* was free of Gibraltar and the prying eyes of the Royal Navy, Adam came on deck to watch the Union Jack flutter in the wind blowing them toward Italy. The foretopman and Ann held him up as he watched the flag in silence, then turned to see the American colors. He gave a satisfied nod.

"I can do this, Thankful," he whispered in her ear. "Where thee is, I am home."

It was a simple matter to go below deck to Loum's cabin, where chairs had been set up. Such crew as were also Friends joined them and seated themselves. Thankful could have wished for a better dress, but that was prideful. At least she still had the handsome grey wool that she hadn't taken aboard the *Tethys*, and two other simple dresses. Her nightgown was gone, but she suspected that Adam wouldn't mind.

The cook had kindly mended the surgeon's service jacket and brushed his trousers. They could find him more clothing in Italy. Thankful herself had wrapped a cleaner bandage around his poor ankle and carefully pulled a sock over the whole foot. It didn't seem right to have bare toes at a wedding, not even one as simple as a Friend's wedding.

She was grateful her dear cousin officiated. Seated side by side, she and Adam holding hands, Thankful suddenly too shy to begin until Loum cleared his throat. He placed the marriage declaration on the table. She and her dear love had drawn it up last night, declaring mutual love, lifelong fidelity, and devotion to their unborn children. Soon they would sign it, and everyone else in the room would also sign to witness.

"Thankful, Adam, thee may affirm how thee chooses."

A long silence followed—no novelty to Thankful. She glanced at Adam to see those silent tears coursing down his cheeks. She didn't dread them this time, because his hand's answering squeeze told her they were not tears of sorrow.

In the peaceful silence, she thought of the voyage begun a month ago. Mama might scold her for the suddenness of this affirmation of her youngest child for a man she barely knew.

No, she knew him well, better than she knew Abner

Whittier and her other two suitors. Her placid life had taken a surprising turn, a jog down dark alleys. Now she would return to sunshine as her life resumed its intended path, but with a difference—time and trial had already welded her to Adam Farnsworth. The matter defied understanding, so she gracefully left it in God's merciful hands. All that remained was solidifying the matter in His watchful eyes.

She stood and helped the surgeon to his feet, her hand in his. "Adam, I take thee, my friend..."

Epilogue

1808, New Bedford

"Thankful, does thee have any plans this evening?"

"None beyond the usual, Adam. Oh, sakes, such a burp! Sam, thee takes after thy father. Hold thy son a moment while I button up. You mean this evening?"

"I thought we could go to the pier to fish and cuddle a bit."

"If we cuddle, we won't fish."

"I'll run the risk. I saw Loum dockside this afternoon while patching that poor lad with an avulsed ankle. I should have summoned thee for that one, love, knowing how thee feels about avulsion, if memory serves me."

"Then thee would be fishing alone tonight, with no cuddling. Loum?"

"Aye. The *Ann* sails with the tide tomorrow. He wanted to know if thee would like another adventure to Italy."

"I trust thee told him that one was enough."

"I never speak for thee."

"Tonight to the pier? I will ask Mercy to stay and mind Abigail. She will do it if Nahum Partridge can sit with her."

"So that's how the wind blows?"

"Aye. She told me this afternoon. Sam will be asleep already. Suppose thee has an emergency?"

"We deal with those, eh? Abner Whittier's wife isn't due for confinement until next week, and all is quiet, medically speaking, at the docks."

"We could cuddle right here and forget the fishing, unless thee is determined to fish."

"I don't really like fish, now that thee mentions it. Let's just go to the dock and cuddle. Not too many fine summer days left for outdoor cuddling, my love."

"Very well. We'll cuddle there, and back here, and then probably upstairs, once Nahum walks Mercy home."

"Have I made thy life boring and predictable, Thankful?"

"Aye. Don't change a thing."

AUTHOR'S NOTE

After the *Ann Alexander* sold her lumber to the *HMS Victory*, the merchant ship didn't sail entirely out of the history books. From 1805 to 1820, the New Bedford merchantman made frequent voyages across the Atlantic as a neutral trader in the Napoleonic Wars. During a trade embargo, she languished in port, as did other American trading vessels.

After Waterloo and Allied victory, the *Ann* continued on her placid way, helmed by Captain Snow and then others. The rise of New Bedford as a major whaling port opened another seafaring door for the ship, and she was refitted as a whaler. These cruises took the *Ann* to more distant whaling grounds in the Arctic and the Pacific, where three and four-year voyages to fill barrels with whale oil were not uncommon. She was one of many such ships plying her trade on faraway seas.

On August 19, 1851, the *Ann Alexander* sailed into and out of history for the final time. In an attack reminiscent of the horror turned on the whaleship *Essex* in 1820, a maddened whale charged the *Ann* as she cruised off the Galápagos Islands and smashed her into a sinking wreck. The men took to their whaleboats, spending a long night in fear of the whale charging them again.

Morning light brought the exhausted seamen the sight of the gallant *Ann*, still afloat. The men cautiously gathered what supplies they could from the *Ann*, then started out in two boats, small specks on a vast ocean.

Fortune smiled. Two or three days later, the *Ann*'s crew was rescued by the whaleship *Nantucket* and eventually deposited in Paita, Peru, into the care of the American consul. The New Englanders, grateful to be alive, voyaged on other vessels from Peru to Panama, and then home to New Bedford.

As it happened, Herman Melville's *Moby-Dick; or The Whale*, was in the process of publication as news of the *Ann Alexander*'s sinking reached New York City. As recorded in his "Reflections," found in *The Ship Ann Alexander of New Bedford*, by C.C. Sawtell, Melville wrote, "Ye Gods, what a commentator is this *Ann Alexander* whale . . . I wonder if my evil art has raised the monster."

—*Carla Kelly*

ABOUT CARLA KELLY

What to say about Carla? The old girl's been in the writing game for mumble-mumble years. She started out with short stories that got longer and longer until—poof!—one of them turned into a novel. (It wasn't quite that simple.) She still enjoys writing short stories, one of which is before you now. Carla writes for Harlequin Historical, Camel Press, and Cedar Fort. Her books are found in at least 14 languages.

Along the way, Carla's books and stories have earned a couple of Spur Awards from Western Writers of America for Short Fiction, a couple of Rita Awards from Romance Writers of America for Best Regency, and a couple of Whitney Awards. Carla lives in Idaho Falls, Idaho, and continues to write, because her gig is historical fiction, and that never gets old.

Follow Carla on Facebook: Carla Kelly
Carla's Website: CarlaKellyAuthor.com

Begin Again

by Josi S. Kilpack

OTHER WORKS BY JOSI S. KILPACK

The Sadie Hoffmiller Culinary Mystery Series
The Newport Ladies Book Club series
Her Good Name
Unsung Lullaby
Sheep's Clothing
A Heart Revealed
Lord Fenton's Folly
Forever and Forever

One

Regina Weathers felt the man watching her from across the ballroom again and wondered how she could *feel* a stare. Despite her knowing full well he was watching, she looked over her shoulder to confirm it. He held her eyes from behind silver-framed spectacles and smiled, giving her the strangest sensation that she knew him from somewhere. But that was unlikely; her world was not so big that she would forget the people she interacted with. Besides, as hostess for her niece's engagement ball tonight, she knew everyone on the guest list and was certain that he had not been on that list. Perhaps he had come with someone who *had* received an invitation?

She turned her attention back to the conversation taking place between Mrs. Dalton and Regina's older brother, Sir Timothy Weathers, regarding the recent changes to the parish church—a remodel that Timothy and Mrs. Dalton had donated funds for. She would ignore the spectacled man and keep her focus on her guests and family who deserved her attention.

"I simply cannot wait to hear the new organ play," Mrs. Dalton said, smiling in a way that even Regina—a spinster of thirty-two years with no romantic experience acceptable for conversation—could see was too effulgent for talk of the instrument. "We will need to decide together what the first hymn will be once the repairs are finished; don't you agree, Sir Timothy?"

"Oh, I shall leave that choice to you, Madame," Timothy said with a slight nod.

The man in spectacles moved into Regina's field of vision and began talking with Mr. and Mrs. Wilson. Regina thought that perhaps she would ask them about him later in the evening.

Timothy continued. "I am sure your tastes in music are far superior to mine, Mrs. Dalton. The only notes I can carry are the ones written on paper and tucked in a pocket."

Mrs. Dalton laughed, and the others in the small group laughed, but Regina just smiled and wondered if her brother realized that Mrs. Dalton was flirting with him. Again. In the months that the two had overseen the remodeling, Regina had noticed the increased attention the widow had shown him, but her brother had not seemed to. Regina had been keeping house for Timothy these four years, ever since the passing of his wife. Should he marry, the new Lady Weathers would take her rightful place in the household.

Regina would not be asked to leave, surely, but it would be best for her to remove herself anyway to allow the family to find their own way together. Except that Regina had nowhere else to go. It was difficult not to think of her circumstance as her fate was ultimately dependent on the graces of her family, but it would be unfair not to help her brother in any way she knew would bring him joy and security. He had been so very good to her and was so adorably naïve regarding the widow's attentions.

"Mrs. Dalton," Regina said, throwing her selfish caution to the wind, "perhaps your family would like to join us for supper sometime next week. I could watch over the children while you and my brother discuss the hymn."

There was a breath of silence as everyone—except perhaps Timothy—seemed to realize the implied intent of Regina's invitation. Within the private conference it could be adequately expected that they would discuss things beyond than hymnal discussions.

Mrs. Dalton's eyes lit up at the suggestion, and she smiled gratefully at Regina before turning her attention to Timothy. "Would that be acceptable, Mr. Weathers?" The peach-colored ostrich feather attached to her satin cap shivered in anticipation of his answer.

"Of course." Timothy's smile was nearly as wide as the widow's, stretching across his face, which even at forty-three years of age was handsome. Regina's heart warmed at his reaction. Yes, seeing her brother happily settled would be a grand thing.

When her dear friend Camilla approached, Regina excused herself, and they were soon arm and arm walking the edge of the ballroom, surveying the décor, and commenting on the attendees. It seemed that everyone of their class within ten miles had come tonight, and Regina could not help but take pride in the success of the evening thus far. She did love to entertain, and the engagement of her niece Julia—Timothy's eldest child—was ample reason to do so.

Regina was saying how much she would miss Julia when she noticed the man in the spectacles again. He was no longer talking to the Wilsons; once again he watched Regina, from the far side of the room. She looked away, increasingly anxious about his attention.

Though she was dressed in a new ball gown, it was not so fine as to warrant such attention: emerald satin with silver overlay and white gloves. She *was* wearing her mother's diamond pendant and silver earbobs, which dangled nearly to her shoulders but her appearance was not remarkable in a room filled with women dressed to the extreme with elaborate gowns, hats, and jewelry too flamboyant for her own, more subdued, style.

For a moment, she wondered if the man's attention could be nefarious—perhaps he was a jewel thief or scoundrel—but why would a scoundrel lie in wait for anyone at a country ball? Or stare with such intent as to give himself away? Regina shook away her thoughts of the strange man; this was not the time to give in to such distraction. Since she was responsible for the comfort of her guests; she needed her senses completely engaged.

When the first strains of the orchestra sounded with a traditional minuet, starting the dancing portion of the evening, a hush fell over the audience. Guests cleared from the center of the ballroom and began casting looks about, in search of partners.

"Will you dance tonight?" Camilla asked as they watched the first couples take the floor.

"Not tonight," Regina answered. Though she liked to dance, she often felt awkward when asked, as though the gentleman was asking because he, or his wife, felt sorry for her spinster status. Tonight, however, she had an excuse to say no, and even better, an excuse to be so busy that no one looked upon her with the usual pity. "I must look in on the kitchens. If you'll excuse me, Camilla."

"Of course," her friend said, already moving to the edge of the dance floor. "If you should need me, *I* shall be dancing." She smiled pointedly, and Regina smiled back.

Camilla was but twenty-four. Not quite on the shelf as Regina was, but certainly past what would be considered prime marrying age. Camilla maintained that whether she married or not, it was no matter to her. Regina often claimed the same. *Better to be content in one's place,* she told herself, whenever regret seeped in. That she had ever expected a different future was something she thought on but rarely, what good did it do to think on what hadn't been?

Regina moved toward the door but actually quitting the room took her several minutes due to so many guests wanting to compliment her on the evening, but finally she pushed through the door and into the hallway, which almost sounded silent compared to the ballroom, though she could still hear music and laughter through the door.

She had taken three steps when she heard the door open behind her. She looked over her shoulder in time to see the man with spectacles slip into the hallway behind her. She turned toward him in surprise and raised a hand to her throat. His hair was dark brown and curly, with strands of grey here and there, but it was his eyes behind the spectacles that drew her attention. They were green and intent and . . . familiar?

"Sir," she said in reprimand, her heart pounding as she remembered her suspicions of him being a thief or a scoundrel. "I must insist that you—"

He moved toward her, reaching out as though to take her hands. She crossed her arms and scrambled backward, staying out of his reach. He came to a stop, and his smile fell. The same sense of familiarity tugged at her mind once again, but in a way that made her think that she'd only dreamed him, as though her potential memory of him was not real.

"You look beautiful, Reggie."

Her breath caught in her throat, and her eyes went

wide. With the nickname came a hundred memories of it being said on those very lips. Those lips she had longed for, pined for, and ultimately cried for and then forgotten. Or so she told herself. The hallway swirled, and Regina reached out to the wall to brace herself, knocking a picture frame askew as she did.

"Ross?" The name had once felt like sugar in her mouth.

His face—older but increasingly familiar—lit up on hearing his name. With his smile came the shadow of the straw-haired, gangly boy he'd been fifteen years ago, a face not as chiseled and weathered. She saw him as he'd looked the last time they'd met by Hanson's wall.

I'll come back, Reggie. I promise I will, and then we'll be together."

Ross had not come back, and the reminder brought the same searing pain to her chest that loving him had caused her back then and in the years since. She narrowed her eyes, lifted her chin, and pointed toward the front door. Inside, she was shaking, but she knew how to hide her thoughts and feelings. Because of him, she'd learned the part well.

"You were not on the guest list, Mr. Martin, so I must insist that you leave. This instant."

Two

Rossen Martin was mesmerized by the fire that lit Reggie's striking blue eyes—eyes he had dreamed about for so long. Her passion was something he had loved in her when they were young and glad to say had not been extinguished in the intervening years. He moved toward her, aching to hold her in his arms again, to touch her skin, which still looked soft and youthful—she had not spent the better part of fifteen years on a ship or a battlefield, as he had. She took a step back from him, and tightened her jaw even more.

"Reggie," he said, almost laughing her name as something akin to giddiness overtook him. He had been in Himley only a few days before learning about the ball and devising his plan to surprise her here, perhaps even lead her to a dance—in public, this time. "It is so good to see you."

"Good to see me?" she repeated, dropping her hands to her hips, which only further defined her figure. She had grown from child to woman, and he could scarcely contain the feelings seeing her stirred within him. Her honey hair was piled on her head with a few soft curls to frame her face. She was an absolute vision except for her expression, which was hard as stone. "I have not seen you for fifteen years, Ross—Mr. Martin. And I have *no* desire to see you now." She pointed to the door again. "Get out."

Though Ross had preferred the fantasy of Reggie falling into his arms and professing her continued love for him, he had known he would have to explain himself at some point. "I realize we need to talk of all that's happened, but can't we, for the moment, simply enjoy being face to face again? It has been so long, yet seeing you makes it seem as though it was just yesterday that we made our promises to each other."

Her nostrils flared, and her hands dropped from her hips as her shoulders came up. "It was *not* yesterday," she said in clipped sharp words. "It was *fifteen years* ago."

She advanced toward him, but he just smiled, entertaining the idea of her perhaps *now* falling into his arms—though her fire was quite invigorating to see. Her temper had been a trial for her parents, but never for him. It was yet one more thing he loved about her.

When she was within a foot of him, she raised both hands, but instead of falling into his embrace, she pushed against his chest—hard. Hard enough that he stumbled backward, catching his foot on the leg of a decorative table and causing a metal bowl of flowers to crash to the floor as he fumbled in an attempt to keep himself upright. No sooner had he caught his balance than she slammed her hands against his chest again, catching him unawares a second time, and sending him sprawling to the ground.

She was yelling, but in his attempt to recover from this *very* unexpected turn of events, he could hear nothing but a word here and there: "Leave . . . hate you . . . Bedlam . . . never . . . ridiculous!"

"Wait!" He finally got his feet beneath him again and backed out of her reach. As a soldier, he knew how to defend himself, but touching a woman in that manner was something he could never do. A collection of servants had congregated behind her, seeming to assess the situation, but he kept his focus on Reggie. He put his hands out, palms forward by way of surrender. "Wait!" he said again.

Reggie stopped her advance, but her hands were fists at her side, and her neck was stuck forward as though she were seconds away from snapping at him with her teeth. If her anger hadn't brought such becoming spots of pink to her cheeks and a brightening to her eyes, he would have been frightened. But he was not frightened. Rather, he was more in love with her than he'd ever been before.

"Can we discuss all that's happened?" he asked, attempting a smile, but her eyes narrowed even more. He realized that his attempts at levity were not helping. He kept his expression unreadable. "So much has happened, Reggie, and—"

"Do *not* call me that!" she said through clenched teeth. She was beginning to take on a somewhat demonic quality, which was no longer so well compensated by her fetching color or fine eyes.

"Very well." His hands were still out in supplication for mercy.

A maid approached and whispered something to Regina, which she waved off. The maid stepped back and spurred the other servants to assist with cleaning up the flowers.

"Regina, then?" he asked. "Shall I call you Regina?"

"You shall call me *Miss Weathers*," she said. "As any other gentleman not of my acquaintance would if he had any manners at all, which you obviously do not have."

"Of course." Ross had not considered that she might not still be equally in love with him. And yet, did not her reaction—extreme as it was—not speak of deep feelings?

"Miss Weathers . . . I should have written."

Her face went red, and her chin dropped another inch, so that she was glaring up at him. Her face had even seemed to swell; he backed away another few feet to ensure his safety.

"You should have written?" she bellowed. Truly bellowed. Like an ox. "You have appeared all these years later, and all you have to say is that you 'should have written'?"

She moved toward him again, and he realized that she might truly hurt him. He looked around wildly and spied a footman approaching quickly from the right. Ross grabbed the man by the shoulders and used him as a human shield.

Regina did not stop advancing, however. In fact, he wondered if she'd noticed the footman there at all as she clawed in the direction of Ross's face and said unintelligible things.

It was the footman who finally grabbed hold of her wrists and calmed her with the use of her name several times. Regina stopped, then backed up and raised a hand to her forehead, blinking quickly. The footman twisted out of Ross's grip and then looked between the two of them as though unsure what to do. The butler suddenly appeared, breathing heavily, as though he'd come at a run. He asked questions of the footman before turning his attention to Reggie and asking her what had happened.

She took a breath, then turned to the side, staring at the wall while seeming to contain her emotions. After a few seconds—with the footman glaring at Ross every other moment or so and the butler looking befuddled—she raised her chin and spoke as though talking to the wall before her.

"Have I drawn the attention of my guests, Shaw?"

"No, Ma'am," Shaw said. "Though I have sent for your brother."

She nodded, and then lifted a hand to her neck, which was red and splotchy. "Shaw, see this man out of my brother's house, and see to it that he does not return."

With that, she turned on her heel and proceeded down the hall, restored to her confident English gentlewoman demeanor rather than the banshee she had been a minute earlier. A man joined her—her brother, Ross assumed since he had never met the man. He looked at Ross quickly before falling in step with her and moving away while they spoke words Ross could not hear.

He watched until they disappeared around a corner, then looked at a glowering Shaw. "I am leaving," Ross said, turning toward the front door.

But the footman took hold of the back of Ross's coat anyway and pushed him along. The butler hurried ahead, and when they reached the entrance, he grabbed the knob, pulling the door open. The footman pushed Ross roughly over the threshold, which he tripped over before tumbling to the ground. All those years of military training, for what?

"If you return," Shaw said, "I shall call the constable *and* the stable hands. Whichever reaches you first will determine how best to punish you for attacking Miss Weathers."

Attacking Miss Weathers? The door slammed, and Ross slowly got to his feet while adjusting his spectacles, which, fortunately, had not fallen off.

Certainly neither the butler nor the footman had been there for the whole of the altercation, or they would have known that he'd been the one fending off an attack. He questioned his choice of not wearing his uniform—would it have earned him some respect? He hadn't wanted to stand out, which is why he'd chosen traditional dress, but could not imagine he'd have been thrown out in regimentals.

His bad knee had struck the cobbles of the porch, and his palms were scraped from the ejection—he'd certainly endured worse, but the injuries still smarted. A number of coachmen stood a short ways away, snickering and looking on, but he simply nodded at the lot of them. He didn't care what they thought as he limped away—what anyone thought, except Reggie. And he felt sure that once he could break through the layer of anger, he would get to the heart of the woman he had fallen in love with all those years ago.

He straightened his coat and brushed off his trousers while regarding the door that had just been shut in his face. His eyes then moved up the front of the grand house—a window at the top of the house began to light up, as though someone had entered the room with a candle. It was reasonable to assume that Reggie had removed to her bedchamber to collect herself before returning to the ball.

It made him smile to know that her thoughts were of him—even if they were not so kind right at this moment. Eventually she would have to come to the happy memories—the ones that had sustained him all these years: of foot races to the bridge and throwing stones in the river, of daisy chains and dancing in the meadow as they taught themselves the steps of the waltz. Those memories could dispel much darkness; he knew that from experience and felt sure she would have a change of heart if she allowed herself to remember.

The front door opened to reveal Shaw's stoic face, and Ross tipped his imaginary hat at the man then hurried away—his actual hat and coat were somewhere inside the estate house, taken when he'd arrived an hour earlier. Retrieving them would be a perfect opportunity to return tomorrow and request a meeting with Reggie once she'd had time to calm down.

Guest carriages filled the drive, but Ross had come on horseback despite his evening dress. With his knee growing increasingly sore, mounting was difficult, but he managed. Some yards from the house, he had the impression to turn around. In the open window of the room he'd watched light up earlier, he saw the silhouette of a woman. He could not see her face, but he knew it was Regina—his Reggie—watching him leave. Perhaps wishing that he wasn't? He put two fingers to his lips, then stretched out his hand to send the kiss to her. The window slammed shut, echoing into the night, and the shadow disappeared, but Ross was not discouraged.

It was impossible for him to even consider the idea that after all that had happened while they were apart, he and Reggie would not end up together.

Impossible.

Three

"I do believe it is beyond saving," Regina said with a frown as she fingered the stain on one of the tablecloths. It was wine and perhaps some gravy, too. As mistress of the house, she was consulted regarding linens no longer fit for use, and the laundress had scrubbed this stain so long the fabric had begun to fray.

"Very good, Miss Weathers." The maid bobbed a quick curtsy and disappeared with the ruined linen, while Regina opened the ledger on her desk, flipping to the page regarding linen supplies so as to make a note. Twice a year she replenished cloth goods with an order to a factory in Leeds. She liked to keep the list up to date.

At the sound of footsteps, she looked to the doorway in time to see Timothy enter. She closed the ledger, returned it to its place in the desk, and faced her brother in anticipation. He did not often seek her out; therefore, he must want to discuss a topic of great importance. She felt sure she knew what it was and her stomach tightened in anticipation.

"Are we quite recovered from the ball?" he asked, nodding toward the ledger.

"Nearly so," Regina said. "We have restocked the larder, cleaned and restored every room, and counted the linens. I shall meet with the steward regarding his thoughts, but I believe we can say, finally, that the party is over."

The party had actually been over for four days—it had taken that long to set the house back to rights. Julia had gone to stay with a dear friend on the other side of town, and the younger boys had returned to school, so the house was all but empty. Regina missed the children, as she always did, but she enjoyed the peace as well.

"Will you take a bit of air with me in the gardens, then?"

As Regina fully realized the intention behind her brother's seeking her company, she was forced to think back to her most embarrassing display at the ball—not that she had ever forgotten it. After Timothy had joined her in the hallway that night, quite concerned, she had assured him that all was well—she'd composed herself rather quickly after the storm of emotion had passed—and promised her brother a conference about it when the household had sufficiently recovered from the ball. Now that their overnight guests were gone and the house had returned to its usual routine, she could not put him off any longer and therefore agreed to the interview with a nod.

"Excellent," Timothy said. "The garden, then."

She kept her smile polite as she took his arm—a rather formal offer on his part considering that it was just the two of them—and walked with him out of the house, to the east side, and into a beautiful garden, which their mother had designed decades ago.

Mama had loved gardens the way Timothy loved horses and Regina loved . . . making things better for the people in her life, she supposed.

After a few minutes, Timothy introduced the topic. "The man at the ball was Lieutenant Rossen Martin, was it not?"

Regina startled and looked at her brother's profile. By the time Ross had come to Himley, Timothy had married, was the father of two children, and lived in London. Since Regina had never spoken of Ross—ever—to anyone, it was a shock to hear Timothy speak his name. "How do you know that?"

"Between the staff and a few select guests, I uncovered the identity of the spectacled man you had thrown out, but I'm afraid that no one knows more than his name. His uncle owned Valor House, did he not?"

"Yes," Regina said simply, looking forward again. Remembering such details of Ross's life was like pulling slivers from her skin; she could not help but think it would be less painful to keep them there. She should have realized that other people would know him, or take note of his name at the ball, but after so many years of him being more of phantom of memory than a man she had not considered it.

"And how are you acquainted with him?" Timothy asked.

Regina wished she could say she did not know him—she had convinced herself that she never really had—but it seemed as though the part of her soul that had festered all of these years, the part with the splinters left behind, was eager to be free of the secret she had kept for so long. "I once believed I would marry him."

Timothy came to a stop and turned to her with wide eyes. She could only meet them for a moment before looking away. "It was a secret engagement," she said. "We were very young."

Timothy continued to stare, opened his mouth, closed

it, and then led her to a bench beneath a trellis. It was September and cool enough that they did not need the shade; however, it seemed that he wanted to hear her tale sitting down. "You have never told me of this." He sounded hurt by the ignorance, as though they were confidantes who often whispered secrets behind their hands.

In truth, Timothy was eleven years Regina's senior; they had not grown up together. In fact, they had not known each other all that well until she'd returned to keep house for him at Crumhall. They had become quite close since then, but what he *knew* of Regina's past was something they did not discuss, and she purposely let alone those parts he knew nothing about.

"I have never told anyone."

"You must tell me now." Timothy directed his full attention to her, though she remained standing beside the bench. "The whole of it."

Regina took a breath for fortitude—it was not an easy story to speak about. "When I was fourteen, Ross's uncle invited him to stay the summer at Valor House. We met on a day I had stormed from the house following an argument with Mama about something I no longer remember. Ross had decided to explore the ruins. We met by accident, but it felt like fate."

Dredging up such memories and speaking them aloud for the first time was disconcerting, and Regina found herself needing to push away rising emotion as she continued to explain: how she and Ross had become secret friends, unrestrained by family or societal expectation. How they had shared smiles at church, left messages for one another at various places around the countryside.

When Ross returned to school, Regina thought she would never see him again, but he returned for the

Christmas holiday and again the next summer. By the end of that second summer, they fancied themselves in love, and when he returned the *next* summer, they began making plans to marry.

"I was nearly seventeen, and therefore of marriageable age. Ross, however, was only one year older. He had no income other than his allowance, which was at the mercy of his parents, and had only just finished his primary schooling. He was expected to pursue an education studying the law."

"He would have been unable to marry for years, maybe a decade," Timothy commented. "He could not support a family until then."

Regina pinched creases into the skirt of her morning gown and nodded. "I better understand the reasons for such requirements now, but at that time, it felt vastly unfair. We decided that the rules about a man waiting for marriage until he was established were simply tradition intended to rob us of our happiness and our youth." She shook her head. "We were so foolish."

"You were young," Timothy said, as a good father would. "Smarter than you'd ever been before, and feeling as youth often do—strong and sure of themselves."

Regina nodded in agreement, appreciating the merciful interpretation. "And believing ourselves wiser than anyone else."

"And no one knew of this secret engagement?"

Regina shook her head. "Part of the excitement was the very secrecy of it; we had a hidden part of ourselves that no one else knew about. I relished it and felt so grown up to have this special connection. But when we decided to marry, we knew we would have to talk to his parents, and then to Papa. We felt sure we could help them see the wisdom of our choices in one another and gain their support. We were in love, or so we thought, and felt sure that it would conquer all."

"What happened?" Timothy asked.

"He wrote a letter to his mother and stepfather." She went quiet, feeling the emotions of that time—the waves of anticipation and then the regret and fear and sorrow.

She explained how Ross's stepfather came for him immediately and carted him back to Kent. Regina had dared not write him due to his quick departure, and she'd spent months in a state of such hopelessness that she'd felt sure she would die.

Then Ross came for Christmas and sought her out, telling her only the barest details of what the months had been like with his parents, how they'd berated him for being a lovesick boy, unable to know his own mind. Not to be silenced, he'd argued back and, in the end, had agreed to take their offer of a commission in the army. They'd said that if he would take two years to establish a career, they would condone the match.

"He would still have only been but twenty years old."

"Twenty-one," she corrected, but then shrugged. "Which would still have been young—I know that now—but our hope was restored. I could not imagine waiting two more years, but I fancied myself so in love with him that it would be worth the sacrifice."

Timothy nodded, thoughtful as he met her eyes once again. "That is why you did not take a Season?"

Regina paced to the other side of the arbor and finally sat beside him on the bench, though it did not remedy her growing discomfort. "It would have felt like a betrayal to Ross." She shook her head. "I am humiliated to think of how stupid a girl I was." She let out a breath. "He said he would write me, but I received only one letter from London before he left for India. He never wrote again."

Ross's words from Saturday night came to mind—*I should have written*—and she had to blow her breath out slowly so as to avoid the intensity of anger she'd felt at his words.

"I remember Mama being quite vexed by your refusal to go to London."

She'd disappointed both her parents by declining the chance to secure a good match. The memory made her sad. "Even so, I remained faithful to Ross. I would not consider the idea that Ross might have abandoned me, and I told myself he'd simply been unable to send correspondence. That was easier to believe, especially when his regiment was sent to France."

Timothy whistled under his breath as he turned to her. "He fought?"

"I saw his name in the reports—that's how I knew he hadn't simply gone to India as he'd expected. After that, I looked for his name in every report that came to the house. As long as he was not in the listed dead, I clung to hope. I immersed myself in books and music, asked Mama for a tutor so I might improve my French. And then, one dark and lonely day, I realized I had not heard from him in *six years*, and I hadn't seen his name in the reports for months."

She had to pause and shake her head. Even having lived it, she couldn't believe she'd waited so long. "I did not know if he was dead or alive, but I could not hide from the fact that either way, he was not coming for me. I still can't believe it took me so long to come to my senses."

"Is that when you went to work for Mr. Corrings?"

Regina made a sound like a growl in her throat. Mr. Corrings was her *next* embarrassment and another way in which she had disappointed her parents—though *disappointment* seemed too light a word. But there was no reason to keep the details from Timothy—not after she'd already revealed so much. Besides, he knew of the scandal—everyone did—only he did not know all of the reasons behind it.

Mr. Corrings was a puffy man with three grown sons, four young children in need of a governess, and two dead wives. Having only recently admitted to herself the level of her foolishness in putting her entire future on hold for Ross's return, Regina accepted the position, which she'd seen advertised in the paper—against the advice of her parents, who were embarrassed to have her work—and six months later accepted Mr. Corrings's offer of marriage.

"I took the position in hopes that a new life would distract me from my old one. Mr. Corrings' offer seemed to be my only hope of having a family, and though he knew I did not love him, his children were sweet, and he and I were both lonely. Love would come in time, I told myself, but after the engagement was announced . . ." She stopped herself, unable to keep the heat from rising in her cheeks as she stared at her shoes peeking out from her hem. "It was acceptable for him to hold my hand, to sit close beside me." She shuddered at the memory of it but knew she needed to clarify before Timothy thought something truly ruinous had taken place. "There was nothing that most couples would not find . . . enjoyable," she said in Mr. Corrings defense. She had once lain in Ross's arms and watched the clouds, and had even allowed him to steal a kiss or two. Mr. Corrings had not expected any more than that.

Those moments with Ross had created stirrings within her, feelings that gave her reason to anticipate pleasure from such things again. But Mr. Corrings was twenty-two years Regina's senior, with a fat stomach and jowls that hung loose below his chin. More than that, she did not love him. When he put his arm around her, she cringed and pulled away without thought, then excused her reaction as nerves and tried to steel herself for his future showings of affection. One night, he'd kissed her fully, and she had been so horribly repulsed by it, that she had sworn off marriage completely, not only to him but to anyone at all.

If becoming a governess, and then becoming engaged to her employer, hadn't been embarrassment enough for her family, breaking the engagement after it had already become public had created a great scandal. Her father had had to make a settlement to Mr. Corrings, and Regina had been sent to stay with a distant cousin in Sheffield.

Eventually, she'd accepted a job at a girls' school near Brighton, where she'd taught French and literature until Timothy's wife had passed away and he'd asked her to return to the home of their youth to help him manage the place. Their father had passed by then, disappointed in his daughter to the end, and Mama had been in poor health.

Regina had returned like the prodigal, determined to make her mother proud by managing the home and her brother's children as well as any woman could. And she had.

By the time Mama died two summers ago, their relationship had healed. No one spoke of Regina's past, accepting that she was a dependable woman with pleasing manners, a generous heart, and admirable skills in household management. It was as though none of the horrible things had ever happened, and, on most days, she could believe it too and be content in her place.

After she finished her tale, they sat in silence for some time, until Timothy cleared his throat.

"And now your Mr. Martin has returned." He did not phrase it as a question, but the statement asked a dozen questions nonetheless.

"Yes, he has," Regina answered. Her discomfort at having already said so much spurred her to stand again. She shook out her skirts and pretended interest in the miniature roses growing beside the trellis. She fingered one of the velvety blooms but pinched it too hard, causing the petals to bruise and break.

"What shall you do?" Timothy asked.

Regina took a breath and kept her eyes on the remnants of the rose she'd just destroyed. Not everything could be put back together. Not roses. Not hearts. "I shall do nothing."

"Are you not curious as to why, after all this time, he's finally come back?"

"Not curious enough."

"Curious enough for what?"

She turned to face him. "I don't know that I ever really loved him—I was a child, and he was as much fantasy as he was flesh and bone. Clearly, whatever it is he might have felt wasn't enough to bring him back as he promised. It was not enough to even induce him to put pen to paper in all of those years. We have both chosen our courses, and there is nothing he can say or do that will undo the years. If I could have my way of it, I would prefer never to see him again."

"I understand that he called on you the day following the ball."

"He came for his hat and coat, then requested an audience, which I refused." Regina had recovered her confidence now that the whole of the mess had been explained. "The staff has been given carte blanche to send him away without consulting me if he comes again. I have no desire for his attentions."

"You did not know that he called again this morning, then?"

Regina startled. "He did?" she said without thinking. "This morning?"

A slight smile lifted one side of Timothy's mouth, and she felt herself blushing as she turned back to the roses, this time crushing one on purpose.

"He was turned away, per your instructions, but he left something for you, and Shaw asked me if he should approach you regarding it. You gave them no instruction on how to handle gifts. Would you like to see it?"

Regina composed herself then turned to face her brother, who held out his hand, palm up, but fingers closed. She knew what he held before he opened his fingers to reveal the small metal key, which looked more like a knob.

"You recognize it," Timothy said, watching her face and surely reading it better than she would have liked.

She wanted to reject the gift, to roll her eyes and stomp away, but instead, she reached out and reverently took the key from his hand. Ross had kept it all these years? The lump in her throat took her off guard, and all of the feelings she had felt during this interview became a bundle of confusion in her mind. "It's a key," she said, stating the obvious. She turned the key over and thought how just a short time ago it had been in Ross's own hand.

"A key to what?" Timothy asked.

"To a music box I once owned."

In her mind, she was taken back to their final meeting at Hanson's wall. She'd already known he was leaving, so she'd brought a token, something for him to return when he came back—a symbol of the incompleteness she would feel without him. The music box had been a gift from her grandmother and one of Regina's dearest possessions.

The swan won't sing until you bring this back to me, she'd said while becoming lost in those green eyes, which made her think of oceans and hayfields and springtime.

"Do you have the music box still?" Timothy asked, bringing her back to the present.

Regina closed her fingers over the key, then looked up at her brother. "I did not take it with me to Mr. Corrings' estate, and when I returned, it was gone. Likely a servant took it, not realizing it was silent without the key." She shrugged as if the loss did not bother her. "Many things are lost over time."

"Yet Mr. Martin did not lose your key," Timothy pointed out.

Regina held his eyes for a moment before looking away. "The return of my key is too late for the music box, and the return of Mr. Martin is too late for me."

Four

The day following Ross's return of the key, Shaw discovered an enormous bouquet of flowers left on the front porch. After a maid delivered the flowers to her room, Regina sat at her vanity and opened the card to find nothing more than a heart sketched onto the paper. The romance of it tugged at her emotions, even more when she recognized wildflowers from the meadows around the tower ruin where she and Ross had often met.

Regina dropped her elbows to her knees and her head into her hands, overwhelmed with old memories and new insecurities. She stayed thus for some time until the housekeeper, Mrs. Williams, knocked to ask if Regina still wanted to discuss the day's menu. They were supposed to have met in the library at nine o'clock.

Regina dressed quickly and met with Mrs. Williams as though this were any other day. When they finished discussing the menu, Regina gave the flowers to Mrs. Williams and asked that she display them below stairs for the enjoyment of the staff. Regina slid the note into a drawer of her desk next to the music box key. She tried all day not to think of the flowers or the note or the key, but, of course, she could think of little else.

At the end of the day, after Regina's maid had finished readying her for bed, there was a knock at the bedchamber door. Regina put on her dressing gown and bade the person to come in. Timothy entered with a vase holding a portion of that morning's bouquet. Regina scowled at the flowers, then at him before dismissing her maid so as to have a private discussion.

When they were alone, she turned to face him. "I sent the flowers below stairs," she said.

"Mrs. Williams asked if you might like some of them in your room, and I thought it a splendid idea. They are yours, after all."

"It is *not* a splendid idea." Regina moved toward her bed, which had been turned down. "And I am quite tired, so I would ask that you leave me and return the flowers to Mrs. Williams."

He ignored her instruction and put the vase on her dressing table. Regina stared at it from across the room, feeling a softening that she could not afford to feel.

"Will you not let him explain himself?" Timothy asked.

She looked from the flowers to his face, speaking with the same level of sincerity he had used. "I do not need an explanation. I am quite content with my situation." A worrisome thought seized her, and she lifted her chin. "Unless you are tired of me and are now intent on pushing me toward Mr. Martin."

"Of course not." Timothy sounded offended. "I simply want you to find the greatest happiness you can—"

"A man who is responsible for so much pain in my life—whether or not I should have put such stock in him in the first place—is not someone who will bring me the greatest happiness."

Timothy looked as though he wanted to press the issue, but instead, he wished her goodnight and quit the room. Regina went to bed feeling a bit disappointed that he hadn't argued the point a bit more, but then convinced herself that it was for the best. She did not want Mr. Martin's attention. She didn't!

On Thursday, Shaw found a poem on the doorstep—her favorite, "To the Virgins, to Make Much of Time," by Robert Herrick. She read the first few lines then spent a great deal of time looking out the window and trying not to remember telling Ross that while she loved all of Herrick's poetry, "To the Virgins" was her very favorite piece. How could he have remembered that all these years? The message of the poem was to seize the day—*carpe diem*—and to not let opportunity pass by unexplored.

"You are playing with me," she said to no one at all. "But you shall not win." She put the poem in the drawer next to yesterday's note. Julia had returned, and the women had much to do to get ready for the wedding. Regina had no time to spare for thoughts of Ross. Or so she kept telling herself whenever she found herself thinking of him, which was far too often.

On Friday, a purple scarf was left for her on the doorstep—he remembered her favorite color? She acted irritated by the gift, as she had with the others, but alone in her room; she draped it across her arms and looked at her reflection in the mirror, conflicted on every side.

He was wooing her, seducing her, in a sense. Did she dare to open her heart again? A few trinkets did not make up for fifteen years of heartache.

She thought back to Timothy's advice that she ask Ross

for an accounting of his silence. Entertaining the idea of meeting with him face to face was quite terrifying, however. In the hallway during the ball, she had felt the most discomfiting—*attraction* toward him, even when she'd screamed like a demon. He'd sent her emotions into a jumble, and she'd lost all dignity.

What if that attraction overrode her sensibilities and put her in a position where she would have her heart broken again? She'd told Timothy that she was not convinced she had ever loved Ross.

Now, she fingered the fine silk of the shawl and knew that she'd been lying, no matter how much she wished it were the truth. Still, having loved him in the past was not the same as loving him now, or trusting him to love her back. She took the shawl from her shoulders and put it in the same drawer in which she'd stowed the other items. She felt more raw every day, more afraid and yet . . . more curious, too.

On Saturday, there was a linen-lined basket with strawberry tarts inside—another favorite. Ross used to steal tarts from the cook at his Uncle's house and bring them when they met.

On Sunday, Regina was up at dawn and wondering what was waiting for her on the porch. She refused to act on her eagerness, of course, and instead called her maid to help her get ready for church. Last week—just two days after the ball—Ross had sat in a back pew and she'd successfully ignored him through the whole service. Would he come to church again today? Had he left a gift on the porch again, or would he skip the Sabbath? When she came down to the main level, Shaw handed her a letter.

She tried to act casual as she went to the library and closed the door.

Dear Miss Weathers,

I hope that by now, you know my intentions are real and that I wish more than anything to be reconciled with you. I have never stopped loving you. Please meet me at Hanson's wall tonight at midnight and let me tell you a story of hardship, toil, lost love, and, I hope, redemption.

Only you can decide how my tale ends. I shall wait for one hour, and if you do not come, I shall not bother you further. But please come. It is my greatest wish to see you in the moonlight once again.

Love,
Ross

Regina read the letter twice through, then folded it and set it in her lap. Would she go? *Should* she go? Did she dare?

Five

Ross turned his collar up at the increasingly cold breeze. Inviting Reggie had been an attempt to recreate their last meeting, but midnight in September was very different from what midnight in July had been. He checked his watch against his lantern's light—the waning crescent moon did not provide much. Twenty minutes after the hour. Was she not coming? He had done everything he could think of to show her the depth of his feelings, with hope that any one of his attempts would earn a response on her part. She had remained silent, however, and this was his last hope.

Perhaps he had spent all those years making more of their attachment than there ever had been. His body and soul recoiled at the thought, yet he could not make her love him, not with memories, not with gifts. That was why he had promised to leave her alone if she did not come tonight. It had been a very difficult promise to make, but he loved her, and because of that, if she *truly* did not want him, he would not press her further.

The glow of another lantern in the distance caught his attention. He jumped off the wall and moved toward the light, attempting to not show the limp that had become more apparent after he'd been thrown out of Crumhall. However, when he made out her form beside the light, he felt the rejuvenation of his arms and legs and heart. They came to a stop before one another in the meadow they'd once danced in. His eyes soaked her in. Her expression was guarded, but she did not look angry, only cautious. Her hair fell in a plait over her shoulder, and she wore a long blue dressing gown tied at the waist, with a thick shawl about her shoulders. The thought that she'd snuck out to see him made him smile.

This was just as it had been when they were younger—meeting in secret, their love belonging to them alone. He longed to return to the time of innocence and simplicity they'd once had.

"I'm so glad you've come, Reg—Miss Weathers."

She looked about herself nervously and pulled the heavy shawl tighter at her neck. "I am unsure why I did, Mr. Martin. This is quite inappropriate."

He wanted to say that she'd come because she still loved him, but he could sense her wariness and did not want to destroy the simple trust she'd shown in coming tonight.

"Thank you," he said. "Thank you for giving me an opportunity to explain myself."

He noted interest in her eyes—only a flicker—but it was there all the same and gave him blessed encouragement. He was of no mind to delay the heart of the matter, therefore he took a breath and dove straight in.

"When I left under the counsel of my parents all those years ago, I thought I would see the world then return with confidence and swagger, as well as a military career. I expected to spend the years of my service running drills in the oppressive heat until I could return to you."

He paused in an attempt not to get too drawn into the memories of what had happened next—it had taken many years not to be haunted by those things day and night.

"Napoleon changed everything. My regiment was one of the unlucky ones called up to fight the ground war, and we were sent to battle after battle throughout Europe, watching our friends be killed and then marching in their places."

He paused, the memories pushing too hard at his defenses to allow him to go into more detail. Better that he skip ahead; besides, she already knew some details from his letters.

"Early in the Fourth Coalition, I was wounded so severely that I was sent to Italy to recover. It was there, while anticipating my return to England, that I heard of your engagement."

"You had been gone for six years by then," she said quickly. "*Six years*, Ross."

She had used his Christian name! His heart soared. But she was not done speaking.

"And you never wrote to me as you promised. I could not wait forever."

"I *never* wrote?" Ross repeated, pulling back slightly in shock. "I wrote you every month unless I was in battle, and even then I wrote as often as I could."

"You did not." She shook her head. "You wrote me when you left London—that is all. You said as much the other night at my niece's ball—you admitted that you should have written."

"I meant that I should have written when I came from London two weeks ago; that I should have warned you of my arrival."

She looked confused, but determined. "I have never received word from you, not since you first went away."

"But I did write to you all those years. I . . ." The words trailed off as he realized that her not receiving his letters explained her coldness, her unwillingness to see him. She'd believed that he hadn't cared for her at all. He reached for the lantern in her hand, and she allowed him to take it and set it on the ground at their feet. He then reached for her hand and relished the warmth of holding it in his own.

"Reggie," he said, daring to use the name he'd called her by all those years ago. "I swear to you that I wrote you often—as much as I could. When I did not get a response I assumed that I was simply not in one place long enough for your letters to reach me."

She said nothing, but he could see that she did not believe him, and her distrust made his stomach tight. She pulled her hand away and used both to clutch at the shawl around her shoulders. "I would have received your letters if you had ever sent them—I was at Crumhall for years after you'd left; I did not even leave to have a Season in London. Whenever I was invited to visit a friend or relative, I was always fearful of missing your correspondence, yet none ever came."

That was impossible! "Surely some were lost due to the war, but not *all* of them. Not every one." There was no reason she wouldn't receive *any* of them. Unless . . . "Did you speak to anyone of our engagement? Did your family not approve, as mine did not?"

"I told no one," she said with confidence. "I kept our secret at first because it was ours alone, then to be protected from judgments, and finally because I was too humiliated to explain that I had believed your word for so long."

The accusation stung, but he remained steady. "The only way you would not have received my letters is if someone intercepted them."

Her forehead creased with worry for a moment but then she lifted her chin and shook her head. "No one knew of our promise to each other; therefore, there was no reason to prevent me from receiving your letters. Writing a soldier was patriotic, if nothing else. No one would have objected."

"But someone must have discovered the engagement and—"

"You were to tell me all that happened." She waved her hand through the air in a gesture of impatience. "I believe you left off with news of my engagement, which did not last even a week."

"Why? Why did it not last?" How he wanted to hear her say that it was because the man was not him, was not Ross— the boy she still loved and who still loved her from afar.

"It is impertinent for you to ask such a thing," she said, looking at the ground. "It was not a good match; that it all. How did you hear of it?"

"From another soldier at the hospital in Italy—last name was Lebelson. His family was from Wolverhampton. Do you know them?"

"Our families have been friends for years; their oldest son went to university with my brother."

"Yes. He'd been there two months longer than I had, enough that his letters had found him, and he had one from home announcing your engagement."

"Which would have been finished by the time he learned of it," she said.

"I assumed it was the *wedding* that was finished by then." He could not push away the lingering pain the news had caused him. "To say I was heartbroken is to put it far too mildly—I was dumbfounded."

"It had been six—"

"I know," he cut in, not wanting her to think he was

angry but needing her to understand. "But I had believed that the reason I had been spared when so many others had not was because of you, because you were waiting for me and we were destined to be together. When I thought that you had married another, I questioned the purpose of my entire existence."

She was silent, looking between him and the ground a few times as she seemed to gather her thoughts. "Did you get *my* letters?" she asked. "I wrote you faithfully for the first two years."

"Some."

"Some?" she asked, looking confused.

"In wartime, people move a great deal, and the mail was unreliable at best. I received six, perhaps, maybe seven in those early years, and how I relished your words—and I could see that I had missed some in between. It did not matter; I was so glad to have your letters. When they stopped, I blamed the continued conflicts, certain that once I was in one place long enough they would catch up to me."

He smiled, but the furrow in her brow only deepened, spurring him to continue. "In Italy, when I learned of your engagement and did not receive your delayed letters, I realized how foolish my hope had been. It was obvious you had moved on, and, as you said, it had been six years—why would you not move on by then? I could not bear to return to England and see you on the arm of another man; so, I agreed to go to Spain despite my injuries, which had earned me a way home if I wanted it. I told myself that I did not care what happened to me next, yet I fared well; investments I had made in India grew, and I was more able to determine where I went and how I served. But even when I tried to distract myself with my duties, I could not stop thinking of you."

He lifted a hand to his face and scrubbed his chin, rough with a day's growth of stubble. "Thinking on another man's wife was sinful and hollow, but the memories of our time together here in Himley could not stay away for long. When life pressed upon me and I could not remember what it was like to feel peace and happiness, it was your face I saw, your words I heard in the air giving me encouragement." He paused and smiled. "There were times I felt sure that I could smell the very scent of your perfume."

She was watching him now, seemingly still reluctant to accept what he'd said, but he felt sure she wanted to.

"Upon learning of my uncle's death three months ago, I sold my commission and returned to London, both fearful and hoping to see you again. And it was there that I learned you had *not* married. No one I spoke to knew the details, only that you kept house for your brother and were still called Miss Weathers. I settled my affairs as quickly as possible and came for you."

He let those words sink in for her, hoping she felt them as well as heard them. He reached for her hand and when she let him take it, caught his breath. "We are here now, Reggie. Together. We can begin again."

"It is not so simple." Reggie looked at the ground, but she had not pulled her hand from his; she was obviously sorting through many things in her mind.

"It *can* be that simple, Reggie," he whispered. He squeezed her hand and brought it to his lips, hating the pained expression his kiss brought to her face. He lowered her hand and leaned in. "We can forgive each other and whoever else might have added to the pain. We can take hold of our futures together and live as we once dreamed."

She was shaking her head before he finished, and he felt his stomach sink even further. She lifted her eyes to meet his while extracting her hand then backing away. "I can't imagine war and battles or the fear and degradation of those things—and I am so sorry that you faced such horror. I do not mean to discount your hardship in any way."

She paused for breath, and when she spoke again, her voice wavered. "However, I don't believe you can imagine what it felt like to be so abandoned. Life for me was just as I'd been before you left, with all of the same expectations and frustrations. I had nothing to distract me from your absence, and I was so devoted to you. So certain. I withstood my parents' anger and frustrations when I refused to pursue a match. I lived as though you would walk through the door tomorrow and make everything worth the sacrifice. But you didn't even write."

He opened his mouth to revive the argument that he *had* written, but she spoke again before he could.

"I cannot express how difficult it was to recover when I realized that you were gone from my life—and what a fool I felt. So yes, I *did* become engaged because my prospects were poor, and I was so very lonely. I thought I could capture at least part of the life you and I had planned, but then I broke my agreement because he was not you. I believed that after loving you so wholly, I could never love another. The complications of that time are without description, though I know it was not a battle of life and death as you faced. My parents were humiliated; I hurt a good man who cared for me and I rejected the chance to have children of my own. It has taken years to find a place of comfort, years to not have you intrude into my thoughts, and to not dwell on all I have lost."

"I am so sorry, Reggie." He wished she would let him hold her. "I am so *very* sorry, and I would do anything to take the pain of those years from you. Does it not help to know that I loved you desperately too, that I never stopped loving you?"

She raised one hand to her head as though it was beginning to ache. "I don't know. I don't know what to think."

"Then don't think." He took a step closer. "Just feel what it is like for us to be together. Allow those years to drop away and let us go back to how we were."

"We can't go back." She dropped her hand and shook her head. "I cannot forget what has happened and though you say you wrote, how am I to simply believe the word of a man I have not heard from for fifteen years? For you to imply that we can simply begin where we ended is unfair. We are not children; we may not even like each other as we are now. So much has happened—we are not who we once were. So much has happened."

"Then we shall begin anew," he said with hope. "We shall become reacquainted with each other and fall in love again."

Emotion rose in her face as her mask of anger slipped, and her tears overflowed. He attempted to pull her into his arms, but she pushed him away, creating even more distance between them.

"You make it sound so simple, but it is not. You are asking me to risk too much, trust too much, hope too much. The last time I did that, my heart was broken beyond repair."

Ross felt his frustration rising. She was so stubborn, so determined not to trust him, and he did not know how to break through the barriers. "I cannot guarantee that there won't be difficulties, but I *can* promise you with my whole heart that I love you, that I am committed to doing whatever it takes for us to find a way. I do not believe I was spared for nothing. I still believe I was spared for you, Reggie. To restore to both of us all we have lost. As soon as I discovered you were unmarried, I knew to my very bones that we were meant to be together."

She regarded him, still crying, then spun on her heel and walked back the way she'd come.

The things he could say or should say raced through his mind, but it was all things he'd said already, yet it seemed as though she had not heard any of his words. He could think of only one thing he had not yet tried.

He ran to get ahead of her, and after passing her, turned to block her way. When she attempted to step around him, he took her by the shoulders and kissed her before she could prevent it.

As his lips connected to hers, a wave of warmth enveloped him, and he begged her heart to hear his and know of his dedication, know of his love for her, and *try* to trust him again.

Six

When Ross's lips touched hers, Regina froze and then . . . she felt his warmth fill her entire soul.

In the years since the last kiss she and Ross had shared here at Nelson's wall, she had convinced herself that the sensation she'd felt had been those of a foolish girl acquainted with too many novels and naïve expectations.

The fact seemed to have been confirmed when Mr. Corrings' kiss had left her with nothing but disgust. She'd used *that* kiss as further proof that she had grown out of such fantasies.

But this . . . this kiss was just as those from their youth had been. Every part of her body felt both alert and relaxed, poised for more yet lost in the moment. She reached for him, releasing her shawl, unable to get close enough to him. His hands cradled her face, and his kiss became insistent. Then he pulled away, leaving her breathless.

"I love you, Reggie. As much today as any other day of my life."

His words washed over her, but as he pulled her in for another kiss, her resistance rose once more.

He might still love the seventeen-year-old girl he'd left behind, but Regina was no longer that girl. None of her arguments had been settled by this kiss. She had worked too hard to protect herself from pain to invite it in again.

Pushing him away took all of her strength, but she stumbled out of his arms and then refused to look at his face, afraid of what she would see there. All she could think was that *she* had to be the one who left this time. She heard Ross say her name as she turned away, but she only lifted the hems of her nightdress and dressing gown and ran, determined to get away from the confusion she felt every time she was with him.

She heard his steps catching up from behind her and when he grabbed her arm and spun her around, she screamed as though he'd struck her. He abruptly let her go and then stared at her with wide eyes.

"I can't do this," she said through her sobs. "Please leave me be. Please let me go." She thought of the letter he'd sent her that morning, inviting her to come—and threw his own words back at him. "You said that if I would come and listen, you would not bother me again. You were not a man of your word fifteen years ago, but *please* be a man of your word in this. Let me live the life I have made for myself. Let me live in peace."

He continued to stare, his hair wild with the wind tearing at it, and his eyes sad. He took a step away from her. And another. "I will let you go," he spoke in tones so soft she would not have heard them if not for the wind carrying them to her ears. They fell like hammers, and she felt the impact of each syllable—would it hurt so much if what she were asking for was right? "And I will not come after you again. I'm sorry, Reggie. I truly thought . . . I am sorry."

He turned back toward the wall—both lanterns were there, muted beacons in the night. She dared not retrieve hers and come in contact with him again. Instead, she turned away and ran. When she was certain she was out of sight, her legs gave out, and she crumpled onto the grass. The sorrow of what could have been but wasn't washed over her in a torrent. Wind howled, and the trees around her bent while she lay there, crumpled and broken and wishing she could purge the pain. She had found a comfortable life, and he had destroyed it. Again.

His words came back to her. "*I wrote you every month unless I was in battle, and even then I wrote as often as I could.*"

"You are a liar!" she cried into her hands, rocking back and forth in anguish.

We can begin again.

"You are a fool," she said. "I could never trust my heart with you again."

She kept crying as she hadn't cried in years, until the tears gave way to a kind of numbed detachment. Her stomach hurt, her chest ached as she pushed herself to her feet and headed toward home, shivering in the cold because she'd dropped her shawl in the meadow. When the silhouette of the house came into view, she felt the draw of her bed and wished she could sleep for a week.

Would Ross leave Himley now? If she was the reason he'd come, would he now go? The idea of seeing him about the village felt horrendous, and yet the idea of not seeing him again felt even worse. She raised a hand to her lips, where his kiss had been, and felt the invigoration of it all over again.

Though her head felt fuzzy, she reviewed their conversation without the defenses she'd had in place when they'd spoken. She thought of all he'd gone through, of the career he had made for himself. What if he hadn't learned of her engagement? What if he'd returned to England and called on her? Would she have married him then?

She thought of the battles he'd survived, of the horrific things he had seen and done in war—yet he credited her to having helped him through?

He believed all along that they would be together? He kept her key?

His letters. They were the missing piece. She'd hoped for one that would shore her confidence—every day for years and years. Ross had seemed so sincere in his insistence that he had written, going so far as to blame someone else for having waylaid them. His parents had not been happy about their plans to be together, but they could not have interfered with *her* mail. If someone had prevented communication from him, it would have been someone at Crumhall—her parents. But no one in her family knew of Ross—she was sure of it.

Yet, if Ross *had* written, interference of some kind was the only explanation as to why she would not have received his letters.

She let herself in through the west door, which she had left unlocked, and walked quietly through the darkened hallways. When she reached the stairs that would lead her to her room, she walked past them and went instead to the library—where her father's journals were kept.

She opened and shut the door quietly, then lit a candle on the mantle and took it with her to the backmost shelves, where the house documents and ancestral items were kept. She ran her finger along the spines of identical black journals before pulling one out to check the year written on the inside page—her father began a new one every New Year's Day. She pulled out one and checked the date—too early. She replaced it and moved up three volumes to the year that Ross had left England.

With the correct volume in hand, she settled on the floor, flipped through the pages and scanned the neat penmanship of the man who had always wanted things just so. It was why Regina was such a cross for him to bear—she had never followed his patterns and instructions but he had always been quick to chastise her when she did not meet his expectations. Because of that it was difficult to consider that he would keep his knowledge of Ross a secret if he knew—surely he would rail against her for it. But if there was any person who would have interfered with Ross's letters, it would have been him.

But how could he? He hadn't known about Ross.

Seven

"Good heavens, Regina," Timothy said from above her. "What are you doing?"

Regina did not look up—a maid had discovered her fifteen minutes earlier, and she'd known Timothy would not be far behind. "The letters." She turned a page and blinked her eyes to keep the words from blurring. "If I had received his letters, none of this would have happened."

"What would not have happened?" Timothy asked, standing over her. "What letters?"

"Ross's letters," she said, blinking again and raising her eyebrows to help stretch out her eyes. She had been scanning the journals for hours, reading of parties and business transactions and now and again, news of the family. Nothing about any letters. Nothing about destroying his daughter's future. The longer she'd looked, the more she'd doubted herself, but without proof, could she simply take Ross's word that he'd written her? "All those years, and not one?"

Timothy's boots creaked as he squatted in front of her

and used his finger to lift her chin. He looked concerned. "Have you been here all night?"

"Last night I met Ross, in a meadow where we used to go." She looked past Timothy as if to see the memory of Ross walking toward her in the night, so excited to see her even as she steeled herself to keep him away. She returned her attention back to Timothy's sympathetic expression and felt her chin begin to tremble. "Why have I tried *so* hard to push him away? Why can I not simply trust him?"

He stared back at her, then grasped her elbow and helped her to her feet. She resisted, but without any sleep to fortify her, and with Timothy bigger and stronger, her efforts had little effect.

"But Ross's letters that never reached me—he said he wrote as often as he could but I never received a single one." She stretched her hand toward the jumbled pile of journals as Timothy escorted her from the room. "Only Papa would have kept them from me, don't you think? But he would have written of keeping them from me in his journals, right? He would have written of his reasons."

"I will search for proof of these letters in the journals."

She looked up into his face as they walked side by side. "You will?"

He nodded. They reached the stairs, where he kept hold of her elbow as she kept misplacing her feet. When they reached her bedchamber, he opened the door and led her in, startling her maid.

"See that she goes to bed and stays there until . . . at least three o' clock."

The maid nodded.

"Oh, I couldn't," Regina said, attempting to stay upright even as he pushed her to the bed. Her thoughts were still a whirlwind, however, and she could not seem to quiet them.

"Ross is so certain—he was so sincere in his surprise that I never heard from him in all those years. Would he have come if he really hadn't written? Would he have approached me at the ball? If Father kept the letters . . . if he knew . . . "

"I told you that I would look for the letters." Timothy pushed her beneath the covers and pulled them over her. "You will sleep—you're being absolutely ridiculous right now, and if making sure you stay in bed until you can think clearly means posting a man at the door, I shan't hesitate."

Regina allowed herself to relax. "If I'd received his letters, everything would have been different. I'd have waited for him as long as I had to."

Timothy smiled sadly. "I'll do my best to find the answers."

Eight

Regina dreamt of India and mail coaches, of Mr. Corrings and empty cradles. The thoughts swirled and burst until finally, blessedly, they calmed into the collection of memories that Regina had tried so hard not to think about all these years.

Moments she'd shared with Ross played out like a story on stage, and they felt so real that when she awoke, she did not immediately remember all that had happened in the years since those days of blissful innocence. She blinked awake and stared at the green and gold canopy over her bed and listened to the rain upon the lightened windows, holding onto the feelings left behind from sleep until she remembered why she was waking in the middle of the day. *Ross.*

She jumped out of bed, then had to hold onto the bedpost to steady her dizziness before running for the door. She stopped half way across the room and went to the bell pull instead to call her maid to help her dress. It was bad enough she'd been in the meadow and the library in her dressing gown; she couldn't go running through the house in her nightdress now.

It was nearly 4:00 when she hurried down the stairs and turned sharply to the library. Timothy was not there, and it took the help of Shaw and a footman to find him recently returned to the stables from a ride . . . in the rain? She waited for him in the library, and when he entered, ran to him.

"Did you find mention of the letters in Father's journals?"

"I'm afraid I did not," Timothy said. So quickly had he come to her that he hadn't taken off his wet outer clothing, which he now handed to Shaw, who then quit the room.

Regina's stomach sank as she sat onto the settee beside the fire. "You found nothing? No mention at all?" Surely if her father had been so opposed to the match that he would destroy the letters, he would have mentioned it in his journal. Or had he *not* interfered? Perhaps Ross *had* lied to her after all?

"I found no mention in Father's journals." He came to sit beside her on the settee while she puzzled what he meant. "Not in the journals, but . . . Shaw went by Henry then, you know. He was our first footman and was in charge of the post."

Regina nodded, bracing herself.

"He does not know the reasons, mind you. All that Father told him was that any letters from outside the country, or any with the name Martin or his regiment, Shaw was to bring to Father, regardless of who they were addressed to. It took some time for Shaw to realize that the only correspondence fitting the parameters were addressed to you."

Regina let out the breath she hadn't realized she'd been holding and leaned against the chair back. "He *did* write to me," she said quietly, and in an instant, a different past played through her mind.

This past included letters now and again, which would have made her miss Ross each time she received one, but then her feelings would have mellowed to a contented confidence. She would have worried over him, prayed for him, but known that he carried her in his heart. She would have watched the papers and tracked his regiment's movements, would scarcely have breathed when a new battle was reported, all the while continuing to hope that all would be well. She still would not have gone to London for her season, but she would not have become a governess, either, would not have become engaged to Mr. Corrings.

Because in this past, Ross would not have gone to Spain; he'd have returned to her. And though it would have been later than expected, she would have basked in his return; they would have married in a church. By this day they could have had children of their own.

She did not realize she was crying until she saw in her mind the final scene of what might have been—her and Ross as they were now but in a home of their own, with a son who had Ross's nose, and perhaps a daughter with Regina's honey colored hair. She raised a hand to her mouth to keep from sobbing, but managed to contain herself enough to remove her hand and ask one final question of her brother.

"Why? Why would Father do this to me?"

Timothy shook his head, his expression pained. "I cannot begin to know. But I've the suspicion that he would have seen Mr. Martin as below your station," he said quietly. "I have sent word to Father's solicitor, and I shall oversee a greater study of his records in hopes of finding an answer, but one may not be there, Regina. We may never know."

She stood abruptly and crossed to the rain-streaked

window. "I could have been so happy." She heard her own words and turned back to her brother. "Not that I am not happy with your family Timothy, I didn't mean that."

"I know," he said. "Do you not think I don't go back in time to when Gwen was here and wish that she still were? Perhaps we would have traveled to France when the war was over, as she'd always wanted to. Perhaps I would not be attending our daughter's wedding alone. There is no sin in wishing for something to be different, Regina. Regardless of why it happened, you were wronged. You are justified in your grief."

His sympathy only prompted more tears to fall. "I have lost so much."

"You have not lost your future, however," Timothy said. "You are not seventeen, or twenty-two, or twenty-six, but is there any good reason you can think of for delaying your happiness even one more day?"

She shook her head. It all sounded so obvious when he said it, yet she thought back to last night and the way she'd left Ross. He'd been so hurt. He'd said he would not come for her again. She dropped her chin and looked into her lap. "I was cruel to him, Timothy. I told him to leave me be."

"So you shall *untell* him," Timothy said. "That is, of course, if you want him. If you don't, then you ought to let things be."

"I want him," she said, feeling the longing for another chance in her stomach and chest even as she wrapped her arms around herself. "I have always wanted him."

"You told me once that you did not know whether you loved him."

"I have tried so hard not to, but I can no longer deny it." She lifted her fingers to her lips again and choked on a sob. "What if he will not have me now? What if my treatment of him has destroyed every good thing we could have had? I have been so bitter—I am not the girl I was. What if he cannot love the woman I've become?"

Timothy smiled, but she found no comfort in it. "I feel sure that after all he's done to prove himself, you need not worry about his not returning your affections once you explain them."

"I did not acknowledge his gifts to me," she said, reviewing all of the things that had

happened. "I attacked him at the ball and said horrible things." What if instead, she had fallen into his arms? What if she had kissed him that very night? It hurt to think of the possibilities. "I was so frightened of trusting him, but what if he cannot trust me now?"

"He is in love with you, Regina. Love is bigger than everything you have spoken of here,

and I believe he knows that; otherwise he would never have come. Yes, you are changed, as is he, but you are not so different—you are not unlovable."

It seemed impossible. After how she'd behaved? "I did not return the affections he has shown to me, and now—"

A new voice broke the silence. "You have not forgotten our kiss already, have you?"

Her head snapped up, but she did not dare look to the doorway for several seconds. The sound of footsteps came toward her, and Timothy rose, putting his hand on her shoulder for a moment.

"I believe I shall leave you two alone." He sounded quite pleased with himself.

Regina blinked as she put together bits of information she had ignored until now; Timothy had come in from the stables because he had been riding despite the rain. Had he gone for Mr. Martin while Regina slept? Had he learned the tale from Shaw and gone about repairing the mess she'd made without saying a word?

Legs clad in grey trousers entered her field of vision. She dropped her head again and raised her hands to cover her face. How long had Ross been here? How much had he heard?

She lifted her eyes to his as he smiled down at her.

"Might I sit?" he asked.

She gestured to the place beside her on the settee but kept her eyes on his as he sat beside her. When he reached for her hands, she let him take them.

"Please allow me to introduce myself." He put a hand to his chest before he continued. "My name is Rossen Barkley Martin. I have of late been serving in the King's Royal Army but, thanks to Napoleon's recent imprisonment, I am back in England and determined to make a home in Himley, a place of many happy memories for me. I am unmarried, but hope soon to remedy that situation if I can find a woman with honey hair and bright blue eyes who will make daisy chains and waltz in meadows with me. Do you, perchance, know where I might find such a woman?"

Regina was laughing and crying at the same time, then took a breath so she could speak. "I make wonderful daisy chains," she said in a whisper; it was all she could manage for the moment. "And the very best dances in my memory took place in a meadow not far from here." He smiled while she took a breath. "But I must also inform you that I am quite stubborn sometimes, and . . . independent—not like another girl you might have known before."

"Ah, that is good to know," he said with a nod. "To be equally fair, I should warn you that I have a knee that bothers me quite a lot; sometimes it gives way completely, and I fall most awkwardly to the ground. I also have a collection of scars I may need to explain in the future, to say nothing of my poor eyesight. While it is not terrible, it is easier to find my spectacles when I need them if I simply keep them on my nose." He tapped the spectacles for emphasis. "I do not always sleep soundly, and I have developed a great appetite for mushrooms, though as a younger man, I hated them on principle."

Regina laughed again, scarcely able to believe that any of this was happening. "I am quite the opposite. I once liked mushrooms, but find that of recent years, I can tolerate them only if they are chopped very fine."

Ross pulled his eyebrows together and seemed to thoroughly contemplate the information. "How about strawberry tarts? Might they still be your favorite?"

"Indeed they are, sir."

"Oh, you need not be so formal with me. It would make me ever so happy if you would call me Ross. And you are?"

"Regina Weathers."

With the introduction, she was unable to resist moving in for a kiss, allowing her lips to linger on his and admit that though she might be a spinster of thirty-two years, her heart was young enough to begin again, just as he'd asked; just as she'd been sure she could not. Fifteen years and he was here again, willing to love the woman she'd become, wanting to share a life with her.

She pulled back from the kiss enough to add, "But you may call me Reggie."

ABOUT JOSI S. KILPACK

Josi S. Kilpack is the author of more than twenty novels, which include women's fiction, romance, mystery, and suspense. *Wedding Cake*, the final book in her Sadie Hoffmiller culinary mystery series, was released in December 2014 and her first Regency romance novel, *A Heart Revealed*, came out in April 2015.

Josi and her husband, Lee, are the parents of four children and live in Northern Utah. In addition to writing, Josi loves to read, bake, and travel. She's completed six half marathons to date, but may never run another because right now she hates running and does hot yoga instead.

Author website: JosiSKilpack.com
Blog: www.josikilpack.blogspot.com
Twitter: @JosiSKilpack

The Affair at Wildemoore

by Annette Lyon

OTHER WORKS BY ANNETTE LYON

Band of Sisters
Coming Home
The Newport Ladies Book Club series
A Portrait for Toni
At the Water's Edge
Lost Without You
Done & Done
There, Their, They're: A No-Tears Guide to Grammar from the Word Nerd

One

The Pembrokes of Wildemoore Hall were hosting a house party with some fifteen guests, if the reports were true, and tonight a ball would honor the party. Families from miles around would attend, including Mrs. Ellen Stanhope and her daughters. Her husband, Mr. Anthony Stanhope, had yet to return from estate business but would in all likelihood arrive home in time to make an appearance.

In three quarters of an hour, the ball would begin, which meant that Ellen and her daughters should be departing at once. If she'd had her wish, they would have departed as soon as Cornsby had brought about the carriage, some fifteen minutes hence, and yet it stood out front waiting, while she stood inside, waiting for her daughters to finish their toilette.

Ellen paced the front hall, wondering whether to send one of the maids up to check on the girls, although Diana's maid, Rose, was already there, of course.

Mrs. Wimbley, the housekeeper, came down the hall and eyed the staircase. "Shall I go see if something is the matter?"

Something inside Ellen's heart tweaked the slightest bit—perhaps mother's intuition—so instead of sending Mrs. Wimbley upstairs, she said, "I think I'll check on them myself, but thank you, Mrs. Wimbley."

"Very well, Mrs. Stanhope," the housekeeper said as Ellen marched to the stairs and went up.

Not a minute later, she opened Diana's bedroom door to find all three of her daughters inside, bustling about, talking in whispers and then laughing at whatever another had said. To Ellen's relief, her two younger daughters, Catherine and Mary-Anne, appeared to be ready—fully dressed, with their hair up, curled and tied with ribbons. Catherine wore a necklace with a single pearl resting in the hollow of her throat, and Mary-Anne had fresh pink roses pinned to her dress and woven into her hair.

But Diana's hair was down, and instead of wearing one of her ball gowns, she stood before a full-length mirror in the corner and held up two gowns, taking turns placing the pale-blue taffeta in front of the brown silk, then tilting her head as she considered one dress, only to switch it with the other, tilt her head the other direction, and bite her lip with indecision.

Her maid stood to the side, holding yet two more gowns and looking flushed. Tendrils had escaped her bun and had curled as a result of the exertion it took to dress her charge.

At Ellen's entrance, the poor maid's face blanched white. "I'm so sorry they're not ready, Mrs. Stanhope," Rose said, bobbing at the knee and lowering her gaze to the floor. "I've been trying—"

"It's quite all right," Ellen said. "It's not your fault that my eldest daughter is suddenly obsessed with fashion." She crossed to the mirror and admired the yellow silk, which Diana was now considering along with the brown, having taken it from Rose's hands after shoving away earlier.

"Yellow becomes your hair," Ellen said. "And that gown has always been a favorite of yours." The words were all true in spite of her motives for saying them—hoping to hasten the decision.

"I just . . . don't . . . know . . ." Diana sighed. "Which color do you think—" Her voice cut off so quickly that her mother knew quite well Diana was hiding something. Had there been any doubt about the matter, the look that plainly showed a fear of discovery, which Diana gave her two sisters, only confirmed her suspicions.

Ellen took the brown dress from Diana's hand and returned it to Rose. "Put this one away as well. Miss Stanhope will be wearing the yellow."

"Yes'm," Rose said, bobbing again, then shooting Diana a worried look before hurrying to return the gowns to the wardrobe.

For a moment, the three young women said nothing, remarkably silent—which might as well have been a flag waving the message that they were harboring a secret. Ellen sat on the small bench at Diana's vanity table and clasped her hands, trying to look at ease rather than rushed and annoyed at the continued delay. Had she known her family would be late, she wouldn't have ordered the carriage already. She hated making anyone wait—or being made to wait, either— and that included the help as well as the Pembrokes.

"So tell me . . . what is the gentleman's name?" Ellen asked, keeping her voice as light as possible.

Catherine's and Mary-Anne's eyes widened with surprise, and they looked at each other, as if shocked that their mother had figured something out—as if Ellen hadn't been young once herself, with the same idealized view of the world and men and romance. She turned her gaze to Diana, eyebrows raised in question. In spite of herself, Ellen couldn't help but be a bit entertained at seeing bright pink buds brightening her daughter's cheeks and Diana averting her gaze from her mother's.

"I . . ." Diana seemed to study the rug's design with an intensity no floor covering could justify, as if she hadn't seen this very rug every day of her life. "What I meant to say . . ."

When her voice trailed off again, Ellen debated whether to let her daughter squirm a little longer but decided to put the girl out of her misery. "I remember," she said gently. "When I met your father, I was about your age, you know."

The words made her heart ache a bit. She missed those days, when, more than two decades previous, she'd believed that she'd achieved what so many other women never had—marrying the perfect man. That he would always set her heart beating fast, whisper in her ear about her beauty, about how she was nothing short of an angel sent from heaven to live among mortals. In short, that she would live happily, in romantic bliss, for the rest of her days.

Of course, such fairy dreams don't last, and as was so often the case, she hadn't thought past the wedding altar. The bliss and euphoria of becoming Mrs. Anthony Stanhope had lasted a few years, but eventually it faded, so slowly, in the face of hum-drum reality that even she hadn't noticed until the bliss had evaporated completely as the morning dew in the sun. Ellen still prided herself on the fact that she and her husband had never had a genuine row. They had never disagreed so hotly that they raised their voices or became so angry that they spent days in simmering silence. She'd known of plenty women who complained of such things.

No, she and Anthony had simply grown apart. First it

was his business trips to London and regarding the estate, which she never resented, of course; a landed gentleman must manage his affairs. And she'd found herself more busy in managing the household, especially as she'd discovered that she had a knack for such things as schedules and menus and budgets and discussing issues with Mrs. Wimbley and Hughes, the butler.

And through those same years, of course, came one daughter and then another and another; Ellen had spent nearly nine months with each confinement flat on her back, unable to bear the smell of food or keep down more than a sip or two of broth and the occasional biscuit with tea. Her maid had ensured that few people ever bothered her during her confinement, which at the time, in her misery, she'd viewed as a good thing. She often wondered now, though, whether Anthony had ever wanted to see her during those months of constant illness. Had he worried over her wellbeing? Had he taken notice of her absence at the dinner table, or had he been so busy with the estate and hosting guests and who knew what else that he'd noted her empty chair but hadn't ever *missed* her?

Their fourth and final child, a boy, had died at birth, and that was when Ellen had wanted her Anthony back. She'd needed to be held in the arms of the one man whom she could cry with, who could hold her in his strong arms and assure her that all would be well, that he would stay with her as long as she wanted him to. But after the stillbirth of baby William, her husband hadn't come to her, at least not in that way. He'd visited her, of course, and when he'd come to her room, he'd spoken in solemn, sad tones.

She'd yearned for him to sit on her bed and pull her into his arms, to whisper into her ear about how sorry he was. To cry with her. But by then, none of that was possible because they'd become near strangers. *Of course* he wouldn't have sat down or done any other such thing that belonged to those who were truly intimate. As they had once been but were no longer. She didn't ask him to mourn with her, and he didn't ask it of her either.

Even now, twelve years later, she didn't know what *he* had felt—what he yet felt—about the loss of his only son.

She still missed the man she married. She missed the woman he'd married too, for that matter. How had she changed so much that her own husband didn't know how to speak to her in anything but cordial, polite tones?

"Mother?" Catherine said, pulling Ellen out of her thoughts.

"I'm sorry," she said, realizing that the girls had returned to their chatter about dresses—Rose had even brought back the pale-blue taffeta for additional consideration. "I got distracted for a moment." She smoothed her dress, cleared her throat, and tried again, although this time, maintaining her composure proved challenging for a reason other than impatience. "Diana, my sweet girl, the color of your dress won't matter. I am sure that, whoever he is, he's already smitten with you. When he sees you tonight, he will see nothing but the stars in your eyes, I assure you."

Truth. A bitter truth, for Ellen remembered Anthony looking at her that way.

Diana smiled softly, clearly pleased, but when she spoke, her voice had a tone of suspicion in it. "Are you earnest? Or are you saying so just to get me dressed quickly? I know we'll be late, but—"

"I'm quite sincere, I assure you," Ellen said. "And yet . . ." She hesitated, not sure if she dared give the advice she so wanted to. After all, at the age of her eldest daughter, she wouldn't have paid any heed to such words.

"Mother, what is it? You seem so serious all at once." Diana handed Catherine the yellow gown, then pulled a short stool closer and sat on it, leaning toward Ellen, an expression of concern etched in her features.

Ellen looked from one daughter to the next, taking in the image of each one and wondering where, indeed, the time had gone. It hadn't been so long ago that she'd held each of them in her arms. She took a deep breath and gave her best advice. "I want you all to remember that a *good* match is what is most important—a man who can provide and care for you and your future children. A man with a reputation and honor to uphold. Emotion and romance is all well and good, but—"

"Oh, I *adore* Lord Byron's poetry," Mary-Anne said, mock-swooning onto the bed. "I could read his romantic poems all night long and never tire of them."

"That is the very thing I am cautioning you against," Ellen said, smiling sadly. She was quite serious now that the subject had been broached. "A man who is worthy of your love needn't be the kind who dances best or who most sets your heart aflutter."

"Oh, Mother," Catherine said with a giant sigh. "Let us have some fun while we're young."

With one finger raised, Ellen went on. "I never said you couldn't enjoy yourselves, only that the time will come when—"

"If memory serves," Diana interrupted. "You were quite smitten with Father. Or so I've heard."

Now it was Ellen's turn to blush. "I was indeed, and he with me, if I may say so. He was devastatingly handsome."

"And a wonderful dancer?" Catherine asked, clearly baiting her. "You married the man who set *your* heart aflutter, and it all worked out. Why shouldn't we do the same? There's no need to pick *either* a good match or being in love. I say, choose both." She turned to Diana. "Which brings us back to the moment. I don't want to miss any more of the ball at Wildemoore than we already will have. Wear the yellow, won't you? Rose can fix your hair in a snap, and we can be on our way."

When Diana seemed to soften, even taking the gown back, Mary-Anne spoke up, clearly wanting to add her own log to the fire. "Besides, I'm sure Mr. Whitcomb will be quite prompt, and you don't want him dancing with too many other young women simply because you aren't there, do you?"

Her tone was teasing, but Diana's reaction was anything but. If looks could sew a mouth shut, Mary-Anne would never have spoken again.

Ellen had been so close to getting Diana dressed, although she considered the conversation a success if only because she now knew the name of her daughter's beau. She tried to ease the tension by first, not reacting immediately to the name, and second, by standing and walking toward the door to the hall.

She opened it, but before going out, said, "Mr. Whitcomb, is it? He is quite handsome, isn't he? He comes from a good family, and from what little I know of him, he might well be a very good match."

She grinned at her daughters and walked out, rather pleased with herself for leaving them speechless. But when she closed the door behind her, a waterfall of memories rushed into her mind, one after the other, bringing with it a wellspring of long-buried emotions.

She remembered times in past years when she'd seen glimpses of the Anthony Stanhope she'd fallen in love with, when she'd felt the same love of old rush forth anew. When she'd seen glimpses of the same love returned in his eyes.

But as sweet as those memories were, the most recent such memories were from several years ago.

I did make a good match, and I have a good life, she thought as she made her way back down the stairs. *It may not be the life I thought I would have, but it is a good one, and I'm happy.*

Then why couldn't she stop wondering if she could have prevented her and Anthony from drifting apart?

And why, a little voice in her heart demanded, if romance was as silly as she'd implied to her daughter, were tears blurring her vision at the idea that she could have lost Anthony's love forever?

Two

Anthony Stanhope had spent an exhausting week away from home and felt quite eager to return to Rosewood. He thought of what food might be awaiting him, for Cook was excellent at her trade. Asparagus with the perfect hollandaise sauce, perhaps. With roasted duck and her special gravy. With bread pudding.

It would not matter much, however, in light of the fact that he'd be eating it alone, and the food would quite likely be cold, for the rest of the family had surely eaten already. He'd be lucky to get a bit before quickly changing and heading out to the Pembrokes' ball. He never had been one to enjoy balls much. Even in his courting days, he preferred other activities, but he religiously attended any ball Ellen did, just to be near her. Heavens, he would have found a way to visit the stars if it meant dancing with her.

Even now he didn't mind the dancing itself—it was the crowds he objected to. He was quite a good dancer, although no one would ever hear him say such a thing. Now, on the unusual occasion that his wife showed an inclination for a reel, he took her to the floor, and otherwise, he did his gentlemanly duty of giving a few women a dance partner throughout the night. Ellen rarely danced anymore; now she tended to sit at the edges of the room, with several old crones who shared the latest gossip, no doubt, though Ellen was neither old nor a crone.

He'd have much preferred to stay home, but tonight he couldn't very well justify doing so when the host was George Pembroke, a man who had been somewhat of a mentor to Anthony when he'd first taken over the estate from his father. He owed much to the old man, and tonight, that meant putting on evening wear and making the trip to Wildemoore alone, hours after the rest of his family had gone, then staying fashionably long enough to be polite.

As his valet helped him dress, and as he rode in the carriage through the darkness, Anthony harbored two hopes: that he could find a way to leave the ball early—perhaps find Pembroke early, chat for several minutes, and make his escape without the host or anyone else noticing; and second, barring a quick escape, that the ball itself would be a relatively painless event. He had low expectations on both counts but decided to hedge his bets anyway.

So after alighting, he instructed his driver not to unhitch the horses unless told to do so. Anthony had every intention of departing within half an hour. "I'll send word if I find I will be longer."

"Of course, Mr. Stanhope." The driver flicked the reins and drove toward the carriage house.

Anthony girded his loins and walked up the steps into Pembroke's mansion.

Inside, the servants gestured the way to the ballroom, bowing as they did so and saying, "Nice to see you," and, "Good evening, Mr. Stanhope."

Anthony nodded and smiled in return, but he didn't strike up any conversation. Walking with quick strides down the hall, he stepped into the ballroom and surveyed the room, looking for the host. To make a proper appearance, Anthony would likely need to dance at least once. He would also need to find his family, with whom he could carry on a bit of lively conversation for others to observe. *Lively* described most things that happened with Catherine nearby.

Such a shame that Ellen rarely danced; the evening would have been far more endurable if he could take her, rather than one of the women from town, to the dance floor. They always seemed flustered, babbling about uninteresting hearsay, as if they believed he would care about whose daughter was rumored to be courted by whom, or which estate had lost money due to poor investments. He'd much rather have a quiet evening by the fire with a book in his lap, a glass of wine in hand, and Ellen with her own book beside him.

His mind flashed to a time shortly after they'd wed, when Ellen had regularly joined him in the library. She'd often read to him, leaning against his shoulder as he listened, sipped wine, and played with the curls at her neck that had fallen from her chignon. He could still remember the softness of her skin, her faint scent of lavender.

His pulse began to pound at the thought, and he paused and took a deep breath to compose himself. He hadn't thought of those newlywed evenings for years. In fact, he'd made a point of forgetting them, because the present hardly resembled them. The only clear commonality was that the master and mistress of Rosewood bore the same names as those of that happy couple. But they no longer looked like the same young, star-eyed youths they'd been when Anthony had carried his bride across the threshold of their home, up the stairs, and into his bedchamber.

A mirror hung on the wall beside him, and he studied his reflection. His hair had thinned on top and had threads of gray throughout. His face now bore a few creases across the forehead, around his mouth and eyes. And the trousers his tailor made for him of late were much larger than before. He turned from the mirror.

The differences in us are more than external. The reminder felt like a stab to the heart. He could hardly imagine Ellen joining him in the library anymore, let alone wanting to be close enough for him to wind her curls about his finger as she read him poetry.

But that was all a thing of the past. Time to return to his duty. He tugged the bottom of his waistcoat, cleared his throat, and stepped forward as if bearding a lion in its den.

No sooner had he taken three steps than he heard a high voice exclaim, "My goodness, Mr. Stanhope, is it really you?"

The voice seemed vaguely familiar, but he couldn't place it. He looked about, trying to find the owner. He needn't have; an older woman in a bright-pink gown and feathers in her hair suddenly stood at his side and had somehow slipped her hand through his arm without his noticing. She walked him forward.

"After all these years! I've been at Wildemoore for a week now without seeing a glimpse of my old neighbor and friend." She leaned in. "Or, I suppose I could say, my old *beau*." She snickered and straightened.

And that was the moment Stanhope knew with no uncertainty the identity of the woman. "Why, Amelia Fletcher. I don't believe we've seen each other for at least twenty years."

"Twenty-one and three quarters," she said. "But who's counting? And it's Mrs. Beauchamp now, of course."

"Yes, of course," Stanhope said, remembering the

wealthy nobleman who'd swept into the lives of their small town so long ago and who had, in the process, swept Miss Amelia Fletcher off her feet. "And how is Mr. Beauchamp? Is he in the party as well?"

"I'm afraid not," Mrs. Beauchamp said, her voice dropping ever so slightly, as if putting on an air of sadness. "Consumption took him two years ago."

"I'm sorry to hear that."

Mrs. Beauchamp shrugged. "My eldest son, Thomas, runs the estate now, and he does a fine job, if I may say so. Well enough that ever since my mourning ended, I've often left for weeks or months at a time, visiting friends in the country or doing whatever else I please. It's quite a comfort to a woman in my position, I tell you."

"Yes, I can imagine it would be," Anthony said, although her words puzzled him. Her laughter and flirtatious behavior seemed entirely at odds with her having lost a husband. Perhaps she was more private than she'd once been, holding back her true emotions until she could find a moment to herself behind a closed door. He well understood that way of going about the world. He'd become a consummate actor in wearing the proper social masks to hide his true feelings.

But he hadn't always been so. Back when he and Ellen used to read together, then discuss their respective books over breakfast the following morning, the show of feelings had been different between them. They'd ridden on horseback together and had picnics. And during particularly busy times, when they couldn't get away for a picnic or spend long hours together in the library, they still exchanged small words, looks, and touches throughout their day. More, they'd shared their deepest thoughts and feelings, whether those were burdens or joys.

When had he last shared a burden with Ellen? A joy? He couldn't remember.

And that, in itself, was a burden—that he no longer confided his heartache and trouble to her. But Ellen did seem to appreciate a strong man who kept the estate's affairs in order and who simply stayed out of her way. So he did.

They moved in entirely different spheres now, ones that did not touch. Were he to attempt to reach across the chasm separating them, and express how much he missed her, she might well rebuff him. He wasn't sure, but the fact that he didn't know proved the point: they'd become strangers.

She'd grown into a strong woman, one he no longer needed to protect as he had when she was nineteen. Now, if he were to admit to sorrow, she might laugh at the supposed weakness of such a statement. Better to remain quiet altogether and hope for his marriage to remain cordial and polite for the remainder of their days. Such a life wouldn't bring him the happiness he'd once possessed over being her husband, but at least he would retain her respect.

That is about all I can hope for now. He had his daughters' futures to account for now. Making sure they had secure futures with good husbands—that needed to be his focus.

"Are you even listening to me?"

Mrs. Beauchamp's voice finally came to his attention, and Stanhope wondered just how long she'd been talking without his hearing a word. A dance ended, and those on the floor applauded the musicians. Not wanting to offend Mrs. Beauchamp by having to answer her question and admit he hadn't been listening, he decided to make his appearance on the floor sooner than later.

Anthony nodded toward the dance floor. "Unless you are otherwise engaged, would you do the honor of joining me in the next dance?"

She put a hand to her breast and batted her lashes as if she were a fifteen-year-old receiving her first offer. "Yes, of course," she said demurely, this time putting her hand out and letting it hang in the air, waiting for him to take it and walk her to the floor.

So he did. The dance felt longer than most. As he led Mrs. Beauchamp through the steps, he wondered if his eagerness for the song to end was simply a matter of being fatigued from his trip, or whether Mrs. Beauchamp and her prattling nonsense were the reasons. Likely some of both.

She hadn't always been this way, had she? He tried to remember, but at first the details of their brief courtship remained hazy; he hadn't thought of those days in far too long. Miss Amelia Fletcher had been the one girl every young man had had his eye on. She'd been like pollen to bees, attracting swarms of young men vying for her slightest attention. A smile aimed in the right direction had often been enough for a young man to float in ecstasy for days. So when she'd expressed a preference for a certain Anthony Stanhope, he'd been the envy of every man within leagues.

As they danced and Mrs. Beauchamp smiled flirtatiously his way, Anthony remembered more. In his youthful immaturity, he'd enjoyed the status that having Amelia Fletcher on his arm had given him, but the excitement had waned quickly.

She had not a single original thought in her head, and no desire to talk about anything he found interesting: art, music, literature, history. For her, conversation, such as it was, consisted entirely of fashion, hairstyles, and balls, with local gossip sprinkled in for good measure. Anthony had wanted to end the whole affair, but he'd always been a bit too soft-hearted for his own good, so instead of injuring Miss Fletcher, he'd determined to endure her, comforting himself with the fact that, from a societal standpoint, theirs would indeed be a good match.

So it had been a great relief for Anthony when Charles Beauchamp had arrived in town and swept Miss Fletcher away in a torrent of poetic passion that rivaled Lord Byron himself. When he read of their trip to the altar not too many months later, Anthony had breathed an enormous sigh of relief.

He'd almost decided to stop attending balls altogether, no matter whom he offended in the process, when he was formally introduced to one Miss Ellen Burton. They'd seen each other at some prior events, and he'd always admired her quiet, yet stunning, beauty—a beauty that didn't call out for others to admire her. She had a way of dressing and speaking and carrying herself that was clearly at home with and confident in who she was, with no pretense or efforts to impress. After Amelia, he'd found such qualities in Ellen to be nothing short of angelic. Upon further acquaintance, she'd proved to be precisely the kind of woman Anthony couldn't help but fall hopelessly in love with.

Yet here he danced again, wishing that Amelia Beauchamp, née Fletcher, now widowed, was his dear Ellen. Instead, his partner continued on and on, chattering about what she believed to be a foolish trend in hats and even pointing out examples of fashion sins in the room.

How could the woman in the blue tolerate wearing a dress a full *three* years out of fashion? And that gown there—the fit on that spinster was positively atrocious; the gold satin looked ridiculous simply hanging on its owner. The girl probably had no idea she looked like a stuffed doll in it.

To his credit, Stanhope never let his smile waver or his voice crack. He nodded when appropriate, avoided responding at all to her verbal barbs at his neighbors, and otherwise endured, grateful for the moments when partners separated, and growing ever more certain that this was the longest dance in history.

When at long last the final strains of the violins ended, Anthony sighed—then hoped Mrs. Beauchamp hadn't noticed. He bowed, holding one of her hands in his. "It was a pleasure to see you again after all this time." Straightening, he moved to walk off the floor, where he spotted his wife sitting with several other women.

In spite of the noise and tumult of the crowd, she quickly turned from her neighbor and looked straight at him, as if he'd called her name. He smiled, and she returned it, although hers seemed more of a friendly recognition than anything else.

"Oh, but I can't let you go so easily as all that," Mrs. Beauchamp said, and again wound her arm about his.

Anthony tried to find some excuse to extricate himself but, loath to offend, flashed another smile. "Oh?"

She leaned in, brought a finger to her lips, and kissed it, then placed the same finger on his temple, which she then drew down his cheek, whispering, "I've missed you so, Mr. Stanhope. I hope that perhaps we may . . . *rekindle* our friendship." With that, she released his arm and walked away, directly in front of him, no doubt so he could see her figure as she departed.

For a moment, he could do nothing but gape, his mouth hanging open. She couldn't possibly think he'd . . .

Even if other men of his class philandered quietly—and some not so quietly—he wasn't that type of man. For Mrs. Beauchamp, of course, a woman who had been married—and well—her good reputation was almost impossible to destroy. She had nothing to lose. Neither did he, as far as reputation. He clamped his mouth shut.

But I do have much to lose in Ellen. Or I hope I do.

How long had he and Ellen been living two separate lives? Until tonight, he hadn't given thought to how things had once been, not for far too long. But now that the memories had been dusted off, they sent him yearning again for the intimacy he and Ellen had once shared.

Would that tonight, they would read in the library, perhaps different novels, but sitting together, pausing to comment on a line before delving back into the story. Perhaps sitting on the settee, with Ellen's feet tucked under her, his arm around her shoulders, her head resting against his.

Or she could read beside him in his bed as they had once done with some regularity. He imagined Ellen fluffing the pillow beside him as he told her of Mrs. Beauchamps' ridiculous hint. He pictured Ellen laughing herself silly, then saying something about how Mrs. Beauchamp was right in envying the life they'd made together. She'd lift her chin and kiss his jaw. He'd take the invitation, kissing her back with the deepest feelings a man could have . . .

He sighed. All of that was far in the past and unlikely to happen again. How it had all been lost, and so completely, he didn't know, although he suspected it was in large part due to the simple neglect of the things he most treasured. He'd forgotten to tend the garden of their love, and when he'd finally come back to it, the weeds had overtaken the glory that had once been there: Ellen's love had withered.

Whatever the reason, their lives were different now, but he would *not* chase the garish "beauty" of Mrs. Beauchamp.

She didn't really mean she wanted to rekindle . . .

No, he decided. He'd misinterpreted her. Women didn't simply fawn over men they hadn't seen in over a score of years. She'd suggested they rekindle their *friendship*, nothing more. He had many lady friends. Another would be acceptable, if not entirely welcome.

Whenever the Pembrokes' house party concluded, she would depart, and he wouldn't again worry about spending another minute with her and her judgments about his friends and neighbors.

Feeling better, Anthony managed a genuine smile. He tugged his waistcoat and moved in Ellen's direction, but he looked at her and saw her stricken face—eyes wide and red, her lips pressed together. He knew that look as well as his own reflection, though he hadn't seen it in a long time; it was the tell-tale sign of her holding back emotions in an attempt to not cry. She looked wounded, and judging by the pain in her eyes, wounded by *him*.

The realization made Anthony paused in his step. What had he done to cause such a reaction? Should he have not greeted her? Should he have not danced with her at all? Did she wish he'd skipped the ball altogether? Had he forgotten some important duty at home?

Baffled, he gave his wife what he hoped was a cheerful smile, but in response, all she did was stand and hurry away.

There had been a time when he would have already known what troubled her. Now, he not only didn't have any idea, but he also had no way to provide a balm for her pain.

I could follow her and ask her to confide in me. But would such an act yield fruit aside from formalities and quiet assurances that she was quite well, thank you very much?

That's what she would say, for that was how they dealt with each other of late.

Yet he wanted to be the one to comfort her, to fix whatever was amiss. *I gave up that right*, he supposed, when he'd let her drift away like dandelion fluff in the wind.

A flurry of brown moved near the doors—Ellen's dress.

With Amelia Beauchamp's figure and voice and fluttering eyelashes completely forgotten, Anthony found himself moving that direction at an increasingly rapid pace, despite the knowledge that he was embarking on a fool's mission.

His aim remained entirely on comforting his wife. His mission might be in vain, but he had to try.

Three

A headache began throbbing beneath Ellen's right temple. She walked faster anyway, needing to free herself of the stuffy, hot ballroom. She needed air. Perhaps a bit of a chill would do her good—it would wake her up from childish fantasies and fairy tales and bring her back to reality. No more wishing for a past that could not return. No more hoping that maybe her Anthony—her intelligent, strong-yet-gentle, and yes, handsome Anthony—still loved her, somewhere in his heart.

Is he my *Anthony any longer?*

The thought forced a strangled cry from her throat; she covered her mouth to hold the sound in, hoping no one had heard. She lifted her skirts and began to run blindly through the corridors. She'd been to Wildemoore many times before but, in her emotional state, couldn't remember where to find one of the balconies, where she could get some fresh air. The door was somewhere upstairs, so she hurried up the long staircase. Her emotions clouded her thinking, and she couldn't find her way in the halls.

The Affair at Wildemoore

All she could think about was how beautiful and young Amelia still looked in spite of the intervening years. How her dress was the height of fashion, how her hair was swept back in the latest style, adorned with beads and feathers. Nothing like Ellen's own simple gown of brown silk, or the plain hairstyle she'd chosen, its only accent being a matching ribbon.

How plain she felt—and old and downright simplistic—compared with Amelia. The two women had never met, but Ellen remembered well the stories about how Anthony had been entirely smitten with her, only for Amelia to run away and marry another man.

Ellen had hoped to go to her grave without ever laying eyes on the woman.

Not recognizing the hall she found herself in, Ellen stopped and looked around. She was lost. While she could likely find her way back, she didn't want to do so anytime soon, for fear that an arriving or departing guest would see her. No, she needed to remain unseen for the moment so she could compose herself.

Fresh air seemed to be out of her reach, however, so Ellen hurried down a hall, peeking into doorways and passing up bedchambers and other private areas she couldn't very well violate. Her slippers padded along the carpet quietly, but her breath had become quick and labored with the exercise—and, quite frankly, with the sudden shock of seeing Amelia Fletcher hanging on her husband's arm. Flirting mercilessly with him—that alone had been hard to watch; yet had that been all, Ellen would have shrugged the moment off and continued her conversation with Mrs. Cooley.

But Amelia's behavior had elicited a reaction: Anthony had offered the woman his most charming of smiles and had promptly asked her to dance, as if he couldn't wait to be near her again.

Silly, Ellen chided herself as she hurried down another hallway. *He dances with many women at many balls.* As did virtually all men, married or not. Nothing scandalous or upsetting there.

But this was *Amelia* he'd grinned at—and had danced with so hurriedly. Amelia, who had always eclipsed Ellen in both beauty and elegance. Amelia, who had a way of speaking and walking that seemed to leave sophistication in her wake. She even had a more elaborate name; *Ellen* seemed horribly plain beside *Amelia.*

Anthony must think so too, she thought, unable any longer to hold back the tears that had been blurring her vision. They tumbled down her cheeks and onto her gown, making dark dots in the silk. *No one must see me this way.* The urgency she'd felt before only increased.

As she rounded a corner, she caught a glimpse of a shadow. Her stomach dropping with dread, she hurried into the nearest room, hoping that whoever the person was, they hadn't seen her and wouldn't follow. By some stroke of luck, she found herself in a library. She snatched a book from a shelf; then, on the toes of her slippers, she hurried to the far end of the room. She dropped onto a wingback chair and opened the book, pretending to read. Perhaps if the person in the hall peered in, they'd see nothing amiss—just a woman reading a book—and continue on their way. Although she had to admit, now that she had the book open, the lampless room was far too dark to read in, and therefore her ruse would be unlikely to fool anyone.

By the door, the floor creaked, as if someone had stepped into the library. Ellen held her breath and moved not a muscle save her eyelids, which she closed, praying that she wouldn't be noted or, if that was impossible, that she would be ignored and not spoken to.

More creaks, followed by the sound of shoes on wood, which meant the person had entered and was walking along the edge of the room, not on the rug as she had done. Ellen forced herself to keep still, to not look over. She comforted herself with the thought that at least her tears would be hidden in the darkness, provided she could keep herself from sniffling. At that realization, and unwilling to take chances, she gently tugged a handkerchief from the cuff of her sleeve and held it to her nose.

"Ellen?"

At the sound of her husband's voice, shock, confusion, and something else erupted in her chest.

He used my Christian name.

That was something not even married couples typically did, something Anthony hadn't done since the death of their little William. She wanted to cry out with her husband's name, but the image of him showering attention upon the flirting, stunning Amelia, made Ellen hold her tongue.

She turned her head in his direction and raised her brows, in spite of the fact that he likely couldn't see her face. "Mmm?" Words would betray her tears and make her cry harder.

Anthony pulled a chair toward hers and sat upon it. "Are you well? You seemed upset when you left the ballroom."

A long time ago, when he used to ask after her wellbeing, he'd always reached for her, touched her in some way. Now her hands ached to be held by his. As a precaution she dabbed the handkerchief against her nose again, swallowed hard to clear the knot in her throat, and managed, "Quite well." Two words with an entirely neutral tone.

Well done, Ellen.

"I see you are reacquainted with Mrs. Beauchamp." The words forced themselves out of her mouth; she hadn't meant to say more, and she wanted to call them back.

"I did," he said vaguely. "Mr. Beauchamp has passed, apparently."

"I see." She didn't yet trust herself to speak more than a few words without her voice cracking. Her mind whirled.

Did Anthony still regret losing Amelia to Charles Beauchamp? Was he even now wondering what his life would have been like with her instead? If he'd have a living heir—or several sons?

She'd heard plenty of stories during their courtship—and after—about how everyone for miles around had been quite sure that Amelia Fletcher would marry Anthony Stanhope.

When Anthony first proposed, Ellen had been so certain of his love. But now she looked at those memories with suspicion. Had he showered affections upon Ellen as a way to nurse his wounds after Amelia had broken his heart and married someone else?

Had Ellen been then—and was she still—his second choice?

"Have you fallen ill?" Anthony asked. Now he reached for her hand, which she let him take, but only just.

She readied herself to snatch it back. "I'm a bit tired, is all." A lie, if there ever was one. The first she'd blatantly told her husband.

But, as she pondered further, not necessarily the only one. She'd hidden her true feelings thousands of times over the years as he'd withdrawn from her to someplace she could not go. After failing to reach him so many times, she'd finally resolved to live in such way that the cooling of his feelings would be of no consequence to her.

She'd had to make that resolution, or she would have gone mad. And while a woman with her social standing could do some things without raising eyebrows or causing a scandal, going mad was not one of them. So she supposed she hadn't been entirely honest with him over the years, but this was her first outright falsehood.

Anthony pressed her hand between his in a gesture so tender that she wanted to curl onto his lap and be held.

"Did you just return from London, then?" she managed.

"I did. I'm a bit tired, but I suppose that my coming was a good thing." He chuckled. "Though seeing Mrs. Beauchamp was quite a surprise."

"Indeed." Ellen slipped her hand out and put it back into her lap with the other. He had to mention her again? "She doesn't look a day over thirty. She's quite beautiful. Don't you agree?" She held her breath in the hopes that he would contradict her evaluation.

"She's exactly as she always was," Anthony said, but Ellen couldn't quite read his tone.

Amelia was exactly as she was when he'd loved her? As beautiful and desirable? Did he still love her, then? Had he only now realized as much?

Many a man of name had a mistress, some openly. Ellen had often been grateful that at least her husband would never do such a thing. But now . . . perhaps she should have expected this as inevitable. If love had dried up in one place, only to appear, resurrected, in another, could she blame him?

Ellen felt as if her heart had been pierced by an arrow. He'd practically admitted he still loved Amelia, for if a man still loved his own wife, he would discount the beauty of another woman. Yet how could he have ever thought that Ellen herself had ever been beautiful? She'd never been plain, exactly, but her features, when compared with those of Amelia's, would always be found wanting.

She hoped she was overreacting, that her husband had no intention of meeting Amelia after the ball or of blowing on the embers of their old love to renew the flame.

She had to ask. Grateful for the darkness, she managed, "Then I assume you'll be seeing quite a lot of Mrs. Beauchamp after tonight?"

He hardly paused to consider the question before saying, "I imagine I will."

She could feel another cry threatening to escape, so she clenched her teeth so hard that her jaw hurt. Better that than showing weakness. She'd never been one to bend or break. She might not be beautiful, but she was strong, and she intended to prove her mettle as much to herself as to her husband.

She stood. "Would please you call for the carriage?"

"Of course," he said, standing as well. "I told my man to wait for word before unhitching the horses; he won't be but a moment."

Anthony reached forward, and in the shadows of the library, Ellen held her breath as a flicker of hope danced through her middle. Would he touch her face? Maybe press a kiss to her cheek? She did not dare hope for more.

But all he did was reach for the book she still held in one hand and take it from her. She expected him to ask what she'd been reading, but with the moonlight through the windows as the only illumination, the lettering was too dark to make out. Besides, they both knew she hadn't really been reading.

He tossed the book onto a nearly table. "Do you remember how we used to read together in the library?" He took a step closer, and Ellen could feel his warmth. She wanted to reach up, to draw his face to hers, to kiss him soundly as she'd once felt she had the privilege of doing whenever she wanted to. She hadn't felt such things in so long that the idea flummoxed her. She wasn't nineteen or twenty any longer. This was all foolishness. She couldn't bear to give her heart to Anthony all over again, only to have him choose Amelia.

"Of course I remember," she said.

She'd never forget the time he'd read a portion of *The Diary of William Pepys* in ridiculous voices, or the time she'd convinced him to give William Blake's poetry a try. She would cherish those memories for the rest of her life.

She rarely saw Anthony disheveled, but now and again, she caught him late at night when his beard had grown in a bit. Such sights always took her back to their nights in the library, where he'd often kissed her, short and sweet at first, then their kisses growing longer and more passionate as they set their books aside. She'd loved the feel of his stubble under her hands as she held his face.

No stubble tonight, surely. No doubt he'd shaved before coming to the ball. Not that she would have let herself touch his cheek to find out. Doing so would likely also entail gazing into his eyes. She would never again let herself be put into such a vulnerable position, not when Amelia Fletcher Beauchamp was trying to elbow her way into their lives.

I wish someone would have told me to truly live every second of my life back then, because those sunny days didn't last. Nothing beautiful does.

Yet she felt puzzled. Why had he mentioned their nights in the library right after admitting that he still found Amelia as attractive as ever? Ellen felt an urgent need to escape, an even stronger urge than in the ballroom. She needed to be anywhere but here, in the darkness, in this soft silence, which filled her with longing for her husband.

"I'm—I'm quite faint," she said, reaching for her chair

and sinking into it again. "The carriage. Would you call for it, please?"

Four

"I—of course," Anthony said. After a moment, he bowed in Ellen's direction, then strode out of the library to find the Pembrokes' butler. "Roberts," Anthony said, "would you please see that the carriage I arrived in is brought around for my wife straightaway?"

"Of course, Mr. Stanhope," Roberts said with a formal nod.

As the graying gentleman went off to complete the request, Anthony stood in the estate's front entry alone, confused, and unsettled. He raised his eyes to the upper floor, where Ellen waited. He'd felt as if he'd been on the cusp of—of—well, *something*. But what? Something lovely. He knew that much. But it had vanished quicker than a frightened doe. Baffled, he thought through the moment he and Ellen had just shared, trying to weigh and measure her every word against his, trying to puzzle out the meaning of what he'd almost had, but had lost.

The butler returned a few minutes later. "The carriage should be here at any moment, Mr. Stanhope."

"Thank you." Then Anthony realized that Ellen would need to be given word to come down, and his gaze moved yet again to the upper floors. He had yet to fathom what had caused her tears and flight from the ballroom. At present he had assurance about only one thing: Ellen did not wish to see him or talk to him. The mere sight of him seem to cause her injury, and he wouldn't injure her again for the world. The butler's form was receding down the hall when Anthony called out to him.

"Roberts?"

The man turned about expectantly.

"Could you send someone to fetch Mrs. Stanhope? She's upstairs in the library. I'm afraid she's fallen ill."

"Of course," Roberts said with a nod. "I'll send one of the housemaids."

Once again alone in the entry, Anthony paced, pondering, but for the first time in months, his mind did not find distraction in the worries about the estate—the tenants who'd had a failed crop and couldn't pay rent, another tenant's loss of two cows, and so forth. Such worries had occupied the whole of his mind for the last week, but now Ellen took their place.

His mind returned to their courtship, of days when he couldn't bear to be apart from her. When they'd spent hours before the fire in her parents' sitting room, reading poetry—her favorite had always been John Donne.

Occasionally, he'd convinced her to play the pianoforte and sing for him. Anthony smiled at the memory of her soaring soprano. But then he remembered how they were now, and he didn't recognize the young, carefree couple in those images.

Could those young lovers yet be found, or were they lost forever?

His brow furrowed, and he paced, hands clasped behind his back, practically wearing a path in rug.

Could it be that Ellen had simply fallen ill? If so, she needed only a physician to be well once more. He thought back to the glimpses he'd had in the ballroom—her flushed face and watery eyes. Signs of fever? She'd been sitting, too, perhaps because she'd felt faint. In the library, instead of stepping behind a bookcase for privacy, if that's what she'd been looking for, she'd first found a place to sit.

Yes. The more he considered the idea, the more certain he became that his wife had a fever and simply felt weak. As soon as he'd seen her off, he'd send a messenger to fetch a physician to Rosewood.

But he quickly changed his mind. First he'd ask Roberts to send for the carriage; hitching the horses would take twenty minutes at best. Then he'd find his silly daughters to inform them that their evening of revelry needed to end prematurely, and they would all head home.

Then, after a few days' recuperation, all would be well.

And I shall spend more time with my sweet Ellen, he thought, feeling lighter already. *If she wants such a thing*, he amended, scowling as he realized that perhaps she preferred his absence. Was her reaction this night a sign of her dismay at his return? At the thought, his heart dropped two inches.

At length, a housemaid appeared, supporting Ellen. The two walked past Anthony and out the front door with only the slightest of greetings and acknowledgment on his wife's part. He stepped through the door after her and watched as Ellen picked her way across the gravel drive to the carriage. The driver handed her up, and still Anthony waited at the door, not moving until the horses had lurched to a start and the vehicle rolled down the drive, around a corner, and out of sight.

Now it was time to request the carriage, send word for a physician, and make his excuses to Pembroke. After accomplishing these duties, Anthony set out to find his daughters in the ballroom. He stood near a column and looked about, quickly spotting Catherine and Mary-Anne standing in one corner, grinning widely as they watched someone on the dance floor. He followed their gaze and spotted their elder sister and her partner, Mr. Whitcomb. Diana seemed to glow with happiness, a sight that made Anthony's middle twist uncomfortably. He remembered Whitcomb from their families' acquaintance, and in Anthony's mind, his daughter's beau was little more than a boy. Yet the young *man* stood taller than Anthony. He wore the side whiskers of a full-grown gentleman and moved about the dance floor as smoothly as any suitor could hope to do.

For the briefest flash, Diana resembled her mother uncannily, and Anthony felt as if he were watching young versions of himself and Ellen dancing. With a start, he realized that he and Ellen had been the very same age, although that seemed impossible.

Zounds, we were young. And so in love. His middle twisted again, and this time he shook his head to eradicate it. No more dreaming of the past. He needed to get home, which meant taking his daughters with him, even though they would, no doubt, protest something awful over the injustice of leaving a ball so early. Like a man on an urgent errand, Anthony marched along the edge of the dance floor toward his two younger daughters. He hadn't quite reached them before someone dressed in bright colors with feathers in her hair stepped in front of him, forcing his own step to come up short.

"Mr. *Stanhope!*"

"Mrs. Beauchamp." Having avoided a collision, he nodded and tried to step around her. "If you'll excuse me."

She smiled coquettishly, shifted her stance to block his way, and tilted her head. "Where *have* you been, Mr. Stanhope? I've been looking for you ever since we parted this evening, but you've been nowhere to be seen. Surely you won't deprive me of another dance?" She stepped closer and unexpectedly slipped her hand through his arm—then held on so tightly that he couldn't extricate himself without making a scene. "Promise me just one?" Again she tilted her head, but this time, her lower lip pushed forward in a pout.

Anthony wondered if ever a man had lived who'd thought such a thing attractive. Had *he* thought so, many years ago, when he'd briefly courted her? He couldn't imagine thinking so, but perhaps when they were both younger, such things were different. Truth be told, *they* were different. Upon reuniting with Mrs. Beauchamp tonight, he knew he'd forever count the match he'd made with Ellen to be one of God's greatest blessings. He couldn't have borne a life with such pouting and flirting garish behavior as Amelia's.

She hadn't spoken an untoward word, yet Anthony cringed, feeling like a prey needing to escape its predator—and hoping no one had seen or heard the woman. Uncomfortably, his eyes darted to Catherine and Mary-Anne, whose gazes were directed his way. Their awkward expressions confirmed that they'd seen and heard the display—and likely knew Mrs. Beauchamp's intentions every bit as well as he did.

His neck burned as he reached for her hand. "I'm quite sorry, Mrs. Beauchamps," he said, trying to unwind it from his arm while maintaining a practiced smile. "But I—"

"Oh, Mr. Stanhope, please" she said, clinging to him

and stroking his sleeve with her free hand. She squeezed his upper arm. "My, you're as strong now as ever you were." She looked up at him with possessive eyes and smiled knowingly, as if Anthony should be privy to her thoughts and intentions.

And my daughters are watching.

"Unfortunately, my wife has taken ill; I must go home posthaste." When she didn't step away, Anthony firmly unwound her hand like a barnacle from a ship's hull.

"Another time, then?" While she made no additional move to capture his arm again, she didn't step back, either. Instead, she reached out and placed an open hand on his chest, stunning Anthony into silence. She raised one eyebrow and smiled. "My heart is beating ever so fast as well. Until we meet again—soon, I hope." With that, she batted her eyes, licked her lips, and sauntered away.

Free at last.

He watched her move away for several seconds, waiting until he was quite certain he'd be able to reach his daughters before she could accost him again. He placed one hand over his heart, which was indeed racing—but not for the reason Mrs. Beauchamp implied.

The music ended, and the crowd applauded. Anthony wove his way through the pressing crowd. At last he reached his daughters just as Diana's beau bowed to make his leave. She bent briefly at the knees and nodded, her cheeks dotted with pink. As she turned to her sisters, she seemed unable to stop smiling.

Another pang, this one in Anthony's chest. He and Ellen had once looked and felt so. His daughter might have found such a match herself already. One day would she, too, lose that smile as her mother had?

Suddenly aware that his daughters were looking at him expectantly, he quickly changed his countenance to one of good humor. He nodded at the general direction Diana's partner had gone. "Should I expect to see Mr. Whitcomb in my study soon, seeking permission to court my daughter?" he asked with what he hoped was a teasing smile.

Diana flushed brighter but still grinned. "I think so," she said. "At least, I hope so." She lowered her eyes and bit her lower lip as if trying to restrain her smile. She began to chatter to her sisters about the possibilities of a spring wedding; Anthony raised a hand to stop her.

"I came to tell you girls that your mother has gone home."

Catherine gasped. "Left? Already?"

"I sent her home in my carriage, and I plan to follow in the other in a few moments. I assume you girls aren't silly enough to want to walk three miles in the dark, so I suggest you make your excuses and meet me at the front doors in five minutes' time. No more dancing tonight."

"Oh, don't make us leave yet," Mary-Anne cried, joining her sister in pleading, hands clasped. "Please, Father. The night has scarcely begun."

Catherine folded her arms, and Anthony expected another plea. "Mother isn't sick," she said instead, and with conviction.

Anthony began his rehearsed retort. "I demand that—what?" He turned to Catherine. "How do you know any such thing? I've been to see your mother only a few minutes ago, and I can assure you, she is quite unwell."

"*Unwell*, perhaps," Catherine said. "But not of body—of spirit." When his look of confusion didn't ebb, she went on. "She is sad, Father. Melancholy. Of a depressed disposition. Out of humor?"

"Do I dare ask if you girls know why?"

Catherine seemed content to answer. "I would hazard a

guess that it's due to watching Mrs. Beauchamp and her... *affections* toward you." She blushed a tad at that, but Anthony hardly noted it, for he was already looking about, wondering who might be listening.

He stepped closer to his daughters and whispered, "Nonsense."

Catherine and Mary-Anne exchanged glances with each other, then looked to Diana, who nodded and answered for the group. "We think Mother is envious of Mrs. Beauchamp. Mother is likely worried, too, after the attentions you gave her tonight."

"The—the attentions—*I* gave—" Anthony spluttered for a moment, confused. "She is an old acquaintance. I had to be polite. A gentleman can hardly rebuff a lady in public. Certainly your mother knows that."

His daughters' implications seemed ridiculous in the extreme, yet he could not banish the worry they brought to his chest. No, they couldn't be right.

But Catherine was nodding emphatically. "I heard Mrs. Beauchamp. She said she wanted to *rekindle* a relationship with you, Father."

Mary-Anne piped up next. "You courted her at one time, didn't you?"

He drew a hand down his face wearily. How did his daughter know so much about things from before they were born? "Well, yes, but that was very long ago, and Mrs. Beauchamp married well before your mother and I—"

He cut himself off this time. A few pieces of the puzzle were still missing, but he could finally make out the image.

Could it be that Ellen thinks I chose her only because Amelia was taken? Anthony found his collar awfully tight. *Then tonight, when Amelia appeared again and hung on my arm...*

All at once, the events of the evening made perfect sense, and with that clarity came a jumble of emotions—a surge of joy that Ellen yet cared enough to feel so strongly for him, a tempering of sadness for the pain she must have felt and must yet feel. Lastly, he felt emboldened by determination to prove his love to her anew.

"Come," he said, motioning for his daughters to follow, no longer willing to wait for them to give their regrets to the host and hostess. "We leave at once. I must attend to an urgent matter—something I pray you three can help me with." The girls followed behind, clearly befuddled. He paused in his step and turned about briefly to add, "And Diana, I'm quite sure your beau will forgive your early departure. If he doesn't, quite frankly, he doesn't deserve your hand."

Diana blanched but quickly recovered. "And if he does forgive it?"

Anthony smiled. "Then perhaps I may take a liking to the boy after all." He gestured toward the doors and clapped his hands. "Quickly now."

 Five

Ellen sat at the edge of her bed, waiting for her maid and wanting nothing more than to don her nightclothes and lay her head on a pillow. She'd sent the physician away without seeing him, hoping to slip into the oblivion of sleep—the only escape from her current turbulent emotions. Sadly, such oblivion would be short lived. Now she wondered whether sending him away had been hasty; laudanum would have helped her sleep.

I suppose I should be grateful that Anthony called for a physician, she thought. *I suppose that he means he cares.* Instead, the physician's arrival had told her something else: Anthony no longer knew her. The man she'd married twenty years ago would have known at a glance that she hadn't become ill. *That* Anthony would have *seen* her heart aching. Yet he'd called for outside help instead of coming to her, being the only one who could heal what was truly wrong— her aching heart. She shook her head disdainfully in an attempt to hold back the tears that had threatened to fall ever since she'd walked past him while exiting Wildemoore Hall.

She glanced at the door, wishing Anthony would walk through it, knowing he wouldn't. He was still at the ball, with Mrs. Beauchamp.

Is she why he was willing to let me go home without protest? So he could spend more time with her?

The tears came awfully close to the surface, and then in spite of herself, they fell. She stood and paced, wiping her cheeks. If she didn't manage to rein in the tears soon, then tomorrow, she'd have a puffed, splotchy face unfit for receiving visitors. On the other hand, if everyone at the ball assumed she'd fallen ill, she had a satisfactory excuse for not receiving visitors.

The thought should have cheered her, but the ball had pulled out her heart from some safe, locked chamber and opened it up. For the first time in years, she'd allowed herself to think of Anthony as she'd once seen him—not just as her proper husband, Mr. Stanhope—but as the man who'd gently won her heart and then had held it in his hands so gently and tenderly that she'd known where she belonged—with him, always.

The feeling was hardly more than a faint wisp of memory now. She remembered feeling and thinking such things, but she couldn't fathom what it had been like to experience them. The memory seemed like a vision of some other person, a mere phantom of someone who vaguely resembled her.

Neither of us is the same person.

So much the sadder. Though they'd drifted apart, Anthony hadn't seemed unhappy with his life, not until tonight, when Amelia Fletcher Beauchamp had glided back into their lives and demanded everyone's attention, including Anthony's.

And he'd quite happily given it to her. He'd danced with her. Smiled at her with his elegant charm.

He's done all of that before with other women, she argued. Yet something felt different about how he'd behaved tonight—she could feel a difference. And *that* was what bothered her. Part of the difference, she acknowledged, was that Amelia wasn't just any woman at any ball with whom Anthony danced to be polite.

After their wedding, seeing the very same scene wouldn't have bothered Ellen at all; she'd been so confident in her husband's love and adoration that questioning whether he yet carried feelings of love toward a former lady acquaintance had never entered her mind.

Well, not usually—only in the occasional moments she'd heard whisperings about town, mostly in the first few months of their marriage. Often from old women who insisted on dwelling on the worst possible speculations. Other times it was gossip spread among young people who saw such torrid stories as the spice that made life enjoyable.

Ellen had always laughed such comments off, holding her head high as she'd marched past the whispers and pitying eyes. Then in the evenings, she'd tell Anthony of what she'd heard, and they'd laugh and laugh. On such nights, he'd often scooted close and recited lines from one of her favorite poems—John Donne's "Valediction: Forbidding Mourning," about a married couple yet in love, to be separated for a time. How their love was so pure that it was heavenly, not like "sublunary"—earthly—lovers' love.

After quoting the poem, Anthony would gently tuck a piece of hair behind her ear, then let his fingers trail down her cheek. He'd set his book aside and press his lips against hers—tender yet firm in his desire and feeling. His kisses had always awakened a thrill in her middle.

When was the last time she'd had such a kiss? She couldn't recall.

Yet at one time, they hadn't been rare. There had been a time when, before Anthony left for business, he'd quoted the same lines:

Our two souls therefore, which are one,
Though I must go, endure not yet
A breach, but an expansion,
Like gold to airy thinness beat.

Before he spoke the next line, she'd often stepped nearer and quoted it with him as their lips neared one another, and they whispering, lips touching, of their love being fine as gold and able to stretch across the miles. Then he'd kiss her, long and deep, before leaving, and she'd cling to the memory of that kiss until he returned.

Many a time she'd wondered if her mother would entirely approve of Donne's poems, which were so full of not just beauty, but of passion.

But maybe she remembered those nights all wrong. She must have read too many of John Donne's love poems. They were why she believed passion and love could endure.

What if, in truth, she'd never had that love? Anthony could have been so heartbroken over Amelia's marriage that he'd simply turned his energies elsewhere. And Ellen had naively assumed his feelings for her to be genuine.

Had he kissed Ellen as if kissing Amelia?

Her heart ached more now than it had all night. She walked to the bell pull to ring for her maid again, wondering if perhaps there was some laudanum in the household after all. She continued pacing, wringing her hands, as she waited. More and more memories from years past came to the fore, and with each came the same, deeply upsetting question.

Was his love for me ever real?

Her door finally opened, and Ellen turned expectantly, but it wasn't her maid at all. It wasn't Anthony, either. All three of her daughters entered, looking ready to burst with excitement.

"What is it?" Ellen asked, walking over. She put on a smile and hoped her tears had dried sufficiently. "Has Mr. Whitcomb proposed?" It was the only thing she could think of that would affect her daughters in such a way.

Diana shook her head.

"No," she said but did so with a smile—a genuinely happy smile.

Perplexed, Ellen looked at Catherine, then at Mary-Anne. Both of them grinned like cunning foxes. Ellen took a step backward. "Why are you home already? Where is your father?" The girls giggled, prompting Ellen to put a hand on one hip. "I insist you tell me—what is the matter?"

Diana was the first obey. "You're needed in the study."

"That's right," Catherine said with a nod. "Father asked for you to come straightaway."

"Your father . . ." Ellen's brow furrowed.

"It's quite urgent," Mary-Anne said, trying—but utterly failing—to maintain a serious expression.

Diane lifted a finger. "But you mustn't ask what it's about, because we can't tell."

Confused and exhausted, Ellen turned about and walked the other way in hopes of regaining composure. What could Anthony possibly want to speak to her about? Why tonight? And why wasn't the family still at the ball? So many questions, and she supposed she wouldn't have a restful sleep—or any answers—unless she went down to the study and faced her husband. Maybe he would confess his long-standing love for Amelia. Dread washed over her at the thought of facing Anthony tonight.

I'd rather beard the lion in its den.

Yet it must be done. After several deep breaths, she returned to her girls. "Tell him I'll come momentarily."

The girls scurried out of the room, and Ellen closed the door behind them. She sat at her vanity table to see if she could do something with her mussed hair and tear-stained face.

If Anthony insisted on confessing his love for Amelia, then Ellen would at least make an attempt to look a fraction as beautiful as Mrs. Beauchamp—and a fraction of how beautiful she herself had felt once upon a time in his arms.

Six

Looking into a mirror on the study wall, Anthony adjusted his cravat for probably the tenth time in as many minutes, then resumed his pacing, also for the tenth time. The longer his daughters were gone—the longer he waited to see his dear Ellen, the longer he dwelt in the misery of not knowing what the future held—and the more worry tightened his insides into a knot. Already his mind had invented a thousand possible outcomes for this evening. He would be able to bear only one of them.

He'd once heard that Raphael was the patron saint of lovers. Despite being Anglican, he half-wished he were Catholic and could therefore call on the saint in this time of need. Yet on second thought, would Raphael bless the venture of this night, or would he instead look at Anthony—middle-aged and graying—then laugh before leaving in search of a worthy, young couple to bless with love?

From the hall, he heard sudden footsteps and laughter—his daughters at last. Was Ellen with them? Anxious over his appearance, he smoothed his hair, rested an elbow on the fireplace mantel, and propped one of his boots in its toe, hoping to appear as if he'd been standing in such a faux-relaxed position for some time. His ribcage hammered like a drum behind a battle line—an apt metaphor, as he was about to launch into a battle of sorts. His heart would very likely be a casualty.

With a flurry of colorful ball gowns, the girls practically tumbled into the room. They all wore sparkling eyes and smiles.

Diana, ever the leader, spoke. "She will be down soon."

"Thank you." He cleared his throat, wishing to remove his cravat altogether; it was strangling him. "If I may ask . . . what is your mother's demeanor?"

Catherine crossed to him and slipped her arm through his. "Do just as we discussed, and everything will be grand."

It didn't escape his notice that she hadn't answered his question. The knot tightened. Anthony glanced toward the bookshelf, where a volume of poetry, bound in red, seemed to glow. "She may not remember half the things I told you about. It was all so long ago."

Mary-Anne joined Catherine at the fireplace, taking his other side. She gently urged his elbow off the mantel, then put her arm about it. "Trust us." She looked straight into his eyes.

He nodded, thinking through the conversation from the carriage ride. The girls had probed for details about their parents' courtship, of anything he'd once done to woo their mother, and, later, what he used to do to show his love. It was oddly comforting that his daughters simply assumed that their parents had a romantic history, that their marriage hadn't always been politely platonic.

Fortunately, they're right.

At the sound of door hinges squeaking, they all looked

over—and there stood Ellen framed by the doorway, the glow of a lamp lighting her face. Perhaps it was the shadows softening the evidence of time, but whatever it was, Anthony felt as if he were seeing her at nineteen again. As his heart had leapt at the sight of her entrance so many years ago, it did so again. He could not take his eyes from her sweet, dear face—one he'd long thought beautiful and in which one could now detect wisdom and knowledge from maturity and hardship.

He instinctively knew what hardship had written upon her features—the same burden that had first brought a change to his black hair, peppering it with silver: baby William.

We haven't spoken of him since he was buried . . .

He wanted to demand from his younger self why he hadn't flown to his wife's side to weep with her. He'd wanted to do that very thing but hadn't known if, after Ellen hadn't wanted to so much as lay eyes on him during her confinement, his presence would have been welcomed. So he'd stayed away and, instead of mourning, had thrown himself into the estate.

He'd been utterly foolish. They'd both been wounded, and by their staying apart, they had grown progressively unhappier over the ensuing years. At least, he had. He only tonight admitted as much. He'd allowed the blinders of responsibility and duty to keep him from feeling or seeing what happened around him. So he hadn't sought out care for his beloved as he'd sworn to do at the altar.

Ellen took a step farther into the room. "You wanted to speak with me, Mr. Stanhope?"

So formal. And proper. Granted, most married couples never used Christian names.

But once, we were different from most.

Keeping his gaze on Ellen's, he spoke to their daughters. "Girls, if you would excuse us, your mother and I have things to discuss."

Ellen stiffened at his words, ever so slightly, and as their daughters flounced past her and closed the door behind them, her face looked regretful that she could not follow. Eyes trained on the rug, she walked to the center of the room, hands clasped. Anthony wanted to speak to her, take her into his arms, and kiss her. But first, he strode to the door, where he turned the key, removed it from the lock, then placed it in a pocket of his waistcoat.

"Now we won't be interrupted," he said, turning toward Ellen, whose back now faced him.

"May I ask what urgent matter you feel we must discuss?" she said quietly.

He took a deep breath and walked to around to face her. He reached out and took her hands in his—they were so cold—and waited for her to lift her eyes. His mind sought to remember the advice of his daughters, but now, standing on a precipice, it all vanished like an ethereal specter. Not knowing what he would say, still holding her hands, he stepped closer. She seemed to brace herself.

"Ellen, I'm afraid I owe you a much-overdue apology."

She raised her head quite abruptly at that. Her face looked pale, her eyes pinched. "What for?"

He'd wounded her again. How, he did not know. *Blast.*

Best to press on. "There was a time I could not imagine going a day without seeing the face I love, hearing her voice, kissing her lips."

"A time long past." She again bowed her head, this time closing her eyes. Tears trailed down both cheeks. "I understand your desire to be happy and the truth that she may give you some of the happiness I have been unable to provide." She sat up taller and drew in a breath as if her spine had turned into a rod of iron. She turned her face to look at him, and this time, her voice was steady and firm, if swelling with an undercurrent of emotion. "I ask just one thing of you: that you be discreet so the neighbors remain ignorant of your liaison. I believe—" She swallowed and tried again. "I deserve at least that much: retaining my dignity by not being publicly humiliated."

For a moment, Anthony was so utterly confused that he was rendered speechless. Then his previous realization lit his mind, and he understood—she meant Mrs. Beauchamp. He held Ellen by the shoulders and tried to look her in the eye. "My sweet, sweet Ellen. *You* are the only woman I love—and the only woman I have *ever* loved."

She shook her head, back and forth, bringing a handkerchief to her nose. "I saw how she looked at you. I saw you—"

"You saw a man trying to be polite," he interrupted. "You saw a man hounded by unwanted attentions from a crass woman." He dared to stroke her jawline with his thumb. Her stiffness softened ever so slightly. Encouraged, he went on. "The brief time we courted felt like a lifetime. I didn't know how to step away. I assure you that when she ran off with Mr. Beauchamp, I was happier than either of them."

Ellen ventured a glance at him quietly. "You—were?"

"*Utterly* happy and relieved, even though half the town had assumed we'd marry. And then I met *you*—far more beautiful and kind and thoughtful. Everything she was not. With you, I could talk of poetry, and you never once pretended you weren't clever enough to understand the words."

She smiled a bit at that. A small flame of hope erupted, emboldening him.

"We discussed literature. We even debated interpretations. And I loved you all the more for your passionate arguments, especially when they differed from my own. You helped me see the world through different eyes, and I found a more colorful, complicated, messy, yet wonderful world than I'd ever known existed."

The smile tugged a bit more at the corners of her lips. "So . . . you never cared for her?"

He shook his head. "Never."

"Not at *all*?" Her eyes seemed to plead for the answer he most readily gave.

"Not with a single hair on my head. To this day, I consider *Mr.* Beauchamp to be the greatest answer to prayer in the history of England."

Ellen sniffed and dabbed her nose. Her demeanor shifted from one of formality, bordering on coldness, to one of guarded hope. Anthony took her by one hand and led her to the same sofa on which they'd spent hours reading together. After she sat, he crossed to the bookshelf, fetched the red volume, and returned to sit by her. Their arms touched, and she didn't move away.

On seeing the book, she reached out one finger and traced the golden letters on the cover. Perhaps she felt the same—that this book could return a portion of what they'd lost. Still in a quiet voice, but one no longer seeped in melancholy, Ellen quoted the beginning of their favorite poem as flawlessly as ever.

> *As virtuous men pass mildly away,*
> *And whisper to their souls, to go,*
> *Whilst some of their sad friends do say,*
> *"The breath goes now," and some say, "No:"*

So let us melt, and make no noise,
No tear-floods, nor sigh-tempests move;
'Twere profanation of our joys
To tell the laity our love.

As her voice trailed off, her body seemed to yield, leaning into his; her shape still matched to his perfectly.

Her head resting on his shoulder, she said, "I remember speaking those words with you before we parted, every time you took a journey from home."

He nodded but said nothing, hoping for more.

"But tonight, those words made me think of something else." Something significant, surely.

"Oh?" He wanted to know her thoughts as he wanted breath but dared not ask what she spoke of.

She took the book from his hands and turned to "Valediction: Forbidding Mourning." Her finger tracked the words as if she was reading to herself. Anthony read along, waiting for her to speak.

"Here," she said, looking at the first stanza. "You and I weren't given an opportunity to say whether his breath was going—or no. *He* never took a breath." She lifted her face to his, and their gazes, at last, met. Hers searched his, and he realized she was speaking of their son. "Did you know that he didn't breathe, not once? But he was perfect, with the sweetest lashes and nose and chubby fingers—even perfect toenails. But he was already gray and cold by the time I got to hold him."

The topic of their son made him catch his breath. "No, I didn't know." Anthony's eyes burned. He'd spent years locking away his emotions and recognized this moment as one upon which everything he'd lost now balanced.

He worked up the gumption to speak the name that had

not passed his lips in as many years. "William was a beautiful child."

Ellen nodded, pressed her handkerchief to her face, and fell into Anthony's embrace, weeping. He, too, allowed the tears he'd denied for years to finally fall, wetting her hair, as he held her close.

After twelve years, they finally mourned their son together. For some time—he knew not how long—they grieved over the son they would never see walk or laugh or run, never see grow into a man.

Against her forehead, he pressed a kiss. More of the poem came to his mind, words that fitted the moment—words of love that had endured difficult times. He whispered in her ear,

> *We by a love so much refin'd,*
> *that ourselves know not what it is,*
> *inter-assured of the mind.*

She shifted, looking into his eyes, then reached up and pulled his face closer to hers. "Care less eyes . . ." She pressed a feather-light kiss to each of his eyelids. "'Lips . . .'" She pressed another to his mouth. "'And hands to miss.'" She took his hands in hers and kissed his palms, then looked into his eyes. "But I *have* missed you—I've missed you so much, even while in the same room."

"And I, you," he said, wiping her tears.

She reached up and did the same to his.

Anthony soaked in her countenance, marveling. "How is it that we came so close to forgetting?"

She smiled again, and this time, although the image resembled the young girl he'd first loved, the expression contained experience, temperance, and wisdom.

Characteristics the older Anthony found even more desirable.

He leaned in and placed a long, tender kiss on her lips. She sighed and kissed him in return, wrapping her arms about his neck as if unwilling to let him break apart. He was quite willing to oblige; they hadn't shared such a tender, vulnerable moment, in years, if ever.

When at last they pulled away, he rested his forehead against hers. "Promise me one thing?"

"Anything," she said, her eyes closed so her lashes fanned over her creamy skin. She kissed his jawline three times, which distracted him for a moment until she asked, "What shall I promise?"

His mind kept returning to the end of the poem, which compared the two lovers to a compass, the type with which a person drew a circle: two pieces connected into one. As one drew a circle, one piece stood in the center, holding a steady position as the other went around, drawing a perfect circle. And then the two parts were brought back together again.

"Be the other half of my compass?"

The crinkle of the wrinkles by her eyes told him she understood the reference. "'Thy firmness makes my circle just,'" she quoted. "We shall be firm for each other from this day."

"Always," Anthony said. He stood, took her by the hand, and led her to the door, which he quietly unlocked. To his relief, he saw no tittering or other evidence of their daughters. Together he and his wife walked, hand in hand, up the stairs and down the hall, until they reached his bedchamber.

At the door, he turned to her, unused to broaching certain topics. But then she spoke, eliminating the need for him to.

"I remember the first time I crossed that threshold as Mrs. Anthony Stanhope." She squeezed his hand and smiled. He squeezed back, pleased, but still unsure if they had fully bridged the chasm.

"Shall I . . . escort you to your room?" His brow raised as if asking a different question. Hardly able to breathe, he waited to hear the answer he so wanted.

"If we are a compass, then this is where we began, isn't it?"

He nodded uncertainly.

"Carry me across the threshold again—'And make me end, where I began,'" she finished, paraphrasing the final line. She raised herself onto her toes and whispered. "Forevermore, our two souls are one, remember? We promised."

Joy warmed Anthony's chest then spread, filling his body. "Yes, we did."

He opened the door, lifted his wife—his bride again—and carried her across the threshold. He closed the door with his boot, then carried her to the bed, where he gently laid her down and sat at her side. Leaning close, he stroked her hair; Ellen reached up and combed his with her fingers; he nearly melted at the touch.

"I love you, Anthony Stanhope."

"Not as much as I love you, I'm afraid," he said with a chuckle and leaned in to kiss her soundly.

ABOUT ANNETTE LYON

Annette Lyon is a Whitney Award winner, a two-time recipient of Utah's Best of State medal for fiction, and a three-time publication award winner from the League of Utah Writers, including the Silver Quill in 2013. She's the author of more than a dozen novels, at least as many novellas, several nonfiction books, and over one hundred twenty magazine articles.

Annette is a cum laude graduate from BYU with a degree in English. When she's not writing, knitting, or eating chocolate, she can be found mothering, reading, and avoiding the spots on the kitchen floor.

Website: AnnetteLyon.com
Blog: blog.annettelyon.com
Twitter: @AnnetteLyon
Facebook: Facebook.com/AnnetteLyon

The Duke's Brother

by Heather B. Moore

OTHER WORKS BY HEATHER B. MOORE

Esther the Queen
Finding Sheba
Lost King
Slave Queen
The Aliso Creek Series
Heart of the Ocean
The Newport Ladies Book Club Series
The Fortune Café
The Boardwalk Antiques Shop

One

Burnside County, England—1821

"I despise my sister," Mabel Russell muttered. She dipped her quill into the inkpot, trying to come up with a nice way to put off her sister's umpteenth invitation to join her in London and take part in the Season. "Perhaps despise is too strong a word."

> *Dear Ethel,*
> *It is with deep regret that I must turn down your kind invitation. For I have come down with . . .*

She stopped and rubbed her temple with one hand. What could she say that she hadn't already used as an excuse? If she claimed illness, Ethel would make the journey home to their country estate . . . well, their former estate. Their father had died six months before, after which the estate promptly went to their father's first cousin, Mr. Lloyd Griffin.

For the past six months, Mabel had not only grieved over the loss of her kindly, if a bit preoccupied, father, Lord Russell, but she'd also endured her childhood home's being invaded by another family. Nothing was the same anymore.

Mabel sorely missed her father. He'd been a gentleman as well as a respected scientist. During his life, extensive collections of insects and birds had been displayed about the house, a fact that had startled many of their guests over the years. Even Mabel's sister, Ethel, had been quite adverse toward them. But Mabel had never known anything different and accepted insect displays about the house as a part of her normal upbringing. Unlike Ethel, Mabel embraced her father's scientific obsessions and started her own insect collections.

Her mother, having died when Mabel was too young to remember her, had no influence on Mabel's upbringing. To avoid her older sister's fussiness and annoying attention to details such as the latest fashions, which ribbons should be used, and how many times one could wear the same pair of shoes, Mabel had naturally followed her father about.

At his side, she'd learned more about insects and birds than any society woman should ever know. In addition to her father's studies, she'd also begun to find an interest in reptiles and invertebrates. Mabel supposed that as the years continued to go by without her attending a Season or securing a husband, she'd be placed in the eccentric category. For now, she didn't want to be categorized as anything. Her greatest desire was to be left alone, to roam the lands she'd grown up on, to create her own collection of species, and study interesting books.

There was just the small matter of the house being occupied by her father's cousin and his family, which, unfortunately, consisted of a nasal-toned wife and three boys under twelve. Loud, obnoxious boys full of questions. Boys who followed her all over the house if she didn't take care to sneak down the back stairs.

Mabel crumpled the letter and pulled out another piece of paper.

> *Dear Ethel,*
> *I regret to inform you that I will not be able to accept your kind invitation. I have found myself quite busy with my new aphid collection, so I plead for your understanding...*

A loud knock on her door startled Mabel into dripping a blot of ink onto the paper.

"Mabel! Mabel!" a young boy's voice cried out. "Tom's tipped over your insects!"

To another person, the words would have made no sense, but for Mabel, the words shot dread straight into her heart. She jumped up from her chair and rushed to her door. Flinging it open, she came face to face with William, a boy of nine or ten.

His eyes widened at her hasty appearance, but he quickly said, "This way! He's in your shed."

Mabel's blood pumped hot as she started to run. No one was allowed in her shed, and she kept it locked tight for that reason. Last week, Tom had released one of her snails and Mabel had never seen it again. When her father's cousin had brought his family here, the first thing his wife had said was, "The insects and all creatures must go."

Mabel had argued and argued until, at last, she was allowed to keep her collections in one of the gardening sheds, whereas her father's extensive collections were shipped off to some museum in London to be enjoyed by the more intelligent masses.

With William behind her, she tore down the stairs, rounded the back hall, and then burst out of the doors that led to the gardens. A couple of servants stopped to stare, but Mabel knew it wouldn't be long before they resumed their duties; they often saw her rushing past them for one thing or another.

When the garden shed came within sight, Mabel slowed a bit so that by the time she'd reached the opened door, she'd caught her breath. She was prepared for the worst—a cracked case or little Tom climbed up on the table. But, no. It was much, much worse. She froze, staring for a moment, unable to completely comprehend.

Five-year-old Tom sat on the dirt-packed ground, holding a preserved praying mantis in his chubby fingers. Around him were the remnants of a fallen and broken display case. The insects that had been part of the set were in various stages of disarray. Broken glass littered the ground. Remarkably, Tom seemed unaffected by it all. But as soon as he looked up at Mabel, his eyes rounded.

Mabel was so stunned, she said nothing. She'd always locked the shed door. How had Tom gotten inside? And then she knew. She looked over at Will and saw guilt flush hot over his face. He must have found the key hidden beneath the rock. When the case had fallen and broken, it must have spooked him enough to come and find her before letting one of his parents discover the mess.

Will's eyes budded with tears, and he started to stutter an apology. Mabel could only stare at him numbly.

"We in trouble?" Tom's small voice rang clear.

Mabel kept her gaze on Will, trying to keep her emotions in check. "Take Tom out of here."

Will nodded, looking a bit relieved that he wasn't getting yelled at and scurried to drag the protesting Tom out of the shed.

Mabel took a few steps forward, then sank to her knees and began picking up the insects one by one. She examined each for salvage-ability. She'd spent months collecting them, then hours pinning and meticulously labeling the species, writing in calligraphy on parchment. And now the display was completely ruined. Her other three cases appeared untouched, but her stash of parchment had fallen to the earth and been stepped on. An open inkwell was overturned, dripping down a table leg.

Her tears fell now, and Mabel didn't stop to wipe them away. She gathered the broken insects as quickly as possible, avoiding the glass. She'd have to sweep it up later.

"What happened in here?" Mrs. Griffin's nasally voice resounded from behind her. "My boys are in tears."

Mabel didn't turn at first, just continued to pick up her insects as Mrs. Griffin stepped into the shed.

"Oh! This is a mess—a dangerous mess," she pronounced. "My boys could have been severely injured. How careless of you, Mabel. I thought Mr. Griffin instructed you to keep the shed locked."

Mabel finally turned, looking up at the woman, who wore a heavy gray silk dress. It seemed that the wife of her father's cousin always chose the staunchest colors to wear. Mabel wouldn't have been surprised to learn that the woman had been raised in a nunnery.

"Tom and Will found the key. Then came in without my permission and broke the case," Mabel said in a shaky voice. "The insects are irreparable."

Mrs. Griffin barked out a laugh. "Irreparable, you say? What were you thinking—that you could have brought them back to life? They are dead, you know."

Mabel hated Mrs. Griffin's ice-blue eyes, small mouth, pale-green complexion, and thin lips. In fact, the woman looked a bit like a praying mantis. Except that Mabel would never do an insect the disservice of comparing it to a woman like Mrs. Griffin.

Rising to her feet, Mabel grasped the table to steady herself as she took a deep breath. "The shed door was locked. Will must have unlocked it, because Tom is too small to have figured out how."

Mrs. Griffin brought a hand to her chest. "Are you accusing my boys of this mess? As if it were their fault?" Her nasal pitch rose a notch. "Boys are curious, and if you had locked the shed, they wouldn't have been exposed to this danger."

"They broke the case, not I," Mabel reiterated, her face growing hot.

"And now you are arguing with me," Mrs. Griffin said in a tone that sounded as if someone had died. "You do realize that you're a guest in our home, and that Mr. Griffin was more than generous to allow you to even keep your insects?" She wrinkled her nose, making her look even more like a praying mantis. "The bugs are morbid, if you ask me. Dead things on display like that, wings and legs pinned to a mat as if you were practicing some sort of poppet doll torture."

Mabel wanted to kick something. She wanted to cry. Scream. Anything that would get her frustration out. Instead, she bent and picked up the last two insects, a dragonfly and black-winged beetle. She set them carefully onto the table, and then she turned to Mrs. Griffin. "I'll finish cleaning up in a moment. I have a few things to attend to."

Keeping her emotions in check and her chin raised, Mabel strode out of the shed and marched up the back stairs to her bedroom.

The Duke's Brother

Dearest Ethel,

I'd be delighted to accept your invitation to visit your home in London. I'll be bringing my collections with me and hope that you'll understand I won't be much in the way of socializing during the Season. I have several projects to work on and hope to find exciting additions to my collections in your beautiful garden and the surrounding parks.

Two

London

Gregory Clark cursed at his clumsiness as he pulled the cravat from around his neck then tossed the rebellious piece of fabric on the floor. He scowled at his disheveled appearance in the mirror. Why was tying a simple knot so difficult? Perhaps he shouldn't have dismissed his valet that morning. At least he'd done so after he'd been shaved.

Crossing to the window of his bedchamber, Gregory found something else to scowl about. The early-morning rain had turned into a steady drizzle. He'd planned to ride on horseback to his brother's London home to discuss the purchase of a new stallion. Now he'd have to take the carriage.

The rain had dampened his already sour mood. Sour because Lady Violet had written again, requesting—no, *insisting*—that he accompany her to a musicale that evening. Lady Violet was a widow of only two years, but already she was on the prowl. Not for another husband, of course, but a male companion.

When she'd learned that Gregory was the younger brother of a duke, she'd practically attached herself to him—an affair between them wouldn't be much of a scandal, she'd said.

"The woman has no heart," Gregory muttered as he picked up the cravat again. He slid it around his neck and looped it once, then twice, then made a flourish, trying to mimic his valet. But when he let go of the fabric, it hung completely and utterly limp.

"Jones!" Gregory shouted.

No one answered. In fact, the house was so quiet that he could hear the clock ticking in the hallway. Jones must have taken him seriously this go around. This wasn't the first time Gregory had fired the man, along with a couple of other servants, but it was the first time that Jones had really left.

Gregory snatched up Lady Violet's letter and stalked out of the room, intent on insisting that Jones come back. It turned out that Gregory did need a valet, if only to make him presentable for the trip to his brother's home.

When his father had died the year before, leaving the title of the Duke of Rochester to Gregory's brother Richard, Gregory had been more than happy to let him take over the country estate, the London holdings, and everything else Richard cared for. Gregory cared for none of it. He wanted only to be left alone and to stay as far from the ton as possible.

When he'd told Richard that he'd like to use his inheritance to purchase a farm to work himself, Richard had laughed. Gregory's face burned at the memory as he descended the stairs and went from room to room, searching for that deviant Jones, or any other member of the staff, for that matter.

He came to a stop at the door of the kitchen—empty. Even Mrs. Brown was not in her usual place.

Where is everyone?

He stalked back to the hall and rang the bell on a marbled side table. *That ought to get someone's attention.* A few moments later, when he heard the patter of someone's footsteps, barreling toward him, Gregory smiled to himself. But it was a young maid running his way, and she almost didn't stop in time.

"Whoa," he said.

Her rosy face flushed even more as she came to a teetering stop and said, "Beg your pardon, my lord."

His mind went blank for a moment. He wasn't sure what this young thing's name was—Pearl, or Ruby, or maybe Jade. She came in the mornings to care for the indoor plants and flowers. "Have you seen Mr. Jones or Mrs. Brown, or perhaps anyone else on the regular staff?"

"Today is their half day, and most of them have gone to church services. They won't be back until this afternoon." She dipped into a curtsy. "Can I be of assistance?"

Blast. She was right. It was Sunday, and that meant his staff wasn't fully running. Why he'd ever thought that giving them time to attend church, of all things, was beyond him. Couldn't they say their prayers right here in the townhouse?

"Can you tie a gentleman's knot?"

The young maid's eyes widened, and if Gregory hadn't been so out of sorts, he might have laughed at her terror-filled expression.

"Never mind," he said, his tone brusquer than it should have been. "I'll go as I am. Would you tell Davey to pull around the carriage?"

"Yes, my lord." The girl dipped into another curtsy, then scurried off.

In the hallway mirror, Gregory caught a glimpse of his disheveled self. His unruly cravat couldn't be helped; he hoped that torrential rain had kept away his sister-in-law's morning visitors. It wouldn't do for him to be seen like this by a member of the ton. But he had to speak with his brother today about purchasing the Parker stallion. If Gregory didn't write back quickly with an offer, the animal would be sold to someone else.

And until his inheritance was transferred to his trust, Gregory had to consult with his brother on any large purchases. He was counting the weeks until his funds would be secured, when he'd be able to leave London for good and never again worry about cravats, valets, or missing housekeepers.

By the time the carriage was brought around, Gregory had donned his coat, hat, and leather gloves. The rain hadn't let up a bit. He hurried into the carriage and sat back in the stiff seat to catch his breath before realizing he'd stuffed Violet's letter into his vest pocket.

Even if concluding his business with his brother took but a few moments, by the time he'd return to the townhouse, it would be too late to pen a reply, which would make him seem callus by making a lady wait so long. He'd need to compose a letter while at his brother's. The thought was far from appealing, considering that Richard's wife, Ethel, was sure to inquire after Gregory's business.

He leaned his head back against the upholstery and let out a great sigh.

Dear, sweet Ethel . . .

His sister-in-law's face could launch a thousand ships, yet her personality would cause them to crash into each other in exasperation. Ethel seemed to know everything about everyone, and insisted on giving him her advice every time they were in a semi-private moment together. And sometimes when they weren't.

For instance, last week, when Gregory reluctantly accompanied the duke and his wife on a picnic to make the numbers even, he'd suffered through an entire carriage ride with her. Ethel had regaled the many fresh-faced unmarried young women he would have the opportunity of meeting during the upcoming Season.

It was now starting—hence the musicale he'd been invited to by Violet—and it would soon be in full swing. All the more reason to hope that his trust would fund very soon. Gregory chastised himself; perhaps he should have gone to church with the rest of his household today. Would it be sacrilegious to light a few candles for himself and ask that his inheritance be rushed?

As he thought of all the dances, dinners, theater excursions, and game nights that he'd be expected to attend as the younger brother of the Duke of Rochester, a low-throbbing headache began. Gregory had always managed to avoid the Season, but it hadn't completely saved him from mindless socializing. He'd still been forced to attend various dinners due to one family obligation or another, and the many matrons had introduced their daughters to him. He shuddered at the memories.

He'd made a point of mentioning his plan to live in the country and run a farm, for that scared away most of the matrons and their daughters. Except for Violet. Apparently, Violet was more than happy to use him for less-than-noble purposes.

Gregory had been quick explain to Ethel that his ambitions as a farmer were not attractive to Society, but she'd just laughed and said, "You'll find the right woman soon enough, and then all of your dreams of milking cows will be long forgotten. You'll want to give her a respectable home and send your sons to the best schools. Mark my words, your priorities will change."

At last the carriage pulled through the gates of his brother's London estate, then came to a stop. Through the rain, Gregory dashed to the front porch of his brother's elegant home, earning only a few drops on his coat as the front door opened. They must have seen him coming.

But instead of a butler standing and holding the door open, he saw someone else hurrying through the door, and, not stopping, run right into him.

Gregory had the presence of mind to reach out and steady the person, but it was too late; he'd been tipped off balance, so he slipped on the wet ground and fell with a thud.

Three

Just as well, Gregory thought, as he lay on his backside on the wet ground, rain drizzling on his face. He didn't expect anything better from such a day than what he'd already endured. He closed his eyes for a moment and let out a breath of frustration.

"Are you all right, sir?" someone said above him, the same person who'd knocked him down.

Gregory peeked out of one eye. It was a woman, one who looked quite familiar, but he couldn't place her. "I am fine," he said, then opened both eyes.

The woman's dark brows were still pulled together, and Gregory couldn't help but notice her deep-green eyes, perhaps because they stared openly at him. This was no reticent female.

"Mabel!" another voice called. "What have you done?"

Gregory looked over. "Hello, Ethel." His normally stoic sister-in-law had arrived and appeared to be on verge of a breakdown. He climbed to his feet, thinking he might need

The Duke's Brother

to help her back to the drawing room and into a comfortable chair.

"I didn't mean to run him over," the woman named Mabel said.

Ethel placed her hands on her hips and let out a dramatic sigh. "Gregory, this is my sister, Miss Mabel Russell." Ethel turned her disapproving gaze on her sister. "Mabel, this is Lord Gregory Clark, Richard's younger brother."

Ah. Gregory understood why the woman looked familiar; she was Ethel's sister. The two were similar in appearance. Ethel was refined and austere, with her brown eyes, fair skin, and deep brown hair, and her younger sister sported the same hair color. But Mabel's eyes had more green than brown, and her complexion was . . . well, touched by the sun and the color was emphasized by a sprinkling of freckles like a dash of cinnamon.

Gregory tried to figure out what bothered him about Mabel. Perhaps it was because everything he'd ever imagined about the sister-who-refused-to-leave-the-country didn't match the beauty peering up at him with an arched brow full of curiosity. He missed his brother's wedding because he'd been traveling the continent at the time, and thus had never met Ethel's family. Mabel was not the shy person Gregory had assumed a country recluse might be.

To be frank, she seemed quite bold staring up at him.

"It's a pleasure to meet you." Gregory bowed his head.

"Please accept my apologies," Mabel said with a smile on her face and amusement in her gaze. "I hope you are uninjured."

Did she find the incident humorous? Gregory had expected her to be mortified. Instead, she seemed quite recovered and free from any embarrassment. "I am not injured," he said.

"Well then." Mabel flicked a gaze at her sister. "I'll be off, and don't worry about the rain. That's what my parasol is for."

Gregory only then noticed she carried a parasol in one hand and a hat box in the other. But it wasn't an ordinary hat box, for the top had been cut out and replaced by white cheesecloth.

Ethel stepped across the porch and grasped Mabel's arm. "No, Mabel. Stay with us." Her words were firm, but her tone was sweet. "Gregory has recently arrived, and it's rude to abandon a guest you've just met."

Mabel's gaze returned to Gregory. Her eyes were the darkest green he'd ever seen—almost unreal. Perhaps her eye color was from all of the time she spent in the country; she'd somehow adapted to her surroundings, like a chameleon.

"You don't mind, do you, Mr. Clark?" Mabel said. "I mean, unless you came to sit with the ladies for morning tea and gossip about what everyone might wear to the musicale tonight?"

Gregory was too stunned to react. And then it happened—an unexpected laugh burst from him.

"See?" Mabel said, turning her attention back to her sister. "He's not here for us at all. Besides, he's *family*. Hardly a guest." She reached out and touched Gregory's arm, surprising him even further. "It was lovely to meet you at last, brother-in-law. I'm very sorry about running into you. If you stay for supper, I'll be delighted to discuss the recent horse races and whether the corn crop should be taxed. But right now I have some pressing matters to attend to before the rain stops. I'll see both of you later. Good-bye, now."

Gregory could only stare in astonishment as Mabel stepped off the porch. She lifted her parasol and opened the flimsy thing, as if it would protect her clothing and shoes from the rain, then strode with determined purpose around the house and out of sight.

He turned to Ethel, thinking they could share a laugh or two, but she had a hand to her mouth. Her normally composed face was flushed with embarrassment, or anger, or both.

"She's charming, if a bit unconventional," Gregory said. When Ethel didn't reply, he added, "Where is she going?"

"Oh," Ethel gasped. Her other hand clutched her middle.

"Are you all right?" Gregory asked, rushing to her side.

Ethel waved him off, seeming to compose herself. "I don't know what I was thinking, inviting her here for the Season. I guess I hoped she'd find a husband . . . but she . . ." Ethel looked up at him, her eyes red and moist.

"What can I do to help?" Gregory asked, feeling uncomfortable around a weepy female. Where was his brother? Shouldn't he be handling this? Gregory didn't have a sister and didn't know how in the world he should behave.

"Would you help? Really, Gregory?"

He cleared his throat. Where was that damn Richard? "Of course. Anything."

"Thank you," Ethel said, dabbing her eyes. "She needs someone to guide and protect her. To take her to social occasions this Season. I'll attend them as well, of course, but she won't listen to me"—she let out a half-sob, half-hiccup—"as you so plainly witnessed. When Mabel arrived last night, she wasn't even wearing gloves or a hat. Judging by her reaction, you would have thought I'd asked her to step on one of her infernal creatures instead of asking her a simple question. Her temper flared as quick as can be."

Gregory had no idea what Ethel was referring to, but he nodded sympathetically anyway.

"If you could accompany her to the musicale tonight, it would such a relief to me," Ethel rushed on. "You can be more discreet, making suggestions on how she should behave among the ton. If I suggest one tiny thing, she does the complete opposite."

While Ethel rattled on, the knot that had formed in Gregory's stomach tightened into a noose. His gaze strayed to the corner of the house that Mabel had disappeared around. What was she doing out in the rain anyway with a modified hat box?

"Gregory!" Richard said, coming to the front door. "Come in, come in! No use standing out in the drizzle."

Gregory shook his brother's hand, relieved to see someone he understood.

"He's promised to help with Mabel," Ethel burst out. "He's coming to the musicale and will introduce her to eligible men, the ones who are more mature, of course, because they are the only ones who will be able put up with her quirky rants . . . or at least, they'll be too tired to care about them."

Richard chuckled and slid his arm around his wife's shoulder, then leaned down to kiss her cheek. "That's wonderful, dear." He turned a gleaming eye toward Gregory. "Thank you for your help with Mabel."

Gregory cast a desperate look at Richard, which only made his brother chuckle even more.

"I assume you're here to discuss the Parker horses," Richard continued. Then to his wife, "We'll join you for tea when it's served, my dear."

Ethel seemed mollified. She squeezed her husband's hand then was off to some other part of the house.

Huh. That's how it works, Gregory observed. A bit of affection, a few sweet words, and Ethel's histrionics were cured.

With Ethel gone, and Mabel outside somewhere, Gregory finally had a chance to return his attention to his errand. "How did you know about the Parker horses?"

"Read about them in last night's post," Richard said, leading the way to the library.

Gregory groaned as he followed his brother. He'd thought his letter to Parker had been exclusive, or close to it. "Then everyone knows about the stallions. We must make an offer on one of them right away."

Richard stopped at the library door and opened it, motioning for Gregory to enter first. "I thought the same thing, although I'd like to buy the pair of them."

Gregory turned to look at his brother. "Both stallions?" Perhaps this day was salvageable after all.

"I'll buy one, you buy the other, and we'll train them together," Richard said, closing the door behind him. "On that farm of yours." He walked to a side table and poured two small glasses of port.

"I think that's the most brilliant idea you've ever had," Gregory said.

Richard grinned. "A toast, then?"

Crossing the room, Gregory took one of the glasses. Raising it, he said, "To the stallions." He drank his portion in a couple of swallows, then set his glass down. "I'll write him now."

"Be my guest," Richard said, crossing to the floor-to-ceiling windows over-looking the gardens.

"Do you think your man could post it right away?" Gregory asked.

Richard gave a nod. "I'll ring for him the moment you've finished."

Gregory scrawled the letter to Parker in haste. Then, with Richard's attention still on the window, he started a new letter, one to Violet, in which he suddenly had an excellent excuse to not accompany her to the musicale. For he was otherwise engaged, accompanying Ethel's sister.

"I think I'll go see to Ethel," Richard said. "She seemed quite upset a moment ago. I was afraid that her sister would wreak a bit of havoc on our peace."

Gregory snapped his head up. "Her name is Mabel, right? What is she all about?"

Richard turned from the window. "Come see for yourself, brother. The view will explain everything."

Four

"There you are, beautiful thing," Mabel crooned to the snail she'd just spied beneath a dripping rose bush. Snails fascinated her. She'd read a study about one that had lived for more than ten years in captivity. Rain trickled all around her, but she ignored it. This was the best weather in which to watch snails in their natural habitat. She'd long abandoned her parasol. The rain was only a light drizzle now and besides, she was already wet.

Another snail appeared from the dark soil and crept toward the first snail.

"Friends. You must be friends!" Mabel exclaimed.

"*Who* are friends?" a man's voice spoke above her.

She froze, knowing it must be Gregory, the man she'd literally run into. It was fortuitous that she'd been on her way to the garden when he'd arrived. She didn't know what to think of the immediate affect he'd had on her: his nearly black eyes flashing at her, his black hair, his tall frame, and his somewhat disheveled clothing had all made him look like he'd just stepped out of a wild forest. And his laugh. It had made her want to laugh too.

Mabel rose from her crouch and looked up at him. He was even taller than she'd first thought. Though she had no mirror, she could guess at her tousled appearance, and for the first time in memory, she felt a bit of remorse that she hadn't pinned her hair properly, had kept the parasol shielding her head, or at least had taken more care with the muddy ground.

She could hear Ethel's fretful words now.

Mabel clarified. "The s-snails," she said. Why did she feel so out of sorts around this man? "They are cohabiting, which leads me to believe that they are mates."

Gregory's eyebrows shot up.

"Oh dear, I'm so very sorry," she rushed on. "My sister hates it when I say inappropriate things, and I have a habit of not remembering to curb my tongue until it's too late."

Gregory's lips quirked. "I won't tell her." He crouched at the place she'd occupied. "I agree. They must be mates, which would indeed make them the best of friends."

Mabel was keenly aware of Gregory's dark curls curving against his collar and his broad shoulders speckled with raindrops. Apparently, he'd come outside with no umbrella. And apparently she was staring at him; her face quickly heated into a full blush.

"My brother tells me that you're a scientist, Miss Mabel," he continued, watching the snails as they slowly pushed their way through the dirt.

"My *father* was a scientist. I'm simply an interested student of science." She crouched beside him, drawn to the snails, which were inching closer and closer together. Perhaps they were about to demonstrate . . . Mabel's face went hot again.

"I'd say you're more than interested," Gregory said, casting a sideways glance at her.

No hope of hiding her blush now. Being so close to him made her feel light and airy, even though the clouds above were oppressive. She reminded herself that he was a member of the ton, brother of a duke, representing everything she'd never fit in with and had hoped to avoid...

At least, until she had no choice but to leave her father's estate.

Mabel watched the snails, giving herself time to calm her consternation before replying. "I am no stranger to drawing-room ridicule, Mr. Clark."

"Miss... may I call you Mabel?" he asked.

His request was unexpected and had the feeling of intimacy. Why couldn't he have left her here, alone, in the rain instead of pursuing a conversation?

"I mean, you are my brother's sister-in-law," Gregory said. "That makes us practically family."

Mabel swallowed against her suddenly dry throat. They *were* family. He was her sister's brother-in-law, so by extension, she shouldn't feel nervous around him one bit. "Of course," she managed to rasp.

"Well, then, *Mabel*," he said, standing and extending his hand.

She looked at it, then up at him. His eyes were as dark as she remembered, but instead of the flashing annoyance she'd seen on the porch, they were... kind. Attentive. Curious. Amused?

"Might you take my hand so that I may help you to your feet?" His mouth drew upward.

He was silently laughing at her, she realized. No doubt he'd also prepared a number of jests to share later in mixed company. Mabel could imagine the resulting whispers. She resolutely placed her hand in his and let him pull her to her feet.

But before she could draw her hand away, he said, "Mabel, what I wanted to say, and what I hope you'll receive with the sincerity in which I intend it, is that I think your interest in insects and snails to be absolutely fascinating."

Mabel stared at him, utterly stared, her mouth open and her eyes wide like a koi fish in a shallow pond. "You are jesting, Mr. Clark."

"Call me Gregory," he said, his fingers tightening around hers ever so slightly. "And no. I am in complete earnest about my interest in your work." Before she could counter or protest, he continued. "Tell me about your hat box. I noticed the top has been cut off and altered."

"Oh," Mabel said, this time tugging quite firmly against his grasp and reclaiming her hand. She turned away from him and gazed at the snails, which were ever so much closer to each other now. Weren't they supposed to move slowly? "I want to capture a snail, perhaps two, especially if they're mates." *Oh dear.* Her cheeks were burning again. "It's said that they can live for years in captivity."

"A hat box *would* keep them captive," Gregory said with laughter in his tone.

Mabel looked over at him, narrowing her eyes, trying to gauge whether this would turn into a joke, like the ones she'd so often heard told about her. But his eyes held no disdain. Instead, he was smiling at her.

She found herself wanting to smile back. "I wouldn't make them live in the hat box," she clarified, her mouth tugging upward on its own accord. "It's just a means of transportation as I collect them in the garden and carry them to . . ." She stopped. She hadn't thought her plan through entirely. She'd brought several of her insect collections with her and set them up in her guest room, but what would Ethel think of having live snails inside her immaculate home?

She looked behind her; surely there was a gardener's shed someplace that she could—

"If you need a place," Gregory said, "I have a small, unused greenhouse at my townhouse. I'm afraid my gardens aren't nearly as nice as my brother's, but the previous resident must have wanted to cultivate plants in the winter months and built the greenhouse."

Mabel felt her eyes sting, as if she might actually grow emotional at such a generous offer. "I-I don't know. I mean..."

And then a surge of joy pulsed through her as she pictured his offer. A private greenhouse. Away from Ethel's scrutiny. All to herself. She smiled at Gregory, pointedly keeping her arms at her sides because she wanted nothing more than to hug him in gratitude. "Where do you live?"

He chuckled, and Mabel realized that his dark eyes were perhaps the most captivating she'd ever seen, far and above those of any of her precious insects.

"I'm only two streets over. A short carriage ride or a nice walk on a sunny day. Although I don't think you're the type of woman to let rain stop you from doing what you want."

She had no reason to blush, but she did despite her efforts. "I would be honored, Gregory," she said. "Thank you."

Suddenly, spending the Season in London didn't seem so awful, not if she would be able to conduct her snail research in Gregory's greenhouse. She bent to retrieve the hat box. Perhaps she could go to the greenhouse now to prepare the place.

"You are welcome," Gregory said.

His voice brought her back to the present. "Why did you come out here? Certainly not to offer me the use of your greenhouse."

"No," he said. "It seems your sister expects us at tea."

"You tell me this now?" she said. "After we've been dallying for a quarter of an hour?"

He didn't seem the least bothered by the delay in delivering his message. "Dallying in the garden, in the rain, seemed much preferable to tea."

Mabel laughed, surprising herself. "I agree," she said. "Unless you are merely teasing me, in which case, I disagree with your teasing."

"I am only half-teasing," Gregory said. "But mostly I am in earnest, and I'm very much looking forward to your setting up your projects in my greenhouse."

Mabel's breath left her for a few seconds. *Hard to believe this man is a member of the ton.*

Gregory belted out a laugh, then wiped off some of the rain from his face. "I might be a member of the ton, but I'm a bit unconventional . . . like you, I suppose."

Mable stared at him in horror. "Did I say that aloud?"

He continued to smile. "I enjoy hearing your thoughts."

Mabel exhaled slowly, her mind spinning in a hundred different directions. "You are not what I expected, Gregory Clark."

Five

You are not what I expected, Mabel had said.

Gregory could say the same of her. She was unexpected. Refreshing. Unassuming. He found himself humming as Jones, his newly rehired valet, tied his cravat.

Now back at home, Gregory had a chance to reflect on his interactions with Miss Mabel Russell. He had never met anyone quite like her. He suspected her to be one-of-a-kind, and he was wholly charmed by her. He could see why she vexed her sister and maddened members of the ton. But he had little respect for the ton, anyway. He was tired of their fussy ways, severe judgments, and frivolous activities and conversations.

When had he ever spent such a delightful morning? And in the rain and crouched in the dirt, no less? He didn't particularly care for snails, but as Mabel had explained their unique lives and habits as they strode back to the house, he'd become quite interested. The most memorable moment of the day was when Mabel had told Ethel over tea about her intentions of moving her projects to Gregory's greenhouse.

Ethel had shown a mixture of delight and confusion. Richard had shot him a questioning look, which Gregory promptly ignored. His brother would become aware of Gregory's interest in Mabel soon enough. He was quickly losing his heart to Mabel—an experience he'd never thought he'd have in this life—especially in London.

Darkness had fallen, and it was nearing eight o'clock, the hour in which his brother, Ethel, and Mabel would come for him. They would attend the musicale, and Gregory was happy to accompany Mabel. He only hoped that Violet had received his message in time and wouldn't be there waiting for him. Or if she did come, that she wouldn't make a spectacle. After all, nothing of note had happened between them. Only a bit of flirting, mostly on Violet's part.

After leaving his brother's home following tea, Gregory had spent most of the afternoon cleaning the greenhouse. He couldn't wait to show Mabel about and hoped she wasn't otherwise engaged the next day. Or the next.

His senses were so alert that Gregory heard the arrival of the duke's carriage below his closed window. He bit back an impatient remark directed at Jones and instead, took a moment to gather his senses as Jones made a final brushdown of his coat. He didn't want to frighten Mabel off with his eagerness to show devotion. In fact, he had better play it casual.

But once he'd climbed into the four-person carriage and situated himself across from Richard and Ethel, which put him next to Mabel, every piece of clothing felt wrong. His collar was too tight, his cravat sloppy, his hands inside his gloves too hot, his shoes stiff . . .

"Have you heard Miss Patterson sing before?" Ethel asked.

Mabel remained curiously silent. If he hadn't known better, he might have thought she was out of sorts about something. But he didn't know her as much as he'd have liked to. Had she noticed how much he was fidgeting? The carriage was much smaller than he'd remembered, and it seemed to have a lack of sufficient air.

"Gregory, did you hear me?" Ethel said, her voice rising. He hadn't realized she'd spoken to him. Why was his reply suddenly so important?

His brother had to be a very patient man. Gregory thought he heard a scoff from Mabel, but he didn't turn to look at her. Yet as the carriage jostled along the road, the fabric of her dress brushed against his leg. And she smelled quite nice. Not that she hadn't smelled otherwise in the garden, or when she'd first knocked him over, but tonight she had a distinct scent of roses, or perhaps another flower. He wanted to see Mabel's face in the light, and to tell her about how he'd cleaned the greenhouse. But he didn't want their conversation overheard.

He felt a sharp jab to his side and was stunned to realize it was Mabel's doing.

"I haven't heard her sing," he said, shaking his head slightly and trying to focus on the conversation inside the carriage. He dared a glance in Mabel's direction, and he could have sworn she was holding back a smile, although he'd only glimpsed her profile.

"She's wonderful," Ethel exclaimed, her voice not as sharp as before, but still had an edge to it. She turned to Richard. "Isn't that right, dear?"

"Yes, my love. She is wonderful." He patted her hand as if trying to soothe a child.

Gregory wanted to be out of the confines of the carriage. Was something going on between the sisters again? He glanced down to Mabel's folded hands resting on her lap and wondered if the sisters had battled over who wore which gloves. If there had, it appeared that Ethel had won out tonight—Mabel was every bit as well turned out as her sister.

The carriage slowed, and as it pulled to a stop, Mabel's arm brushed his, only the barest brush of Mabel's arm against his, yet the sensation had traveled straight to his heart. Gregory's pulse leapt. He closed his eyes and blew out a breath. It was going to be an interesting evening.

"Are you all right?" Mabel asked in a soft voice.

He opened his eyes. "I am," he said, knowing that he was acting like a young fool, reacting so strongly to a slight touch from a woman.

Richard stepped out of the carriage and helped Ethel, then Mabel, down. Gregory alighted last and offered his arm to Mabel. She slipped her hand around his arm without hesitation, as if it were the most natural thing.

Ethel's brows arched sky-high as she looked over at her sister. "Remember what I said, Mabel."

Gregory cringed at her tone; he'd been at the receiving end of it more than once.

"I will," Mabel said.

But Ethel persisted. "Your behavior tonight is imperative. You'll make your first impressions and may wipe away all gossip from last year's drawing room disaster."

Mabel's fingers tightened on Gregory's arm, and she stood straighter and stiffer.

"I said I'll remember," Mabel said, her voice quiet but firm. "Must you bring that up every chance you get? I'm not a child, Ethel. If you recall, I'm here by your request. I would have been perfectly happy to stay in tonight."

Ethel flushed, but she raised her chin, eyes glittering. "I remind only so you'll take more care, and to make sure you don't laugh too loud or start talking about—"

"I know, Ethel," Mabel cut in. "I won't talk about any insects, alive or dead, and I won't discuss about how upset I am with father's cousin for running us out of our own home, or about how wasteful the members of the ton are, spending their days purchasing the latest fashions and drinking imported French wines while beggars are starving a few streets away—"

"Mabel!" Ethel said. Her piercing gaze turned to Gregory. "Tell her. Tell her how important it is to not create a stir."

Gregory wished to climb back into the carriage. He looked at Richard, who seemed to be taking everything as par for the course. Either he was used to the sisters' arguments, or Ethel didn't put Richard in the middle of them.

Gregory looked down at Mabel, and she met his gaze. He expected to find her upset, or at least ruffled, by her sister's words, but her expression was one of challenge, as if she were challenging him.

He held back a laugh, for now. "Your sister only wants the best for you," he said, drawing Mabel toward the walkway, out of the way of the next approaching carriage. He called back to Ethel, "Don't worry, I'll keep her out of harm's way."

Ethel must have been satisfied with that, as she began talking to Richard about one of their neighbors. Gregory took the opportunity of her distraction to lean close to Mabel and whisper, "I would love to hear about your father's unscrupulous cousin and the evils of indulging in French wine."

A smile lifted the sides of Mabel's mouth. "Don't let my sister hear you say that."

"And please do tell me of the terrible fashions Society enslaves itself to."

Mabel's nose wrinkled as she eyed him. "Don't tell me you're willing to get rid of your cravat?"

"Do you want me to?" He lifted his hand to his throat as if to untie it.

She blushed furiously.

Gregory realized he'd taken the teasing too far. Fortunately, they had arrived at the main doors of the musicale. The doorman held the door open for their party, and soon they were swept up in greetings by old friends.

Mabel released his arm but stayed close as Ethel made introductions. He caught Mabel's eye more than once, and each time, she looked away quickly, her lips pursed but her eyes twinkling. And Gregory wondered how on earth he could learn how Mabel had been involved with the "drawing room disaster" the year before.

Six

Gregory appreciated the refreshments that were brought around before the start of the musicale. He looked on as Richard and Ethel introduced Mabel to several men and the guests began finding their ways into the music hall and to their chairs.

"I knew your father," a man named Mr. Weathers said to Mabel. He bent over her hand with a decided sniff. He reminded Gregory of a hound. "His papers were very thought-provoking," Weathers continued.

Mabel gave the man a genuine smile.

Gregory's heart hitched a little.

While Richard and another man were talking to him about their purchase of the Parker stallions, he tried to listen at the same time to the conversation between Mabel and Mr. Weathers.

"He used to dictate his findings to me." Mabel's voice had become bright and cheery.

"How wonderful," Weathers said. "You must have quite the intellect."

When a blush rose on her cheeks, Gregory felt himself frowning. Weathers appeared to be a decent sort of man; his clothing was well tailored and his mustache neatly trimmed. If it weren't for his pointed nose and habit of constantly sniffing, Gregory might have approved of the man. Or was it sniffling? Did the man have a cold?

Gregory realized he hadn't heard a word they'd said for several moments, and when he paid greater attention, Mabel was speaking.

"You really can't discount winter," she said. "Many insects and critters hibernate, but others quite enjoy the cold."

"Ah, interesting," Weathers said with a smile that further confirmed Gregory's first impression of a hound dog. "If you would like to sit by me during the performance, I'd love to hear more about winter-loving insects."

And then Weathers glanced down at Mabel's bosom.

It was one thing to constantly sniffle, but quite another to ogle. Mabel wore a fashionable dress with a snug bodice, but that was all Gregory had allowed himself to notice.

"Miss Mabel will be sitting with me," Gregory interrupted. "I wouldn't want her to catch cold." He stared at Weathers, who looked as if he'd been struck on the side of the face.

The man's mouth dropped open, and then, as if in confirmation of Gregory's implication, Weathers sniffed again. "I am quite well, thank you," Weathers said, lifting one of his shaggy brows. "Have we been introduced?"

"Not formally," Gregory said, holding out a hand. "I'm Gregory Clark."

Weathers' eyes widened a fraction. "Ah, the duke's brother. I've heard your name."

They stared at each other a moment, and then finally

Weathers said, "Nice to meet you . . . both. Perhaps we'll have a chance to talk more during intermission."

Gregory gave a distracted nod and guided Mabel to a set of chairs behind Ethel and Richard. Ethel saw them approach and flashed a hopeful smile at Gregory. He nodded, indicating that Mabel had behaved properly.

"That was quite rude to whisk me away from him," Mabel whispered as they sat down.

"*He* was rude," Gregory whispered back.

"How? By showing interest in my studies and asking questions?" Mabel folded her arms and kept her gaze straight ahead.

A man at the front of the room began a recitation of the many talents and virtues of the night's singer, Miss Patterson.

Gregory leaned close to Mabel. "He was *staring* at you."

She went very still, then looked at him from the corner of her eye. "Is it so terrible for a man to take an interest in me? Isn't that why I'm here, to get married off so my sister will no longer need to endure my idiosyncrasies?"

Laws, this woman didn't have trouble speaking her mind—something Gregory found completely refreshing. "He was staring at you in an entirely inappropriate manner."

Her head turned a fraction of an inch toward him, so Gregory could see more than her profile. Heaven help him, she was blushing again.

"Well, Mr. Gregory Clark, how *should* a man look at a woman such as myself?"

He fought to keep a somber face. The introduction of Miss Patterson was over, and another woman began to play the opening notes of a song on the pianoforte. In only seconds, Gregory wouldn't be able to say another word for a while.

Leaning slightly closer than was perhaps entirely proper, he whispered, "A man should look at a woman with the respect she deserves, especially one as beautiful as you."

Mabel turned to look at him full on. Her eyes gleamed with amusement, as if she considered what he'd said a great joke. "You, Gregory Clark, are a flirt."

He was about to deny her accusation when Miss Patterson opened her mouth and started to sing. Mabel turned her attention to the singer. From the start, Miss Patterson's voice was pleasant and captivating, and Gregory could understand why Ethel found her so engaging.

Gregory sat back in his chair, and Mabel leaned forward attentively, apparently taken with the performance. He had called her beautiful, and he'd meant it. He hadn't been teasing or flirting, merely stating a fact. But she was so much more than a beautiful face, and when he dared think it, a lovely figure. The music hall was filled with beautiful women, yet none captured his attention like Mabel did.

While she watched Miss Patterson, Gregory watched Mabel. As long as he continued leaning back, he had a nice view of her profile—her eyelashes, the rosy blush high on her cheeks, her dark hair arranged in an expert coif. He tried to look past Mabel and focus on the performer—he sincerely did—but every time he took his eyes from Mabel, they invariably strayed back only seconds later.

Miss Patterson finished a song, and Mabel burst into fervent applause. Gregory applauded as well. A few heads turned at Mabel's enthusiastic response. Even Ethel glanced back, her lips in a tight line.

Miss Patterson sang two more songs, and then the attendees broke for intermission.

Ethel turned to them with a smile. "I saw you speaking with Mr. Weathers at quite some length," she said to Mabel. "He's a fine gentleman."

Mabel nodded. "He is. Did you know that he's read much of Father's work? We had a lovely conversation about the temperatures in which some insects thrive."

Ethel's brow pulled down. "Oh, Mabel," she said in a hushed voice. "Please don't tell me you put him off."

"It was all quite civilized," Mabel said, keeping her smile. "Ask Mr. Clark."

Ethel turned an inquisitive eye toward Gregory.

And again he was caught between the two sisters. "Mr. Weathers seemed quite taken with Mabel," he admitted.

Ethel beamed and clasped her sister's hands. "He's a good catch. Be sure to seek him out before the end of the evening so he'll feel compelled to call tomorrow."

Mabel returned her sister's smile, making Gregory's heart sink. How could she be interested in Mr. Weathers? His nose was too long and pointed and those inferno sniffles couldn't be born, not to mention his straying eye.

"Would anyone care for a stroll on the veranda before the second half of the program begins?" Gregory asked. "It's quite warm in here."

Ethel linked her arm through her husband's. "We must speak with the Chatsworths. I haven't seen them in ages."

"I'll come with you for a walk," Mabel said to him.

Gregory gave a single nod as the thought of Mabel coming with him on a walk made his heart hammer. Mabel placed a hand on his arm, and it was all he could do to keep from staring at her as they walked to the Venetian doors. Once outside, the cooler air did him immediate good, although his heart rate didn't slow much.

A few other couples were strolling about, seeking the same break from the stuffy music hall. A nice breeze had picked up, and Gregory wished he could loosen his cravat to enjoy the full effect.

"Now," Mabel said, her hand playfully squeezing his arm. "Why are you so against Mr. Weathers?"

"I'm not *wholly* against him," Gregory hedged.

"*Partially*, then?"

He couldn't help but smile at her wit. They'd reached a low wall that surrounded a garden. Gregory stopped and turned to face Mabel. "I can see why your sister becomes so vexed with you."

She returned his smile. "Do you know something about Mr. Weathers you aren't telling me? Perhaps a dark secret too horrible to divulge in front of a lady?"

Gregory studied her face. In the moonlight, she looked positively ethereal. "There's nothing horrible about him, at least, not to my knowledge. We met for the first time tonight. But . . ." He paused as another couple strolled by, and they exchanged brief greetings.

"But?" Mabel prompted when they were alone again.

"But he is not good enough for you. He does not appreciate you like I—" Gregory closed his mouth. He'd been about to get himself in trouble, a lot of trouble.

Mabel's brows simply arched. "Do *you* appreciate me, sir?"

Seven

Mabel had been bold to ask the question; such had been her nature since she was a little girl—her father had told her about all her wailing she did if she didn't get her way immediately.

The way Gregory looked at her now made gooseflesh rise on her arms—not in fear or wariness, but in the most warm, delightful manner. She enjoyed Gregory's quips and discomfiture over Mr. Weathers. It was only natural for her to tease him about it. Or perhaps she had deeper reasons for drawing him out and getting him to confess that he was interested in *her*, however unbelievable such a thing might be to some.

It would certainly be unbelievable to Ethel, who could comprehend only a fortunate match for Mabel if she took on the persona of a woman who spoke merely when necessary, and only about inane topics.

Unfortunately, Gregory Clark, brother of the Duke of Rochester, was a member of the ton. And although Mabel found him handsome, good-natured, and decidedly charming and affable, she would never marry someone from the ton. No, Mr. Weathers was much more to her liking—a non-descript man who lived a quiet life in the country.

In fact, she felt quite excited at the thought of establishing herself as the lady of a manor, in which she could come and go as she pleased. No one would question her penchant for insect collections if her husband supported her desires.

Besides, Gregory had very specific opinions, likes and dislikes. She had no use for that sort of man.

His mouth turned up in a smile as he held her gaze. "Of course I appreciate you. You're Ethel's sister."

"So it's your duty, then, to appreciate me," she pressed. "A family obligation?"

"No," Gregory said. His eyebrows had risen as if he was surprised at the question and didn't know how to respond. "I mean . . . perhaps that's part of it."

Mabel turned from him and looked out over the shadowed garden. "It's almost time to return to the hall. Don't you think Miss Patterson has a lovely voice?"

Gregory moved closer. "Mabel," he said in a low voice. "I must explain myself."

She held very still, not looking up at him.

He was close enough to feel the warmth of his body. "Mr. Weathers is a fine gentleman, as your sister said." He hesitated and reached for her hand.

The move surprised Mabel, but she didn't resist. She didn't move at all, though her hand was quickly warming in his.

"When he looked at you as if you were a prize—assessing your figure and studying your manner—it bothered me."

Mabel looked up at him. "Isn't that what all men do?

Especially those of the ton?" She pulled her hand from his and folded her arms. "Mr. Weathers is like you and all of the others who decide if a woman is worthy of marrying based the way she dresses and the people she's connected to."

Gregory looked as if he'd been slapped, and Mabel hid a triumphant smile. This was exactly why she hated musicales, balls, and other formal events—the pompous opinions, the judging of merit based on appearance, and the heated debates with handsome men. Well, maybe the heated debates weren't typical, and maybe she shouldn't be so stirred up by a few comments made by one she'd only recently met.

A woman's voice cut through the night air. "Gregory! There you are!"

He turned, seeming stunned that someone had interrupted. Mabel turned too. A woman in a shimmering violet gown practically sailed toward them. Her limbs were long and elegant, her movements graceful. If Mabel hadn't known better and recognized the telltale appearance of someone of high station, she'd have thought this was a dancer from one of the London stages.

"Darling, I've been looking for you everywhere," the woman said.

Gregory took her proffered hand and bent over it, bestowing a kiss. When he straightened, Mabel eyed him curiously. His face had flushed, and he didn't look particularly happy to see the woman.

"Who is this young thing?" the woman crooned.

"May I introduce Miss Mabel Russell, Ethel's sister," Gregory said. Then he turned to her, but his eyes were a bit unfocused. "Mabel, this is Mrs. Violet Muller."

"How wonderful to meet you," Violet said. "So kind of Gregory to escort his sister-in-law." Her eyes went back to Gregory, and she took a step closer. "I admit that when I first received your note, I was distressed. I hoped that nothing was amiss between us."

Mabel's chest tightened as Violet ran her fingers up Gregory's arms.

He gave Violet a faint smile, but that didn't matter. Surely he was more than affable toward Violet when they were alone.

"Will I have the honor of meeting your husband, Mrs. Muller?" Mabel said.

"Mr. Muller passed on two years ago," Violet said, not taking her eyes off Gregory. Her simpering smile didn't seem to indicate any lingering grief over her dead husband.

"My condolences," Mabel said, but Violet barely acknowledged her. Mabel felt the heat of embarrassment creep up her neck. Who was this woman, and what claim did she have on Gregory? She tried to shift the conversation. "Do you know my sister, Ethel?"

This time, Violet did look over at Mabel. "Ethel? Why, no. We have not yet been introduced. Perhaps Gregory will do the honors." She linked her arm through Gregory's, with a familiarity that seemed more than a casual friendship. It had an intimate feeling to it, as if . . .

Mabel exhaled with the realization. As if they were more than acquainted. As if they were lovers.

"If you'll excuse me," Mabel said. "I'm sure Ethel is looking for me." She hurried away before she could hear Violet say one more thing to Gregory.

Mabel had hoped, perhaps had even believed, that Gregory might prove to be different from the others, even though she'd accused him of being the same as the rest of the ton. She blinked against a burning in her eyes as she stepped into the music hall, not wanting to speak with anyone. But there was no way she could avoid conversation after Ethel had spotted her and waved her over.

Coincidentally, Ethel and Richard were speaking with Mr. Weathers. It was just as well. At least he hadn't a woman, dressed in a color to match her name, hanging on him.

"There you are," Ethel said, all smiles. "We were getting acquainted with Mr. Weathers. Did you know he raises sheep on his country estate?"

Mabel returned her sister's smile, then greeted Mr. Weathers. He beamed at her. What did it matter if his gaze strayed a bit too low? She pushed away thoughts of Gregory and what he might be doing with Violet in the gardens. All men were indeed cut from the same cloth. If marry she must, she'd prefer a quiet life in the country with someone like Mr. Weathers. The conversation continued around her, and she contributed here and there, but decided that she wouldn't be fool enough to expect a love match if she were to marry at all. Mr. Weathers would do just fine.

Eight

Two Days Later

From his bedroom window, Gregory stared out at the drizzling rain and swore. The night of the musicale had been a disaster, and it seemed the heavens above wanted to add in their two bits. His heart had nearly stopped when Violet had appeared in the gardens and interrupted his and Mabel's conversation.

Violet had immediately homed in on Mabel and latched onto Gregory. The moment Violet had done so, he'd wanted to shake off her steely grip, but she hadn't been easy to deter. And after Mabel had left them alone, it had been all Gregory could do to not chase after her.

Gregory's teeth still hurt from gritting them. Eventually, he'd been able to politely escape Violet and take his seat by Mabel. But there had been no more soft smiles or sideways glances. Mabel had remained stiff and silent.

And at one point, she'd leaned over and said in a quiet,

furious tone, "You're just like all of the other men of the ton."

For the second time that night, he'd felt as if he'd been slapped.

Had they not been surrounded by so many people, all with eager eyes and loose tongues, he would have marched her out to the veranda and . . . what? Told her that he was not like the others? That he was sorry about Violet's insinuations? That he had an offer in on a country estate where Mabel could explore and collect all of the insects her heart desired?

Gregory cursed for a second time and let his head fall against the cold windowpane. How could he have become so wrapped up in Mabel? He'd only just met her. He could imagine her reaction if he were to declare himself . . . or worse, Ethel's. Richard would simply laugh. And laugh.

But heaven help him, Gregory couldn't stop thinking about her. Not after she'd remained silent in the carriage as they drove him home, not after he'd climbed into his cold, empty bed that night, and not while he'd tossed two nights in a row, with her spiteful words echoing in his mind. Not when he spent the whole of yesterday traveling to and from the Parker estate to sign the purchase agreement for his pair of stallions. And certainly not this morning, when he'd awakened with a blistering headache.

Gregory turned from the window. It was nearly noon, and he'd accomplished nothing. He hadn't even let his valet dress him. Jones probably thought he was on the verge of being fired, again. Crumpled paper lay strewn about the floor where Gregory had discarded letter after letter to Mabel. The only correspondence he'd successfully completed was a letter to Violet, effectively breaking all ties with her. She would be upset, but he hoped she'd forget about him. He couldn't allow her pursuit to continue.

He used the bell on his desk to ring for Jones. When the valet entered, Gregory said, "I need to dress quickly. I'm going to my brother's house."

Twenty minutes later, Gregory's mood did not improve when he pulled up in his carriage in front of his brother's home, only to see another carriage out front. He'd hoped to speak to Mabel without a lot of people around.

As it was, he reached the doorstep the moment the door opened and Mr. Weathers came striding out. Gregory stopped and stared. The inferno man looked much too pleased with himself—so pleased that Gregory wanted to swing at him to get the smile off his face.

And behind Mr. Weathers walked a beaming Ethel and smiling Mabel.

Drat. Had the man already proposed? Gregory nodded to Mr. Weathers but otherwise ignored him. When Mr. Weathers was finally tucked into his carriage, Gregory turned to the women.

"Gregory, how lovely to see you," Ethel said, the remains of her smile still in place. "Richard isn't here at the moment, but—"

He held up a hand. "That's quite all right. I've actually come to invite the both of you to my home to tour my newly renovated greenhouse."

"Oh. How . . . kind," Ethel managed, her eyebrows drawing together in confusion.

Gregory looked past her to Mabel, whose smile had fled; her expression was utterly blank.

"I've, uh," Gregory started, clearing his throat. "I've cleared it out. And now it's simply waiting for new occupants." He looked from one sister to the other. At his words, a bit of light had crept into Mabel's eyes, giving Gregory hope that she didn't completely hate him.

"That was very generous of you," Ethel said, turning to Mabel. "Don't you think so, dear?"

Mabel gave a slight nod, but said nothing.

"Well, then, if you aren't otherwise engaged, would you like to come in my carriage?" Gregory said in a casual tone, trying not to sound too eager. "I know it's a bit drizzly, but my horses are at the ready."

"Well, I . . ." Ethel said, glancing again at Mabel, who made no indication of her desires.

The seconds moved slower than snails.

Finally, it seemed that Mabel's curiosity prevailed over her disapproval with Gregory. "Now is as good a time as any," she said. Her voice sounded dull, but Gregory noticed her eyes had again livened just a bit.

The women called for their cloaks, and within moments, everyone was settled into his carriage. The drive to his townhouse was punctuated by light conversation, mostly with Ethel's inquiries about Gregory's trip to Parker's the day before. Mabel remained silent, but more than once, he caught her gaze on him.

He couldn't very well count that as a victory, not yet. First he needed to apologize if he expected anything to return to progress. He hoped she'd give him a chance to explain about Violet. Gregory realized that even if his relationship with Mabel had no hope of progressing, and if, heaven forbid, she became engaged to Mr. Weathers, he valued Mabel's friendship above all else.

By the time the carriage had stopped in front of his townhouse, the rain had also stopped, and the clouds had parted enough to let the midday sunshine through.

Mabel stepped out of the carriage and turned her face toward the sun. "I thought the sun would never come out," she declared to no one in particular.

Gregory took the opportunity to hopefully draw her out. "The sun must have been waiting for you to come."

A slight smile played on Mabel's face, but she didn't answer.

"You've kept us in suspense long enough, Gregory," Ethel said. "Lead the way."

So he did, through the side gate and around the townhouse, to the small garden area and greenhouse. He had to admit that in the sunlight, it looked quite nice surrounded by trees of dripping green. He opened the greenhouse door for the ladies and followed them inside.

Ethel wrinkled her nose. "It smells as if this place has been locked up for ages."

"It does," Gregory said, looking over at Mabel. Her opinion was the one that mattered.

She'd walked farther in than her sister and now stood in the middle, gazing about.

"What do you think, Mabel?" Gregory ventured.

She seemed startled that he'd spoken to her. When their eyes met, her expression was sober. Gregory's heart lurched at the depths of green in her eyes. They were like something from a forest, as if she'd lived a former life as a nymph.

"It's adequate," Mabel said.

"Adequate?" Ethel's voice pierced the air. "What's ever gotten into you, Mabel? The other day you were in raptures just thinking about this place." She gave a sniff, then wrinkled her nose again. "I think I'll go and speak to Mrs. Brown about tea. Is that all right with you, Gregory?"

"Of course." His fortune today had turned out to be greater than he could have hoped. He'd have a chance to apologize, to explain, to—

"I'll come with you," Mabel said, leaving Gregory's side and crossing to her sister.

Gregory stared after the two women as they left the greenhouse. He wasn't sure exactly what had happened or why, but he felt as if he'd just had his heart trampled on.

Nine

"Thank you, Bess," Mabel said, dismissing the maid who'd finished arranging her hair. The young woman scurried from the room, probably excited to have a few hours off.

Mabel glanced at the sealed envelope on her dressing table, which she'd been ignoring ever since its delivery that morning. It was from Gregory, and she had no idea why he'd written her. Well, that wasn't entirely true. It was probably some sort of apology, explaining who Violet was and most likely insisting that the woman was only a friend.

As if Mabel could ever believe that.

She'd turned down Ethel's pleadings to attend a rout the night before, knowing that Gregory would be there. But she couldn't turn down the masquerade ball tonight. Ethel had insisted she attend, seeing as Mr. Weathers had inquired specifically after her.

Mabel had no doubt that Gregory would attend as well, and even though everyone would be wearing masks, they wouldn't be concealment enough for a man as tall and broad as Gregory.

Mabel let out a sigh. She knew she was being stubborn. Perhaps she should get it done with and let the man apologize. She couldn't avoid Richard's brother forever. Gregory would always be around, in one capacity or another.

Mabel picked up the letter and slid her finger under the seal. She scanned the words quickly, feeling her face heat as she did so. Then she leaned forward on her dressing table and read more slowly.

> *Dear Mabel,*
>
> *I hope this letter finds you well and happy. I also hope that I am not being too forward in what I want to say to you. I realize it may be difficult to have a private conversation in the near future, as it seems you are determined to not speak to me.*

Mabel's face flushed at his accusation. She *had* been stubborn. Embarrassingly so.

> *First, I hope we can be friends, no matter your thoughts after you read this letter. I truly hope we can have the best sort of friendship. We will often be in each other's company, seeing as your sister is married to my brother. But it's more than that. I greatly esteem you, and I hope you'll believe my sincerity in saying so.*
>
> *Mrs. Violet Muller was widowed two years ago as you know, and since my arrival in London a few weeks ago, she's taken a decided interest in me. She is a pleasant woman, I'll admit, but she is not for me.*
>
> *You accused me of being like other men of the*

ton. I want to assure you that whatever else you may think of me, I am not like other men in this regard. To be blunt, in hopes that you appreciate direct speech, I do not and have not had an intimate relationship with Mrs. Muller.

Were these pretty words from a pretty gentleman? Mabel wanted to believe that's all they were, but her heart said he was sincere. And that meant she had wrongly accused him and selfishly judged him. Her stubborn heart softened as she realized that the man she'd hoped Gregory to be, might in fact be the man he actually was.

The second point I feel I need to address is that my offer of the greenhouse has no conditions of use whatsoever. You may come and go as you please, with no obligation to meet with or speak to me. I've informed my staff that you have free rein and are to be made welcome any time you should arrive.

Mabel smiled to herself even as guilt crept in. He was too kind, too generous. And she did not deserve such consideration. Not after the way she'd practically thrown a fit like a jealous woman. He'd treated her with the same respect she should have given him. And for the first time since meeting him, and becoming mesmerized by those dark eyes, she allowed the barriers around her heart to lower.

Yes, he was a gentleman of the ton, but he was so much more. His station didn't have to define him, just as hers didn't define her. He was offering an olive branch to her, a woman who least deserved it.

The third point, and perhaps one that will be less

well received than the others, is that I was not entirely honest about the reasons behind discouraging your interest in Mr. Weathers. I did—and still do—hold you in high esteem. I am enamored with your character. And, I also must confess, you have captivated me. Not only with your beauty, which is plain for every man to see, but also with your openness, your honesty, your love for what really matters, and your impatience with what doesn't.

Mabel brought a hand to her heart, her breath growing short. Was it possible? She wondered. Possible to fall in love with a man through the written word? Or had she already loved him from the moment he'd crouched beside her to examine the snails in the garden? If her heart had turned toward him on that day, then she had not allowed herself to accept such a possibility.

But now . . .

Mabel, if you haven't already ripped this letter to shreds and burned it to ash, I'd like permission to be your friend. And if I may be so bold, I'd like to ask for the opportunity to court you. If I must compete with Mr. Weathers for your good favor, I will gladly do so. I ask for no promise from you, but only a fair chance, if you'd be so generous to allow it.

Yours,
Gregory Clark

Mabel touched her cold hands to her hot cheeks. And then she laughed. It turned into a giggle, and soon she was crying. *I've lost my mind.*

She read the letter again, but then suddenly, she

couldn't read it anymore. It was too personal, too dear. She scanned her bedroom for a place to hide the letter and settled on slipping it beneath the lining of one of her insect collections.

Then she took out a fresh piece of paper from the bureau and began a letter to Gregory.

Ten

Gregory couldn't stop smiling. He was a fool, and he knew it. But he was also in love, and didn't that allow for one to play the fool? Standing on the outskirts of the main crush at the masquerade, he waited for Mabel to appear with her sister and Richard.

They were late, which only made his heart pound harder. Ethel was not one to be late, so, of course, Gregory started imagining all sorts of arguments between the sisters that might have caused the delay. But mostly, he just smiled as he recalled the letter he'd received only an hour before from Mabel.

The script had been hastily written, which perhaps meant she hadn't read his letter until that evening. The thought of her incessant stubbornness had only made him laugh. In her letter, she'd told him of the infamous drawing-room disaster, in which she'd worn a tiny—living—lizard as a brooch to a soiree. She'd secured a jeweled collar around the creature's neck, then pinned the collar to her gown.

The men had all been quite interested, and many had

asked questions. But the women had been mortified, and one had even screamed and fainted. Gregory chuckled, remembering Mabel's description of the debacle:

> *Mrs. Christensen scared my lizard so thoroughly that the poor thing had an unfortunate accident on my silk dress. Ethel was so horrified at the woman's screams and my spoiled dress that she ushered me home immediately. News of the incident was printed in the society papers the next day, and Ethel forced me to write an apology to every single person who had been in attendance that night. After writing so many letters, my hand ached for days.*

What hadn't been so humorous was when Mabel recalled being referred to as "lizard-lady" for weeks afterward.

Mabel's letter had continued:

> *But if you can live with courting lizard-lady, then I suppose I will give you a running chance against Mr. Weathers.*

And thus the smiling.

None too soon, Mabel arrived. Even in her jeweled mask, Gregory immediately knew it was her. She wore a gray silk dress edged in dark green. Her mask was of silver as well, and adorned with dark green feathers. He waited a moment, while Mabel and Ethel and Richard greeted the hosts, then he moved through the crowd. He paused until he was sure that the person Mabel seemed to be scanning the crowd for was him. When her gaze landed on him, and her mouth turned slightly upward, he knew it was time.

He crossed the room and when there was a slight lull in the conversation between Mabel and Ethel, he stepped forward just as the first waltz started up. "May I have this dance?"

She turned to him, with Ethel at her side. Plainly, Ethel didn't know who he was, but judging by the shy smile from Mabel, she clearly did.

He held out one hand, and as she placed her hand in it, she squeezed his fingers.

As they joined the others on the ballroom floor, he asked, "Whatever happened to that lizard?"

She smiled up at him, her lips the softest pink, her eyes a deep green peering from behind the mask, and Gregory knew that his heart would never land back on earth.

"I released it in the wilds of Hyde Park, to forever frighten ladies and cause them to faint."

As he led her through the steps Gregory chuckled, then lowered his voice and leaned a bit closer. "I think I've seen the little fellow from time to time."

"You have?" Mabel gave a soft laugh, her breath sweet. "I'd love to visit him."

"Then we shall," Gregory declared as they moved to the music and around the couples on the floor. "I will pick you up tomorrow in my curricle." He held her gaze. "Unless . . . you have another suitor coming by?"

"I have no other suitor," Mabel said, moving a touch closer to him.

"What about Mr. Weathers?" His heart drummed. Had she put Mr. Weathers off already?

"It's a long story," she said with a dramatic sigh.

They danced another few measures, Gregory waiting for her to continue. When she didn't, he said, "I love a long story."

She blinked at him, amused. "Perhaps I'll tell you one day."

"One day? What's wrong with right now?" The music drew to a close, and the dancers were leaving the floor arm in arm. Gregory could dance no more than twice with her in the same evening, unless they were engaged. Since they weren't, he'd have to give her up to dance with some other fellow within moments. "Has the next dance been spoken for?"

"No, but I cannot dance with you twice in a row," she said, stepping out of his hold. "What would Ethel think? Or better yet, the ton?"

Gregory smiled and offered his arm. "No one will even know who we are."

"You *are* a flirt," she said as they began to walk to the edge of the ballroom. "I knew it from the moment I met you."

"You mean the moment you ran me over?" Gregory said as the music struck up for the next number, a quadrille.

"I take exception to that."

"I take exception to your calling me a flirt," Gregory countered. "If I have ever been in earnest about any one thing, it is about you."

"Then take me out to the garden where the air is cool," Mabel said in a low voice. "And we can discuss your earnestness away from the crush."

Gregory happily led her to the garden. "Shall we hunt for snails?" he asked conspiratorially.

"Tempting," she said, looking over at him.

The moonlight made her look like a fairy . . . like a moon goddess. "When are you bringing your snails to the greenhouse?"

As they moved through the garden and passed another

couple, Mabel said, "Well, since we're speaking to each other again, I suppose I'll bring them tomorrow."

Gregory grinned. "Before or after our ride in search of your lizard?"

"Before." Mabel slowed and pulled him to a stop near a bramble of roses. "Or perhaps we should take the snails with us and introduce them to Mr. Scales."

"*Mr. Scales*? I hadn't realized he had a name," Gregory said, looking down at her. They stood close enough that her breath warmed him in the cool night.

"Not a very original name, I admit." Mabel reached up and lifted his mask. "I like you better this way."

At her touch, Gregory inhaled. She was closer to him than she'd been while waltzing. She smelled of rain and flowers. He lifted his hands to her face. "May I?"

She gave a slight nod, so he slipped his hands behind her head and untied her mask.

She held very still, not moving, but he felt as if every part of him was alive at her nearness.

"Tell me about Mr. Weathers," he said in a quiet voice, lowering his hands.

She didn't turn her gaze away, and he realized that he could get lost in her eyes for a very long time.

"There's really nothing to tell," she said in a casual tone, but Gregory recognized the amused gleam in her eye.

He tilted his head, waiting for her to continue. The music coming from the ballroom had changed again—a new dance had started up, so the garden was virtually abandoned.

She let out a soft sigh. "Very well. This evening, I wrote two letters. One to you, and one to him."

Somehow his hands found hers, and he interlaced their fingers. "A devastating set-down, then?"

"An honest one," Mabel whispered, swaying toward

him. "I told him I would be courting you—and only you."

Gregory raised a brow, both surprised and delighted. "Am I the first to know of this news?"

Her hands tightened in his. "You are. But we should probably tell my sister and your brother soon. They'll certainly notice."

"Hmmm," Gregory breathed, lowering his head. "They will need to be notified very soon, perhaps as soon as this evening, especially if I kiss you . . . right . . . now."

Her hands released his and moved to his chest. Her fingers curled around the lapels of his coat, tugging him slightly forward. It was all the encouragement he needed.

Gregory kissed her, his hands sliding up her arms and over her shoulders until they rested on her neck, his thumbs brushing her jaw. She tasted of sun and rain, flowers and grass, warmth and coolness—all of nature wrapped into one. Her arms slid around his neck, and he felt absolutely lost as she returned his kiss.

It took a bit of effort to regain his senses, when moments later, and all too soon, she drew away.

Her body still nestled against his, she said, "Are you flirting with me, Mr. Clark?"

"Definitely not," he whispered, resting his head against hers. "That was for keeps. Forever and always."

She let out a contented sigh, and he wished he didn't have to let her go, that neither of them needed to return to the ballroom.

"Did you know that swans are monogamous?" Mabel asked suddenly.

He chuckled. "I didn't, but it doesn't surprise me." He lifted his head and gazed into her eyes. "Swans live on the country estate I'm looking at purchasing."

Her eyebrows lifted. "Ethel told me about your farm."

"It's not mine yet," he said. "It still needs a final inspection before I sign the papers. Before that can happen, my inheritance must fund."

"Swans on a farm sound quite lovely," she said, her eyes bright.

"I was hoping you'd think so." He reached for her hands again, intent on asking her a question. "I was also hoping you might come along with Richard and me when we do the inspection. We'd bring Ethel, too, of course."

She paused, but not for long. "I'd love to."

"Then it's settled." He released her hands and retied her mask, then his own. "You'll court only me. You'll come with me to my new country estate and give it your blessing. And you'll be my swan."

She laughed. "I think I will dance a second dance with you tonight, Gregory."

He smiled as they made their way back toward the ballroom. "Tonight, nothing would make me happier."

ABOUT HEATHER B. MOORE

Heather B. Moore is a *USA Today* bestselling author. She writes historical thrillers under the pen name H.B. Moore; her latest is *Finding Sheba*. Under Heather B. Moore, she writes romance and women's fiction. She's one of the coauthors of The Newport Ladies Book Club series. Other works include *Heart of the Ocean, The Fortune Café,* the Aliso Creek series, and the Amazon bestselling Timeless Romance Anthology series.

For book updates, sign up for Heather's email list: HBMoore.com/contact

Website: HBMoore.com
Facebook: Fans of H.B. Moore
Blog: MyWritersLair.blogspot.com
Twitter: @HeatherBMoore

Dear Timeless Romance Anthology Reader,

Thank you for reading this anthology. We hoped you loved the sweet romance novellas! Heather B. Moore, Annette Lyon, and Sarah M. Eden have been indie publishing this series since 2012 through the Mirror Press imprint. For each anthology, we carefully select three guest authors. Our goal is to offer a way for our readers to discover new, favorite authors by reading these romance novellas written exclusively for our anthologies . . . all for one great price.

If you enjoyed this anthology, please consider leaving a review on Goodreads or Amazon or any other e-book store you purchase through. Reviews and word-of-mouth is what helps us continue this fun project. For updates and notifications of sales and giveaways, please sign up for our monthly newsletter here on our blog: TimelessRomanceAnthologies.blogspot.com.

Also, if you're interested in become a regular reviewer of the anthologies and would like access to advance copies, please email Heather Moore: heather@hbmoore.com

Find us on Facebook for our latest updates.

Thank you!
The Timeless Romance Authors

MORE TIMELESS ROMANCE ANTHOLOGIES

www.ingramcontent.com/pod-product-compliance
Lightning Source LLC
LaVergne TN
LVHW021755060526
838201LV00058B/3107